A
New Map
of Love

Abi Oliver has spent much of her life in the Thames Valley. She studied at Oxford and London Universities, has worked for a charity, as a nurse, on Indian Railways and as a writer. She has also raised four children and lives in Purley-on-Thames. This is her first novel as Abi Oliver.

A New Map of Love

ABI OLIVER

PAN BOOKS

First published 2017 by Macmillan

This paperback edition first published 2018 by Pan Books
an imprint of Pan Macmillan
20 New Wharf Road, London N1 9RR
Associated companies throughout the world
www.panmacmillan.com

ISBN 978-1-4472-8403-1

1 3 5 7 9 8 6 4 2

A CIP catalogue record for this book is available from the British Library.

Typeset by Ellipsis, Glasgow
Printed and bound by CPI Group (UK) Ltd, Croydon, CR0 4YY

For M, with love xx

FEBRUARY 1964

One

1.

It was never George Baxter's intention to run off from the funeral. He had not planned to be first out of the car park at the Crem, driving like the clappers despite the weather before the others had finished admiring the flowers. Nor did it seem at all the thing to be whistling on the way home from laying your wife of twenty-six years to rest, let alone if what you found yourself whistling were tunes from *South Pacific*. But he was not himself. He seemed to have lapsed into a *Scouting for Boys* reflex from his upbringing. A Scout Is Always Cheerful, No Matter What. And he couldn't stand the silence in the car – a silence that would now go on forever.

The windscreen wipers beat time. Fat snowflakes slopped against the glass. He kept an eye on the rear-view mirror to see if the pack of mourners was catching up, but there was no sign. They would be taking it more carefully.

In his grey saloon he dashed through the villages until, from the brow of the hill, his own came into view at last. Greenbury was a cosy huddle of dwellings round a square church tower, tucked in at the toes of the chalk down. Today the snow had reduced its thatched cottages and cob walls to a few black lines, like a Victorian engraving. He swooped downhill between rows of snow-laden elms, roared into the gravelled yard and braked beside the pea-green Morris pick-up.

The house, screened from the road by laurel and hawthorn, was cream-faced with a beard of Virginia creeper and stiff whiskers of winter roses, which in summer would scale to the roof in a rampant wig of gold blooms. Unlike the cottages at the heart of the village it was only about a hundred years old, the roof tiled, not thatched. At the drive's entrance, hanging from a gas lamp, now electrified, was a sign announcing, **CHALK HILL ANTIQUES – Geo. Baxter Esq.**

George jumped from the car, slamming the door as he strode to the front door. One hand grasped his black trilby, the other fumbled for keys in a trouser pocket that was suddenly unfathomably deep.

'Damn it.' There was the usual tussle with the lock, the dog barking inside. Door open at last, he took a frantic glance behind him in case the black-hatted pack had caught up. Thank heavens he had taken his own car.

'Hello, old boy,' he said to the hound before racing up to the bedroom, a tall, fleshy man taking the stairs in doggy bounds. Bedroom: jacket off, must hang, good quality suit. Trousers down, onto a wooden hanger and hooked on the wardrobe door. George felt his face take on a look of bewilderment. Where had his clothes gone? His real clothes? He performed several laps round the room in his vest and long johns, staring fruitlessly at the bed and the seats of chairs. Dangling from the back of the Windsor chair was an orphaned pair of braces. He picked them up and gazed at the perished elastic. At last, in an indignant outburst,

'Winifred! What in God's name have you done with my trousers?'

The faint rebound of his voice met only silence. Winifred Jane. Win . . . He sank down on her side of the bed. She was not going to answer. She would not be answering ever again. Now the silence weighed upon him: he sat, as if winded. Feelings jostled inside him, vibrations of long-ago abandonments. He gave his thighs a vigorous rub.

'No good – this is no good at all.'

He was about to get up when he caught sight of the basket on Win's bedside table in which she kept her hair things. George reached over for it and heard himself let out the 'ughnm' sound which these days seemed to accompany his bending or stretching for anything. The basket had once contained a gift of lavender soaps. Win kept it tidily stacked with the hairpins, rollers and kirby grips with which she used to 'put my hair up' every night of their marriage even though he longed for her not to. The only time she had let all this go was a few winters back, when she had that terrible flu.

'I must look a sight,' she apologized through a haze of Vicks VapoRub. 'I'll get my rollers in as soon as I'm better . . .'

As if she must do it for him. Her hair was still black as the inkiest blackbird then. Every day it was immaculate, the tight curls tamed by hairspray and waving back away from her forehead, the way the Queen wore hers. He squeezed one of the rollers in his hand and winced. It was all wire and mesh, like a bit of fence from a prisoner-of-war camp. Fancy sleeping with that pinned to your skull every night. When her hair faded she began to tint it. She wasn't dyeing it, she insisted, just 'giving it a wash through'. She didn't manage all that by the end – nor the curlers. She had been natural then in a loose nightgown. Beautiful in his eyes. She rose to meet death, old Win did. She rose and grew as never before while moving daily further out of his reach.

He put the basket back on the bedside table and sat staring at the window. Might the two of them, had they both lived long enough, eventually have grown back together in some fashion? He saw them reaching out, connecting first at their fingertips, slipping a palm round each other's wrists in playful union, her white inner arm sliding along his until they were lime trees, pleached into a seamless . . .

Lord God, how long had he been sitting here?

He leapt from the bed. He had to find his . . . It came to him: the washing basket. Of course – he'd put his trousers in the laundry as usual, thinking someone, *someone* would wash them.

One pair of oil-stained trousers the colour of cattle dung safely retrieved and flung on the bed. A blue striped shirt, a favourite navy jersey, both elbows out – Win had not been up to darning lately. As he fastened his shirt buttons he went to look out at the drive. The pack would be here any minute, surely? It was quiet, the snow marked only by tyre tracks and the dark trail of his footprints. From up here they looked small and lonely, an uninhabited archipelago in a desolate sea.

He hurried downstairs, the hall tiles icy under his feet. Standing on the kitchen's grey lino, George eyed the table, humped as a camel under a white cloth. Beneath it, he knew, was Vera's spread. Any minute now, she and the rest of Win's cronies would all be swarming at the house. Of course, he had had a word with them all at the Crem, before the need to take off seized him so abruptly. And now, here were the expected funeral bakemeats. For a moment he tried to persuade himself that he could manage it, stay and face them all – Rosemary, Pat, Eunice and the others, all full of *poor Win*. And of course Vera – oh dear God, Vera – whose every act made him feel guilty or inadequate. He felt stretched to the end of himself, the thought of it all unbearable.

Nose twitching, he reached forward to lift the edge of the cloth, keeping his body well back as if there might be something dangerous underneath. He examined the mounds of sandwiches and hams, the trifles involving glacé cherries, the inevitable pies, all laid out lovingly by Vera, marvellous Vera, who had started as a cleaner in the shop and now seemed to run his entire life.

'I can't,' he stated, dropping the edge of the cloth. 'Just can't.'

Lifting it again, he poked his head underneath and ferreted about like an old-fashioned photographer. After scooping a few offerings into a linen napkin he turned, performing a sudden swivel to avoid tripping over the dog whose nose was wiffling hopefully beside him.

'Get out of the damn way, Monty – oh Lord God Almighty.' He looked down at himself. Navy jumper, shirt tails, long johns. 'My trousers!'

Upstairs, and after a dangerous moment of entanglement with his fly buttons, he seized some socks – 'Damn it, they'll be here' – and tore downstairs again. Sandwiches, coat (flask already in pocket), boots, dog. Where was his pipe? No – too late for that.

George opened the front door and peered out. Coast still clear. The Morris had a hat of snow on its cab roof.

'Right, Monty . . .' He couldn't leave the dog here. He'd be raiding people's plates and humping their legs. 'In you get.' Opening the cab door he picked up the grumbling basset hound and heaved him onto the front seat. 'Too many pies,' he told him. 'That's your trouble.'

Jumping in, he started up the engine – 'Come on, come *on* . . .' The windscreen wipers swished. No cars appeared, no black hats. He'd made it. He eased the pick-up out of the drive, turned on to the Didcot road and drove away with the speed of a fleeing burglar.

2.

He parked the Morris at the crest of the track that cut along the side of Greenburton Hill. Everything was white now except for the fresh tips of winter wheat, a rectangle of threadbare corduroy across the sloping downland. Flakes collected steadily on the windscreen. Every so often he switched on the ignition to move the wipers.

In the quiet, George sat beside Monty, chewing slowly and gazing out at the falling snow. The dog's attention was torn between the whirl of flakes and the fast dwindling beef and horseradish sandwich in George's hand. The sandwich was winning.

'You look about as cheerful as I feel,' George addressed Monty's mournful countenance. 'Eh – Mr Glum?' he added, aware that the dog's expression was permanent rather than any great sign of sensitivity to events. 'A right pair we are.'

Sandwich suspended in hand, he examined himself in the rear-view mirror. The wide, pink face staring back at him was that of a man of fifty-six years and two months. Its features showed signs of losing life's long tussle with gravity. Large grey eyes, nose a strong wedge of a thing which had embarrassed him when he was young. Now he rather hoped the eyes looked soulful and the nose distinguished. His biscuit-coloured hair was swept into clumps, giving the appearance of having recently encountered gale-force winds. He gave it a futile pat with his free hand. The sight of his own face seemed only to add to George's creeping sense of shock.

'What the hell have I done, Monty? How on earth did we end up here?' He had run off from his wife's funeral do like a bolter fleeing a wedding. Here he was, hiding away from all the people who had cared for Win. The very people he should greet and thank; from whom he should accept sympathy. He was sure they already thought him a toad, all those blasted females. He could see it in the way they looked at him. They already thought he had neglected Win. And now look – he had done a bunk. 'What kind of man am I?' he groaned at this evidence of his own derangement.

Monty, eyes pleading and a string of drool dangling from his jowls, followed the sandwich looping in the air in George's hand.

'Here you go old boy.' George lobbed this last crust. Monty snapped it up like a performing seal. 'Oh, and look what I've got – your favourites.' Monty's gaze snapped towards the rustling in his pocket. The ancient, comforting joke: 'Bassetts for a basset.'

He selected a liquorice and white sugar sandwich from the little box and flicked it upwards. Monty caught it in one.

'There – and don't go pinching them from my pocket.'

George wiped his hands on his trousers and reached into his other tweedy pocket for his hip flask (silver, L.G. Birmingham 1892 – not really antique). He pulled off its cup, surprised at how much his hands were trembling as he poured a tot of the amber liquid. Its scent made his nostrils flare; that cognac glory-hallelujah of copper-pot stills and oak barrels. He sat back, so far as it was possible to sit back in the upright seat and stared out at the bloated sky.

'Oh dear God, Monty, how am I ever going to face them after this?'

Monty offered no further comment except a grunt as he settled on the seat, eyes half closed, resigned to the fact that there was no sign of any more liquorice allsorts.

George laid a hand over his pounding heart. 'You should be ashamed of yourself,' he lectured himself. He drained the silver cup, then resorted to swigging straight from the flask. The alcohol slid down, burning pleasantly in his stomach. His muscles slackened. Gradually, his agitation faded. He became reflective. The least he could do, he thought, pushing himself woozily upright again as a mark of respect, was to drink a private toast to his wife.

'Poor little devil,' he murmured, pouring another snifter into the cup. 'We didn't have a clue, did we?' After further thought he added, 'I've been a shocking bad husband.' He shook his head. 'Good sort, you were, my dear. You deserved much better.' After another lengthy pause he raised the cup high. 'Well, I suppose we gave it our best. Cheers, Win old girl.'

He was downing the contents when in the fading light he saw movement ahead on the track. A man in a brown coat was coming slowly up the rise, a scarf muffling his throat. He was looking down, talking to a child who was holding his hand as they stumped through the snow. Both of them had on navy-and-white-striped bobble hats, as if someone had knitted them a matching pair, and wellingtons. The boy's – somehow he seemed a boy, in his blue anorak – were red.

George felt a bit of a fool sitting there. On the quiet hillside he could just hear the man talking in an even voice and the child's chirping replies. The lad had wide eyes which seemed to take in everything in a trusting sweep. It was his openness George noticed first. With a pang he saw that the boy could have been himself fifty years earlier: round-faced, pink-cheeked, solid. He was always big for his age, making people think he was older than he was, that he had more courage and substance than was ever the case.

Hearing them, Monty leapt up from the seat and started barking. The father and son stopped, startled, then smiled. The boy said something and his father picked him up and brought him along the passenger side of the van to look. At this Monty went berserk, snarling with gums rolled back like some mythical beast, scrabbling on the seat and sending trails of slobber down the window. George caught a glimpse of the boy's face, mouth open in surprise, the smile gone.

'Hello!' George waved in a way that he hoped would appear jolly. He's friendly really, he wanted to tell them. It's just his territory. The father, pale and serious, gave a brief nod and moved further away, stooping to put his son down.

'Steady on, Monty – you'll burst a blood vessel.' George was filled with sudden anguish, as if he and his dog had struck the wrong note, spoiled some innocence of the afternoon for the man and his boy.

In the mirror, he watched the two of them recede slowly down the track into the village, two figures side by side. Himself and his father, a nervy schoolmaster. Himself and the spectre of the son that never was, for himself and Win. The ghostly image of a whole past that might have been different.

He put the cup back on his hip flask, feeling warm and muzzy, yet desolate. His feelings opened by the drink, by the man and his son, he looked out over the muffled hillside. The longer he sat there the more the tracks and familiar landmarks were being reshaped by snow, so that this place, so near home, now felt only half recognizable. It felt as if his life had been filling with snow these past months. He had thought it would just continue, its paths and crossings, its knolls and slopes, more or less predictable as before. It had been a limited existence to which he had resorted and by which he had often felt dulled and constrained. But at least life with Win had been familiar and safe. Now, dear Win was gone. Win, who had been slipping from his grasp finger by finger, so that she had left him some time before death took her. Gone: every gentle reproach, every quiet breath and valiant smile. And he was left adrift.

Realization throbbed in his mind: here he sat, George Oswald Baxter, alone with his unfortunate initials and ridiculous dog. He had not one blood relation in the world. Alone with no compass in this explorer's blizzard, all landmarks effaced. Alone, and . . .

No, that could not be right. Strange sensations jostled inside him. Feelings that seemed utterly out of place. Seconds later, it crackled through him, a bolt of elation so fierce that he had to seize the steering wheel. His heart started banging like a tom-tom as a shameful excitement stole his breath and filled him to the back of his throat. This was terrible. He was going off his head, first running off and now this . . . He gripped the steering wheel. For heaven's sake, man . . .

But yes, *yes* – it would not be denied. *The life force. He* was not the one who had died. He had life in him yet. And how he wanted it – all of it! Wanting stormed through him and made itself his whole condition. It yanked his ears and dragged him by the ankles. It was a primitive hunger gripping and filling him: a greedy, mindless, ravenousness for life.

Possibility swirled before him. *Life*. It meant walks holding hands in meadows freckled with buttercups. It laid before him dishes of ripe peaches, carafes of wine and evenings swimming naked in the river . . . It swept him across grand landscapes; it meant riding bareback over the plains . . . No, maybe it didn't . . . His imagination stalled for a moment. He found horses utterly terrifying. But it did mean seeing a wider world. And a world in which he could share a bed with a lovely woman, a woman who would fizz and leap and undulate and make him laugh and – without malice – laugh at him.

He felt so lost, and his longing was in such crazed collision with anguish and remorse that he folded forward under the force of it until his head touched the steering wheel. His body heaved. For the first time since a summer morning in 1944, on an Italian hillside, he wept. Eyes closed, his sobs rumbled up and overcame him; tears ran onto his hands. Only gradually he became aware of something wet and whiskery and faintly liquorice-scented nudging at his ear.

'It's all right,' he said. Still weeping he sat up, extricating himself from Monty's concerned nose. 'You sit down – that's it, boy.' His arm round the dog, comforted by Monty's stinky warmth, he looked out at the darkening afternoon. 'We should just drive off over the hills, and never come back. Are you game, Monty? You and me?'

The dog gazed gormlessly at him. George wiped his face and blew his nose, cold reality settling on him again. What the blazes was he thinking? He had only just taken leave of his wife. It was no good doing something rash. He had to get his bearings – and in the meantime he had a business to run and a dog badly in need of a tin of Winalot.

He started the engine and let it idle for a few moments before letting off the handbrake.

3.

He had to face the house. Even now it seemed inconceivable that Win was not coming back. If he were to walk in and find her in her apron by the cooker it would not feel strange. Her sickness and death would fade like a dream. Life would go on. Existence, anyway.

Closing the front door, he paused in the hall, listening, just in case. Monty's toenails clacked ahead along the tiles, then stopped. He turned with a baleful glance as if to say, 'Well come *on*.'

George felt the dark silence weigh on him. As he passed through the house, he found himself switching on all the lights. The front was devoted to the business. His office was to the right of the front door. He did not go in there, but stepped into the showroom on the left and clicked the switch. Light gave the large room back to him, the sheen of polished walnut and rosewood, the sweet smell of Antiquax polish. Leaving it lit up, he went along the hall.

Their living quarters were at the back, the sitting room the most private refuge. Customers occasionally strayed into the kitchen at the end of the hall to the right. They seldom got as far as this room. It was extraordinary the way people felt entitled to wander and poke about in your house. They had resorted to a sign at the bottom of the stairs saying PRIVATE, after Win once met a man coming out of their upstairs bathroom. At weekends when it was busy, they even hung a rope across the stairs.

Turning on the kitchen light, the sight that met George took him aback. The humped feast was gone and instead there sat one white plate overturned on another. Beside it, a dish containing a whole, enormous pie. A note in careful, looped handwriting was tucked under the edge of the dish:

Dear Mr Baxter,

Here's a bit of supper for you. Just pop it in the oven about 25 mins, not too hot, say 150. No one touched the pie so I thought you'd like it. I'll be in tomorrow.

Vera

PS. We all understand.

George looked under the top plate. Beneath lay a generous portion of liver and onions, mash and sliced rounds of carrot. Only now, seeing the food, he realized he was famished. Replacing the cover, he slid both plates into the oven and switched it on. He peered at the bevelled edges of the pie. A give-away seepage of pink juice confirmed his worst suspicions.

'Rhubarb – dear God – in February.'

Vera was a great preserver and bottler. Plums, gooseberries, rhubarb, apples and pears were to be had at any time of year at the snap of a Kilner jar lid. Win loved rhubarb. What she had never got round to mentioning to Vera was George's violent aversion to it. Monty, who could never be described as finicky in this regard, came in for a lot of leftovers.

'It's such a waste, George,' Win would tut as Monty golloped down yet another slice. 'And heaven knows what'll happen if he eats too much rhubarb.'

'Well it's just as wasted inside me, I can tell you,' he would reply. 'At the least the dog gets some enjoyment out of the darn stuff. He only eats the pastry anyway.'

'She *means* well,' Win would insist.

As this oft-repeated conversation ran through his head, George sank onto a chair by the table. Monty's collar rattled against his bowl as he scrabbled for the last scraps of food. George stared at his hands, which looked huge things against the pale blue Formica. Women. Why did they always make him feel so helpless? With women he felt like a scrap of cork being borne along by a prevailing tide. Yet how bleak and inconceivable to live without a woman in his life. Tears muddled his vision again.

Once he had eaten, he washed up the plate, knife and fork and left them on the rack to drain. Worried in case the lit-up state of the place might encourage people to call on him, he quickly went round turning lights off again. In the sitting room, he sank into his baggy green chair. Monty settled beside him. Two other dogs, in chipped, Staffordshire earthenware, regarded George with a melancholy air from alcoves each side of the fireplace.

The quietness of the house pressed in on him. Was this how it would be now, night after night, always? He lit his pipe, packed with St Bruno, comforted momentarily by this aromatic ritual. His mood tilted this way and that. For a time, he was filled with desperation as he looked into the void of his emotional life. Win had been a wonderful woman – everyone said so. But their marriage had become a delicate balance of habit and avoidance. There had scarcely been a day over the past twenty years when he had not thought, is this all? Looked at other couples – happy, laughing, physically close, it seemed – and twisted inside with longing. And that longing, the desolation of those days when Win was so ill that she was no longer herself, had led to Maggie, to . . . Oh God. Thank heaven Win never knew.

But that was then. Now, he scarcely knew who he was, which way he was facing to begin this uncharted path into grief, into a new life. He could not think straight about anything.

Reaching over the side of the chair he found Monty's warm ear and sat stroking it.

4.

It was late when the phone rang. George had dozed off in the chair, jacket draped over him, and found himself jangled awake, chilly and discombobulated. He flung off the jacket and moved automatically to the hall telephone. It did not cross his mind that he could leave it to ring.

As he picked it up the ringing stopped. More silence came down the line. Then he heard someone take a sharp breath.

'George?'

It was her. Maggie.

'Um?' A strangled utterance forced its way out of him.

'Sorry it's so late.' She was speaking very quietly. 'I had to wait for John and Rick to go to bed. I just . . . I didn't want to come to the funeral . . . Not when – well, you know.'

He could see the flinty track up to the farmhouse, himself walking up it, Maggie Wylde's arms opening to him. An ache spread across his chest.

'I just wanted to make sure you're all right, lovey. You must've had such a terrible day . . .'

'Yes.' He cleared his throat, attempting to sound in command. 'Quite all right, thank you.' There was a division, like a wall, between how things were in bed and not in bed. He couldn't talk to her now.

'I could come down . . .' But she sounded doubtful.

'No!' He tried to soften this abrupt refusal. 'Don't do that. It's late. And you mustn't.'

'No. I suppose not.' He heard her sigh. 'All right, Georgie – as long as you're OK.'

The silence went on so long that he was about to put the receiver down. Her voice came again in a desperate burst. 'George? I want to be with you . . . Properly . . .' She sounded tearful. 'Oh God, I'm sorry – I wasn't going to do this.'

For a second his being leapt with hope. A woman in the house! Lovely Maggie. She would only have to move down the lane. He need not be alone after all. A second's further thought brought disaster crashing round his head. John Wylde, their three grown-up children: divorce, shame and disaster.

'No, Maggie.' He spoke sadly, but with a firmness that surprised and even impressed him. 'You know that's not right.'

A stifled sound came down the line. Eventually she said, 'I know. Really. But . . .'

'Maggie – don't. Please. I'm going to put the phone down. Goodbye, my dear.'

'Bye,' she just managed.

He replaced the receiver. For the first time he noticed the cold from the tiles seeping through his socks.

'You mustn't,' he instructed himself. 'Never again.'

'Come on, Monty.' In the sitting room, the dog was sitting up, eyeing him in a guilty, sidelong manner. There was a black tinge to his jowls and in the middle of the floor, near his jacket, lay the torn remains of a yellow and white box.

'You bad boy . . .' Monty cringed theatrically, showing the whites of his eyes. 'You've polished off the lot!' He hadn't the energy to be properly cross. He was too taken up with Maggie. He gathered up the torn remains of the liquorice allsorts box. 'Come on, you wicked creature – out.'

Two

1.

Waking the next morning, the first thing he felt was the heaviness of the blankets, pressing down on his own sadness and disorientation. He was also lying awkwardly on his left arm. As he turned onto his back, opening his eyes, he was filled with a momentary rush of excitement. It felt as if everything should be different. The snowy hillside – his revelation.

All subsequent moments confirmed that things were not different. At least not in terms of the possibility of ripe peaches and swimming with naked abandon. Nor, he realized, in terms of the prospect of amiable and available women flocking to his door. Bleak days of sadness and loss – they were what lay ahead.

But things were altered. For one thing, the room was full of an eerie, almost visionary light from the snow. And the guilty sense of freedom was still there. He stretched, toes pushing against the winceyette sheet with a sensation of spreading out to inhabit all of himself. He imagined this was how you would feel when washed ashore after a shipwreck; limp, mortally exhausted, but full of a maddening sense of hope.

He stepped out the back into a glittering morning. Frozen spiderwebs sagged from the washing line. Monty cavorted across the snowy back garden like a pup. Narrowing his eyes against the glare, George watched this portly vision in brown and white lumbering back and forth, ears flying, giving off ecstatic woofs.

'Silly old fool,' George muttered. 'You'll do yourself a mischief. Come on – got to open up.'

It was a comfort, getting back to business. He walked round the house, out of their private flower garden. Win preferred that no one could see their smalls hanging out, so this was well screened by a wooden lattice sprawled over with honeysuckle and climbing roses. Beyond, at the side of the barn was his vegetable patch and a space for a rusty iron table and chairs where the men ate their sandwiches when it was warm.

In the yard he knocked snow hats off the stone dogs by the barn door and turned the key. Inside he breathed the building's musty wood smell. To the right, behind a partition, was the workshop, with windows facing over the vegetable garden. The rest of the barn was the overspill showroom.

George looked across the array of furniture. Both showrooms were carpeted in a deep, blood red. The house showroom was set out more like a proper room, but the barn lent itself to a selection of small tableaux. He arranged things as if on little stages from which the players had temporarily strayed for a cup of tea. To his left a collection of chairs – a Windsor in yew, two French rococos with rose and cream upholstery and an upright farthingale – encircled a mahogany Sheraton tripod table as if awaiting the seated bottoms of social occasions. The farthingale had sat in someone's shed for about thirty years, the wood dry as bone. The lads had done a marvellous job. It had a sheen on it now. Beyond that was a mahogany dining table, a set of Regency Trafalgar chairs tucked round it and on top, a silver candelabra. This seemed off-centre to George and he went over to move it.

Antiques were not mere objects, in his view. Nor dead museum pieces. Hands had fashioned them with effort, with mood and feeling. He knew this by the life in his own hands, from the years he spent at the bench, learning the skills of restoration. And the more you arranged things to support an understanding of their vitality, the more life they embodied. Even in the barn he never just crammed things in the way some dealers did. Like that philistine Lewis Barker over near Twyford with that warehouse of his – everything shoved in anyhow and dusty as hell. Lewis had a good eye all right, but visiting his place was the most cheerless dealing George ever did. That lumpen fool might as well be selling second-hand lawnmowers.

In the house showroom he gathered the lighter woods, the walnut, rosewood, satinwood. The room was a feast for the eyes with the morning sun streaming in across their warm grain, catching the gleam of porcelain and glow of ruby glass which he displayed on the furniture. Sometimes customers gasped with pleasure at the sight. That was the best sort of customer: someone who would enter into the spirit of things, not just see a cold profit in the making.

For the moment the tools in the workshop lay silent. He had inherited two of the three men who worked there from Arthur Bagnold when he took over the business after the war. The place had been in a right state then. Arthur had grown old and wandery in his mind. When George bought the property so that he and Win could settle here, he had to start almost from scratch, repairing the house and outbuildings and getting the business going again.

Like George, the two more senior men had been away to war. Clarence, two years older than George, returned from the Royal Berkshires and Alan, Vera's husband, from RAF Coastal Command. Both had begun their working lives with Arthur Bagnold. Arthur had trained Clarence, who in turn instructed Alan. Six months ago, now things were busier, George had taken on another lad. Kevin, the seventeen-year-old apprentice, had the features of a faintly animated potato and a naturally gormless demeanour (adenoids were a problem). But he did profess eagerness. 'I'm ever so *keen,* Mr Baxter. Keen as mustard. Honest I am.' And keenness, George thought, was to be encouraged.

When he himself had first been apprenticed to Old Man Arkwright in their Suffolk town, no one had had many hopes for him. His father packed him off to Arkwright when everyone, George included, despaired of his schoolwork. He was a great, floundering boy with a physique that looked fitter for lumberjacking than the painstaking restoration of wood. Old Arkwright eyed him up and gave him a chance. Those joint-of-meat hands were found to be dexterous, his nature sensitive to the grain of wood, the rightness of curve and angle.

'Well, bor,' Arkwright told him in broad Suffolk, after six months, 'I reckon you've found your pond.' And a happy duck he had been.

Kevin, also belying appearances, had hands sympathetic to wood as well as a willing nature. He seemed to be finding his pond too. Every so often those vegetable features launched themselves into a smile of bemused satisfaction.

George strode out into the snowy yard again. 'Come on, Monty!' He stamped his boots on the front step. 'Breakfast – before the troops get here.'

2.

Since Win became too ill to get up, he had got into the habit of making breakfast alone. It made him feel manly, as if he was back in the army. He was no longer using the silver toast rack on which Win had always insisted. Today, extraordinarily hungry, he fried three eggs, four thick back rashers and threw in a handful of mushrooms. After downing this with a pile of toast like a block of flats and a pot of tea, he began to feel ready to face them all.

'Keep busy, that's the thing,' he said to Monty. 'Keep the business up to scratch.'

The dog gave a long, dozy grunt.

'If you didn't agree, you'd say so, wouldn't you?' George said, stepping over him. Monty had forever to be stepped over as he was forever right in the way.

He stacked the plates in the sink, musing on the business. Win had always been the one to help out with the accounts, taking telephone messages and dealing with customers on days when he was out and about. Unofficially they had been in it together. During her illness, Vera had mucked in and helped where she could. Now he had to face up to it: he was going to have to take someone on – a book-keeper at least. In his fragile state this felt like a mountainous task.

He was beginning to consider that he might wash up, when he heard, 'Coo-eee? Hello? Mr B?'

'In the back, Vera!'

'Righty-ho.' There was a small kerfuffle as she took her coat off. Vera and Alan lived only a few minutes' walk away on one of the roads down into the village. The house, opposite one of the pubs, was a new bungalow which, after prolonged deliberation, Alan had decreed should be called The Bungalow.

The untouched pie was still on the table. George whisked it away and into the back of the refrigerator with a second to spare. Vera's face arrived round the kitchen door. A roll of hay-coloured hair loomed over her forehead and a similar wide-bore kink bounced each side of her face. Clearly Vera did something with hair rollers. Whatever it was, it was different from what Win did with them. Vera had honest blue eyes and square, widely spaced teeth which made her look amiable the second she parted her lips. Her shapely body could achieve a great deal of activity very fast – especially on the pie-making front. She reminded George vaguely of a very clean pit pony.

'Hello, Mr B,' she said with her usual Berkshire verve, though muted by an awareness of dealing with the bereaved. 'How are you today? (No don't slobber on my skirt, Monty, there's a good boy.)'

'Oh . . .' George rammed his hands into his trouser pockets. He had a suit on today in a rather loud brown and green tweed. The one Win used to say made him look like a bookie. 'I'm quite all right, thank you, Vera.'

As he spoke he wondered, did that sound crusty? Maggie said he was a crusty old thing – but only on the outside.

'Are you?' Vera came up close, still holding the basket she

brought in every day containing Vim, folded dishcloths and other mysteries. In a motherly way she looked into his face. There was something unnaturally pink about her lips. He was used to Win wearing red lipstick, which appeared obviously like lipstick and suited her dark looks. But the pink stuff just made lips look more like lips, only with some sort of raging inflammation. He caught the familiar, chemical smell of hair-spray.

'You *poor* thing,' Vera went on. 'Oh I did feel bad for you yesterday. That you felt . . . Well, that you couldn't . . .'

'Ah, yes.' George looked down again, finding a couple of sixpences to chink in his pocket. 'Yes. Sorry. Couldn't really . . . You know . . .'

'Oh don't apologize, Mr B, we all understand.' Vera put her basket on the table and pulled out the pink rubber gloves she wore to do almost everything. 'Really we do.'

One of the gloves was inside out, the reverse side an unnerving flesh colour.

'Oh dear,' Vera sighed, pulling on the left glove, which was the right way round. 'Poor Mrs B and poor you. She was such a lovely lady.'

'She was.' It was true, he knew.

'You must feel *dreadful*. I mean if anything happened to Alan . . .'

'Yes,' George agreed. He shook his head as if he had run out of words, mainly because he had. 'But thank you for the meal last night. And another delicious pie.'

'Oh it's nothing – you're more than welcome.' She put her mouth to the other glove's opening and blew into it. A pink rubber hand inflated momentarily in front of her face. 'If there's more I can do, you just let me know.' Both gloves on, she started running water into the sink, swishing in the soap. 'I'd best get on.'

'Yes – get on. Good idea.' George released his hands from his pockets.

'No one holds it against you that you're opening today,' Vera remarked over her shoulder.

Until that moment it had never occurred to him that they might. Heavens, was this another sign of his callousness?

'I thought I would,' he said uncertainly. 'No point in – you know – moping.'

Vera turned with a sudden sweet smile. 'No, of course not. You're very brave, Mr B. That's what I think. The others all said how brave they thought you were.'

'Ah?' George doubted this in the extreme.

'They said they'll all pop in and see you're OK.'

Who? When? Oh good Lord!

'How kind. Right – well, I'd better be off. Clarence'll be here.'

'Oh,' Vera chuckled. 'He certainly will. Like the weather.'

As George reached the door he paused. 'I suppose now I'll have to advertise for someone to help run the place.'

Vera's frame seemed to stiffen. Slowly she turned to stand sideways on to the sink in her flat black shoes, one hand still in the washing-up water.

'The thing is, Mr B, I know I've only been filling in and that, but I'd . . . I'd really like to carry on,' she said, a blush seeping up through her cheeks.

George was startled. Vera was the cleaner and he had not got any further in thinking about it than that. He had to admit, though, she had far exceeded what he'd expected. He had hoped for a bit of dusting, being civil to customers and answering the phone. But she had shown a real prowess with people and had taken on the books, Win teaching her what was needed.

'If . . .' she added hesitantly. 'Well, if you don't mind. Course, I'm probably not what you want.'

Surprised, George perceived before him a creature with a need.

'Won't it be too much for you, Vera?' He stepped closer to her again. 'What with all the other things you have to do – cooking, cleaning?' She had taken to cooking for him as well, bringing platefuls over.

'Oh I can do all *that*. That's nothing.' She sounded dismissive, irritated almost and glanced away, out of the window. For an alarming moment George thought there were going to be tears. But she looked back at him, her eyes serious. 'I just . . . I don't know much about the business. I feel a proper chump sometimes when the customers come in – 'specially ones like that Lady – whatshername . . .'

'Byngh.'

'With an "h",' they both said, and laughed.

'Oh you don't want to take any notice of that old trout,' George said. 'Terrorizing everyone in that Daimler of hers. She's a blasted menace.'

Giggles burst from Vera. 'She is a bit. But the thing is, I'd like to learn, Mr Baxter. I've never done much and I was never any good at school. And all the things here are so old and beautiful. I love working here. I think I could learn everything if you'd teach me – and you didn't mind?'

This solution had not occurred to him but until now he had

not got around to thinking of any other. During Win's last months they had all just muddled along. He felt relief at this notion and touched by her feeling for the trade. For an awful second he found himself wishing that Vera was not married to Alan, or to anyone and that they could just . . . But no. *No.*

'Everyone has to start learning somewhere,' he said. Vera, still blushing, was listening as if her entire future happiness depended on him. 'I don't see why not. Let's give it a try.'

'Oh *thank* you, Mr Baxter!' She brought both hands up to her chin as if in prayer, Sqezy bubbles sliding frothily down her right arm.

'Not at all.' George, turning to go, paused again. Was this the moment to ask whether a pie filling other than rhubarb might be a possibility? But courage failed him. They had made enough progress already this morning.

'Mr B?' Her voice was sombre now.

'Umm?'

'If you'd like any help, when it comes to it – with Mrs Baxter's things?'

Things? Of course. He hadn't thought. There'd be clearing out. Organization needed. Wherever did one begin?

'Thank you, Vera. That might well be a great help. Perhaps just not quite yet . . .'

'No,' she said gently. 'Of course not.'

3.

Clarence dismounted from his bike at the gate as he always did. He wore, as he always did, a black gaberdine mackintosh, tightly belted, and a sludge-coloured tweed cap. His one concession to the weather was a hand-knitted scarf in sulphurous yellow – the wool unravelled from goodness knows what previous garment – tucked in most precisely at the neck.

Barring the war years, Clarence had been cycling over here to work from Wallingford, six miles away, since the dawn of time. Possibly earlier.

'Morning, Clarence,' George saluted him from the front step, his breath unfurling white into the air. Monty barked as usual. As usual Clarence ignored him. 'You managed to get here then?'

In fact there had been no more snow overnight. George was trying to flatter his efforts, even provoke that most rare thing in Clarence – a smile.

Clarence nodded curtly, his greyhound features not altering. 'Don't know as I'll be able to get back though, come this evening.'

Optimism was not part of Clarence's repertoire. Nor, in general, was conversation. Today though, instead of passing straight to the workshop after this garrulous outpouring, he wheeled his black bicycle over to George and looked up at him, eyes dark as the flints scattered across the chalk hills.

'Sorry not to come back to the house like, yesterday. Only Edith didn't feel up to it. Upset her a bit.'

When George had stepped into the chapel at the Crem the day before, he saw Clarence and Edith Collins standing right at the back like two testy-looking rooks. Clarence, startlingly, wore a black trilby while Edith, in a black and white dogtooth-patterned coat and black pork-pie hat, wept quite violently into her handkerchief throughout the short ceremony. Edith was several years older than Clarence and at least three times his girth.

'Not at all, Clarence,' George said, omitting to mention that he had not even been at the house himself. 'It was good of you both to come. Win would have been very grateful.'

Win had in fact thought Clarence was a 'miserable old acid drop'. However.

Clarence nodded. He looked as if he was about to say something more, but clamped his lips over yellow pegs of teeth and wheeled his bike off to the side of the barn. His right trouser leg was tucked into a mean-looking black sock. George saw him yank the trouser free of the sock as he walked and straighten it out with an irritable kick.

George noticed that everyone was behaving gently with him. Alan, Vera's husband, a slender, black-haired man who also spoke after long intervals of deliberation, came over as he arrived, took his cap off and shook George's hand.

'Good to see you, Mr Baxter,' he said, as if George had been away somewhere worrying for several months.

Even Kevin the apprentice – who had not, so far, been

notable for his fineness of feeling – said, 'Mornin', Mr Baxter. You doing all right, are you?' in such a stirringly tender voice that George found himself almost tearful and had to hurry back into the house.

4.

Business was slow because of the weather. George found it hard to settle. He wandered between the workshop, where he got under the men's feet, to the house, where he got under Vera's. Finally, mug of tea in hand and Monty at his heels, he slunk out to the garden shed. He had a workbench in there where he sometimes did fretwork and other repairs. There was a comforting smell of wood shavings and varnish. Keeping the door ajar so he could see out, he lit the paraffin stove and soon got a fug up. He settled in the wicker chair with his pipe, a rug over his knees, took off his tie and undid his top shirt button. Monty sprawled on an old blanket.

If George leaned forward he could just see the tarpaulined nose of his boat, *Barchetta*, sticking out from beside the shed. Thoughts of dipping oars, of sunny afternoons on the river at Wallingford cheered him. The arches of climbing roses that in summer screened the shed completely were winter sparse, so that through them he could make out the lawn edged by crammed, rose-filled borders, the washing line slung across from end to end.

'I know you're hiding from me out in that shed,' Win used to say in occasional fits of choosing to examine their marital realities. 'That's why you planted all those roses.'

'Not hiding,' he would fib, to her doubting eyes.

'Don't pretend to me, George. It's so silly. You obviously feel you have to get away from me. You'd rather spend your time with that dog of yours.'

A huge silence would open in him like a cave. Where to begin? What words for what he really felt? He was doing his best just to get by.

'Getting out from under your feet,' he resorted to. 'So you can have your cronies in without me hanging about.'

'Don't call them that. It makes them sound like a coven.'

There was no safe response he could make to that either, so he'd get it in the neck all over again. They were her friends. At least *they* wanted to be with her. And so on.

Twenty-six years. Well, the war sort of counted, though he was away nearly four years. Already it all seemed like a dream. She had been there, all that time, and now she wasn't. He missed her. Of course he did. All those years they had spent together. Yet, shameful, in a way he could hardly admit, was the realization that she scarcely seemed to have touched him – not deep down . . . This lack, he felt, must be due to some grave fault in his nature and stopped that train of thought before it went any further.

He polished off a few Lincoln biscuits with the tea. Exhaustion weighed on him. Perhaps he was wrong to have opened the shop today. It was gloomy in the shed, though the door and window gave him strips of brightness. After laying the pipe in a saucer on the floor, he closed his eyes. On the screen of his eyelids he saw a leaded library window, lit by sunlight; the full, pink head of a rose pressed against it, seeming to watch over him, smiling. The image warmed and loosened him and, for a while, he dozed.

Half waking, he heard the telephone ring but no one came to trouble him. In his drowsiness, the new state of his life was gradually becoming apparent, not now in an ecstatic vision, but in melancholy. The truth of being alone sank into him: no wife, no children, no brothers or sisters to reflect back his childhood. He stared muzzily at a small patch of sky before his eyes slid closed again. Perhaps he should get out of the house. Would it be wrong of him to go to the pub this evening?

5.

Very late that night, he walked Monty along the lane behind the house. The snow, now frozen, crunched under his feet. From an icy, cloudless sky, a three-quarter moon looked down with what George felt to be an aloof, mocking gaze.

Monty was sniffing about somewhere out of sight. Just ahead was the beginning of the track to the Wyldes' farm. George stopped, feeling the cold air sting his nostrils, the heavy sit of his coat and the general befuddlement resulting from several pints in the Barley Mow. He thought back to the smoke-hazed light of the bar and gave a groan.

For a start, as well as the usual drinking crowd – his pals, Bill, Roy and the others – John Wylde, Maggie's husband, had come in. He didn't drink there often. As a farmer he was early both to bed and to rise. John came up and shook George's hand. He was a stocky, earnest-looking fellow with a shy manner. When he did look at you he had a rather penetrating gaze. Tonight, George mistook this for an ability to see into his own mortified soul. Fortunately, John put George's bumbling inability to construct a sentence down to the incoherence of grief.

'Sorry to hear about Mrs Baxter,' John said, as he held out his hand.

'Eeurgh . . .' George began. They shook hands, solemnly.

'Well . . .' John left a masterfully timed pause before nodding towards the dartboard. 'Team's waiting.'

George sat with his pipe lit, listening to chat about the impact of the weather on Bill's car, the carelessly thrown cigarette butt that had set unfortunate Graham Sellers' thatch on fire, the potholes in the Didcot road. Now he was on to his third pint he was gathering courage. That woman was behind the bar tonight – Barbara. He could see how it felt talking to a woman who was not known to him. After all, it had been a long time . . . Through the smoky air he kept seeing glimpses of her black hair, parted in the middle and fixed up at the back, a sheen on it under the lights. She wore a Windolene-pink sweater. He kept thinking about her. She must be at least, what, thirty-five? She was a compact woman, with a handsome if forbidding face with strong black eyebrows. So far as he knew, she lived somewhere on the other side of the village and he had seen her once or twice along the lanes. Though she often worked in the pub these days, he had never had anything resembling a proper conversation with her. Maybe, he thought, now was the time.

'My round.' George rose, gathered orders – a half of mild, one cider and three pints of Morland's – pulled his shoulders back, straightened his collar and advanced on the bar. He aimed to look masculine, noble and boyishly appealing all at once. He rested one arm on the bar while Barbara pulled a pint for some bloke in a swanky leather jacket. George's eyes moved, seemingly beyond his command, to her chest area. The sweater was a polo-neck, ribbed and tight, emphasizing even more the interesting apparatus at the front . . .

'So d'you want a drink or not?'

It seemed not to be the first time she had asked. She had moved to face him across the scattered beermats on the bar, a jar of maraschino cherries and a pot of cocktail sticks. Her arms were tightly folded across her chest as if she could read his mind. George retreated a step for a second, driven by the force of her glower.

'Er . . . Ah, yes! Of course.' He leaned on the bar again. 'Hello – good evening, Barbara, dear.' He smiled, waiting for her face to do something more encouraging than it was currently. But the glower deepened.

'My name's Brenda,' she snarled.

George was so flummoxed by her terse reaction that he clean forgot what the orders were and had to go back and ask. The others weren't slow to cotton on.

'Ha ha – is she giving you a hard time? George's gone and riled Brenda – look at 'er face! Go on, George – she won't bite you!'

He received plenty of ribbing over this and laughed along with them. But he still felt clownish and humiliated, which, in the presence of women generally, was no novelty.

Following Monty's progress through the darkness, he thought of Maggie with mournful longing. Maggie was the one woman he had ever known who had not made him feel like a fool. Even with Win, the least intimidating woman he had been able to find, it had happened eventually. Slowly, increasing over time, he had felt inadequate and forever in the wrong.

He stopped at the end of the farm track. He could see no lights. Maggie and John must be tucked up together. Suddenly he felt cold and very sober. He and Maggie had slipped into their little arrangement, just for a short time. And now they had to slip out of it again. He was not in love with Maggie Wylde and he did not believe she was in love with him. But at the thought of never lying in Maggie's arms again, his heart buckled with sorrow. Because – and what an admission – in his fifty-seventh year, it was with Maggie that he had discovered a joyful freedom in lovemaking that he had never known before.

'Monty? Where've you got to?' He pulled his torch out of his pocket and clicked it on. The beam of light soon picked out Monty's testicles swinging jauntily a few yards ahead.

'Come on – home now,' he called quietly. 'Best not come this way again.' As they strolled back he said, 'You seem to get by without the females, old boy. Perhaps I should take a leaf out of your book.'

Three

1.

Win was never quite sure about Maggie. 'I do wish she'd do something about her hair,' she said once or twice. Nothing harsher. Maggie was too warm a person to invite criticism. But there was something about her that unsettled Win. George could see why. She was, he thought, what you might call 'a natural'.

Wylde's was mainly a dairy farm with a few fields of wheat and barley. But Maggie also kept hens and her hens ran free. She was appalled by the idea of penning them up in battery sheds like some farmers were doing now.

Win loved eggs and used to go and buy half a dozen from Maggie quite regularly. But when she was too weak and off colour, George began to go instead.

Maggie wore skirts, always, despite the chores she did around the farm. Some women were taking to wearing trousers these days, which in the main George regretted. It was the war that started it, of course. All those forces girls. Even Win sometimes wore slacks, as she called them. She had a couple of neat navy pairs, 'for all that clambering about you make me do'. She was never too keen on the boat either.

Maggie did not clamber. Except on the hottest days of summer, she seldom wore anything on her feet but black wellington boots, whether prodding cows into the milking shed or collecting eggs. Above the boots would be the skirt and over that a thick cardigan which she often hugged around her, unwittingly emphasizing her curvaceous figure as she walked along. When it was cold, her hands would be invisible inside the sleeves. That first time they were together, the cardigan was a chunky thing the colour of marrowfat peas. And her skirt was brown. Though nothing exotic, it shimmied over her hips and buttocks in a way that gave a fulsome impression of the undulations beneath. Her thick hair, always loose, hung over her shoulders. No rollers or kirby grips – just her, loose and natural.

That time was not the first occasion when he had been to buy eggs. He had started going last autumn, after Win was taken bad again. There had been a period of grace after they took the breast off, before 'it' was back – in the liver. He never took Monty after the first time because his arrival sent the black and white farm dogs into a proprietorial apoplexy. They looked set to maul Monty's ears to ribbons.

George had been in an odd state then, he could see, looking back. He did not really recognize it at the time. Win shrank into a world of her own. He could never think what to do for the best for her. He was, though he hardly knew it, lost and achingly lonely. What happened that afternoon was never his conscious intention. Even so, he was not especially surprised by it. In his experience – most of which he had never shared with a single other person – women behaved in ways that were quite different from how they were expected to or were portrayed as doing. He knew that one of the reasons he'd married Win was that she *did* seem to behave in the ways women were expected to.

Maggie sold the eggs from an outbuilding across the yard from the house. It had turned cold and a bitter wind was blowing, forcing the stink of cow dung into George's nostrils as he followed her across the yard. She hugged herself loosely, as usual. He watched her haunches with appreciation. Before egg-buying became his task, he had hardly ever set eyes on Maggie Wylde, but now he found himself appreciating her pink country face, high cheekbones and wide mouth. Not a pretty woman exactly but lovely, a hint of childhood freckles still across the bridge of her nose.

'How's Mrs Baxter?' she asked over her shoulder. Her hair was caught to her neck by a green knitted scarf.

'Not so good,' George said, recovering himself as his boots slipped, almost landing him in a dark patch of slurry.

'Oops-a-daisy,' Maggie said, laughter in her voice at the sight of his flailing arms. Her laugh, he noticed, was wonderful; low and gurglingly naughty.

It was good to be in the outhouse, sheltered from the wind. The papier mâché trays of eggs were stacked on a table. Beside them were the boxes with lids, ready to be filled.

'Dozen or half?'

He asked for a dozen size twos. Holding the front edges of her cardigan with her left hand, Maggie reached for the boxes with her right and started to pop eggs into the slots, two at a time. Some were white, some a rich brown. A few were muddy and had feathers stuck to them. Watching, George noticed that Maggie bit her nails. The tip of her nose was pink with the cold. With both hands now, she closed the two boxes, put one on top of the other and slid them over to him. For the first time she raised her eyes to look at him, a slatey-blue gaze as he passed coins into her hand. She glanced down, counted the money and tipped it into a black cash box. Looking up again, she paused for a second, a questioning sympathy in her eyes and said, 'There's no one here but me.'

It was almost wordless, that first time. Maggie came round the table and gently jerked her head. He followed her, already overcome by a sense of surrender, out into the wind, to a barn the other side of the milking sheds.

Two sick heifers had been kept in from pasture in a pen divided off by rows of bales from the main straw stack. Maggie must have explained this to him, but afterwards he could not recall her speaking at all. What he could remember was the cool strength of her hand as she led him to the corner and the highest part of the wall of bales, her hands guiding his up under her blouse, the throaty sounds she made as they locked together. His own need rose fast, to a startling pitch. Her head tipped back, her hands gripping his arms. He could see her throat working, her chin pointing at the rafters as he rocketed up in her with what seemed unprecedented force. As they calmed, she righted her head and pulled on his arms. She pressed him close as he slid from her, glad to be able to straighten his legs. In the quiet he became aware of the young beasts' breathing. He stroked Maggie's thick hair. He felt mellow and released and grateful.

'I'm here a lot of the time,' she said, adjusting her skirt. 'On my own, I mean.' Into his silence she added, 'Nothing'll happen. I've got those pills.'

'*Have* you?' he said, astonished.

She moved her head and smiled up at him. 'I'm more of a modern girl than you'd take me for.'

2.

It only ever happened twice more. It was a long time before he dared go back. He was ashamed of his own wrongdoing and afraid of facing Maggie – of what she would want, or wouldn't. But one afternoon in the new year, feeling lonelier than ever in his life before, he did go. He had seen John Wylde drive away in his van earlier and thought perhaps today she might be alone. It was just before Win went into hospital and she had friends with her. He tried to persuade himself that they needed eggs, even though the real desperate, aching need, for comfort and reassurance, was his own.

'John won't be back for hours,' she said, leading him into the kitchen, which smelt of cattle-meal and dogs. 'He's gone to Aylesbury.' The three farm dogs sniffed round him suspiciously until Maggie ordered them away.

'Not your bedroom,' George protested as they climbed the stairs with their runner of green carpet. He felt a primitive revulsion at the idea of sharing sheets with John Wylde.

'Don't be silly.' Maggie's skirt was undulating in front of him. 'There's Linda's old room.' Of her three children only the youngest, Rick, lived at home and he was at work. 'It's spare now – there's a little heater in there.'

At the top of the stairs she reached for his hand again. She looked at it for a moment and gave that low laugh in her throat, then reached up and kissed his cheek. 'Come on.'

She took him into a room at the far end of the landing: pale green walls, a single bed and chest of drawers. It was almost bare of possessions, except for a few china animals on the chest – elephants, a glass fish. The floor was brown lino with a bar of winter sunlight across it.

What surprised him most, in all the feverish, life-giving relief of it all, was the amount of laughter between himself and Maggie. For a start, there was her reaction to the sight of him naked. There he was, stripped down to his Adam suit, she standing before him, pink and rounded and lovely, her hair loose over her shoulders. Suddenly Maggie sank down on the bed and laughter poured out of her like spring water, gurgling across the floor to meet him.

'What the hell's so funny?' he said, wounded.

'You!' She made attempts to recover, wiping her eyes. 'Oh, deary me – sorry! Just *you*, Georgy-Porgy.' With a grin of pure affection she opened her arms. 'Come 'ere then.'

Lovemaking in a single bed made them feel like naughty kids. Maggie's body was – if not a surprise, since lately he had spent much time imagining – a wonder to him. Her limbs, like her hair, had a heaviness that he found strong and reassuring, as if she was a wall he could lean into.

From the beginning there was a relaxed, nuzzling playfulness. Their eyes kept returning to each other's gaze, seeing each other, her face amused, affectionate, aroused. At last she slipped over him, both of them rocking together until she was panting and he could not hold back from letting the stars burst and reel away from the taut universe of his body and for those moments he could forget all the helplessness and desolation of Win slipping away from him.

When they had both quietened and lay together, sweat slicking between them, then they were at their most serious. That was the day the talking began.

George leaned up on one elbow and looked down at her. He traced a wormy stretch mark across the side of her belly with his finger. Maggie patted her stomach as if it was a friend.

'Home to three,' she said. 'Bit like a tent – the big top. Seems funny now – as if it never happened.' The thread of a sigh came from her. 'They're all gone – nearly, anyway. And here I am – still just here.'

George stroked her thigh, saying nothing. This was outside his experience. He and Win had somehow never had children. He had never experienced the terror of getting a girl pregnant that other blokes seemed to be forever worrying about. Win had never needed those pills. Not that he blamed her in any way. For all they knew the fault might just as well lie with him. They had never checked to find out and it was a sadness that lay silent between them. But Win seemed to assume that hers was the lack and suffered in quiet, undramatic ways that he could not reach.

For a second the troublesome memory of Argentina and Inés Lester needled in his mind and he pushed it away. A woman who had confessed her barrenness to him. A long time ago, he thought. And a long way away.

Maggie raised her head and looked at him, wide-eyed as a child. 'You're a nice man, George. I hope you don't think badly of me.'

It had not crossed his mind to think badly. At this precise

moment he was lost in a state of worship for her. He was the villain of the piece – a man unfaithful to his sick wife. He told her so and she smiled sadly.

'You're not a villain. We all just need more than we've got most of the time.' After a moment she rolled a little apart from him and wiped the inner bends of her elbows then rubbed her hands on her thighs. 'Phoo – it's hot. Shall we switch that heater off?'

George got up, stretched and ambled over to switch off the heater, which was blowing hot air into the room. He felt a festive sense of reprieve, of aliveness, naked in the warmth, the air stroking his skin. A guffaw came from the bed.

'You've got a nice bottom, Georgy-Porgy.'

'Have I?'

'Very *ample*.'

He strode back to the bed. 'And you, madam, are a very cheeky girl.' He tickled her and she writhed and wobbled so deliciously that he felt another hoik of desire. Lying down again, an arm crooked across her, he spoke, like someone breaking out of a cell.

'I'll never understand women. Queer cattle, one of my army pals used to say. Very queer.'

He expected her to laugh or protest, but she drew back on the pillow a little and looked carefully at him. 'What d'you mean?'

'You want me to say – really?'

'Really. I do.'

He eased round on to his back, resting his hand against her warm belly. She laid a palm on his chest as if to feel his heart.

'The thing is . . . This is going to sound as if I'm bragging. It's not that – it's just, I've found that women have come to me in the past. Taken charge.'

Except Win, he thought. Not her. That had been another of her attractions – she waited for him to make the first move.

Maggie made that small sound of amusement in her throat. 'You've got come-hitherish eyes, George.'

'*Have* I?' News indeed.

'Oh yes. You have.'

He was still trying to take this in when she said, 'What was your mum like?'

George lifted a leg, crossed it over the other. Such freedom: naked, talking. A slack, joyful feeling.

'She died when I was quite young,' he said. 'I was five, just. They must have taken me away that day, to a house somewhere. There was a grey cat, very big with yellow eyes. I didn't like it – it didn't like me much either. That's all I remember.'

'But you remember *her*?'

He thought for a moment. A pink rose glimpsed through the leaded casement of a school . . . 'She's always just out of reach.'

Maggie lifted her head and looked down at him. 'You poor little devil.' Her country accent made it all the more tender. 'What about brothers, sisters?'

'Just me. My father was a schoolmaster. Sometime after that he managed to get a job in the college – a boarding school, so that we could live in and I'd have companions. There was no one my age to begin with, but in the end I was given some sort of scholarship there.'

'That sounds posh,' Maggie remarked, lying down again. 'That's why you talk like that.'

'Like what?'

'Nicely. Properly. Not like me.'

'I like the way you talk. But yes, I had a better chance there. I was never any good though. Always better with my hands. Dad could see it and as soon as he could get me out, he sent me to Arkwright's to learn cabinet-making and restoration.'

'Didn't you run away?' She moved her head a little, her hair caressing his skin. 'From school? I thought that's what you do if you're shut in one of them places.'

'My father was there – where would I have run to?'

'I dunno – away to sea! I would've done.' After a moment she said, 'Don't you just want to run away from here? Go anywhere, see things? The furthest I've ever been's Devon – just once.'

Devon. Win's favourite holiday spot. 'Why don't we go abroad, for a change?' he used to say in the early days. He had seen a few other parts of the world already and it had widened things for him.

'Abroad?' A grimace would accompany this. 'Why ever would you want to do that when it's so nice here? We can go to that clean little boarding house – such a pleasant couple . . .' Year after year. He stopped asking.

'You must've been places, Georgie – in the war?'

'I was in Italy – Service Corps. And before the war I went to New York – and Buenos Aires.'

Her head shot up again. '*Did* you? Why?'

'Oh – business.' He wasn't talking about that. Business!

'New York – I'd love to go there. What was it like?'

'It was . . . extraordinary.'

That was one word for it, he thought. A collision of disquieting feelings arose in him when he touched on these memories: New York; Argentina, the Lesters. He wasn't going into all that now. He turned on his side again and took Maggie in his arms. She felt big and limp and warm. Now he was calmer though, and released, he could feel the cold gnaw of guilt beginning. He must leave. He shouldn't be here, should never have come.

'So you're a local girl?' As if it wasn't obvious. But he wanted to change the subject.

'Oh yes, local,' she said flatly. 'Grew up in Cholsey. Married my schoolroom sweetheart. Sometimes I look back and think, why was I in such a hurry? I married him when I was eighteen. I could've done all sorts – taken off in a car, travelled the world. I want to *see* things, George.' She began to sound almost tearful. 'Not just cows and chickens.'

'Maybe you will, one day.' He kissed her forehead, feeling he ought to extricate himself from her but not wanting to hurt her feelings. 'Tell you what – why don't you come out with me on the river?'

'What – at Wallingford?' She soundly intensely unexcited by this. 'Hardly seeing the world, is it?'

'Well, change of scene . . .' He smiled at her. He noticed, now, the sinking light outside. 'I must go, my dear. Must get home.'

Maggie kissed his cheek. 'You must.' Their eyes met, smiling, and they held each other again before he climbed out of bed.

3.

They never did go out on the boat together. There were just those two afternoons (the first time hardly counted, he felt). The second time, only a month ago, she had passed him in the morning as he walked the dog. I'll be on my own, she told him, without stopping.

There was that pale green room again, the two of them taking refuge in each other, with the winter afternoon going on distantly outside. It felt to him as if the real unfaithfulness lay in the talking, even though he knew that Win was really gone from him already. Even in the short periods when she was awake now, she was far, far away. She seemed more comfortable with her nurse than with him. He was deeply fond of Maggie, touched by her longing, and its clash with her loyalties. She needed to talk as much as he did, to work things out.

That second afternoon, as they lay under the covers, not having bothered with the heater, heads on the shared pillow, Maggie raised her head, looking down at him. He saw her pause for a moment, as if worried by what she was about to say.

'Have you ever been in love, George? Really in love?'

He looked up into her eyes, shocked by the question. He loved Win, of course he did. But in a barely acknowledged, secret part of him, he knew what Maggie was asking. Have you been *really* in love: to the absolute depth of your soul? And was that real and possible or just something in stories? He hardly knew how to answer her because he hardly dared ask himself.

'Well – in a funny way, yes,' he decided to say. Maggie was settling again, up close to him, but her head popped up when he said, 'I don't want you to get the wrong idea about this.' He laid a hand on her head and gently pressed her down.

'I told you I was in supplies in the war. Remember Cassino?'

He felt her nod. 'Course. That monastery.'

'February '44 was when it happened. God, what a winter. Rain and more freezing rain, pouring down those mountains, great towering, jagged things. The Germans were dug in up there. All the roads were like swamps. You couldn't drive a truck in anywhere near the front line. So they used mules. At the time a mule was more use than a tank. They went round the farms commandeering mules off the locals. They're astonishing animals, tough as anything, noble . . .'

'Anyway—' He could feel a smile tugging at his cheeks. 'For a few days up there, I was assigned to go with a Mule Company carrying supplies up to the front. Now, this wasn't exactly music to my ears because I've never got along with horses. I didn't have much experience of them and what I did have had put me off even more. Vicious buggers, all teeth and hooves, out to get you. Most of the handlers who looked after the mules were Indian lads – good fellers. They seemed to know what they were about, which was more than I did.'

He heard an amused snort from the region of his armpit.

'While we were loading up, I was talking to one of them, a lad called Rajesh – a thin chap, very cheerful. He was holding this mule by its halter. She was a splendid creature;

mealy-coloured muzzle, great long ears. "She is called Clotilde," the chap said. "But we call her Lottie. She is a very good mule."

'We were standing there in the drizzle, the mule just behind us, chatting about what needed doing. After a time I felt something fondling my backside . . .'

'I told you you've got a nice backside,' Maggie mumbled into his arm.

'Yes, but then I felt teeth sinking into me. It didn't hurt exactly because I had thick layers on, but I whipped round all right. Rajesh was looking at me, eyebrows up. "She bit me!" I said – I was quite put out. But d'you know, by the time I'd turned round, that animal had turned her head and was staring in the other direction as if she'd never been anywhere near my backside. Rajesh was grinning from ear to ear. "I think she is tricking you," he said. "Lottie is a very naughty girl."'

Maggie raised her head again, her eyes full of merriment. 'She bit your bum and then pretended she hadn't?'

'You've never seen an animal look more innocent. As I spent those couple of days with her I realized she was a marvellous character. You could chat to her – tell her your woes, sort of thing. She never bit me again. But she definitely had a sense of humour. If you were standing anywhere near her she'd stick her neck out and just breathe down your ear. Rather as if she was kissing you. And those mules are tough as anything: they brought the casualties down, a stretcher hanging each side. And the loads they carried up the mountains – astonishing.'

He felt his chest tighten. Surely he wasn't going to weep again – not after all this time?

'It's a daft thing, I know, but she made me feel safe. I stuck near her all the way. It was bloody frightening up there. The paths were incredibly narrow in places, wet, slippery. It was hell for the infantry, no other word for it. Lottie was – I don't know – she was loving, she made you laugh – she was *life*. Sounds ridiculous, doesn't it?'

'No,' Maggie said. 'Animals are better than us, most of the time.'

'We toiled uphill for hours, the rain pouring down. You could hear the guns. And with no warning there was the biggest explosion of all, right behind me – blew me over. I thought my heart was going to split out of the top of my head. And she'd gone—'

'Lottie?' Up Maggie came again.

'Trod on a mine. De-bollockers, they called them. Bits of her all over . . . And . . .' He stopped, not sure how his voice was going to come out.

'Oh!' Maggie held him, motherly all of a sudden, or how he imagined a mother might be. 'How awful!'

'Rajesh howled. Both of us, there on that mountainside, blubbing away like kids.'

'Oh Georgy-Porgy,' Maggie said.

'That daft mule going like that – it was like the whole war, all of it; the bloody awful, cruel stupidity of all of it.' He felt Maggie stroke his chest. 'Is that love?' He tried to give a laugh, wiping his eyes. 'It felt like it. Dear old Lottie.'

'Why shouldn't it be love?' Maggie said. 'If it gets in your heart like that.'

George took a deep breath, taking in the musky scent of Maggie beside him. The choking sensation started to recede. He felt limp, and once again, grateful. He laid his hand on the top of her legs.

'Queer time, that,' he said. 'Everything lit up, very bright.' After a moment he added, 'I've never told anyone that before.'

Maggie rolled onto her stomach, her hair tickling his chest. 'No one?'

'No one.'

She pulled herself further up to press a kiss on his lips. 'Thank you,' she said in a tender voice. 'For telling me.'

Win grew sicker. He tried to be with her as much as possible. Every week, though, she became more withdrawn and in the days before she finally went into hospital, he found it harder and harder to approach her. Guiltily, he supposed she was angry with him. Was she pushing him away to prepare him for her absence – or did she sense some new physical satisfaction in him? To hurt her was the last thing he wanted. But was everyone in the know, in fact? He had seen Maggie so little that it was hard to believe anyone could have found out. He had never met a soul on the farm or on the way there or back. But women always seemed to know things, as if they had film recording machines everywhere you went. What about the Cronies, Rosemary and Pat, Eunice and the others? He became convinced that they knew.

But was he really sorry? Win seemed to have long left him behind as she travelled on to a place where he could not follow. And Maggie had given him new aspects of himself as a man: joy in his body, unashamed and celebratory. He and Win could claim to have had an intimate life all right. She had always been game (that seemed the word which summed it up). But she always approached intimate relations as she might tackle a pile of ironing – see to it briskly and fold it away again, just the way, afterwards, she would tuck herself into a tightly belted floral dressing gown. She preferred him to be covered up as well. And none of it was ever to be talked about. He knew Win cared about him, as he did her – fondly and always, until now, loyally, over all these years. But somehow he had never felt free in this area of life, as if he must be endlessly polite and on his guard.

Maggie, bless her, had sparked a revelation, shown him a new way he could be – one day, eventually. If he could just find someone to be it with.

Four

1.

For the next few days, life in the shop went on as usual. George secreted slices of pie alternately into the dustbin and the dog at a convincing pace until it was all gone. Its effects on Monty, already a liquorice enthusiast, were not overly volcanic. The snow gave way to days of slush, so that most people who advanced on the front door did so perilously in wellington boots. After a tactful period had elapsed, the wellingtons that began to stride up the drive were those of the Cronies.

They arrived at exquisitely paced intervals. George guessed there must have been a conflab among them to work out the ideal tincture of well-intentioned visits. Each was timed comfortably after closing at five thirty, when everyone else had gone home and night was drawing in.

Rosemary was the first. George was in the kitchen in his slippers, munching a cheese and pickle sandwich and wondering how his homebrewed ale was getting along. There was a sharp assault on the front-door knocker. The dog roared. George ushered him grumbling into the kitchen, where he barked furiously before giving up to sulk. George switched on the hall light. Opening up, he was met by a glistening black wall of umbrella – it had started to drizzle – from under which emerged Rosemary's face, like that of an embarrassed tortoise.

'Ah – Mr Baxter!' she exclaimed, as if no one more surprising could be discovered on his own doorstep.

Rosemary, a couple of years George's senior, was wide-hipped and full-breasted with a scrubbed-looking complexion, faded hair permed into tight curls and bossy brown eyes. She had spent most of her life nursing – 'I did my training at Barts, you know . . . I rose to Matron!' – which explained the sense of impending enema George experienced in her presence. Win told him he was being ridiculous, but nevertheless. There had been a break in this career for a short period when Rosemary married. No one knew what had happened to her husband, other than that this episode involved the word 'horrors' and was swiftly over. You Don't Ask, Win said, seeming rather amused despite herself.

'Ah,' George said. 'Hello Mrs, er, Miss . . .' What the devil was her surname? 'Rosemary,' he resorted to. He clutched at his pipe in his jacket pocket.

'I thought I'd call,' Rosemary announced. Later, when the others started turning up, he realized she had probably volunteered to Go First. As a Professional.

'Come in?' He stood back.

'Oh no; no need . . .'

'But it's a rotten night.'

She relented with a girlish laugh which took him aback and a moment later they were standing in the hall, the point of her umbrella dripping onto the tiles. She was in fact wearing a pair of huge black galoshes. Only now George also made out that she was holding something bulky-looking under her left arm. Above the hefty footwear was a camel coat from under which peeped a hint of box-pleats.

'Do come through . . .' He waved a hand towards the back of the house. 'Have a drink – cup of tea, perhaps?'

'Oh no. Really.'

'Well – or coffee?' What was the right thing? Cocoa? Gin?

'No, I won't stay.'

George thought he made out a blotchy effusion of colour making its way upwards from beneath the woman's collar. He was not sure what to make of this. She was undeniably flustered. With Win she had never been flustered. She might toss a 'good morning' to him, as if he were a passing acquaintance who she vaguely remembered. But flustered, no.

'I thought I'd better see if you needed any help,' she said, standing her ground in the hall. 'I know Vera's marvellous, but she has plenty to do with her own little brood and sometimes, well . . . A professional eye – I'm sure you understand . . .'

'Ah?' He played for time. He hadn't the least idea what the woman was on about. She really seemed rather odd. He was also suddenly aware that his breath smelled of pickled onions, which didn't seem to set the right tone.

'I didn't mean to disturb you. I know Vera's taking very good care of you.'

'Oh she *is*,' George said, thinking guiltily of the remains of the pie hidden in a bag at the bottom of the dustbin. There were limits to how much even Monty should be eating.

'What I really mean in the way of help . . .' Rosemary stepped towards him slightly, appearing to steel herself. 'Was with Win – with Mrs Baxter's – things. I thought you might need a female eye on such, well, *intimate* tasks.' She was blushing furiously now.

'Yes indeed, thank you . . . I haven't quite got to that yet . . .'

'No of *course* not – one mustn't rush these things. All in due season. But if and when . . . Well, must be off! Oh!' she exclaimed, seeming to have forgotten the chunky object she was clutching. 'I thought you might like this. So important to keep oneself properly fed . . .'

George found himself holding a large tin. 'Oh – thank you! How kind.'

There was a fumbling moment as both of them made a move for the door and ended up jammed so close together with the tin between them that there was scarcely room to manoeuvre.

'Oh dear me!' George leapt into reverse as Rosemary exclaimed, 'Oh heavens – sorry!' and hurtled back as if the door handle had given her an electric shock. They were now back where they started but in an even more awkward state.

'After you,' George said, giving an exaggerated stage bow and feeling a complete fool.

At last, between them, they managed to get Rosemary out on to the step, where she put her umbrella up again. But she still didn't move.

'We, er . . .' she sputtered. George waited. What on earth now? 'We are all very . . . well, so upset. Win and so on . . .'

For a few seconds the memory came to him of them all round Win's bed, the Cronies. All her loyal female friends whom, he assumed, she felt loved her better than he did.

'And you being left alone,' Rosemary was saying. 'You know, not right really, a man and so on. Very sorry. You know where I am – any time . . .'

'Oh thank you!' George said for what felt like the umpteenth time. 'Very good of you.'

He watched her stumping off into the darkness of the slushy drive, slightly bent forward under the umbrella, and realized that contrary to the impression given, he had only the vaguest idea where she lived. Somewhere near the church, he thought.

'Funny woman.'

Determinedly he put all of it out of his mind and went to the cellar to fetch one of his crocks of mild. He left the woman's gift on the side in the kitchen and did not give it a thought until the next morning when Vera arrived. She stopped, coming in through the kitchen door.

'What's that?' she said, eyeing the foreign item on the counter. It was a square Huntley & Palmers tin, 'Cocktail Assorted' biscuits.

'Oh, I don't know,' George said. 'Rosemary . . . You know, *Rosemary*, brought it round last night.'

'Abbott,' Vera looked quite put out. '*Did* she now? She's a proper bossy boots, that one.' She put her bag down and picked the thing up for a moment, weighing it suspiciously. As she lifted the lid, George went to look. Squeezed diagonally across the square tin was a fat Swiss roll, seeping jam at each end.

'Gracious,' Vera said, staring at this offering. The way she said it seemed freighted with significance, though George couldn't make out for the life of him what the significance might be.

To his astonishment he saw a grin spread across Vera's face. 'What kind of roll is *she* after, I wonder?' She started giggling, a hand over her mouth.

George recalled that odd flush moving up from Rosemary Abbott's neck. A small, terrifying chink of light began to dawn on him.

'Good Lord – *no*? Vera, really – you're having me on.'

'I wouldn't be so sure.' Vera restored the lid to the cake tin and went to the sink. Chuckles kept breaking out of her. 'Dear oh dear, we're going to have to look out for you, Mr B.'

2.

Pat Nesbitt, Win's best friend, arrived two days later with her brown and white springer spaniels. George was caught unawares, with the front door open. The first he knew of the visitation was that Monty, who did not approve of other dogs appearing in his front garden, launched himself out into the gloom in a frenzy of rage.

Pat and her husband lived in a clematis-festooned cottage at the heart of the village. Pat, blue-eyed, with just about still blonde curls and a toothy smile, was an ex WAAF. Husband Bill, ex RAF, was something at Harwell (this was how Win always attempted to explain it). Something not on the scientific side. And she described the Nesbitts' marriage as one in which they 'rubbed along'. And against? George always wanted to ask, but knew better than to. Pat always seemed cheerful enough, whatever kinds of rubbing she was experiencing. This despite their one daughter having moved so far away. Since the girl married her Yorkshireman, Pat and Bill had given themselves up to weekend golf with what George considered to be immoderate enthusiasm.

'Monty!' George roared, leaping out into the crazed confusion of barking and dogs' tails. He seized Monty's collar, his hands immediately bespattered with slobber and hauled on it, but only seemed to proceed with Monty attached to the other two dogs in a snarling mass.

'Oh dear!' Pat exclaimed cheerily. 'What a commotion!'

Pat was one of those Englishwomen who accompany most statements, however doom-laden, with horsey eruptions of laughter. 'Looking very bad, isn't it?' Nya-ha-ha! 'Backs against the wall – fancy that, we're really up against it now!' Aha-ha-ha-ha!

'I think Lulu might be coming on heat!' she shrilled across the sea of heaving fur.

'Ah! – Oh!' George yelled. Why the hell had the silly woman brought her here then? This all made even the most basic social intercourse impossible, except for Pat's insistent thrusting of a jar of marmalade into his hand.

'Thick cut!' she shrieked. Hauling on the spaniels, she let out other snatches of noise. 'Made last year . . . Seville oranges . . . Hope you're coping . . . Vera – marvellous . . .'

Having managed to fit the marmalade in his jacket pocket, George yanked a lathered-up Monty off one of the springers' backs. He was towing him over to the house when Monty ground to a halt and slipped his collar. Pat and the spaniels were receding towards the gate. 'So sorry! Back another time!'

It took Monty's slow-chugging brain several seconds to realize that freedom was his and he turned and started off again after the juicy spaniel.

'For heaven's sake, Monty!' George flung himself after the dog. Tripping over into something that became a rugby tackle, he landed half on top of Monty, hands wrapped round the animal's neck. Both of them grunted, winded. Something stabbed into the right side of George's ribs. He realized he was lying prone on top of not only a large basset hound but also a jar of thick-cut marmalade. Struggling to get up and hold on to the frantic animal at the same time, he let out several emphatic army expletives. No sign of broken glass. The marmalade had survived.

'Silly bloody woman,' he grumbled, manhandling a heart-broken Monty into the house. Once the door was closed, the dog tipped his head back, baying in frustration. 'What the hell did she bring them for, eh?' George felt along his ribcage, wondering if anything was broken. He decided to assume not. 'To torment you, old boy.'

But he realized, with some gratitude, that Pat had brought the dogs as cover, so that they would not have to talk, which he did not want to do any more than she did. Pat Nesbitt was a good sort really. Beneath all the neighing, she was kindly and down to earth.

'So,' he muttered, leaving Monty in a despairing posture on the front doormat. 'Who'll be next, I wonder?'

3.

He had to wonder only until Sunday afternoon, when the last of them appeared. Perhaps the Cronies had calculated – rightly – that this was a day when things would be difficult for him.

George had a snooze by the fire in the sitting room after lunch. Then he busied himself, with a newspaper spread over the card table, gluing together the parts of a Meissen plate. During Win's illness he had begun to get used to the house being so quiet. Now though, as he pieced together the delicate coloured fragments, enjoying the smell of Araldite, the clock seemed to tick so loudly that he almost wanted to move it to another room. He tried to keep his attention on the work before him.

He had the kettle on and was letting Monty out at the front when a gaunt figure walked into the drive wearing a calf-length navy coat and matching brimless hat. His first impulse was to act as if he hadn't seen her, to slam the door shut and pretend to be out. These options being blatantly out of the question, he went to restrain Monty's friendly indignation in the face of another visitor.

'Yes, yes that's right – you keep guard,' the woman said in her deep, cultured voice as Monty rushed at her legs. She stooped to pat him. Within seconds the dog was silent as a monk and casting adoring looks at her.

'Sorry, Miss MacLean,' George said, glad that at least this time he could remember the name. Eunice MacLean lived in one of the narrow Tudor terraces just along the road.

'Oh we're old friends, Monty and I,' she said, straightening up. She was carrying a cloth bag which looked as if it contained an enormous jar of jam.

'Do come in,' he invited, discovering in himself for once an enthusiasm for company.

'I don't wish to disturb.'

'No, no,' he said. 'Do come along. I was making tea.'

He led the tall rod of a woman into the hall. Under the coat, which he took to hang up for her, was a straight, grey dress with an edge of lace at the neck.

'A cup of tea?'

'How nice. Though I should prefer coffee.'

The door of the showroom was open and she lingered, looking in. George eyed her from the back. She had steel-grey hair, cut in a severe pageboy and wore black shoes with a strap and button. In her way, he realized, she was rather chic. She reminded him of a period piece from the 1920s and her old-world manners only increased this impression.

'What a beautiful room this is, Mr Baxter.' She spoke in a slow, measured way. 'Such an artistic arrangement. And this – exquisite.' Moving to look at a lady's rosewood desk, she smiled wistfully. 'So pretty and well proportioned. If only one had the funds.'

'Nice piece, isn't it?' he agreed. The woman had a good eye. 'I'll, er, make that coffee.'

She turned. 'Oh, please don't go to any trouble.'

'No trouble,' he said, already halfway to the kitchen. How else were tea and coffee to be made? he wondered wearily. The fact that he had lost his wife made people seem to think he was incapable of lifting a kettle.

Sitting opposite Eunice MacLean once he had directed her and a tray into the sitting room, he was struck, once again, by the look of her. As well as being stylish in an old-world sort of way, she moved with grace. Looking at her now, her strong, almost manly features, blue eyes and arched, slender brows, he realized she may once have been rather a stunner, if perhaps an intimidating one. Now, though, she was so far from anything that was attractive to George in a female that he found himself feeling quite relaxed with her, as if she was another man, or perhaps a Chippendale chair.

'It is difficult to know quite when to call on someone,' she said in her precise English. She followed this by taking a ladylike sip of coffee. George saw the clench of her gristly throat. 'But it is not good to be left completely alone when one has suffered a great loss.'

George swallowed his mouthful of tea, surprised by the rich sympathy in her voice. 'No, I suppose not,' he said. He held out the little tea plate. 'Bourbon?'

Eunice declined with a disdainful flick of a hand. She was sitting very straight on the chair, feet together like a prim schoolmistress. While she seemed to George an alien creature, there was nevertheless something fascinating about her.

He took another gulp of tea and fingered his pipe in his pocket, at a loss. He had never been alone with any of these women while Win was alive. They passed frequently in and out of his house, and Win in and out of theirs. He scarcely knew them at all, other than in transit and from the remarks Win had made about them now and then. He tried to remember anything she had said about Eunice. There was a connection with France. Some tragedy. He didn't think Win knew the details.

'I have brought something to show you,' Eunice said, reaching down for the bag and the pot of jam. The jam, which required both hands for her to manage its weight, turned out to be a clock. She stood it on the table, turned it towards him and he was faced with an outburst of beauty.

'I say!' He sat straighter with genuine pleasure. 'What a marvellous piece. Those decorations – Sèvres, would you say?'

He could see that the clock was French, a rich assembly of gold, red, white and a vivid royal blue. It was constructed like a portico, the clock face hanging as if in a gateway, suspended from the golden roof with a decorated column on each side. The lower edge of the clock was joined, by a gold strip, to a round, ornate picture of a nymph. Down each column and across the top it was inlaid with the rich, glowing colours.

'They are Sèvres in style, I believe,' Eunice said. She gave a smile of pleasure which decreased the ruminant character of her face. Her eyes, he saw, were extraordinarily full of life and feeling. 'It was made, I'm told, sometime mid-way through the last century.'

'Eighteenth century in style, though.'

'Yes.' She seemed pleased. 'Papa – my father – gave it to me.'

'Your father was French?'

'Oh no, it was my mother who was French. Father was Scottish. Presbyterian.'

Of course. MacLean. George waited to see if she would say

more but she did not. He didn't like to pry. If there was some tragedy, he was clearly not going to discover what it was. He cleared his throat. 'Were you hoping for a valuation?'

'No, *no*,' she said, tetchily. 'I have no intention of selling it. I thought it might be of interest, that's all.'

'Oh it *is*.' He smiled now, without reservation. 'Marvellous. So much better than jam.'

'Jam?' Her brow wrinkled.

'Yes, er . . .' This insight was impossible to explain and fortunately Eunice let it go. She was sliding the clock back into the bag.

'I know others will have asked,' she said, holding the bag on her lap. 'But after a death there is a lot to do. I would be happy to help, if you need any assistance.'

'Thank you, Miss MacLean,' he said sincerely, feeling that if he had to resort to accepting any of these offers, he might in fact prefer hers. 'It's very good of you. We men on our own—' He gave a laugh. 'Not the most practical. But I think Vera will be able to help when necessary.'

'You know . . .' She looked up from the bag with the clock, held on her lap. 'I don't wish to pry, Mr Baxter . . .'

Heavens, George thought. Now what was coming? He assumed a neutral, interested expression.

'Win was a marvellous person in her way,' she began. 'Full of practical kindness.' George nodded. Yes of course, of course. A kindness from which he had benefited every day – her cooking, her care of him. With a sudden pang, he longed for her to walk into the room. It had been good, so much of it, had it not, day to day? Getting by together – was that not the very heart of marriage? Images of her arrayed themselves in his mind: Win in the garden, hanging clothes; walking the beach in Wales, dark hair blown to one side; their wedding day, the look she had given him at the altar, those trusting eyes. A good woman. And thinking back to the young man he had been when he married her, would he not do it all over again?

'But . . .' Miss MacLean looked at him with such disconcerting directness that George found it hard to hold her gaze, especially with tears threatening to rise in his eyes. But she seemed to think better of whatever she had been about to say. She paused. 'I'm sure you have a lot of life to live yet,' was all she said, with a gentle smile.

'Yes. Let's hope so.' He tried to smile back, blinking away his emotion.

When they had finished their drinks, chatting a little more, he saw her to the door. After stepping outside, she turned, placed her feet precisely together and said, 'I wonder, Mr Baxter, if you would like to come to the cinema with me one evening?'

George was so taken by surprise that he stood with his mouth open for several seconds while his lulled brain cranked into action. Was this . . . ? Had he read the situation all wrong? An image of the rather disturbing Swiss roll brought by Rosemary Abbott elbowed its way into his mind. Was that . . . ? Did it mean . . . ? Oh dear God.

'The Regal in Wallingford often has a good picture showing,' Eunice said, unperturbed.

He was absolutely stumped for anything to say.

'It's all right, Mr Baxter,' Eunice said. He was sure he did not imagine her withering tone. 'I was simply asking if you would like to go to the pictures, since we both now live alone. I was not making any other sort of suggestion. I am almost fifty-three years old – quite ancient enough, I think you would agree, to be past flightiness. A trip to the cinema is, for me, simply a trip to the cinema.'

'I'm sorry,' he managed to utter. 'Truly sorry. Bit of an odd state at the moment. Peculiar time. Yes – thank you . . . I mean, perhaps . . .'

She held a hand up. 'No need to decide anything. It was just a passing thought. Thank you for the coffee, Mr Baxter.'

'No, thank *you*,' he gushed, idiotically. 'And for the jam – clock, I mean!' He watched her walk off into the darkening afternoon, shamed by her solitary dignity.

'You clumsy fool,' he ranted at himself. Shooing Monty inside and closing the front door, he sagged, leaning his back against it. 'Women,' he groaned. But there were those words she had laid before him, like a gift. *I'm sure you have a lot of life to live yet*. And all he could feel was gratitude. Her words sparked in him – they were an affirmation. As if she had in some way granted him permission for life.

He closed his eyes for a moment, then rallied. 'Right, Monty – what about some of those sausages?'

Opening the refrigerator, he let out a yelp. 'Oh no – oh Lord!' How had he missed seeing it when he came to fetch the milk? And how . . . ? When . . . ? Vera must have popped in some time this morning. Gracing the top shelf, with beautifully crenellated edges and tell-tale pink oozings, was another very large pie.

MARCH

Five

1.

George sat at his desk in the office at the front of the house. It was a Saturday morning, the wind buffeting outside. Through the window he could see daffodils leaning first one way, then another, like old biddies nosing out of a window.

The small room was crowded with his desk, shelves and filing cabinet, the worn remnant of deep red Persian rug concealing the only remaining patch of floor. It, in turn, was mostly covered by Monty, sprawled in a pose of exaggerated relaxation and giving off doggy pongs. Although this was normal, George was starting to wonder if this was what was contributing to the swimmy, not-quite-right feeling he had today. He pushed the window open a crack.

The ceiling-high shelves to his left were mostly filled with old ledgers, interspersed with other things. At his eye level were two photographs, the first of his and Win's wedding day, he standing tall, bluff and, he thought, pretty ridiculous-looking. Win, small and neat beside him in a long white dress and veil, had been captured wearing her reserved smile. The other was a studio portrait of Win, taken ten or so years ago, with the same curled hair, that modest yet closed smile, as if she was longing to look anywhere but at the camera.

High up was the open-jawed skull of a Bengal tiger, which

had arrived with an assortment of items from a house auction. From another sale he had bought the reproduction of Canaletto's Grand Canal in Venice, which hung to his right. He had passed through Venice in 1945 as they made their way up Italy, and the place had filled him with amazement.

A ledger lay open on the desk in front of him, but concentration was nigh on impossible. Vera was dealing with a couple of newly-weds – or was it about-to-be-weds? – in the showroom across the hall. The young woman's operatic laugh kept intruding on him through the closed door, further jangling his nerves. He was definitely not right today. His legs felt peculiar and his temples were throbbing. He stared at the sheet of accounts. Business was not bad, though he needed to get out and stock up. Things were picking up. But he did feel thick-headed and slow. Had there been something dodgy about his homebrew last night, or was he in fact sickening for something? He couldn't be sure.

Vera was talking. She sounded quite commanding, he thought with admiration. Gazing out at the lurching daffodils – all life felt as if it was rocking about this morning – it occurred to him that there was something different about Vera these days. He spent a few seconds trying to work out quite what it was, before giving up. He was in no state to think.

All the same, things with Vera were going rather well. They had come to an arrangement about her duties: there would be a certain amount of cleaning, but increasingly she would take on responsibilities in the shop. In fact Vera had startled him by mentioning that if the shop started to occupy a great deal of her time and he needed a char, then perhaps the best thing would be to take on someone else?

Above all, George had pledged that he would learn to cook. So far his repertoire had expanded from bacon and eggs and beans on toast, to include:

Sausage and mash

Chops, pork or lamb with potatoes and cabbage

Kippers (though they didn't half send a smother through the house and Vera advised against – 'we don't want to put the customers off')

Mushroom omelettes

'What you need,' Vera suggested, 'is to cook a joint. Then you'll have something to last you through the week. And there's always macaroni cheese. Nice with a dab of mustard.'

The supply of pies had abated. To his relief she had been alternating with fruit crumbles.

Another arpeggio of laughter floated through the door, followed by some cooing observation. He expected the woman to break into an aria at any moment. They were just by the door of his office now. Vera seemed to be ushering them outside. Resting his aching head on one hand he heard the 'ting!' of the front doorbell and Vera saying, 'Yes – in the barn, look. There's plenty more to see – do go on over. We'll be with you in just a moment.' He heard their footsteps on the thin gravel outside.

The office door opened.

'Mr Baxter?'

Hearing the strained tone of Vera's voice, he turned immediately. She whipped into the room, shut the door and leaned against it, her face working.

'I think, if you don't mind . . .' she began. George was filled with alarm. Heavens, was Vera about to burst into tears? 'You'd better . . .'

Crumpling, Vera pressed her hands over her face, her shoulders shaking, and a small squeal escaped from her. She removed her hands again, flapping them about in front of her as if this would somehow enable her to speak. Which it didn't. Her face was puce, tears of long-suppressed mirth welling in her eyes. Soon, at the sight of someone so perilously tickled, George was laughing as well.

'Oh, I'm sorry!' Vera managed to squeak, as little channels of mascara trickled down her cheeks. 'Oh I can't – you'll have to deal with them . . . Just can't! Oh – talk about Love's Young Dream.' More laughter surged in her and in this vaporous condition she pointed towards the barn. 'Gone – over there . . .'

'All right,' George said good-naturedly. 'I'll go.'

He found the young couple standing side by side in the barn, apparently overcome by the sight of a mahogany sideboard which he had bought from a dealer in Henley a couple of weeks earlier. It was a beautifully proportioned, serpentine-fronted thing to which Alan had added repairs and Vera elbow grease to perfect its elegance, fit for a graceful and spacious home. The backs of the two people he could see, their hips just touching, suggested to him a couple of schoolchildren. The girl's blonde hair hung almost to her waist and she had on something that appeared to be a navy gymslip. His nibs was in a brown suit, a flick of fair hair just visible at the side of his head. His arm rested round the girl's waist.

'Nice little piece, that,' George ventured, not wanting to appear impressed that someone apparently just out of short trousers could contemplate affording such a thing.

The pair swung round to face him. George found himself facing a wide-eyed English rose with a radiantly soppy expression and beside her the strangely limp-looking young man with very large teeth and a blood-orange-coloured cravat tucked into the neck of his shirt.

'Ew! Hellew!' the girl warbled. 'Ew my Lord – we didn't hear you come in!' This was followed by the glassy chime of laughter he had heard before.

'Can I help you, sir, madam?' George said, with the exaggerated courtesy he often found necessary to adopt when faced by such people.

'Ah well,' the young man informed him, somehow managing to negotiate utterance around those teeth. 'You see, Marina and I are engaged to be married—' maarrd, was what he actually said, extending a soft, gripless hand. 'Gerry, by the way. We're in the process of furnishing our prospective home in Bourne End – we're going to make it *absolutely charming*.'

'Oh it will be!' Marina echoed, clinging to the young man's arm and beaming up at him with what George considered extraordinarily unwarranted adoration. 'It's *so exciting*!'

'How fortunate,' George said agreeably. He gave a small bow.

'Oh petal,' Gerry said, gazing at her. 'We are such lucky, *lucky* little people, aren't we?'

George cleared his throat. He clasped his hands behind his back. Surges of pain passed through his head.

'Daddy says we mustn't spend *too* much,' the young woman went on. 'But Gerry thinks – and of course I think so too – that one must buy quality, *invest* for the long term. Wouldn't you agree? And of course we do want to spend our lives surrounded by beautiful things . . .'

'How old is this?' Gerry pointed at the sideboard.

'George the Third,' George said.

Gerry's face enacted contortions which intimated that this information was somewhat lost on him.

'About 1790,' George told him. 'Mahogany. Very fine.'

'Is it *the one*?' the girl asked earnestly.

'*Well* . . .' Gerry – who, George surmised, clearly had not a clue about this, nor possibly a whole range of other things – swiftly passed the baton. 'What do *you* think, my petal?'

'Oh no, darling – what do *you* think?' She clung tighter to his arm, looking up at him with huge blue eyes.

'I think it would do all right.'

'Well whatever *you* think, *I* think. You know best, darling. You're in charge . . .'

Dear God, George thought. This young milksop *was* probably already in charge – of a bank, or in charge of something anyway. Such people always were.

He was on the point of suggesting that they spend a little more time looking round, when the chesty rasping and revving of a large motor car grew louder outside, tyres crunched on the gravel and a klaxon-like hooter sounded repeatedly. Rescue – if it could be called such – was at hand.

'Will you excuse me?' George said. The two of them barely seemed to notice whether he was there or not.

'Mr Baxter!' Alan appeared from the workshop in his blue overalls. 'It's Lady Byngh – she's, well, she's *here*.'

'Thanks, Alan. I heard.' He moved outside on legs that did not feel like his normal legs at all.

In the yard, seeming to occupy most of it, was Lady Byngh's black and red Daimler, of a vintage sometime long before the last war. Even at first glance the thing seemed to have more than the usual accumulation of scrapes and bumps along the side. One of the headlamps was smashed and the front number plate dangled, clinging on by one end. The engine wheezed into silence.

The car contained four creatures, all of them barking.

'Baxter!' one of them commanded. 'Come round to the chauffeur's window!'

Lady Byngh liked to preserve the fiction that she still had a chauffeur, even though it was at least a decade since her funds had been able to run to one and it was she in the driving seat.

As he ambled round to the other side of the car, George caught sight of Vera, who appeared in the doorway of the house, took a quick look then withdrew, closing the door with the speed that would be required to block out a cloud of poison gas.

Lady Byngh's pugnacious face presented itself at the open window from under a crushed-looking hat of black straw. At the sight of George's face, the two bloated Cairn terriers hurled themselves like cannonballs with teeth and moustaches against the back window. An equally paunchy golden Labrador gazed desperately at him from the passenger seat through a haze of smoke. Clearly Lady Byngh was not intending to get out of the car today so he was not to be treated to the sight of her cigarette-scorched tweeds or oddly matched stockings. He had once seen her in one brown and one orange stocking; surprisingly shapely legs pushed into ancient but elegant shoes.

'Ah there you are, Baxter!' Lady Byngh bawled above the yapping. Her vocal register seldom deviated from that of someone addressing the last living man high in the rigging of a storm-tossed ship. 'Do shut *up*, both of you!' she roared over her shoulder. Not that this made one iota of difference. The conversation continued at maximum volume. Smoke whorled out of her mouth with her every utterance. As George leaned closer to the window, the combined stenches of tobacco smoke, whisky and dog rasped up inside his nostrils like smelling salts.

'My man will bring over the Hepplewhite,' Lady Byngh announced, as if George should already have a precise idea what item of furniture this might be. Having so far evaded the pleasure of a visit to Greenburton House – Lady Byngh's, by all accounts, scrofulous abode in Aston Parva, the next village – he had no idea to what she was referring.

'I want it seen to.' She took a hungry drag on the cigarette, sucking her cheeks right in. 'Wedding present – my nevew.'

'Ah?' George tried to sound obliging. 'A, er, dining table, perhaps?'

'No, *no* – the bureau. Marvellous thing. Priceless. Want the boy to have it. He's in tea, of course – Assam, you know. Wedding's in Kent – don't s'pose I'll be going. Have to ship it.' She took a last frantic suck on the waning cigarette and stubbed it out on the dashboard, dropping the stub somewhere on the mulch of the car's floor. 'So – you'll fit me in.' Not a question. 'My man will be over.'

She started up the car and the yard was once more full of engine clatter and a pall of blue exhaust fumes. Without any further speech, or indeed acknowledgement of George's existence, she drove off. He saw the silhouette of her hat as the car bounced out of the drive again.

The front door opened as he approached it and Vera peered out. 'She gone?'

George indicated the empty drive. He was feeling increasingly weary and strange.

'Gives me the heebie-jeebies, that one,' Vera said as they went into the house. It suddenly came to his notice that Vera was wearing high heels, tottering navy ones. 'And she always looks so . . . *scruffy*. You'd think, her being titled and everything . . .'

'She chucked her cigarette stub down into the car,' George said. 'I thought the whole thing was going to go up in smoke.'

'Oh no,' Vera contradicted. 'I bet the inside of that car's damp as a barmaid's armpit. Nothing'd burn in there.'

Once again left speechless by one of Vera's observations, George went to the kitchen and thought about lunch. Defeated, he sank down at the table. Then he thought about collapsing into bed.

2.

A quiet knock at the bedroom door woke George later that afternoon. He turned over, which produced an unpleasant, thudding rearrangement inside his head. His face was burning but his feet felt cold as stones. Win's clock said it was five thirty.

'Yes?' He sounded quavery to himself, like an old man.

Vera appeared round the door. 'Brought you a cup of tea, Mr B. And a couple of aspirin.' Her heels tick-ticked across the floorboards, to be mercifully muffled by the bedside rug. 'Ooh dear – you look as if you got the flu.'

'I, er . . .' he croaked. His throat felt as if someone had been let loose on it with a circular saw. As he shifted in bed he caught a sweaty whiff from his pyjamas.

'Dear oh dear.' Vera smiled anxiously down at him. It seemed to him that her face was bigger than he remembered. He was very pleased to see her though. 'Look, I'll get you a jug of water – here are the aspirin. And I'll feed Monty and give him a little walk, shall I?' She hesitated. 'D'you need me to stay the night, Mr B? I mean I could do Alan's tea and come back . . .'

He shook his head emphatically, which turned out to be a regrettable move. 'I'll be perfectly all right. I'll let the dog out again later. I say – those two this morning . . . ?'

'Oh yes – they bought the sideboard.' Vera's face twitched

with amusement. 'My goodness – what a daffy pair.' She leaned over him. 'Come on – let's get some of this tea down you.' She hustled him into a sitting position. In his limp green pyjamas, George felt both pathetic and enjoyably mothered.

'A hot water bottle would be nice,' he ventured. 'If it's not too much bother.'

'Course I'll get you a hottie-b!' Vera seemed glad to be asked to do something. 'And some Fisherman's Friends, by the sound of it.'

Tucked up with the rubbery smell of the hot water bottle drifting to him, his body piebald with burning and freezing patches, he drifted back into the weird sleep of fever.

The clammy winceyette sheet twisted itself about his torso. He decided at some point in the evening that a barrow load of wet sand had been dumped on his legs and surmised, unreasonably, that this must be Kevin's fault. Then he dreamed that a conveyor belt-like device made up of fat brown boxing gloves was moving closer, up and over his chest, determined to stifle him. He thought about his white ankles and how insignificant he was in the vastness of the world, before waking, panting in the dark and wringing wet.

Must let the dog out, he thought, with weird clarity.

Too hot even to think about a dressing gown or slippers, he staggered down to the kitchen. The linoleum was a sudden horror, tormentingly cold. Dear Lord, if the floor was that cold, how would the lavatory seat feel? The kitchen light was like knitting needles shooting through his eyes and into his brain.

Monty raised his head blearily.

'Come on you old bugger. Out you go.' He prodded the dog's

rump with his foot. The hair on Monty's firm derrière felt warm and reassuring.

George switched off the stark kitchen light and clicked on the one outside instead. The cold night doused him in an instant and he started to shiver. Rain was falling steadily, the wind gusting. Monty did not approve of rain. He cast a gloomy eye outside, trundled down the step and peed magisterially on the grass before hurrying back in.

The door shut again, George collapsed on to a kitchen chair in the dark, his teeth chattering. He had a momentary urge to search his pockets for Monty's liquorice allsorts and gobble some. A second later the idea sickened him. The task of climbing back up the stairs to bed felt well beyond him.

'Oh dear . . .' He laid his arms on the table and rested his head on them. 'Just sit here, a minute . . .'

'George, what on earth are you doing out of bed?'

He lifted his head again. His body seemed to be frozen solid. Was he awake? Someone was standing beside him in a long dressing gown. Without looking up, he knew that it was Win.

'Come on now, we can't have this. What you need is a nice hot drink and some aspirin. And back to bed!'

He wanted to tell her that Vera had already given him aspirin and that they were upstairs by the bed, but he could not seem to muster a voice.

'Let's get you upstairs, George dear.' Win's no-nonsense delivery had softened into a more motherly tone for which life had given her little practice. She took his hand and he followed her slowly up the stairs, putting both feet on each step, comforted by the sight of her, the familiar floral material and the movement of her neat rump inside it. She tucked him into bed, stroking his head until he slept.

He dreamed about a woman on horseback and he recognized her immediately: the beauty of her flowing hair and direct gaze, the perfection of the rearing horse's bronze limbs moved him almost to tears. The exquisite bronze rested on a marble mantelpiece. I've found her, she's here, he kept trying to tell them, a whole roomful of them. Early seventeenth century – look, over here . . . No one would listen.

Later he woke, hearing rain spattering hard against the window. He wanted Win still to be there. There was no one else in the bed. She must be out of sight somewhere, perhaps asleep in the chair. By the time dawn came, seeping and grey, there was no sign of her and he ached for her to come back.

3.

'You're not missing anything out there, I can tell you,' Vera said the next morning. 'The daffs don't stand a chance in this.'

Her hair looked flattened, despite the umbrella. It dawned on George, somewhere in the depths of fever, that it looked flattened generally. Those big kinks were no longer. The front section of hair was brushed back from her face and fastened with a clip at the back, while the lower part hung loose. What was going on, he wondered vaguely. Though he felt that whatever she had done, it suited her better.

'You don't look too good to me,' Vera said with worried eyes. 'D'you want me to get Dr Bell? You might need penicillin.'

'No,' George whispered. 'Don't bother him. I'll either get over it or I won't.'

Vera seemed amused by this martyrdom. 'Oh I expect you will,' she said, 'on balance. But don't you worry, Mr Baxter. We'll look after you. If you need Alan for anything more . . . you know . . . personal, you let me know, all right? I'll keep a good eye on things downstairs.'

Apart from at night, Vera became his nursemaid. She took over the running of the shop, carried up to him jugs of water, hot water bottles, Vicks VapoRub and a potentially endless supply of cups of tea. All George could do was stew in his sick-bed in a state of sweaty and shivering gratitude.

For the first two days he drifted in and out of feverish sleep, making the occasional challenging visit to the bathroom. He had to gear himself up for these events for a good half-hour before, trying to raise the energy. He held on to every piece of furniture on the way as his head lurched about inside. The lavatory seat felt as gruesome as predicted.

Sounds swam in and out of his consciousness as he lay abed – Monty barking, the sploshing crunch of a car coming into the drive, the front door opening and shutting, voices. He started to hear the tinny sound of music coming from somewhere. He thought he was hallucinating again until Vera told him she had started bringing a little transistor radio in to listen to in the kitchen – she did so love those Beatles! He didn't mind, did he? No, he duly agreed, he didn't.

One morning, some filly-like sounds outside resulted in a small jar of snowdrops appearing by his bed. From Pat Nesbitt, Vera told him. They were delicate and beautiful. Sometime on the second day, just as he had collapsed back into bed after one of his expeditions to the bathroom, he heard an altercation just below his window.

'You may think that – nevertheless, I am a professional and in my opinion . . .'

Who the hell was that? The voice sounded familiar.

'I'm sure you are,' Vera was saying. 'But everything's perfectly all right. Mr Baxter has everything he needs and he said expressly' – had he? He didn't recall having the energy to say anything *expressly* – 'that he does not want to see anyone.'

'All the same,' the voice pressed on, louder now, 'I insist that you let me in to look him over. You don't know as much about influenza as I do, and believe me, I've lost a number of patients to it . . .'

Rosemary Abbott! Recognition jolted through him. What if she had come up here while he was on the toilet? He grasped the top edge of the sheet in horrible suspense. Please, Vera, his mind implored, don't for God's sake let her in. He lay waiting for the sound of authoritative footsteps on the stairs, Rosemary in Charge of the Light Brigade mood, thermometer in hand.

Vera was saying something so quietly that he could not catch it.

'Well,' Rosemary sounded very huffy, 'I think you're being very foolish. I hope he's seen the doctor. But really, after all my years of experience I would be the best person to see to him.'

Footsteps did come up the stairs then. George turned his eyes to the door without moving his head, his nose poking out above the sheet. Vera still had her arms folded across her fluffy, broad-bean-coloured sweater, presumably part of the way she had warded off Rosemary.

'So,' she said. 'Did you hear? That was Rosemary Abbott.'

George eyed her. 'I didn't think having half her patients dying was much of a recommendation,' he said.

Vera laughed, releasing her arms as she bent down to tuck in the blankets at the bottom end of the bed. 'She said she wanted to see to you.'

George moaned, faintly. Seeing Vera there, leaning over his bed, he was momentarily tempted to ask her to hop in for a cuddle. It occurred to him that he might be fractionally better.

Vera looked up, grinning. 'It's all right, Mr B. No one's going to get past me.' Pushing on the bed to help herself up again, she said, 'How about a boiled egg?'

As she went downstairs again, he heard her singing that new song, 'Can't Buy Me Love' . . . or as she was singing it, 'lu-urve.'

The next day, as watery sunshine elbowed the grizzled clouds out of the way, he heard the sound of a large engine grinding its way into the drive. The vehicle braked right outside and a cab door opened, then slammed shut. A genial male voice called out, 'Delivery for you!'

He heard Vera's voice and then Clarence's creaky utterance as well, though he couldn't make out the words. The noises that followed – the squeaks of the wagon doors being opened; laborious shiftings, grunts, thumps and shouted instructions – all indicated the transfer of a heavy piece of furniture from one place to another.

George lay, frustrated. I can barely raise my head, he thought, let alone run my business. He felt limp and floaty and devoid of all energy.

'That was Lady Byngh's bookcase thing arriving,' Vera announced, placing a cup of tea on the table beside him, oblongs of shortbread wedged into the saucer.

'Shelves top, drawers bottom?' he asked, pushing himself to sit up. Vera moved as if to help, then retreated, seeing that he could manage.

'Yes – glass at the front. You're getting better, you are.'

'Called a *bureau bookcase*,' he advised.

'Right you are,' Vera said. He knew she wouldn't forget. She never forgot anything.

'I didn't hear the old girl,' he said, sipping the tea.

'Oh no, it wasn't her – nice chap in a wagon. Clarence says it'll have to wait a week or so – they've put it in the back of the barn.'

George frowned. 'When's this wedding?'

'Not till July, apparently.'

'That's all right then.'

'Oh – there was a note with it, hang on!' Vera ran downstairs and came back with a creamily thick envelope.

'I say.' George eyed it. 'Top quality, that.'

Vera slit it open and handed him the sheet of cream paper. Ornate handwriting in blue ink looped its way down the page with a rightward lurch.

Baxter –

Herewith delivery of my Hepplewhite. You're to carry out all necessary to make fit as a gift for my late brother's boy, Roderick Storr-Mayfield.

I shall expect you to telephone me as soon as it is ready and my man will come to transport it.

Sincerely,

An inscrutable scribble was followed by the printed words:

ELEANORA AGNES LUCINDA BYNGH.

4.

On Sunday afternoon he felt well enough to potter about downstairs, with the prospect of a peaceful afternoon to himself. At this first appearance on the ground floor, Monty gave him the sort of hero's welcome that implied he had been absent for several years.

'Careful old boy, you'll have me over,' George protested over the mighty woofing and crazed tail-wagging. 'Yes, yes – I know you're pleased to see me.' He bent over and gave Monty's ears a fond waggle. 'Come on – I need some lunch.'

He had told Vera he would absolutely be all right on his own. He experienced an exhilarating sense of freedom in being able to stand in his own kitchen and knock up an omelette without interference or undue conversation, other than with the dog. Adding quartered mushrooms, a slick of baked beans and sawn off chunks of bread with a slab of Anchor butter, he sat at the table amid the smell of frying with a sigh of happy anticipation.

Better not start on the beer yet, I suppose, he thought. Arms and legs still aren't quite right. They felt distinctly tremulous. To his surprise he could not manage to eat all the bread and butter. His trousers felt loose at the waist. This wouldn't do.

'Right-o, Monty,' he said, stacking the washing-up in the

sink. 'Let's see what's been going on while I've been in my sick-bed.'

Monty clicked along behind him into the office. George lobbed him a liquorice treat.

'There you are – that's your lot. Settle down now.'

Monty subsided with a grunt behind the chair, head resting on his paws. George opened the current stock ledger and sat up straighter with surprise.

'My goodness!' he said. There was quite a list of sales in Vera's infantile handwriting. As well as the serpentine-fronted side-board purchased by Love's Young Dream, a mahogany dining table and chairs had gone – and even that huge oak tallboy that had been sitting there for weeks. The buyer was not a name he recognized. Passing trade perhaps.

'Well, well,' he said. 'Good old Vera.' She had told him this, come to think of it, but he had not been in a state to take it in. There was no need to have worried. Vera was clearly keeping everything in order.

He sat back, his thoughts untethered. He had the whole afternoon – he should get on with something. Should he make a start on sorting through Win's things, while he had private moments without all these women insisting on helping? But his mind shied away from this, as much from the resulting emptiness of drawers and cupboards as from the task itself. No. Too final. Gratefully, he remembered her presence with him during his fever. He couldn't start clearing out her possessions while it still felt as if she might walk in at any moment.

Easing his chair closer to the shelves, he picked out a couple of old ledgers and flicked through them, looking at past years of trading, items listed in his own faded handwriting. He could remember a good many of them, where he had bought them and from whom; who had bought them off him.

The two clippings fell out from one of them as he riffled the pages, their paper sulphurous yellow, a rusted staple holding them together. It was a moment when his younger self met him as if round a bend in the road and it took him some seconds to recognize what he was seeing. He stared, frowning at the grainy picture. It was of the Prince of Wales, before all that palaver with Mrs Simpson. He was opening the British Trade Fair in Buenos Aires, surrounded by ripples of flags and a blaze of lights, in March 1931. That's why he had cut it out, evidently. It was three years after he had been there himself.

The other was the picture of him, taken that day by Joe Black, his London employer, which had ended up in one of the Sussex newspapers. He stood, posed in front of an ornate marble mantelpiece.

George gazed, half unbelieving now, at the stolid eighteen-year-old in a tight suit, hands clasped in front of him. He could almost feel the blush that had risen in his cheeks that day in Lord Buckleford's grand house as Joe Black instructed, 'All right lad, keep it still.' Behind him, arranged close together on the mantel for the purpose of the picture, were the Allodola Bronzes, Mars and Venus, each on horseback. They were exquisite pieces from the Florentine workshop: two of the most beautiful pieces he had ever seen. When he first caught sight of them, he had felt the hairs stand up on his skin, so lovely were they, so perfect. And he must have been one of the last people to see them together, that day in 1926, before the blunder that had separated them. The papers came to Joe for the photograph eventually, as they tried to track the missing Mars down, but it had been too late.

How strange that this should come to light just when he had had that dream. He knew where Mars was all right. Mars had found his way to the Americas. But it was the exquisitely beautiful Venus who had cantered through his dream the other night. Venus, whose tragic loss of her pair had seemed an extension of all the tragedy suffered by the Buckleford family.

Lord Buckleford's three sons had all been army officers in the Great War. None of them returned to their Sussex village. By 1926, Lady Buckleford had also died and, with his heart in tatters, Lord Buckleford was selling the manor. In the division of what should be kept, what sold, Mars was mistakenly packed up and – as George had discovered when he came upon the bronze two years later in in Paul Lester's *estancia* in Argentina – exported. Venus, it seemed, had been subsequently sold off in haste. Without Mars, she was of far less value. But George had always wondered whether the loss of her other half had been too painful a reflection for Lord Buckleford of his own solitary state. Venus disappeared from view. For over thirty years now, since rediscovering Mars, he had longed to find her again. Somewhere in his mind, he had been keeping an eye out for Venus's beautiful form, her swathes of hair and downcast eyes, ever since.

APRIL

Six

1.

When is it going to warm up? George wondered, pausing to look out as he washed up his morning porridge pan. A harsh wind was shifting the clouds across the sky with unusual speed, the sun flashing in and out.

'Porridge,' he said, resting the saucepan on the rack and clearing bits of onion-skin out of the plughole. 'That's the thing.' Eating porridge was like pouring concrete into foundations and he could certainly do with some in his. Over the ten days since he had climbed out of bed, wobbly as a newborn calf, his recovery had been slow. He kept thinking about the need to plant his potatoes and onions, but even now he still felt muzzy of head and cotton-woolly of leg.

'It's the Result of Bereavement,' Vera counselled, in a way that suggested this was something she had just read somewhere. 'It's not just a mental thing you know.'

Vera was being especially authoritative these days. And not without reason. She had been so busy selling off the stock, and at good prices, that the place was beginning to look frugally furnished rather than offering the atmosphere of elegant profusion for which George aimed. He really must get out buying. Tomorrow – that's what he'd do. He'd get the van out – and there was that auction over near Marlow . . .

He was just pulling on his old tweed jacket when there came an urgent knocking at the back door. He found Kevin on the step, Holland overall hanging open to reveal a waywardly buttoned shirt. Evidently he had been sent to deliver a message so pressing that he was still in the middle of his elevenses – or as it happened, half past nineses – which consisted of a cheese and onion sandwich. Arduous feats of chewing and swallowing had to be undertaken before he could utter a syllable.

'Clarence says –' he managed, before having to pause, his Adam's apple bucking alarmingly.

'Take your time, boy,' George advised.

'He says you'd best come,' Kevin declared after a last, challenging swallow. His face brightened at this achievement. 'Bit of bother.'

The workshop, which usually gave off sounds of hammers and chisels, the rasping circular saw and shouts of male voices, had fallen silent. George stepped inside to find the familiar sawdust and varnish smells, and his men, Alan and Clarence, standing beside the mahogany bureau bookcase which Lady Byngh's 'man' had brought in a couple of weeks earlier. As one would imagine to be the case with most of Lady Byngh's possessions, it was in urgent need of succour.

'What's the trouble, Clarence?' As usual, George found himself addressing Clarence with a joviality verging upon the idiotic, to dispel the aura of sepulchral gloom that Clarence generated around himself.

Clarence, sleeves rolled up, prodded the piece of furniture with his right index finger as if to warn it what was coming, then folded his gristly arms and stood back, staring at it. Everyone waited for him to utter.

'That,' he said at last, with a grim nod at the thing, 'is mated.'

George looked in consternation at the tall piece of furniture, with its glazed cupboard doors – some panes missing, others cracked – its elegant broken pediment cornice, the wood of the back and drawers all gasping for cleanliness and nourishment but which should eventually polish up nicely. The piece that Lady Byngh had called 'my Hepplewhite'.

The thing about Clarence – however galling – was that he was almost never wrong.

'You'd better show me.' George realized that as he had been ill in bed when it arrived, he had never even had a look at the thing. 'Are you sure?'

Clarence uncrossed his arms and again prepared himself to speak.

'It is Hepplewhite, surely?' George pressed him, impatient for this verbal event to begin.

'The top part might be,' Clarence declared at last. 'The state it's in dun'elp. Covers a multitude of deception, all that filth on it. But look 'ere.'

At the point where the top and bottom met, in one small place at the side, he scraped away at the coating of decades of grime, nicotine deposits and ancient furniture polish which covered it like a sick man's sweat. After a moment, horrified, George saw it appear: a definite join. Together they tugged out the lower drawers, having to stop for a bout of sneezing brought on by the dust. Close up, everything about the bottom half of the piece screamed 'pastiche'.

'And the feet—' Clarence pointed a spindly finger. 'Those feet should have cried out to us.' The bracket feet, though on the face of it in the right style, were ill proportioned and too large.

George stood up slowly, fingering the sticky veneer. I've had my eye off the ball, he thought.

'It's a clever match,' he remarked, while he tried to think what else to say.

'It is,' Clarence agreed. 'But she's a pup all the same.'

George rubbed his hand back and forth through his hair as he did when he was bothered.

'You wouldn't expect it – not someone like her, would you?' Alan said. He sounded unusually sullen.

'She said it had been in her family for generations,' George said. Foolishly he realized that as Lady Byngh occupied the tip of some branch of the aristocracy, however attenuated, he had not questioned whether the piece would be genuine.

'I'd say that bit is a good forty or fifty years younger than the top,' Clarence said.

'Yes,' George said humbly, 'I can see you're right. I'm most grateful to you, Clarence.'

A slight flexing of Clarence's lips indicated a certain satisfaction with himself. Sour old bugger, George thought fondly.

Kevin stood watching, picking shreds of onion out of his teeth with a wood splinter.

Alan, who was leaning against the workbench, arms folded, said, 'Well – are you going to tell her? She wants it sent back to her before she ships it off, you know.'

This presented a rare dilemma. Neither George nor Clarence had any interest in deception or charlatanry. Normally it would not even be a question. Genuine was genuine and their pride lay in affirming it. But this was Lady Eleanora Byngh. It was as if she was there in the room with them suddenly, in her singed old tweeds, her bird's-nest hair and random stockings. She had brought the best that she could find to them, having raked through her frowsty house and the remnants of her pride to find a gift of some standing for a distant young relative, who presumably had no idea of the state in which she lived. The bureau bookcase would be taken to Kent, where it might sit tight for decades before anyone discovered that they had been endowed with a Hepplewhite mule.

'No,' George said quietly. 'I don't think we are. It's the restoration she's paying us for. Just do your best for her. Let her enjoy it for a bit. And let's hope that'll be that.'

The men's eyes met – except for Kevin's, which seemed to be, for the time being, in a state of post-sandwich vacancy. They all nodded.

2.

'Off out, are you, Mr Baxter?'

'Morning, Kevin!' George sloshed a last bucket of water over the front of the car. It was an elegant Standard Vanguard saloon and he enjoyed the sight of its grey paintwork dripping and shiny clean. He couldn't have gone out with it in the deplorable state it had been in – you could hardly tell what colour it was. You had to make a good impression, best foot forward on parade and all that. He turned towards the house with the empty bucket. 'Yes – off to an auction. Need to stock up.'

Kevin loped after him. 'Could I come, d'you think? Just this once? I've never been to one of them auctions. Never been nowhere much at all.'

'Well—' George turned at the door, stalled by this tragic admission. 'Yes, why not? There's nothing that can't wait today, I don't think. I'll be ten minutes. Go and tell Clarence – and bring your sandwiches with you.'

'Oh *thanks*, Mr Baxter!' Kevin, enraptured, disappeared across to the barn with an unprecedented turn of speed.

George changed into a tweed suit which he considered made him look rather racy. He had recently had a haircut, was trying to pull himself together. Got to start somewhere after all. He gave himself what he hoped was a winning, dimply smile in the mirror. Downstairs he found Vera close up to another mirror in the hall.

'Ju' 'eeing 'o 'y 'ace,' she mumbled, in the process of applying more of the pink lipstick.

'I'll have to leave Monty here today,' George said. 'He'd be no help at all where I'm going.'

'Oh that's OK,' Vera said to his reflection. She rubbed her lips together. 'He'll be all right.' She turned round and eyed George. 'Ooh – you're looking smart today, Mr Baxter.'

'Thank you, Vera.' Gratified, he examined her in turn. She was wearing a well-tailored navy suit with her clicking heels and that hair was definitely different.

'So are you,' he said. It was true. She looked more . . . What was the word? Sophisticated?

'Well . . .' Vera smoothed her hands first over her hair, then over the collar of her jacket. 'I can't go about looking like a cleaner if I'm in the shop, can I?'

'No – of course. You're quite right.' He felt a wave of gratitude towards her. It was true, the addition of 'my tranny', the little transistor radio that had joined the other items in Vera's basket, made his kitchen a rather noisier place these days. But goodness knows she did bring life and vigour with her. Bashfully he added, 'You're doing a fine job, Vera.'

She blushed with girlish pleasure. '*Am* I, Mr B? Truly? I'm really, really doing my best!'

'You're doing excellently,' he laughed. 'Why d'you think I'm having to go and stock up today? You seem to have sold half the shop since I've been out of action!'

Vera radiated gratification at this praise. Then her face

became anxious. 'And you don't mind that . . . Well, I'm not cooking as much, and . . .'

'But I can cook now, thanks to you! Though I'm sure Alan's glad of a meal now and then.'

'Oh I can do *that.*' Her expression became solemn. 'I just mean – well all the extra things I used to do. I just don't seem to get around to all my bottling, and I'm not making as many pies and all those sorts of things. Alan's getting a bit . . . Anyway, I thought you might mind?'

The extent of George's relief was like an iceberg submerged beneath his smile. 'Vera, my dear – we've enjoyed your pies for many a year. But you're moving on to other things. Pies will have to come second. Of course I don't mind.'

Vera's pink mouth spread wide. In fact there was much mutual beaming. 'Oh I knew you'd understand, Mr B. And I'm so lucky to have such a nice boss!' She was just moving off again when she turned.

'By the way – Mrs Linklater still hasn't paid her bill.'

'Ah,' George said absently. 'Perhaps I'll call in on her in a day or two, when I'm up that way.'

The thirty-mile or so drive to the auction rooms was a pleasant one. They crossed the river at Wallingford, skirted the Chilterns at Nettlebed and recrossed the Thames in Henley. There was a spring lightness to the air, the sunlight growing in strength. The first boats were appearing on the river, which flowed London-wards, as it eternally did. The fields, furry with shoots, seemed to throb with quickening life; the trees were softening to green and the blackthorn was white with emerging blossom.

Kevin, face turned to the window, began on his first cheese and onion sandwich of the day before they had gone five miles. Oniony smells filled the car. George glanced at him, irritated. It would be better company having Monty with him because at least then he could make inane comments to the dog or sing to himself. A stabbing self-pity seized him. Was this to be his life now – Monty and Kevin? It was hard to say which of them was the more animate. Here was spring coming with all its promise – light, new life! He could just about recall that in his own life, the brief spring part. But what had happened to his high summer? It had been rained off and slumped, unfulfilled into autumn.

After the sandwich had receded and on the way through Crowmarsh Gifford, George decided to banish his own longing thoughts and make an effort.

'What line's your father in, Kevin?' he began jovially. He knew little about Kevin, he realized, except that he lived somewhere near the edge of the village. His mother, a plump, harassed-looking but pleasant woman who he seemed to remember was called Sue, had accompanied Kevin when he first came looking for a job.

Kevin turned his head. 'No dad,' he said.

The succinctness of this response rendered it somewhat uninformative.

'Ah?' George thought that was the end of the conversation, but more followed.

'He went. There's just Mum and me and my sister. I don't even remember him.'

'Your poor mother,' George said.

The boy nodded and looked back out through the window.

A long silence followed, before Kevin turned to him and said, 'Mr Baxter – can I ask you something?'

George was startled. Heavens, did the boy need him to have one of those conversations that fathers were supposed to have? Fill him in on certain facts? Not that his own father had in any way obliged with this. An image of himself at Kevin's age came to him, a huge, galumphing, clueless boy. He would have been working for Arkwright about then, pursued by the blonde and curvaceous Ellen, old Arkwright's bold seventeen-year-old daughter; he at once horny as a stag and scared out of his wits. If only he'd had someone to ask at that time of terrifying confusion. The thought of trying to find the right words was appalling, but if it had to be done . . .

'Yes of course, lad.' He forced warmth into his voice and pulled his shoulders back, bracing himself.

'I – the thing is . . .' Kevin stumbled.

'It's quite all right, Kevin – fire away,' George encouraged breezily.

'I'm just trying to understand a whole lot of things,' Kevin began. 'For one thing, Mr Baxter, is it right that the only English porcelain made in the eighteenth century that's *not* soft paste is Plymouth and Bristol – so all the others like Chelsea and Derby and Worcester *are*?'

George swivelled his head to face Kevin with the look of a man whose horse has just asked him to tell him the time. He wrenched his attention back to the road just in time to avoid swerving into an oncoming dustcart. Kevin was still earnestly awaiting an answer.

'Er, yes, that's about the size of it,' George said. He was no specialist in porcelain but he had a working knowledge. 'I, er

. . . But you're apprenticed to carpentry and cabinet-making, Kevin – what's all this about porcelain?'

'I know. And that's all right. I like that. But I do like *china*.' He had now become quite bouncy in his seat. 'I got these books, from the library in Wallin'ford. I like the colours – they all *mean* something, those colours! And I like the words! Qing dynasty! Tea-dust black! Celadon glaze!' His face was pink with excitement. '*Famille rouge*! Majolica! I don't even know how you say most of 'em. But they're lovely, aren't they, Mr Baxter?'

And George, moved by this rough-hewn enthusiasm, could only agree that they were.

'We'll have at least an hour with the catalogue before it starts,' George said, braking in the yard behind the auction room. 'Why don't you go on ahead and have a look round?'

'All right, Mr Baxter!' Kevin, genuinely excited, slid out of the van and hurried round to the entrance.

George let out a long breath, holding on to the steering wheel. He glanced in the car's rear-view mirror at his shorn hair and crisp white shirt. The gesture reminded him of sitting in the van that snowy afternoon when he had had his vision, his sobbing realization of what he most desired, and it filled him with despondency. Though it was only two months ago, two months since Win's passing, it seemed a long time now, as if all he had done since was stagnate. Where was his energy? He sat up straight, taking in a meaningful breath.

'To it, George,' he said. You never knew who might be at one of these do's – they drew in people from all over.

The auction room gave the impression of the main living room in an eccentric household where all activities, barring the very most intimate, were crammed into the one space. At the far end the auctioneer's dais, draped with a tapestry showing hunting scenes, announced on an unfurled poster down the front: 'Fine Antique Furniture: For Sale by Auction'. A chattering assortment of the coated and hatted, clutching sale catalogues, were milling, peering, poking and exclaiming around the large pieces of furniture which in turn were being used to support the display of smaller items. Upon and round the walls were hung and stacked paintings, fire screens and objects too heavy to be inflicted upon another piece of furniture. In one corner sat an ornate, marble-cased clock and next to it, what appeared to be a lead safe.

George paused at the edge of the room, looking around with approval and excitement. He was in his element, confronted by this array of beautiful things. He nodded to a couple of other dealers he knew across the room. His practised eye roved over the sort of antiques to which he was drawn: the wood and fine furniture, the silver and mirrors, the occasional painting. Almost never did he buy glassware or china – so breakable – unless it was too beautiful to resist.

He had ticked several items on the catalogue as being of interest and set out to find them: a Queen Anne bureau in walnut, a gilt-framed Chippendale mirror, a pair of William and Mary stools . . . He moved through the jostling, excited crowd, looking from left to right over the items. And in the far corner something caught his eye, resting on a chest of drawers. A horse – a bronze – could it be . . . ? She must be somewhere . . . Perhaps today . . .

He shouldered his way over, swiftly, to find not Venus but a military male with moustaches seated on horseback. Disappointed, he moved off in search of Lot 107, a walnut bureau. With dismay, however, he saw that standing in front of it with an already proprietorial air was Lewis Barker from Twyford.

Lewis, a sweaty ox with a butcher's complexion, who George knew (from Lewis's relentless boasting) to be a dedicated, prolific and not especially secretive philanderer, obviously already had designs on the bureau.

'Ah, George!' He raised a plump hand. 'See this – got my eye on this, I have.'

And a lot more besides, George thought. A depressing image came to him of the bureau shoved somewhere into the loveless jumble of Lewis's warehouse. He was damn well going to outbid him for it.

Lewis pushed his hands down into his jacket pockets and leaned back slightly, head on one side. 'Only thing is . . . No – can't be . . . It *is* an English piece, wouldn't you say, George? I'm almost sure . . . Only that shaping round the doors, and the cornice – unusual.'

If there was one thing that was certain about Lewis, other than his preference for English over foreign furniture, it was his tendency to disagree with anything you suggested. George stepped forward and pretended to examine the piece more thoroughly, looking this way and that.

'You know,' he announced, through an intuitive strike of inspiration rather than any precise information. 'I'd say it was Dutch.'

'Dutch?' said Lewis incredulously. He took a step back as if for a better view and sucked in air through his teeth. 'No – you're wrong there, George. That's English, that – bulldog and roast beef, that one. *Dutch!* Don't be a fool. If that's not English I'm, well, I'm a Dutchman!'

As George was enduring Lewis Barker's bellows of laughter, his senses were abruptly distracted by a sensuous aroma, tingling through the other smells of stale wool, mothballs and furniture wax. His nose twitched. Perfume – something French, Chanel, perhaps? There she was, passing him without looking in his direction, amid the old-time dealers with gnarled faces, well-to-do retired couples in search of bargains, the usual auction moochers and no doubt the odd criminal: a slender woman in a powder-blue coat. His eyes followed as she moved between the baggy old tweeds and gaberdines. Lewis Barker and his nonsense were forgotten. His very being was focused on her glossy hair, the colour of newly hatched conkers, swept up into a pleat from a face of which he had not yet even caught a glimpse. In seconds he had entered a primitive state. His mind, body and very being were orientated towards one thing: woman. All that was baboon-like within him was crying, *move towards her!*

The other lots he had been intending to view quite forgotten, he pressed through the crowd. The dark, coiffured head was bent over some items on a table. What, among all such objects – the candlesticks hung with glass prisms, the silver-topped cruet sets, ormolu clock and Chinese snuff boxes – would catch her eye? He caught sight of her in profile, seeing a fine, arched eyebrow, flawless skin and retroussé nose. Why didn't everyone just get out of the damn way so that he could get near her?

Driven by this compulsion, he tried to shoulder his way through the knot of people blocking his path, a number of whom were gazing into a glass dome that contained two stuffed seagulls.

'Well I shouldn't want that in my sitting room,' a woman in a brimless felt hat remarked.

'There wouldn't be much point in going on your holidays if you had that, would there?' her companion said.

George, just on the point of pushing through the final obstacle, without a thought in his head about what he was actually going to do once he had, found himself greeted suddenly, at considerable volume, from behind.

'Oooh! 'Ello, Mr Baxter!'

George closed his eyes for a second. His shoulders sagged. There was only one person who spoke in that voice and that loudly.

He turned. There she was, all four foot ten of her in button-boots, a peacock-blue frock and shingled hair the colour of withered horse-chestnut leaves, in every way a relic of her pomp in the 1920s. Her smile revealed a flawless set of dentures. Maud Roberts was unceasingly cheerful, sweet-natured and deaf as a stone dog.

'Hello, Maud!' he greeted her, not without pleasure. He would have been wholeheartedly pleased to see her had it not been for two things. Firstly, that his call-of-the-wild instincts were still trying to haul his attention back to the elegant woman in the blue coat, and secondly, that all communications with Maud had to be conducted at the top of your voice, which in a crowded room was embarrassing. He glanced over his shoulder. The woman in blue was moving further away. He forced his attention back to Maud Roberts.

'Nice to see you, Mr Baxter – how are you getting on without your lovely wife?' she enquired in broad Cockney, so that the entire room could hear. She kept digging the point of her slim, rolled umbrella into the floor.

George stepped closer to her. He had always liked Maud. Once an East Londoner and a lady's maid, she had married a dealer called Dudley Roberts. They travelled the world together in their prime, had several times taken ships across the Atlantic. It was one of the things they'd had in common, George and Dudley – they had both been to America. In later years, before Dudley died, he had become a front-room dealer from a small house in Marlow. Many a time on his rounds George had enjoyed a cup of tea, closely followed by a quick snifter for the road, with Maud and Dudley, in their little back room stuffed with souvenirs, the electric-bar fire going full pelt. Dudley had died two years ago, leaving Maud bereft but irrepressible. Her blue eyes twinkled at him from behind her specs.

'I'm doing all right, thank you, Maud,' he replied, at the highest volume he could bear.

Maud's thin face crinkled and she cupped a hand round one ear. 'EH?' she shrieked.

Oh dear God, George thought. Instead of attempting more speech he raised one thumb and gave reassuring nods and smiles.

'Oh good! It's terrible when they go, isn't it, but you have to keep cheerful. You must come and see me, George, now we're both poor lonesome old things!'

George glanced round. This was not a definition of himself that he was anxious to have broadcast about.

'I've missed our little get-togethers – you come over and see me, won't you?' She laid a hand on his arm for a moment and announced to all present, 'You always know how to cheer me up.'

George was nodding in helpless agreement when he saw Kevin shouldering his way through the crowd, hugging something to him, his face shimmering with eagerness.

'Mr Baxter, look! Can we bid for this? Can we?'

Lot 49 was thrust under his nose, a plate about fifteen inches wide in a gorgeous blend of green, black, coral red and gold.

'It's *famille verte*, isn't it?' Kevin said in raptures. 'Oh *can* we? They're starting in a minute.'

George suddenly felt as if he was the father of a very small boy.

'It's a good one,' Kevin babbled on. 'See at the edge there – see the way the glaze is against the white? *Iridescent*. That's what they say – it must be a good'un!'

'Well . . .' George felt he could hardly say no in the face of all this effusion. 'It does look to be a very fine one . . .'

'Who's this?' Maud screeched.

'Oh – this is my workshop apprentice, Kevin . . .'

'EH?'

'KEVIN!'

There was an abrupt hammering from the dais at the front, which for a second George thought must be his fault and he jumped round. But he saw that the auction was about to begin.

'Ooh, better be quiet, hadn't we?' Maud advised at the top of her voice, a finger to her lips.

George nodded goodbye to her and seized Kevin's bony arm. 'Come with me – I want to keep an eye on Lot 107.' He realized that what with one thing and another he had hardly looked at any of the other lots.

'So can we . . . ?'

'*Yes*.' For heaven's sake. This must be what having children was like. 'Yes, Kevin – we'll bid. Now for God's sake put that thing down before you drop it.'

As the crowd settled in expectation, George looked round for Lewis Barker. He spotted his loud checked jacket not far away, just ahead of them. A second later, at the front close to the dais, what felt like an ocean distant, he glimpsed a finely coiffured head and soft blue coat.

Kevin stood beside him, aquiver with anticipation as the bidding began. Lot 10, Lot 11 . . . George found himself in a state of trance-like involvement. He never tired of the excitement of an auction: the item displayed at the front if it was not too heavy to be moved, the starting price, looks and gestures rippling round the room, the tension when the bidding speeded to a frenzy. Finally, after a pause in the auctioneer's liturgical chanting, eyes darting round to find a last-minute bid – bang! The gavel down and everyone letting out a breath at once.

There was a prolonged session over Lot 19, a painting of horses in the style of Stubbs. It was nothing like as fine in George's opinion, but still old and desirable. Two bidders – one an agent, George realized – became locked in combat. The price rose and rose. George felt his body tense with primitive excitement. Kevin seemed about to explode. He kept hopping from one foot to the other. When the gavel came down at last he exhaled like a deflated balloon.

'Oh that was good, that was!' he cried. 'Oh, this is the best day of my life! Aren't you going to bid for anything, Mr Baxter?'

George smiled at him. 'As a matter of fact there are a couple of lots coming up I think I'll go for.'

They were staples he knew he could sell. One lot consisted of old fire irons, which, despite central heating coming in, still sold like mad. They reminded people, he supposed, of evenings round the hearth. And a box of spirit decanters. He'd take those to a silversmith he knew and have him fit silver flanges on the rim. It made them look very nice and they'd sell – they always did. He won both bids.

Lot 49 was coming closer.

'Are you going to?' Kevin kept on, as Lot 48 was declared sold.

Seeing the lad's tallow-coloured face and intent brown eyes straining with appeal, George knew he could not refuse. In any case, Kevin, full of surprises, was right – it was a lovely piece of Chinese porcelain.

Bidding was brisk at first. Hands moved, nods and gestures were made. Kevin's face turned puce. The price rose and the number of bidders quickly dwindled.

'Go on, Mr B, don't stop!' Kevin urged in strangulated agony.

George was beginning to doubt the wisdom of this. They were already up to £20. There were now three of them bidding: himself, someone to his right and another close to the front. Then two – and then it dawned on him, as he saw a pale hand rise to bid, and the edge of a familiar blue sleeve, that he was bidding against *her*.

All eyes were moving between the two of them. Kevin was standing with his arms bent close to his body, hands bunched into fists. The price rose, five shillings each time, then ten. Twenty-five, thirty. The small white hand darted up each time with no hesitation.

She's just going to go on and on, he thought. He felt trapped.

How high was she prepared to go – forty, fifty, higher? The thought of paying fifty or sixty pounds for a plate was dizzying. He neither wanted to lose face nor disappoint the eager boy beside him. But the woman was not going to give in. It was he who would have to stop.

Another new bid – George nodded his head to a new and last price: forty pounds. The white hand flitted up again without a pause. The auctioneer was notching it up more gradually now: forty-two. George lowered his eyes, drawing in a breath of relief.

'Going, go-i-i-ing – Lot 49 sold to the lady here!'

The gavel banged. The crowd relaxed. Kevin let out an anguished groan but recovered himself. 'I s'pose it was getting rather high. Ooh, but it was close – and you was bidding like a good'un, Mr Baxter!'

George laughed, oddly affirmed by this impudence. He was impressed by Kevin's good nature.

'And we wouldn't want to disappoint the lady, would we?' He wondered if this might give him an excuse to speak to her. 'But tell you what, Kevin – I'm going to get Lot 107, if it's the last thing I do!'

Lot 107, when it came, was announced as 'George II, walnut, English'. Lewis Barker turned and leered knowingly at George. George nodded back amiably. *Was* the bureau English? He eyed the thing, which was placed to their left. He still thought not. Something in his gut told him, though he could see why you might assume it was. It was waist high, no cupboard above, with a steeply angled desk flap and beautifully crafted ogee feet, which placed it in the late eighteenth century. It was an austere piece, with none of the bulbous curves and embellishments that Dutch craftsmanship often displayed. And yet . . . Damn it, he thought. Whatever the hell it is, I can't let Lewis take it back to that black hole of Calcutta of his in Twyford.

They bid, faster and faster. Sixty, eighty, a hundred. He and Lewis were soon the only two left bidding. Between bids, Lewis kept turning with a smug grin that clearly said, soon that will be mine. But his head stopped turning, his bidding slowed.

'Go on, Mr Baxter, go *on*!' Kevin kept urging *sotto voce*, as if this were the Grand National.

'Any further bids?' The gavel hovered. One hundred and seventy-five – a huge sum.

'Yes? Do I have one seventy-five?' Lewis was back in at the last moment. 'One seventy-five. Any advance on one-seven-five?'

People were murmuring around them. George kept his eyes on the auctioneer. All other eyes were fixed on him. He let the tension mount for a second more as the gavel rose and hovered. He gave a small but definite nod.

'One-eighty! Any advance on one-eighty?'

The next two seconds felt like an eternity. For all his bluster, George knew that if Lewis kept this up, he was going to have to stop. The bang cut through the room's silence.

'One hundred and eighty pounds?' A last look round. 'Sold! For one hundred and eighty to George Baxter.'

Kevin let out a cheer. If he had had a hat he would most likely have thrown it in the air. 'We won!'

'It's not really a race, Kevin,' George said, though he was feeling very chuffed with himself.

'Well,' Lewis muttered, shuffling over to him. 'Glad to see you've got such a taste for English walnut, George.' He shook his head, as if he had just witnessed a great act of folly. 'Steep price you've paid there though. Over the odds, I'd say.'

George refrained from pointing out that he had paid only slightly more than Lewis had been prepared to offer minutes earlier and gave a serene smile.

'It's a good piece,' he said. 'Good day's work.'

In the distance he caught sight of a blue coat moving towards the door.

'Ooh look, Mr Baxter – that's pretty, that is!' Lot 108 was a slender *bonheur du jour* women's writing table, edged with ormolu, the drawers decorated with blue and white porcelain plaques. 'Shall we bid for that?'

'Er, what? *No!* Just one minute,' George said to Kevin and Lewis. 'I must just . . .'

Impelled by he knew not quite what bonkers instinct, George followed the woman in blue outside. She walked round to the car park at the back and he followed, admiring her shapely, gossamer-stockinged legs. He was drawing closer when she stopped beside a sleek sea-blue Bentley, the passenger door of which was being opened by a uniformed chauffeur who seemed ready to hand her into it. George skidded to a halt, but it was no good. As she turned to get into the car she could not miss seeing him.

'I, er, good afternoon madam,' he said.

An oval face of alabaster forbiddingness was turned to him. She was a woman of about thirty and of frosty chicness. Fool! His more sensible self bawled at him in his head. Dunderhead!

The woman made one of those sounds that people of her class seemed capable of producing which does not quite constitute verbal communication.

'You bought the, er, plate – the *famille verte*,' he floundered on. Her gaze, with eyes as blue and hard as crystals, did nothing to encourage him. 'Only it was me, bidding against you. I just, er, wanted to wish you well. With your plate,' he petered out, idiotically.

Another undecipherable 'ew' sound issued from the woman's throat.

'Ah well, good afternoon,' George said, attempting to raise his hat before realizing he wasn't wearing one and finding himself making a vague, aerial gesture instead.

The woman slid into the car, sinuous as a cobra. The chauffeur closed the door and walked round to the other side without a glance at George.

Hurriedly, George moved away. His inner voice seemed to have run out of words of self-castigation. It crouched in silent mortification.

'A hundred and eighty pounds?' Vera said when they got back. The words *well I suppose you know what you're doing* seemed to hang unspoken in the air.

'It was – it was magnificent!' Kevin said, skipping away towards the barn.

Vera stared after him. 'What the heck's got into him?'

Clarence did the pick-up from the auction house the next day, in the green Morris. When they unloaded the bureau in the drive, Clarence looked at it, head on one side.

'Nice. Very nice. Is it English?'

'They said so,' George replied. 'I'm not sure though. Can't put my finger on it. When I looked at it I thought, Dutch. Anyway, I kept it out of the hands of Lewis Barker.'

Clarence gave a mirthless chuckle. 'Just as well. It needs a good polish. Kevin!' He gave the lad a gimlet-eyed look, as if daring him to exhibit any more residues of excitement from the preceding day. 'C'm'ere and help me!'

The next morning, Clarence appeared in the office holding a scrap of paper. He stood in the doorway like a bird of doom.

'What's up, Clarence?' George said breezily. He was in fact feeling gloomy and comfortless himself today, but it didn't do to encourage Clarence.

'Lady Byngh's bureau,' he said with an air of distaste. 'She's coming up nicely.'

'Oh, good,' George said. There was obviously more.

'That other bureau,' Clarence announced, with a little jerk of his head. 'I've got started on it.' A considerable pause followed to enable Clarence to fold his arms. 'There's a little compartment inside, secret like – you can see it must be there from the dimensions . . . I was feeling my way around the inside and it slid open. Look – this was inside.'

He released his left arm to hand George the scrap of paper. It was thick, yellow, old. The few words on it were in faded blue ink and a long, looping script. Following a short paragraph George could not make any sense of were the words *Jan de Vroom, Nijmegen, 1788.*

He looked across at Clarence.

'Reckon that's Dutch, that is,' Clarence said. 'Nijmegen's a Dutch place.'

George felt a grin spread across his face. 'Yes, it is, isn't it?'

MAY

Seven

1.

George pushed the boat off from the steps by the bridge and climbed in with the smoothness of long habit. He perched on the back seat and let *Barchetta* glide into deeper water before pulling the outboard's starter cord.

Monty, who had tumbled in before him, settled along the duckboards at the bottom with a long-suffering groan. Monty did not approve of water.

'Complain if you like,' George addressed this large brown and white bolster of resentment. 'But you wanted to come.'

Monty closed his eyes, ears arranged on the warm wood, as if dissociating himself from the whole dismal business.

Setting the engine to a puttering speed, George sat back, holding the tiller and drew in a deep breath. Ah, the smell of the river! It was his first outing of the year and the sun was blazing down. It seemed set to be a good summer. He felt better, as if having the flu and recovering had brought him through a gateway into a place where he was lighter in himself as the year was lightening. He had been out in the garden, planting, tidying. The roses were all in bud and this in itself was a mark of happiness. Every place where he could plant roses, he had done so – yellows, golds and cream at the front; pinks, whites and crimson in the back, sprawling and climbing everywhere, over lattices, the fence, the house: the smile of their beauty everywhere.

Now, with a swelling sense of wellbeing, he looked around him. He had left the Nautical Wheel pub behind him, below which he and two helpful bods had eased *Barchetta* off the trailer and on to the water. He passed the civic paddling pool, the sounds of screams and splashes in its bright, shallow blue; the swimming pool and campsite, where a few camper vans and tents were already pitched. The town lay behind him, the slender spire of St Peter's needling the sky. In front, the river eased quietly between pastures of vivid green freckled with buttercups and the ghostly spheres of dandelion clocks. Here and there, to his left among the black and white cows, a few lumps of the old castle stuck up in the field like snapped-off teeth. The willows drooped in on either side and all that was before him now was the quiet green of the water.

He did not feel the need to go far. Soon he drew in on the left, the same side as the towpath and tied up to a young willow, the boat resting in its shade. Monty half roused himself and looked blearily round.

'No, you're not getting out. Lie down.'

Monty eyed the bank with lethargic longing but decided to do as he was told.

'Right – time for some lunch.'

George wobbled along the boat to retrieve his bag, stowed safely out of Monty's reach, and brought it back, hearing the tell-tale clinking of bottles of Morland's pale. Sitting back in the shade, he took the top off one with a promising 'fssutch!', poured the contents into a tumbler and sipped.

'Aaaaah. Good old Vera.'

Although it was Sunday, she had packed his picnic when he said he was planning to get the boat on the water.

'You go and have a nice day out,' she said. 'You're looking quite pale and peaky still – and it's not been an easy time, has it? I'll sort you out, Mr Baxter.'

Poking around in the canvas bag, he found ham sandwiches – plenty of mustard – chicken legs, tomatoes and a packet of cheese and onion crisps. There were a couple of apples and – a slice of pie. Rather more than a slice, in fact: it was about a quarter of a pie. Peering at the side of it, George was encouraged to discover that the filling was apple.

'Wonders will never cease.' But he smiled. Vera's pies had been in short supply lately. Dear Vera, he thought, mellowed by ale; she was, among all her talents, particularly good at pastry.

Another of Vera's good points was patience. She had waited until George said he was ready. They spent a few sessions, over three days, sorting through Win's things. Vera seemed to sense the times when she should be there being practical and the moments when it was right to stay away.

At last he ventured to open the other door of the large bedroom wardrobe that he and Win had shared for eighteen years. Below the neatly hanging clothes, which gave to the air whiffs of old scent and body odour, lay a modest row of her size four shoes. It came home to him again that he was alone, not just at that moment, but *alone*. Still he felt as if he was in the blizzard, lost with no map.

He stood holding the edges of the wardrobe doors in each hand as if he were about to ask it to dance. Everything inside it was navy blue or a shade of brown, with the exception of her cream blouse, a pair of black fleece-lined boots and the peach-pink frock that she wore to the very occasional drinks parties they attended. Her summer clothes, dresses in pastel greens and pinks, were packed away in the suitcase on top of the wardrobe. The shoes were paired neatly side by side, like people sitting in a church pew. So familiar. So . . . Win. Each shoe, each garment bore her shape, the imprint of her concise movements. They might almost step out and speak in her voice.

His arms felt suddenly so heavy that he had to lower them. His shoulders drooped. Twenty-six years . . . Her smell, the shape and textures of her clothes were so intensely familiar. His wife. A woman who, on the face of it, was beyond reproach. Yet the essence of this woman in whose company he had lived for almost half his life was fast receding into the past, into an unknown strangeness.

'Don't go.'

He heard the words spring out of him. Too late. He could see Win's life as a whole now, the top and tail, the alpha and omega of it. Win, wife, whose body he had loved, or enacted love upon, at least. But her soul, her self? Weren't souls supposed to touch and spark life, like the fingertips in those paintings in the Sistine Chapel? He and Win had never had arms long enough, somehow, even when they were younger and were stretching out, trying. They withdrew and continued with their arms at their sides, as if extending them was a forgotten indecency. Carried on, amiable but unignited.

George breathed heavily for a time, pushing against the tightness of his chest. He remembered the way the Cronies had gathered round Win's bed, better at loving her than he had been. They were leaving him alone now, perhaps felt they had done their duty. But he had run into Pat Nesbitt a couple of days before. 'How *are* you, George?' she said sweetly. 'Oh you do so miss her, don't you?'

Did he? Of course he did. It was true, he missed her in all the shades of every day – he felt lost.

Standing here now, he felt the present sink into him. Onward – that was what he had to do. Releasing the wardrobe, he went to the door.

'Vera?' he called. 'I think we can get started now.'

As winter passed into spring, through the crocuses, aconites and daffodils, through the frosts and rain and weaving through the daily life of the business, he mourned Win. Grief had no end, it just kept reminding him, often unexpectedly, in many moments of the unremarkable life that they had shared. He felt the acute lack of anyone in the house wearing a pinny. Even Vera hardly wore one these days. Washing which he put in the basket remained there until Vera suggested he have a go at the twin-tub. The sight of a pair of his socks drooping on the clothes horse by the fire in the back room could flood him with despondency. He missed her humming as she went about the house, her delicate snores and the soft movement of her breathing beside him in the dark. He even found he missed her friends and the female clucking which commenced once one of the Cronies tapped on the door. He had spent many nights by the fire with the television on, watching *Z Cars* and *Dixon of Dock Green*, eking out cans of ale and stroking Monty's ears.

Then spring proper arrived. The colour was turned up in everything. Green became greener, buds appeared and the first pale flecks of flowers opened into frothing sleeves of blossom.

There was work to do in the garden. Day by day he walked Monty in the village, safely away from the farm or Maggie. He was grateful to her for keeping away from him. He stopped for chats in lanes of thatched cottages and streams sprigged with watercress. People were polite and kindly, constantly asking if there was anything he needed. He could hardly reply, 'Someone I can love to the depth of my soul, please.'

The temperature rose. The trees were bursting into matrimonial garlands, caterpillars wiggled fuzzily along the twigs of hawthorn hedges and the birds along the river flapped and honked in a hormonal frenzy. It was warm and it was glorious with lilac and columbine, laburnum and cherry. In tune with the sheer buddy, sappy, blossoming of everything, George's spirits began to rise and, with them, a recaptured sense of youth.

'I still have spring in my heart, you know,' he announced to his shaving mirror one morning. He gave himself a dimpled smile and turned his newly scraped cheeks this way and that. Wiping the last dabs of shaving cream from under his nose he thus presented a more dignified and, he thought, winning façade.

George settled in the back of the gently shifting boat, sipping Morland's and looking around him with a mellow tenderness. What could be more lovely than this? He had a feeling of calm and accomplishment. The business seemed to be under control. Clarence had done a fine job on Lady Byngh's bureau bookcase (known among them now as 'the pup'). Her 'man' had come to collect it and deliver it back to her. Soon after, George received another of her imperious notes: *Thank you, Baxter – very satisfactory*. At least she'd said thank you. And she wasn't slow to pay. He smiled at the thought of her with a mellow pity. Poor old girl.

He could hear larks high above the pastures behind him. *Allodola*, he thought. The skylark. It was the tiny mark, always somewhere on pieces from the workshop of that time, which distinguished them – the tiny black outline of a bird, close to one of the front hooves of Venus's horse . . . A branch bobbed in the water close to the boat, seeming stuck. Every so often, lime-coloured flowers dropped from the willow to the water's surface, sending out tiny, sunlit ripples. Though the boat was not comfortable enough to sleep in properly, George grew snoozy and his eyes slid closed.

A plash of oars and a giggle woke him. He opened his eyes to see a rowing boat approaching, heading towards the town and the bridge. A couple, their backs to him, were squeezed onto the rowing seat, each working an oar. Though they were apparently trying to keep time with each other, the girl kept giving up in fits of laughter, letting her oar sag and break the water so that the boat skewed.

'Don't, Sal!' the young man ticked her off. 'You'll have us going round and round again. You have to pull when I do!'

Beyond them, in the distance, George saw a white sail approaching.

'I can't!' the girl gurgled. 'I dunno 'ow to do it!'

As they approached, George saw that she was a fulsome girl in a pink and white candy-striped dress, her hair pulled back into a swinging tail.

'You take it all so *serious*, Philip,' she wheedled. 'I only 'ave to look at your face and it sets me off again.' Her voiced turned low and seductive. 'Don't be like that, Philip. That's it – you put your hand on mine. Give us a kiss.'

Her arm round his back, she turned her plump lips up towards him. George watched, feeling foolish. They seemed to have no idea he was there.

'Oh, *you*,' the lad said. Stowing the oars he wrapped his arms round her and a fervent bout of kissing began as they drifted on past. The girl stroked the back of the boy's neck in such a way that George could almost feel it at the nape of his own. Oh heedless youth! To be twenty, to be out in a rowing boat on a balmy day with a luscious girl. Oh God, oh God . . . !

'Oi!' A shout came from the sailing boat which was now almost upon them. It was tacking with the gentle breeze with only a mainsail, trying to avoid the vagaries of the rowing boat.

The lad seized the oars and began to row like mad out of the way. They just avoided a crash and the sailing boat shaved past, steered by a rugged-faced man with almost white hair. Seated on the bow of the boat was a little girl, cross-legged and apparently lashed loosely to the mast. She looked about six years old, her hair in brown bunches. His granddaughter, George thought. Alarmed by the situation, the child twisted round and turned a solemn gaze on the man.

'Daddy?'

'It's all right, Jenny,' he called to her. 'You just sit tight.'

The child nodded and turned to face the front again, as if returning to her dreams.

Her sweet self-possession tugged at George's heart. And her father – older than he was himself, surely? How extraordinary to feel the arms of a little girl like that around your neck; Daddy, Daddy . . . His hormones jangled. His soul howled. The day seemed intent on parading before him all that he lacked. The river was quiet again.

'Right,' he said. 'Lunch.'

At the first crackle of the packet of sandwiches, Monty surfaced like a whale from the deep. George bit into a ham sandwich and reflected soberly upon his desires. Just because you decide what you want, does that make it any easier to get it?

A single swan came rasping through the air and launched itself upon the runway of water with a perky adjustment of tail feathers. Registering another presence nearby, its head swivelled and its gaze took in the consumption of grub in the boat. A-*ha*, you could see it thinking.

'Oh no you don't,' George said, putting his sandwich down.

With the chilly arrogance peculiar to swans, the creature advanced upon the boat. Within seconds, its neck connected with the side, head peering over like a puppet. Monty bayed at it in outrage, skittering about in the bottom of the boat.

'Steady on, Monty, you'll have us both in!' George grabbed one of the oars. Monty was roaring, the swan was hissing, its head drawn back. 'Get off – go on – git!' He made clouting motions at the swan, struggling to handle the heavy oar and managing to sock himself on the chin in the process. 'Clear off!'

The swan lurched into reverse with much affronted hissing and slid away, its neck at a snooty angle.

'Damn thing,' George muttered, feeling sweaty and ruffled. 'Oh give it up, Monty, for pity's sake.'

'I say!' A chandelier voice assailed him from the towpath over the relentless woofing. George became aware only then that something else was barking, a yap like a scraping in the ear. 'I don't think one is supposed to hit a swan! After all, they are Her Majesty's property.'

A blonde, sinuous-looking woman was on the bank in a white blouse and green tartan slacks. The shrill barking, at the end of a thin lead, was coming from something that looked like an off-white feather duster.

George groaned, and not silently. Not another woman hell-bent on telling him what to do . . . He leaned over and tried to grab Monty's collar. What with the swan and now this yapping domestic implement, he was lathered up and couldn't seem to stop.

'Madam.' George attempted to sound humble, which is hard when shouting. 'That swan was attacking my dog. We can't have that, can we?'

The female looked at Monty, who, remarkably, stopped barking. His face sank into an injured expression. George tugged gently on the boat's painter to bring them closer in to the side. It seemed safe to let go of Monty now.

'I suppose not,' she acknowledged. Monty eyed her dog, which was still letting out intermittent noises, whirring on invisible legs towards the boat and then backing off. 'Only when I saw you waving that oar around I couldn't help but think . . .'

It happened in a matter of seconds. With the boat pulled close to the bank, Monty detected a chance of escape. As the woman was telling George what she couldn't help but think, Monty launched his front half towards the bank, leaving his rear section hooked over the edge of the boat, which immediately began to open a distance up between itself and the bank.

'Monty!' George shouted, trying to grab him. The boat keeled violently. Monty's front half then parted company with the bank as well and the muscular rear basset legs scrabbled at the edge of the boat before disappearing with a splosh.

'Oh my goodness!' the woman exclaimed.

George, knowing that he would never be able to manage Monty from inside the boat, jumped in after him. The main channel of the river banked away quite steeply just a yard away, but here he was only up to his thighs. Monty was panicking, his short legs scrabbling at the bank and letting out frantic woofs.

'Come here, you stupid animal!'

Bending over, and in doing so losing his hat into the water, George wrapped his arms round the dog's soaked torso. Feet straining to free themselves from the sucking sludge below, he lugged Monty onto the bank – whereupon the most almighty commotion broke out when Monty, his pride injured beyond endurance, set about the canine witness to his humiliation.

'Well, really!' The woman grabbed her yowling furball and set off along the path with fast, furious steps.

'Stupid blasted female,' George erupted. 'Spoilt the whole damn afternoon! Where's my hat?'

The hat had fortunately drifted into the stuck branch and was resting serenely on the water. George retrieved it, ploughing through the mud and slime.

'Damn woman. Ridiculous, wretched bog-brush dog!' he complained. Turning to the bank to get out, he said, 'And as for you, Monty . . .'

It was only then that he noticed another pair of feet in white shoes with little heels standing beside Monty. Above the shoes were deliciously plump white-clad thighs, a sugar-pink blouse, a complicated assemblage of dark hair and mascara-laden lashes. From beneath these, huge brown eyes were watching him with what seemed to be lively amusement.

From the face came a voice with soft, country twists to it and underpinned by laughter. 'Is there anything I can do to help?'

2.

Saturated from the waist down, the lower portion of his legs covered in stinking slime, George stood holding his dripping hat. Monty, taking in that there was another newcomer to the scene, plodded over to sniff her ankles.

'Oh!' she yelped, shuffling to one side as Monty pursued her. 'Get him away from me, will you?' She jumped about, giggling. 'His ears are dripping on my feet!'

Monty decided this was the moment to shake himself thoroughly, spraying river water and slobber. The woman retreated further, squeaking. George felt as if his soul had turned to mud. Just at this moment, when he was in pining need of female attention, such a shapely glory had to turn up when he was mud-befouled and Monty at his most disgusting.

'Monty, come here! So sorry,' he said, grabbing the collar. He became aware that his legs, with the soaked trousers clinging to them, must look ridiculously puny and squatted down beside Monty to try and disguise the state of himself. The putrid smell from his legs rose to meet him like the death of expectation.

'It's all right.' The guitar-shaped vision edged closer again. 'It's just, I'm nervous of dogs, and that one is rather . . .' Her voice felt like a caress.

'Yes,' he agreed. 'He's disgraceful. Doesn't mean you any

harm though – do you, old boy?' His mind was whirring. Friendly, attractive woman. How old must she be? Forty? Maybe not even that. But bound to be married, *bound* to be. 'The thing is' – he felt he owed an explanation for his general dishevelment – 'he decided to jump out of the boat and ended up in the drink. I had to follow on . . .'

The woman giggled. A dimple appeared to the right of her mouth, making her look even more attractive. George could feel himself tilting inwardly. She was standing at ease now, her hands clasped behind her.

'You do look as if you've been in the wars, the pair of you. Is that your boat? It's lovely.' She inclined her head to read the name on the bow. '*Barchetta*. That's pretty. After the song?'

George looked up at her with a swell of pleasure. 'Yes! Fancy you knowing that!'

In a strong sweet voice, she sang: '*Venite all'agile, barchetta mia – Santa Lucia, Santa Lucia!*' She finished with a mock curtsey, smiling to show small, even teeth.

George was beginning to beam at her when he saw her face fall into tragic lines.

'My first husband, Lionel, taught me that song, before the war,' she said. 'And then he was in the Italian campaign and it became *ours*. He said to me, every time I hear it or sing it I'll think of you. Such a romantic, he was. He was killed in 1944.'

'Oh dear,' George commiserated, rearranging his face. In addition to the muddy smell he was conscious of the increasingly tight cling of his underpants, but this was not the moment to fidget. 'I was there too, as a matter of fact.'

'*Were* you?' This seemed to fill her with delight. 'Well fancy that. You and my Lionel . . . What's your name?'

'George – Baxter.' His legs were beginning to cramp. He stood up to offer his hand, judging it safe now to let go of the dog's collar. 'Sorry – bit damp.'

'It's all right.' A small, plump hand arrived in his and lingered. Those eyes looked keenly into his. George felt a small ignition inside him, like a pilot light coming on. It was the way she looked straight into his eyes like that. Her own were so big and wet-looking, like a lost puppy's. 'I'm Sylvia Newsome.'

'Charming to meet you.' She was still holding his hand. 'So your husband was Lionel Newsome?' he deduced.

'Oh no!' She withdrew her hand, without haste. 'No. I married again after the war.'

'Of course you did,' he said, his thoughts spilling out loud. 'I mean yes. How good – a happy thing.'

Sylvia was gazing at the boat. 'I know it's cheeky of me, but – could I have a ride? I often walk down here and think how lovely it would be to be on the water.'

'Yes, of course – delighted!' George said.

She looked him up and down. 'Oh but you're all wet – and the dog.'

'Soon dry off!' George averred breezily. A married woman, he was telling himself. All above board. A nice bit of company and after all, it was she who had asked.

'Just need to get this chap in.' He bent over Monty. 'If you could hold the painter tight, that's it, that bit of rope. Hold us in close to the bank . . .'

She leaned back, holding on to the rope. 'Got it, captain!'

'Don't dirty yourself . . .' He stooped to grab Monty.

Dog clasped in his arms, George stepped out recklessly over the side, immediately making the boat rock so that he was fighting for his footing. He swivelled with a light-footed panache that he would later have time to congratulate himself on and lurched forward to deposit Monty towards the bow, ending up sprawled across the middle seat, Monty in a petulant heap in the bow. He heard a giggle from behind him.

'There –' He rose, straightening himself out and trying to look as if all this was quite normal. 'Now – let me help you aboard.'

The soft hand arrived in his and Sylvia Newsome nipped onto *Barchetta* like a fleshy little goat. As she landed beside him, George caught a pleasant whiff of perfume – something heady, French perhaps? She clung to his hand to keep her balance and for a moment they were joined, hands clasped between their suddenly very close chests. Her chest, he allowed himself to notice fleetingly before having to look away, was all you could dream of: rounded, jutting but not aggressive. She looked up into his eyes and the intensity of her gaze was like having a bright light turned onto him. He felt a shiver of goose pimples. Close up he could see that she had a healthy complexion, though marked by more filaments of age than he had been able to see from a distance.

'This is going to be such a treat.' She was still looking into his eyes in a way that made him feel ruffled inside. 'I'm so grateful, Mr Baxter.'

'George, please,' he protested. 'Now my dear – you sit there, in the stern.'

Only as she sank gracefully on to the back bench, smiling up at him, did she let go of his hand.

*

George slid the oars into the rowlocks to paddle away from the bank and gently upstream. It was no use starting up the outboard; they would cover the distance far too quickly and it was noisy and lacking in romance. From this position, facing the back of the boat, he could gaze at Sylvia Newsome as much as his already besotted heart desired.

Monty, worn out by all the exertions of the day so far, slumped his head down on his wet paws and emitted the occasional mournful whimper. His fur was herringboned all over with damp clumps.

Sylvia sat with her knees together, the little white court shoes also neatly side by side, hands resting in her lap. George saw that each of her nails was painted coral pink. She looked about her with every sign of thrilled enjoyment as he paddled along. He had donned his damp hat at what he hoped was a devil-may-care angle.

Nature was offering its very finest sunlight bright on the ripples and bringing out the dark sheen of Sylvia Newsome's hair as they moved in and out of the shade. She really was, George reflected, subtly taking in the curving shape, the pouchy prettiness of her face, a most remarkable bombshell of a woman.

'This is lovely, Mr . . . George, I mean,' she said on a sigh, as they progressed between the breeze-ruffled willows. 'It's so very kind of you to offer little old me such a treat.'

Again, he felt the intense beam of her look upon him. Today of all days, when he was in any case dressed in his oldest trousers and a frayed shirt, not to mention now stinking like a swamp, he had to meet a woman like this. This delicious, fulsome, womanly woman. An ache of longing had begun in his chest. For a few moments he had to make special efforts to breathe. It crossed his mind to wonder whether he was falling in love or on the point of having a heart attack, and was there a difference?

'Has your husband never thought of getting a boat?' he asked, pulling manfully on the oars. After all, rowing was a manly activity, and one that it seemed this husband of hers had not mastered. This fact made him feel rather good, despite his vague concerns about his heart. 'After all, just a small rowing boat isn't much trouble when you live so close to the river.'

Her eyes widened. 'Husband? Oh, you mean my David, the poor darlin'. I should've explained. David and I married in 1952. He was actually . . .' she lowered her voice confidingly '. . . *divorced*. Yes, I know – three children as well. Terrible, really – I remember how upset he was about it all when it happened. Not good for a solicitor, so prominent in the town and everything.' For a moment there was a rather prim correctness to her tone. 'He was my boss, you see – I do shorthand and typing.'

George realized then that the name Newsome was familiar to him: James, Son & Newsome, Solicitors. He even had a vague memory of David Newsome, who he had seen about the town – a florid sort of cove with a jaunty moustache.

'David was a good deal older than me, but it never mattered one bit.' Once again her eyes became stricken pools of remembrance. 'We had ten magical years together and then . . .' A handkerchief appeared from some previously invisible pocket. 'He passed away very suddenly one afternoon. They said it was his heart, that it must have been very quick and that he wouldn't have known anything about it. But I wasn't with him. I was in

Petits. I must have been buying buttons just at the moment when . . . I can't forgive myself for that.' She looked up at the impassive sky, as if hoping for extenuation from above.

George stopped rowing, oars left sticking out each side. Win had scarcely ever displayed her feelings. The sight of such passionate grief and self-recrimination filled him with a reckless urge to pull Sylvia Newsome into his arms. Just as this urge was taking hold he was discouraged by another lugubrious whiff of the mud plastered on his trouser legs. He was in no fit state to go near her.

'You poor girl,' he cried, grasping the oars again, his heart skittering with hope. She wasn't married – she was a widow. 'Twice – how terrible for you.'

'I know.' She wiped her eyes. 'Sometimes I wonder what I did to deserve all this. Lionel and I were only married for five years and he was away for three of them. He was a marvellous person. And then David, so generous and lovely to me . . . To tell you the truth, you remind me a little bit of him, George. You seem such a kind sort of man.'

'Well, er . . .' George flushed and made vague paddling motions with the oars. The boat was beginning to drift slowly back downstream and into the bank again. He had largely ceased to care what it did.

'Your wife is a lucky woman,' Sylvia said, stowing the handkerchief away again.

'Oh well – I *was* a lucky man,' George said, feeling that he sounded faintly unctuous, but trying to maintain the reigning tone of the conversation. 'But I lost my wife – just a few months ago, in fact.'

Two deep chocolate pools fixed on him with tragic attention.

'Oh, you poor dear! Oh I do think it's a terrible thing for a man. When we women lose our man – well, of course we're so sad and defenceless on our own. But for a man! So dreadful for Adam to lose his Eve – isn't it?'

'Er, well, yes,' George agreed, ablaze within. He had never met anyone like this before.

'So we're both alone,' Sylvia Newsome said. Once again, her eyes looked deeply into his. 'Well – fancy that! Perhaps this meeting is in our fates.'

At that moment there was a gentle thump as the bow of the boat steered itself into the bank again. Both of them laughed, startled. In the silence that followed the stilling boat, a silence that seemed to have become loaded with meaning, George said the only thing that came into his head, which was, 'Would you care for a piece of pie?'

When they left the river, the low sun weaving light through the willows and slanting across the meadows beyond, he offered Sylvia a lift home.

'Oh that is kind, George,' she said. 'It is a little walk away.' He liked the way she used his name such a lot. *George*. Did he imagine the tone of caress in the way she said it?

'It's on my way,' he assured her, though he only still had a vague idea of where she lived. He only knew that she worked in the office at Green's, the town's garage and mechanic.

'I do feel rather tired,' she said. 'It must be all the fresh air.' She cast a doubtful look at Monty, who George had been keeping away from her all afternoon.

'Don't worry.' He looped Monty's lead even more tightly round his hand. 'I'll put him in the back. He won't bother you.'

'So good of you.' Sylvia laid a hand on her chest. 'It's not that I don't like him – I'm just a bit frightened of dogs. Oh –' she stopped, eyeing the stately grey curves of the parked Vanguard with approval. It looked especially large in this narrow street, George saw, with satisfaction. 'Now that's *very* nice.' An added warmth suffused her tone. 'Oh yes – *very*. But you don't need to go all the way – just drop me off in St John's Road. Oh, you are a nice man, George, giving me a lift.'

'No trouble.' With mesmerized pleasure he watched, holding the door, as she manoeuvred her curves into the front seat. He shooed Monty into the back and presented him with a couple of sweets.

'Liquorice?' Sylvia said. 'Do dogs like that?'

'This one does,' George said as Monty gobbled. 'It's the way to his heart. And to distract him.'

As he drove, praying that the breeze was carrying away the stench of mud, he glanced at Sylvia as often as he dared. She sat looking attentively forwards. Tendrils of her dark hair curled in front of her ears and across her forehead, a striking contrast to her candle-pale skin. She looks like a woman in a painting, he thought. Renoir, perhaps?

He soon became aware of the movement of Sylvia's hand, gripping the side of the seat close to the handbrake. Her thumb, with its coral-painted nail, kept stroking the leather. The movement was constant, in the corner of his vision. Otherwise, she sat quite still, her knees and feet placed neatly together. Long after he had dropped her off, after issuing his invitation for Friday and her accepting it; both waking and in his dreams, he kept seeing exciting images of hands with coral-tipped fingers.

Eight

1.

George steered the Morris pick-up off the road into the lush shelter of a gateway and switched off the engine. The atmosphere of the fields seemed to bulge in through the windows; breeze and birdsong, the scent of barley and hawthorn blossom from the hedge. He was not far from Dorchester and the gateway afforded him a view of Wittenham Clumps, two rounded, copse-topped hills side by side.

'There you go, Monty – you go and have a wander.' He leaned across his snoozy dog to open the door. Monty half jumped, half lolloped out, sniffed his way to the field gate and disappeared with a slither underneath it. George smiled. It was good to have Monty's company on his Monday buying jaunts.

He reached into his old army knapsack for the brown paper bag that had ridden in there since Henley. Inside were two rosy Italian peaches, the first of the season. Taking one out he squeezed it. Still a bit hard, but no matter. He was just about to sink his teeth into it when he heard Win's voice: 'Have you washed that, George? You don't know where it's been . . .' He rubbed the peach up and down his trouser leg as a gesture and took a bite.

'Oh lovely – *bellissimo*!'

The peach was riper than he had feared, the flesh pale, blood red around the stone. He closed his eyes as the taste transported him back to the south of Italy. Dirt poor and war-torn it may have been, but it was a country he had taken to his heart. Another bite sent juice dribbling down his chin.

'*Molto bene*,' he murmured, through juicy lips.

It had been a busy morning. First Henley, where as well as peaches, he had bought a tallboy which he and the dealer had just managed to wedge in the back of the pick-up. He considered going on to Marlow, more as a kindness to Maud 'EH?' Roberts than for any serious buying. But having Monty aboard and at the thought of Maud's tiny, crammed house, he abandoned that idea. Instead, he braced himself and drove to Twyford.

He would gladly have abandoned his visits to Lewis Barker, that bumptious know-it-all who kept two sets of accounts: the official ledger and the biscuit-tin version. Lewis employed no Clarence or Alan to tend to the pieces he bought – he just had a storeroom, acting shabbily as a shop. Everything about Lewis, from his sweaty, ham-coloured face to his treatment of beautiful things grated on George. But over the years he had bought many a good piece from Lewis, so he tried to keep in with him. He was a well-known dealer, and there was no avoiding him, either in the local area or at British Antique Dealers' Association shows or meetings. Lewis certainly knew how to put himself about. George saw his role as rescuing antique invalids from Lewis and nursing them back to health, as well as turning a better profit than Lewis for his efforts.

Lewis's storeroom was next to his house, on the fringes of Twyford. As George braked in the drive. Lewis appeared, a cigarette jammed to the left side of his mouth, jacket swinging open to exhibit scarlet braces and a fuzz of chest hair in the neck of his shirt.

'Morning, George!' Lewis tweaked the fag out of his mouth. 'I see you've got that old mutt of yours with you! More trouble than he's worth, isn't he? Worse than a woman!' His florid face appeared at the driver's window along with the stink of sweat and stale smoke.

'All right if I let him wander?' George said. 'He won't go far.'

Without waiting for an answer, he opened the passenger door.

'I'll open up.' Lewis ground the cigarette butt under his heel and lumbered off towards the storeroom.

Monty sniffed his way to the patch of grass and dandelions edging the entrance to the drive. Knowing the dog would follow in his general direction, George crossed the drive, littered with old cigarette butts, to the inelegant breeze-block storeroom. Its few grimy windows were veiled with cobwebs. It was a bloody disgrace, George thought, already feeling oppressed. Stepping inside felt like entering a sub-standard orphanage. Whispers of 'Help us, *please*,' seemed to emanate from the chaotic assemblage of wood, never-dusted glass, upholstery and dull brass fittings.

Lewis, thumbs in braces, trailed round after him, prattling on: 'Saw old so-and-so the other day. He's a silly old fool. Paid well over the odds for . . .' George struggled to ignore him. As fast as he could decently manage he picked out a couple of pieces: a stylish French sofa, its rosewood frame decorated with intricate marquetry, poked away in a dark recess with an oak corner cupboard dumped on top of it. This had its keyhole half hanging off and its base was badly denting the seat of the sofa. George bought the cupboard as well, guessing he could squeeze the two into the remaining space in the van.

As he was writing out a cheque on the cluttered table that served Lewis as a desk, Lewis, with a smug expression, said, 'Have you sold that bureau you bought the other week yet?' He sucked breath in through his yellow teeth, shaking his head regretfully. 'I don't suppose you've managed much of a mark-up after the amount you forked out for it, George?'

'Ah!' George straightened up briskly, handing Lewis the cheque. 'Thanks for the reminder – I've something to show you, Lewis. Knew you'd be interested, you having such a fine eye for craftsmanship.'

'Ah, well . . .' Lewis acknowledged this compliment as his due. He stashed the cheque away in a tatty black cash box. George drew the yellowed piece of paper from his breast pocket.

'Here we are, look.'

Lewis, doing his best to appear unimpressed, took it from him.

George watched as Lewis read, '*Jan de Vroom, Nijmegen* . . .'

'Old Clarence found it in a hidden drawer in that bureau – must have been there since it left the makers. In Holland.'

Lewis handed the note back with a dismissive laugh. 'There we are – Dutch. Said I thought it might be, didn't I? You're not going to shift that in a hurry, old lad – no one wants Dutch furniture these days, do they? Much better off with English.'

Sitting in the Morris, the taste of peach still on his tongue, he entertained himself with beguiling visions of Lewis Barker being mown down by an express train, or perhaps tipped purposefully off a cliff. These musings kept him quite happy for a few minutes until the overriding thought that constantly interrupted any other these days came nudging into his mind: Sylvia Newsome.

2.

George was strolling across to the rosebud-swathed house the next morning, having unlocked the barn, when he heard Vera's heels approaching fast across the gravel. Since the weekend he'd been almost permanently immersed in reveries involving Sylvia Newsome, but now he hauled his thoughts into the present.

As usual Vera was carrying her basket over her arm. What was not usual was her sharp-lined dark green suit which he could not recall seeing before and her hair, which was now clipped short round her ears and arranged in neat, bouffant layers. She was walking head down and with busy steps so that he had no more than seconds to take in this transformation before they coincided at the front door.

'Mr Baxter,' she looked up at him and announced, with no preamble. 'I've come to a decision.'

'Oh?'

Vera squinted up at him. She looked younger, rather stunning in fact. Her cheeks seemed firmer, eyes bluer. The upturned tip of her nose was pink. She must have caught the sun in the garden of The Bungalow yesterday. Her expression was solemn. He had a pang of unease. 'Nothing too dangerous, I hope?'

'I feel,' Vera announced, standing tall in her court shoes, 'overburdened.'

'Oh.' George thrust his hands into his trouser pockets. 'Oh dear. But –' He frowned. 'You made a pie.' This was symbolic in his eyes for having enough time for things.

'That's just it,' Vera said. 'I made *a pie*. One. We had to share it – a piece for you and the rest for us.'

'But that's—'

'It's terrible, I know. You see up till now I've kept up, but I had to *drown* Alan's in custard every time to make it last the weekend. Alan gets quite difficult with me if he doesn't get his pie.'

This was an aspect of Vera and Alan Day's marriage of which George had had no previous inkling. Granted, Alan had seemed sullen lately, but he was a silent man in any case so it was hard to tell.

'You shouldn't have given me any if you were so short,' he told her, adding heroically, 'I can get by without pie.' He recalled guiltily that Sylvia Newsome had tucked into a good portion of the picnic pie and Monty had polished off the thick edge bit of the crust.

'The point I'm making, Mr Baxter' – Vera's tone became suddenly imperious – 'is that I need help. I did warn you I might. I want to take on a char.'

'Oh yes, of course – *that*.' This came as a relief. He had begun to worry that the conversation was about to become intensely tricky, the way it so often seemed to with women. One minute you were paddling in the shallows, the next you had stepped into an unexpected chasm in the seabed to find the waters of competence closing abruptly over your head. But this was a straightforward enough request and the funds would certainly run to it. 'That's perfectly all right with me, Vera,' he said warmly. 'You go ahead.'

'I've asked Sharon Jenkins,' Vera steamed on. 'She's after some work.' Seeing George look blank she shifted her basket to the other arm and added with slight impatience, 'You know – Brenda Jenkins's daughter.'

'Brenda Jen—?'

'Barmaid. The Barley Mow.'

Cogs clanked. Brenda. Barmaid. Terrifying.

'Oh, that Brenda! Does she have a daughter? I never knew she was married.'

'Well I presume she must've been once,' Vera said, turning to go inside the house. 'Or not. Anyway – Sharon.'

'Yes, yes, Sharon. You do exactly what you think best, Vera,' he said to her back. 'By the way . . . You look very nice today.'

She turned, smiling with radiant suddenness, as if surprised by her success. 'Thanks, Mr B.'

'Er, Vera . . .'

She was on the step, looking down into his eyes now.

'Would it be . . . I mean, I think I've done something a bit rash.' Vera waited with a neutral expression. George eyed his brown brogues. 'I've, er, asked a lady to come and have some . . . Well, to come and . . . I thought I'd take her to the Bridge Hotel.'

'Have you, Mr B?' Vera's tone was so hard to read that he looked up into her eyes to determine whether she was scandalized or just interested and pleased for him. Neither of these emotions seemed to the fore. Instead, what he read in her eyes was *intensely curious*.

'D'you think it's all right?' he asked. 'Does it seem a bit soon?'

Vera folded her arms, the basket crooked in her left elbow. 'Only you can really decide that,' she said carefully.

They stood a moment longer before, almost deafened by the unspoken questions broadcasting from Vera's expression, he felt compelled to spill all.

'Her name's Sylvia Newsome. Met her on Sunday, on the river, sort of thing. She's a widow. Thought I'd take her to the, as I say . . . Friday.'

Vera raised her eyebrows. Gradually her lips followed into a slow smile. 'Newsome,' she echoed, in the manner of someone trying to recall a half-remembered song. 'Newsome . . . Hmm . . .' She turned away. 'Well, that's nice. I hope you have a lovely time.'

3.

As the week passed after his mention of Sylvia to Vera on Tuesday morning, George became aware of a sort of vibration growing around him. At first Vera had blatantly fished for information.

'Newsome,' she mused again, moments after this disclosure as she returned, temporarily, to her rubber gloves in the kitchen – the new char was to start any day. 'Is that by any chance the Newsome of James, Son & Newsome?'

'I imagine there might be a connection,' George said, laying his eggy breakfast plate in the sink.

He felt a sudden desire to obfuscate. Why had he told Vera anything so soon? Why had he given anyone else even the slightest access to information about Sylvia Newsome when, in his new, unproven state, his own mind was so unstably hooked on her? She had become like a constant electric current in his head, sparking pictures of her – of him *and* her together – of her carrying his child . . . How wondrous she would look! Might all the desires shouldering in him like yokels at a hiring fair, be met in her, this glorious, fecund-looking woman?

'She must've been the one who was married to Newsome,' Vera was saying. 'He died some time back, didn't he?'

'I believe so,' George said vaguely.

Vera moved her washing-up cloth over the plates in a silence that George found even more unnerving because for once she had not switched on the radio. He turned away with an air of being preoccupied by something of intense commercial importance.

'Now – must just go and . . .' He escaped the kitchen before any more questions could follow.

After closing time the following day, he was walking Monty round the village when on the narrow path around the church, he came upon two of the Cronies, Eunice MacLean and Pat Nesbitt with her dogs, blocking the path. The women were in intent conversation, close to the two rose-decked almshouses on the corner. George thought for a split second about turning round and creeping back the other way. But Pat's dogs of course noticed him immediately and started heaving on their leads. The two women swivelled round and he was in their sights.

'Ah, Mr Baxter!' Pat called, leaning back like a water-skier to restrain the spaniels. 'How lovely to see you!'

'Good afternoon, Mr Baxter,' Eunice MacLean called to him. Of the Cronies he found her by far the most bearable, but even she had a gimlet-eyed look of curiosity this afternoon. Thank God Rosemary Abbott wasn't there as well. Her attitude to him seemed always to be one of reproach for something he was not especially aware of having done, other than not wanting her to appear beside his sickbed. Had he not thanked her ardently enough for that jam Swiss roll? Surely he had? At least he never seemed to run into her these days.

'Lovely afternoon,' he called. Monty, his ally on this occasion, started barking at a volume that drowned out almost everything else.

'I'll, er – go back the other way,' he shouted.

'No – do come past!' Pat protested. 'We were rather hoping for a word . . . We hear you've got some news . . .'

'Quite all right – no trouble . . .' He backed away, pretending not to have heard her last comment. He was convinced that when he appeared, they had already been talking about him. 'Come on, Monty.' He dragged him away.

What could they possibly want to speak to him about? Not Sylvia, surely? But it wasn't as if he had any other 'news' he might want to discuss. How could they possibly know about her already? He entertained a moment's dark thoughts about Vera. He had only mentioned it to her yesterday. How the hell did news get transmitted so quickly?

But his mind soon leapt back to Sylvia. Sylvia . . . Every time he thought about the prospect of meeting her on Friday, his innards started churning like one of those new automatic washing machines.

4.

'Mr B – what's this?' Vera, who had just gone to the sink, turned round, chuckling. It was Friday morning. She laughed even more at his dazed expression.

George went over, wondering what he'd done now. In the sink, neatly side by side, sat his brown suede chukka boots. Luckily there was no water in there. He frowned at them.

'Did I put those in there? I don't remember.'

'Well I certainly didn't,' Vera said.

'Hang on . . .' He sifted his mind for some association . . . What had he been doing? 'I think . . .'

Behind the back door, in the place where he normally left his shoes, was an egg-smeared plate with a remnant of bacon gristle on it and a knife and fork.

In a tone stranded between amusement and irritation, Vera said, 'What on earth's come over you?'

What indeed? This was not exactly something he could explain. Well, Vera, you see, it's like this: ever since I met Sylvia Newsome I've been in an almost permanent state of sexual hunger and expectation. And the fact that every woman within a mile of here seems already to have a view about the news that I'm meeting Sylvia on Friday is bad enough, but it is as nothing compared with my own terror at the prospect. It's more than two decades since I courted a woman – and in any case, she was a very different sort of woman. It's just not very easy to concentrate, you see, when you feel like this.

He made vague noises of apology and departed in the direction of the barn as if to have urgent words with the men. But he veered away, remembering that Kevin had been keeping on, as only Kevin could, about going with him to another auction. He ended up standing in his shed in the back garden, gasping in deep breaths of the oily air, trying to calm himself down.

5.

She was waiting, as she had said she would be, an unmistakable egg-timer figure in an emerald frock, something pale draped over her left arm. Good heavens, George thought as he drew up to her. Were women really wearing their skirts that short these days? Her hair was piled on her head, the soft little bits curling round her forehead and ears. For a local woman she had a bold sense of style. George worried as to whether he would measure up.

He had dressed up in a light summer suit the colour of milky coffee. He decided to wear a dashing red bow tie and now wondered if that was all wrong and he should have worn a black evening suit, but it was too late. He had given the car a thorough brush-out to rid it of traces of dog hair and driven over with the windows open just in case. Braking just short of where Sylvia was standing, he leapt out and hurried round to open the passenger door.

'Hello, George.' Her voice was like the breath of a fan heater on the already warm summer air. To his considerable pleasure, she stepped right up and kissed his cheek. 'Ooh, you do look smart,' she said.

A few minutes later he was cursing himself. He should have told her how nice she looked. But he was overwhelmed by sensations: that perfume again, like bells jangling in his nose, the general fleshy press of Sylvia's closeness and a sticky hint of her lipstick on his cheek. By the time they were both in the car, he had still scarcely uttered a word.

He drove with a sense of awe, as if he had a rare bird, falcon or eagle, captive on the seat beside him. As they drove the few miles across country to the Bridge Hotel, he made agreeable replies to her airy observations about the beautiful evening light and how nice it was of him to take her to such a lovely place and did he think there was going to be a storm? It was so close . . .

They turned into the car park of the hotel, a graceful, riverside place, its mellow walls woven across with wisteria in full bloom. The lights were warm and welcoming. A row of sumptuous cars – a Bentley, a Jag – were parked outside. George took it all in in surprise at finding himself here. His sort of pub was a bolthole for a pint or two where he could take Monty and relax in a smoky corner with his pipe. Win would not have approved of the Bridge Hotel. It was swanky and involved unnecessary expense. 'I could cook that at home for a fraction of the price . . .' But Sylvia gazed at it as he helped her from the car, with the expression of someone who has at last arrived home in their rightful place. She adjusted her skirt in a dainty manner. My goodness, George thought, that dress was daringly cut. Whoever made it had certainly not squandered any material in the process.

'Oh George,' Sylvia breathed, lips curving up in carmine delight and bringing out her dimple. George's insides felt warmly viscous at the sight. 'This is such a treat. You really know how to spoil me.'

As they went to go in, she reached for his arm. He stood straight as a general and they proceeded inside, George with a certain jauntiness to his walk.

'Shall we start with an *aperitif*?' he asked, amazed at himself even as he said it.

'You must meet such interesting people in your line of business, George,' Sylvia said, once the waiter had settled them at their corner table in the restaurant.

It had seemed dark to him as they first walked in. The long room had one chandelier hanging right in the middle, a rococo-style thing with candle-shaped bulbs and draped glass beads and prisms. The walls were graced with lights on wall brackets, their shades a rust-coloured brocade. As he walked between cloth-draped tables across the deep red, slightly sticky carpet, his eyes adjusted to the shadowy intimacy of the place. Any moment now, he would be sitting facing her, not in the crowded bar with its squirting soda siphons, clink of glass and prattle of other people, but at their own table, a distance from the other diners.

Sylvia had given the waiter an engaging smile as he unfolded a linen napkin onto her lap and waited for him to produce the wine list before she asked this next question. She was full of questions.

'Interesting?' He knocked back the last of his G and T, which he had brought with him from the bar. 'Oh – yes. Very varied really.'

He took in the sight of Sylvia almost as if he was in a dream. The dim light stripped the sheen from her dress, making its green more subdued, and shaded the hollows below her cheekbones, the soft fold under her chin. She sat with her left arm resting on the table while the fingers of her other hand loosely grasped her glass of Martini and soda. As he spoke, she watched him, her eyes fixed with rapt attention, so that his every utterance seemed to attain more importance than he felt it really should have done.

'I suppose I meant . . .' She gave a little laugh, tilting her head. 'Titled people. You know, those wealthy people you read about in the magazine, lords and ladies. So romantic – or I think so anyway.'

'Oh yes. Those people.' He found her naïve deference rather touching. 'Some, yes, of course.' The first titled person to elbow her way into his thoughts was Lady Eleanora Byngh. 'Although it's not all quite as glamorous as you might think. I can think of one or two who are dreadful old ragbags really. They're not all necessarily rolling in money, you know, or not these days. What goes up must come down!'

His chuckling was met by a solemn look of incomprehension. Eleanora Byngh was not perhaps the kind of society person Sylvia had had in mind.

'My David used to have some very interesting clients like that.' In a voice of hushed reverence, Sylvia said, 'I remember when the Linklaters came to live at that beautiful house near Benson. They'd just come back from Africa, I believe, and they needed David's help with all the legal aspects of the house, the conveyancing and so on.' George was starting to notice that whenever Sylvia spoke of her former husband's work she began to speak in the tone of secretary to the Great Man. It rather amused him. 'Do you ever come across them?' she went on.

'As a matter of fact,' George thumbed the wine list open,

thinking this was a test he could actually pass for once, 'I paid a call on Mrs Linklater just yesterday.'

'No! Did you really?' Sylvia sat back in her chair with such vigorous enthusiasm that she almost knocked the menus from the hands of a waiter approaching behind her. There was a pause while they deliberated. Sylvia was quick to make up her mind.

'I'll have the lobster,' she instructed the waiter, without a trace of indecisiveness.

George felt a shock go through him. He was so used to Win, who never looked at the top end of any menu, however humble. She always worked up from the bottom, and not very far at that. Sylvia, however, ordered as if this was a life to which she was born, with no compromise. Grudgingly he admired this, though he felt that a moment's hesitation, a hint of 'would it be all right if . . . ?' would have made him feel warmer towards her, made him feel he wanted to grant her anything at all.

His eye was roving further down, to the steak-and-kidney regions of the menu. But damn it, he felt like steak and kidney, even if it didn't seem very glamorous. He'd have to up his game on the wine list though, not go for the Yugoslav Lutomer Riesling, the cheapest, that he had had his eye on.

'We'll have a bottle of Châteauneuf-du-Pape – the white, please,' he said breezily, as if this was a run-of-the-mill sort of decision rather than one that was making him feel distinctly heady. A guinea for a bottle of wine – good God! 'That'll go very nicely with your lobster.'

'Oh you are kind,' Sylvia said.

'Not at all – cheers.' He held up the last of the gin. 'Here's to a lovely evening.'

He was met by a smile so fervent that he decided it was worth every penny.

'You were saying,' she prompted him, 'about Mrs Linklater.' Her eyes pressed into him, hungry for knowledge.

'Well, I was sitting in her dining room, yesterday afternoon – sharing a magnum of champagne, to be precise.' He produced this information feeling like a magician revealing a rabbit.

'*Were* you?' She leaned forward, her face avid. 'Oh do tell me all about it, George. About the house? It's very big, isn't it? I bet it's beautiful, like a palace inside.'

He agreed that it was. In fact that afternoon could have been mortifying in the extreme, had Mrs Linklater not been a woman of such good nature.

Shown along the flagged hall of the ample Georgian house by 'Cobb' the maid, he had been greeted by the plump figure of Mrs Arthur (he never had discovered her own name) Linklater, in a loose lilac dress. Her – he could only guess – dyed hair, pale blonde, was caught back in a loose chignon, tied with purple ribbon in a playful bow. She was scarcely five feet in height and tottered about in little cream shoes with thick heels. Mrs Linklater must have been in her early sixties, and her round face, wide grey eyes and purring voice all reminded him of a large, indulged pussycat.

'Ah, Mr Baxter, do come in! We're rather at sixes and sevens today – I've a little man in seeing to my electrics.' She led him to the oak table occupying most of the dining room. Placed along it was a series of dainty bowls containing the garish colours of infant sweeties. The one closest to him held Smarties. 'Have a jelly baby – do!' She held one out towards him. 'No?' She popped a yellow and a green sweet into her own mouth and urged squelchily, 'Sit down – do!' Once perched on a chair, at the head of the table, her feet did not reach the floor. She gave one of her wide, disarming smiles.

'Now, Mr Baxter – I'm so glad you've come to see me at last. I have been a faithful customer of yours, have I not? Now, about this bill for the armoire which I bought, in March, I believe.'

George nodded encouragingly. Vera had, so far as he knew, sent her the bill three times.

'I've heard that your, er, woman, the one who does for you . . .'

'Vera Day, yes.'

'She issues the bills now, I gather? The thing is, Mr Baxter . . .' Mrs Arthur Linklater folded herself in towards him, resting her chest on the table in a manner that he found somehow comforting. 'I paid the bill there and then, when I bought it. I believe in getting these things out of the way at once, you see. So I think you had better take a look at your accounts.'

She sat back, her feline smile fending off George's horrified apologies.

'Just a minuscule mistake, Mr Baxter. Already forgotten! A difficult time for you, your lovely wife and so on . . . Now – I'm sure you've time for a drink with me. You can tell me all about your new exciting purchases and see if you can tempt me with anything.' She slid from the chair and went to the door. 'Cobb! A magnum of champagne to the dining room – two glasses please!'

By the time George staggered squiffily back to the car after a half-hour of amiable chatter with Mrs Linklater, the whole business of the bills seemed to be forgotten.

'Now that,' he had announced, pushing down the hand-brake, 'is what I call a *lady*.'

This he recounted to Sylvia Newsome. The story was greeted with rapture.

'She sat and drank champagne *with* you,' she breathed. 'Oh, don't you think that's the mark of a real lady. Champagne any time you want!'

George could hardly disagree.

'And what's her house like? I bet it's *gorgeous*.'

He described the details he had managed to take in while still sober: the ample table, thick, silky curtains at the window, the silver-edged rose bowl on the table with pink rose heads floating in it.

'Oh, how lovely.' Sylvia's hands went to her cheeks in rapture. 'Pink roses, in a bowl? Oh, it'd be so nice to live like that. Don't you think so, George?'

They ate their starter, honeydew melon with a sprinkling of ginger and moved on to the main courses, each with a glass of the clear, cool wine. The dining room filled gradually and soon they were in a convivial atmosphere of clinking glass, the scrape of cutlery on plates and spiking above the flat seam of conversation every so often, guffaws of laughter from a huge, whiskery gent encased in tweeds, seated under the chandelier. Spots of light reflected in the pool of baldness at the top of his head.

All the time, Sylvia asked questions and George, loosened by the wine, unfurled under her interest. In fact he could never before remember meeting a woman who had shown so much concentrated fascination in him. She extracted information in just the way she prised slivers of lobster from its shell. And she declared every other mouthful how lovely it all was, what a treat! He watched the movement of her plump hands, the curves of her arms, the way she paused, her lips shiny with the food, apparently drinking in everything he said. She would ask a question, then another, and off he went, the words prattling out of him.

He found himself telling her all about working for Joe and Walter Black's big firm in London. He had moved on there from Arkwright's when he was seventeen, wanting to branch out, needing more from life.

'There I was, a real country boy, suddenly let loose in London,' he said, sitting back with his glass, expansive after his handsome plate of steak-and-kidney pie. 'They taught me everything they knew, though – I even ended up travelling overseas for them: America, Argentina . . .' Seeing her eyebrows lift, he back-pedalled quickly. He didn't want to go into all that now. 'Every so often, when I first started, they used to send me out into the East End to the butcher's down the street . . .'

'The butcher's?' Her eyes widened. 'Why – for lunch?'

'No, no,' he laughed. 'The butcher's used to wrap the carcasses in muslin covers, which would take in the fat from the animals. It was . . .' He paused, disconcerted. What was that underneath the table, something pressing against his leg which felt remarkably like one of *her* legs? 'The muslin was . . .' His right calf was being nuzzled by something. This was not something he could blame on Monty on this occasion. Sylvia had finished her lobster. Her elbows were on the table, chin resting in her hands with an expression so rapt it was – almost – impossible to believe that she could be engaging any other part of her body. But there it was again.

'It was used for polishing the furniture.' Muzzy with wine, he was beginning to wonder if he was hallucinating. For a moment the sensations stopped. Sylvia sat up straighter.

'I suppose they were Jewish boys who made their fortune,' she said with sudden crispness. 'And you learned everything from them. You must be *so* knowledgeable, George. What a good business you chose to go into, mixing with all these wealthy people. You've obviously done very well for yourself.'

'Oh I wouldn't say I've done anything all that . . . You know, I just go along . . .' He felt another definite caress, softer this time, at the side of his right leg. She must have slipped her shoe off. Her eagerness was almost childlike, at odds with whatever was going on under the table. 'I mean, wealthy people aren't all that interesting you know. Not necessarily anyway. It's no good doing things just for money.'

No, he thought. He certainly didn't want to start talking to her about Argentina. But in those seconds, looking at her avid face, he knew how much it had marked him. She was so innocent, he thought fondly, with this childlike awe of money. In Argentina he had met people whose blood seemed to pump round their bodies for the sole purpose of accumulating wealth. Everything could be bought, down to the dust of the land. No one seemed to think of anything else. This driven singularity – how it had bored and repelled him to the point of nausea.

'It's no good doing what I do for money,' he lectured. 'You have to love it – the wood, the artistry of it.'

'Oh yes,' she said fervently. 'Of course you do, George. I only meant that you're so lucky to earn your living from it as well, because you're so *clever*.' She gazed at him. 'I'd so like to come and see it all – your business, I mean. It must be so lovely and so interesting.'

George reached for the wine bottle and topped up their glasses. He moved his feet so that they were tucked primly under his chair. The balance of the evening needed restoring, he felt. He had talked as if pouring liquid into an empty vessel. He had, in fact, been rather rude.

'Now, Sylvia.' He sat back and lit his pipe. 'I've been keeping on for far too long. You must tell me about yourself. Do you live all alone?'

Sylvia swallowed a mouthful of wine and carefully put the glass down, though she kept the stem nipped between her second and third finger. George saw a flicker of a sharp expression cross her face which he could not read, but in a second it was gone and the brown eyes seemed to fill with sadness.

'Oh no, where I live is my mother's house.' She ran a red-tipped finger round the foot of the glass. 'When David passed away . . .' The napkin was hurriedly dabbed at her eyes. 'The thing was, George, I couldn't bear to be alone in our house. I just couldn't stand it. And mother's not too well. She needs help now and then. My sister Jean lives with her – she's never married, you see. I didn't really want to move in there. It felt like going back to being a child again. I didn't like that. But I thought, why stay here feeling so lonely and upset when I could help my old mum? She needs me, George. And it's important to be needed, isn't it? Otherwise I feel as if my life's not worth anything much at all.'

'Oh my dear,' George said, moved. The brittle person of a few minutes earlier had melted into this soft, vulnerable woman whose eyes were looking at him with sweet appeal. He shifted his foot forward again and felt her leg come to rest against his. 'But I'm sure you *are* needed.' He saw a chance to slip in the question he had been hoping to ask. 'Did you and your – Lionel and David – did you not have any children?'

The look of tragedy increased. 'No. You see, Lionel and I didn't want to bring a child into the world at the beginning of the war when things looked so dangerous and never knowing what was going to happen. And then of course it was too late . . . And David already had three . . . I would have loved to have children of my own – I'm quite a maternal person, George, you see.'

George, gladly, did see.

'But David didn't want any more. In fact he was adamant. He'd had . . .' Again her voice sunk to a whisper, '*the operation*.'

George was startled. He had never yet met anyone who had admitted to having 'the snip'.

'I was very sad about it, but I could see how much his other children demanded of him. And he and I were so happy. Sometimes when a baby comes along it spoils everything. That's what he said about his first wife anyway and I didn't want it to happen with me. But I haven't been a mother, George, and that's a very hard thing for a woman.'

'Yes, I'm sure it is.' He thought of Win, knew she had mourned silently for her lack of children; as had he, in his way.

'I'm so glad I've met you, George dear. One of those unexpected things.' She laced her fingers together on the cloth. 'I don't expect much of life these days. But I sometimes feel as if I've had at least a taste of good things, even if they were all snatched away from me.' She looked down, as if needing to gather herself to say something, before raising her head again.

'We can be a little bit of a comfort to one another, can't we, George?'

She reached across the table between the glasses, her eyes never leaving his, as if inviting him to take her hand, which with his heart pumping hard, he did.

'Let's stop, George, shall we?' Sylvia laid her hand on his arm as they drove back into town. 'Just for a few minutes? Let's walk by the bridge where we were the other night. It's such a lovely evening.'

'Well yes, all right.' He braked in his parking spot. He felt carried along like a piece of willing flotsam on her will, and on the general alcoholic haze of the evening.

The 'desserts', as Sylvia called them, were peach melba, followed by coffee and liqueurs – Cointreau for her, a generous Rémy Martin for him, along with a good plug of tobacco in his pipe. Long before he had seen the bill he knew this was by far and away the most expensive meal of his life. He imagined Win's tight-lipped expression. But he felt defiant. He could afford it. Not every week, obviously, but this time. And there were other ways to live. Wasn't he in search of a new life; new paths opening out in front of him? In between stirring coffee and sipping drinks, they had linked hands across the table, their legs pressed close. And now, walking under a new moon, he took her hand and rested it over his arm and at last something was openly acknowledged.

They set off along the path beside the bridge. George's mind was divided between the hazy, oceanic feeling he had of floating along on his own fate, and a piercing sense that everything was intensely heightened and vivid. The weight of Sylvia's plump arm resting on his and the smell of her perfume awoke in him physical memories – the touch of a woman, scented, glorious in shape . . . Raw longing built in him, so intense that he could not distinguish between the emotional and the physical. He needed. He ached to fold his arms around this woman, to find his gaze met by hers.

'So pretty, isn't it?' Sylvia said, stopping on the path. George hauled himself out of the cave of his desire to acknowledge that yes, the arches of the old bridge, the water rippling in the shreds of moonlight were indeed pretty, though pretty was not a word he would ever have chosen.

She turned to look up at him. In this dim light, close as he was, he could only just make her out. Her eyes looked very large in the shadowy shape of her face. She was wearing her pale shawl thing over the green dress now.

'I've never had an evening like this before,' she said. 'It's the best of my life, George. I can hardly believe it. And it's all thanks to you.'

He was utterly taken aback by this admission, by the suddenly vulnerable tone in which she delivered it. How could this be – what of marvellous Lionel and my darling David? Surely she had had many glorious evenings?

'You're an absolutely lovely man, George.' There was something mesmeric in the way she kept using his name. 'I'm so glad I've met you. I thought my life was over, I really did. I feel like the luckiest girl alive.'

A swell of gratification passed through him like a warming blush. He had done it right. She was pleased. And he was touched by her admission, by this sudden frailness which made him feel rather manly and rock-like.

'Well, I'm glad you enjoyed it,' he said.

'Have *you* enjoyed it, George? I know you're such a clever man and I'm just – well, you know. I'm just a little country girl, really. Not like you, working in London and travelling the world.'

'Oh, I have. And you're a dear,' he added expansively.

'Would it be wrong, d'you think . . . Oh dear.' She turned her head away with a girlish giggle, then looked back at him. 'I'd like to give you a kiss, George. After all, we're hardly beginners, either of us, are we?'

'No, well quite,' he agreed, his blood pounding. 'I'm sure that would be . . .'

Sylvia's lips met his before he could formulate anything sensible to say. He was pulled into the moist heat of lipstick and Cointreau and the electrical sensations produced by Sylvia's fingers caressing their way along the back of his neck.

6.

When he opened the front door next morning to find Alan Day, Vera's husband, waiting outside, George concluded for a few seconds that he was hallucinating. It was, he thought, just that his mind was scattered as a flock of startled pigeons. Yet, even as it struggled towards lucidity, he still felt that Alan did not belong on the doorstep at eight o'clock on a Saturday morning. But this particular hallucination, unlike his high-voltage dreams about Sylvia Newsome, did not vanish as soon as he blinked.

Alan was brown-eyed with well-defined cheekbones and trimmed black hair. His eyebrows were dark, questioning arcs. As ever he was dressed in black trousers and white shirtsleeves.

'I just wanted a quick word with you, Mr Baxter, before the others get here.'

He seemed nervous, a state which George found suddenly infectious. A tremor passed through his innards. What was this about? Why the early arrival – was it pistols at dawn, sort of thing? Surely – terrible dawning thought – Alan didn't imagine there was anything untoward going on between himself and Vera? Or was this all about fruit pies, or rather the sudden dearth of them in Alan's previously well-regulated life?

'Why don't you step inside, Alan?' he invited in a cordial tone.

'No, it's all right, Mr Baxter. I can say what I need to say just as well out here, man to man like.'

This really was ominous. George waited in the doorway, thrusting his hands deep into his corduroys and did his best to appear amiably interested.

'Thing is . . .' Alan's hands joined in the exploration of the interior of trouser pockets. He looked down at the doorstep. 'It's Vera.' With a sudden outrush of passion, he pronounced, 'She's changing. She's not like the girl I married any more.' He looked up at George with terribly serious appeal. 'D'you see what I mean, Mr Baxter?'

George did, up to a point. 'Well . . . Her hair looks a bit different. And I suppose she's not making quite the same amount of pastry she was before,' he ventured.

Alan seized upon this evidence of fellow feeling. 'Oh yes, there's the pastry – but what I mean is, she's getting above herself; selling this, bossing about that. Full of it, she is. All those' – he paused to add a disgusted weight to his utterance – '*pop songs* she listens to.' He shook his head in the face of this deviancy. 'And there's this girl she's taken on! I mean, my Vera, hiring and firing right under your nose, Mr Baxter. That doesn't seem right to me. Not right at all.'

The girl in question appeared later that morning. Though George spent quite some time reassuring Alan that his wife had not turned into a power-crazed insubordinate, but that he had himself sanctioned the employment of Sharon Jenkins, he was still startled to encounter this young and – like her mother – glowering presence in his kitchen.

He had been outside and was crossing the drive quickly to avoid Kevin and his, 'Oh, Mr Baxter, can I come with you to another auction soon? *Can* I? Oh *please*!' He knew he was going to cave in and let him sooner or later, but on this occasion, Clarence appeared in the doorway of the barn in his overall. He beckoned with a skeletal finger like the Grim Reaper. 'Kevin – get in here, boy!'

Rescued, as Kevin veered away, George hurried inside. As he did so he became aware, over the transistor's mutterings, of Monty barking, somewhere at the back of the house. In the kitchen he saw a figure washing up at the sink who gave an overall impression of brownness: blouse with immensely strong-looking, tanned arms emerging from the sleeves, skirt, hair, shoes, all a variation on chocolate.

'Ah, Mr Baxter.' Vera was in there too. She had the presence of mind to click the radio off so they could hear each other. 'This is Sharon. I'm just telling her what's what. We've had to put Monty out in the garden though. He was bothering her.'

George could hear his dog making affronted sounds beyond the back door. The brown apparition swivelled slowly round. Clamping her right hand to her waist, left leg crossed over right, she leaned back against the sink in a manner that could only be described as challenging. Like her mother Brenda, she had a short-bodied compactness which emphasized her chest. Sharon had a mane of very dense, curling hair, and dark, emphatic eyebrows. In fact everything about her was emphatic: the thick, pouting lips, the strong cheekbones and large eyes of some indeterminate colour which were fixed on him with what could only be interpreted as smouldering resentment.

'Can't work with that dog,' she announced, in a voice surprisingly light for her build. ''E bothers me.'

Monty let out a heartrending howl from outside.

'Never mind – he can stay out there while you're working,' George said. He felt quite unnerved by the way the girl was glowering at him. It would take him weeks to get used to the fact that that was just the way her face was.

'She's just learning the ropes today, aren't you, love?' Vera seemed quite relaxed with her. 'I'm going to show her everything this morning.'

'I'll just make a cup of tea and get out of your way,' George said.

Sharon turned slowly – he was also to learn that slow was her exclusive pace – back to the sink.

When he escaped out to the back, Monty greeted him with hoarse jubilation as if, since breakfast, he had had a spell away at the South Pole.

'Come on, old boy, we'll go and sit in the shed. Don't you worry, she's only going to be here once a week.'

Later, Vera reported that, though not the fastest thing on earth, she thought Sharon would do. And it would be twice a week.

'She'll learn,' Vera said. 'Slow but sure.'

'She can't be only seventeen, surely?'

'Oh she is,' Vera said. 'Same age as Kevin. Would you believe it!' She hovered, though all her work was done. 'Off anywhere nice tonight, Mr B?'

George realized he was being pumped for information. 'No,' he said, with an air of bemusement. 'Why?'

'I just wondered.' Vera picked up her bag. 'Oh –' She turned back. 'By the way – I suppose you managed to get that Mrs Linklater to pay her bill at last, did you?'

'Ah – no, no,' George said. He folded his arms, speaking gently. He didn't want to sound as if he was blaming Vera. 'We cleared the matter up. Said she paid up front. She was jolly nice about the fact that we've been pursuing her actually.' He chuckled. 'Even opened some champagne for me.'

'Did she now?' Vera was staring at him, unsmiling. 'Well, I've got to hand it to her – I suppose you swallowed all that, did you?'

George's smile faded. 'How d'you mean?'

'Mr Baxter . . .' Vera stepped closer. 'That woman did not pay for what she bought. I was there. I remember. If she had, I would have written it down, like I always do. Have you ever known me not to write it down?'

'Well, no . . .'

'And she didn't pay – so we'll have to bill her again.'

'Vera – we can't,' he said, appalled. 'Not after yesterday. I mean it's all over – really, I can't possibly ask her again.'

Vera stood with one hand on her hip, looking thunderous. 'Funny how there's one rule for the rich, isn't it? Well, if that's how you want it, I can't argue.'

George opened the door for her and watched her walk away down the drive in her smart suit and shoes. Did he imagine that she even walked faster these days? He felt a twinge of fellow feeling with Alan for a moment. Vera could be fearsome. But you can't just hold someone back, he thought. I suppose I felt held back by Win. He remembered Maggie and wondered if married couples ever stayed long on the same level as each other. Keeping pace, that was the problem. He saw Vera disappear behind the trees edging his land and hoped she would not, in the long run, outpace Alan. He shook his head. He was going to have to write off the sale to the scheming Mrs Linklater.

But closing the door, his mind was once more with Sylvia. Over and over again he replayed their kisses in his mind and felt weak with expectation. Two days he had to wait before he could see her again. Two whole days. He would have to work hard in the garden to distract himself.

JUNE

Nine

1.

'Oh George, this is heaven!'

Sylvia sat on the starboard side of the boat, gazing over the tranquil meadows near Day's Lock with a rapturous expression. They had pootled north away from Wallingford, passing the Bridge Hotel – 'Oh!' Sylvia cried on seeing it, 'that's where we began, George, isn't it?' – towards Little Wittenham and the Clumps. Before they reached the lock, he cut the engine and let the boat drift into the reed-edged bank, the warm silence billowing about them, broken only by the anxious pipping of a moorhen. The sun was still burning off the haze and the fields seemed to exhale moisture and the pungent scent of elder-flower.

George looked across at the twin hills with their dark crowns of trees. He felt blessed by the beauty of the landscape. And here was this heavenly woman beside him.

He had left Monty at home today. 'Sorry, old boy – but you hate water anyway. And the womenfolk don't really appreciate your disgusting habits.' He bent to fondle the dog's ears before he locked up. 'You have a relaxing afternoon. Shan't be too long.' Monty, sprawled on his bed in the back room, looked up blearily from beneath crumpled brows, before abandoning himself to an afternoon of ease.

'I thought we might have our picnic here,' he said. The bags of food were stowed up towards the bow. 'Seems a good place.'

'Oh, it's *lovely*,' she agreed.

George assessed the state of the pasture beside them. There were no swans about, but the grass was dangerously pock-marked with cowpats and there were sizeable thistles.

'Stay in the boat, I'd say,' he remarked.

'I'll see to the food,' Sylvia offered, ever anxious to please.

She was dressed today in a pair of calf-length navy trousers, striped sort of top like a burglar and black shoes with low heels. George took full advantage of the opportunity to drink in the shape of her as she eased herself forward and leaned to gather the bags. As she reached over, an ache spread through him again. *Just come here and take me in your arms, woman.* If only they could be inside somewhere for an afternoon of fleshy tenderness and release. All this necessary pursuit was rather tiring.

'Ooof!' she giggled. 'Got it!'

Righting herself, she shuffled onto the middle bench. He tried not to stare. The striped top, like most of Sylvia's blouses, was cut low enough to reveal the cleft between her breasts and so was endlessly distracting.

'I hope you like what I've brought, George,' she said humbly. 'I'll have to learn what things you like, won't I?'

He found this sweetly disarming. She had insisted on bringing the picnic. 'You've been so kind to me – it's the least I can do. Oh, and look – I brought these for you-know-who.'

She held up a box of liquorice allsorts. George had told her of Monty's adoration for sweets and these in particular.

'It's a shame he's not here,' she said valiantly. 'But you can give him one from me, all right?'

George was very touched. He knew the sweets were aimed more at pleasing him than the dog, but it was a kind thought and he said so. 'Oh he'll be *very* pleased with those,' he added.

'Well, I know how much you love that dog – and he's a fine old boy,' she said, turning with a smile as she laid a rug over the duckboards and brought from the bags a succession of Tupperware boxes stacked in descending order of size. George wondered what was in the really enormous one at the bottom. From the other ones she brought out onto melamine plates sandwiches – egg mayonnaise and beef – chicken drumsticks, Scotch eggs and cocktail sausages, tomatoes, cucumber and celery sticks and from another box, a deep green tangle of watercress. There were packets of crisps and bottles of Watney's Pale Ale. ('You like a nice ale, don't you, George?' Said with the sweetest of smiles.)

Once everything was laid out she sat up, hands on her thighs. 'There – how's that? And I made a strawberry gateau.' She pointed at the biggest box. 'Can't have you going hungry, can we?'

'What a treat!' he said.

'Come and sit here.' She patted the bench beside her. He smiled and shifted over, carefully, to the middle of the boat.

Sylvia turned to look coyly at him. 'There's something else you haven't said, George. Haven't you noticed?' She patted her head. 'D'you like my hair?'

George examined her with a sense of disquiet. The hair – was it different somehow? More of it, perhaps, or curlier?

'I had a perm.' She shook her head so that the dark curls rippled loose around her head. 'I hoped you'd like it.'

'Oh I do,' George agreed fervently. He did like it, he realized, though he would have approved however she wore it. 'It makes you look very youthful,' he said.

She laughed, pleased at this. He longed to reach for her, to press his face into the shadowy little crannies round her neck and collarbones and altogether fold himself round her.

This was already their second meeting since the dinner at the Bridge. On Sunday night they had sat outside at the Nautical Wheel pub by Wallingford Bridge – more vermouth for her, a couple of pints for him. She had gazed at him with that dreamy attention she gave him when he talked. She asked about Win and he told her what he could, casting Win in the kindest light possible. After all, there was nothing wrong with Win. He had always felt that the fault lay with him – for wanting and needing more, for settling for less than that. But he did not say this. He did say, 'She was a good sort. Lots of friends – you know, active in things in the village.'

Sylvia's eyes became liquid with sympathy. 'It's terrible, losing the people you love, isn't it?' She reached for him for a moment and stroked the back of his hand. 'It's the worst thing. Oh I do *know*, George.'

He was gratified, melted, by the attention she paid him. He was not used to such attention – only from Maggie, ever. Of course in some ways she was foreign to him, the way she seemed preoccupied with how much things cost to a degree that he found positively alien. And those girlish mannerisms . . . But, he reminded himself, people had to get used to each other. And what about him, with his pipe-smoking and his dog who liked sniffing people's backsides? If they were to get used to each other then each of them would have to forgive the other for their age, their habits.

That evening as the dusk fell about them, and her eyes remained the brightest part of her, giving back the strings of light outside the pub, she told him about her father.

'He left us.' She looked down as if in shame. 'Just went off and left Mum and Jean and me. I can barely remember him – I was only three. Jean was six. Poor Mum; she set to and started baking her own bread and cakes, selling them out of the front room to make ends meet.' She raised her head. Her face had changed. George thought he had never met someone with such expressive features. There were no tears, but a puckering of pain. 'I haven't been very lucky with men in my life, you see. I mean, with them ever staying to take care of me. I suppose that's why I never rushed into having children – not even with Lionel, though as it turns out I was right to feel . . . you see, I never felt safe enough.'

This soulful vulnerability and her sheer fleshy loveliness sent desirous, protective feelings swilling round George's body.

'You poor girl.' This time he reached for her hand. 'You've been so unlucky, haven't you?'

'Oh George.' Sylvia's words rode on a sigh and she tilted her head to one side. 'You're so kind to me. Of all the men I've ever met, I really think I feel the very safest with you.'

As they sat side by side, close to Day's Lock eating her picnic, she plied him with questions.

'Oh George, you're such an astonishing person, such a man of the world. You must tell me about New York.' This was gratifying to hear and George, feeling short on gratification, swallowed her words like the first summer strawberries.

What he was in fact eating at the time was a satisfyingly large mouthful of Scotch egg, enjoying the promising press of her thigh against his. After chewing and swallowing, during which he rapidly calculated how to unpack this particular drawer of memory, he decided that glamour was the key.

'Old Joe and Walter, the Black brothers, knew how to do things in style,' he said. 'They sent me over as an agent for them – put me up at the Waldorf Astoria on Fifth Avenue.'

He heard Sylvia gasp, just as he himself had when he saw the place and realized that he, gauche country boy, was really to stay in such a looming palace of a place. He had walked round it every day, dazed by its vast opulence.

'That was the old Astoria, of course – they pulled it down the year after. But oh my, you should have seen – the dining room, the luxury of the bedrooms . . . Telephones – can you imagine?'

Glancing at Sylvia, he could see that he had her rapt.

He told her about crossing the Atlantic Ocean, on the SS *Aquitania*. Once installed in the Waldorf Astoria, in the company of Edvin Helle, his aptly named contact in New York, he held meetings with dealers and antiques buyers, some of whom had driven, or 'travelled the railroad' – he enjoyed saying that – from the surrounding states, to sit sipping expensive coffee and perusing the seductive catalogues Joe and Walter had sent with him. Thick vellum pages arranged with photographs purveyed fine craftsmanship of the old countries for which the buyers hungered and with which they might grace their homes and company offices. He met imposing, athletic men who looked to have eaten well from birth, with sharply pressed suits, slick hair and debonair self-confidence. Only one, he remembered, a stunted fellow from Pennsylvania with hollow cheeks, wire-framed spectacles and a diffidence covered by loudness, looked to have thrown off the pinched horizons of poverty.

'I'd wire their orders through to the Black brothers – or requests. Could they find this piece or that? Something French, or . . .' He thought he noticed spores of boredom beginning in Sylvia's expression, rather like mould beginning to bloom on a peach.

'Sorry – rambling on . . .' He looked down at his shoes feeling foolish; a boring show-off.

'*No*, George!' She laid a hand on his arm and kept it there. His hairs rose as if lifted by static. 'It's all so interesting. But tell me more about the place itself. I'd love to see it. Is it as different as they say it is?'

'Oh, it is.' Her hand still on his arm, he tried to capture it: the soaring tallness, the way looking up at the buildings made you feel dizzy. 'The lads who build those things, the skyscrapers, are called "sky boys". Imagine it, working all the way up there.'

'Ooh,' Sylvia gave a shudder, which transmitted in a pleasing way through her whole body.

'And the people there – you've never seen so many different types and accents and languages! Rich, poor – everything seems to be *more* than here. And the music – oh, it was a whole new world for me, I can tell you.'

He did his best to make himself sound an adventurer, a lad with more conviction than the callow twenty-year-old he had been. In reality, almost all his memories of that escapade the other side of the Atlantic were tinged with humiliation and a lingering disgust. New York had only been the beginning, before he was invited – commanded, more like – to Buenos Aires, by Paul Lester. But New York, though it was undeniably exciting, had disquieted him in ways he would never admit to Sylvia. It would make him sound unmanly. It was the crazed, loud pace of everything, the way that, because alcohol was prohibited, it had become an obsession. He even drank soup laced with some hooch or other. And – harder still to admit – that music, the raucous, wild signature tune of the 'jazz age' horrified him. He had heard it snaking and blaring its way out through doorways, or beating on his temples in those places – clubs reeking of hooch and sex and incipient violence – to which tedious, prurient Helle insisted on taking him. Helle, into whose company he was forced during those days.

Helle, six years his senior, worked for a prominent New York dealer. He was a gangling creature with a thin fuzz of hair atop a long face, white as a fish's belly. He wore a drooping moustache which he seemed to imagine made him sexually irresistible.

'Come on, Sonny Jim,' Helle repeated in lofty tones. He said 'Sonny Jim' aggravatingly often. 'I'll take you to a speakeasy. You can't leave this city of ours without a taste of the high life.'

For two evenings George managed to avoid him. All he wanted each evening, after days of strain and new faces, was to stroll about the streets. He wandered in Central Park with its soothing lake, his unaccustomed eyes free to drink in this heaving, modern place. He wanted to sit somewhere quietly and look around him. Boring, perhaps, but he had grown up in a town where a passing motor car was an event that sent children scurrying out to wave and stare.

By the third night he had run out of excuses.

'So . . .' Helle said as they stepped out of the Waldorf on a warm, April evening. Helle was sweaty and excitable. His breath stank like fermented apples. 'Out on the town at last! You might want to cut your teeth – *or rather*, spill your seed' – a nudge which made George long to punch him on his stupid, bony jaw – 'Sonny Jim!'

Helle led him along various side streets. He seemed soon almost lost and childishly excited. 'You can drink all you like where we're going, Sonny Jim!' Pinching George's arm at the elbow, he led him along streets of soaring, narrow tenements and down steps to a gloomy basement. George loathed it all from the moment they stepped inside, the way the walls seemed to close in, containing air thick with cheap perfume mingled with hooch and other primal stinks and an atmosphere of licence and looseness.

Helle pushed him across to a table. A dark-haired woman was sitting astride the lap of a man whose features George could not see, since her face was pressed to his as she rocked up and down. It took moments for it to dawn on George that they were actually . . . They were . . . He tried not to look. As soon as Helle had a drink inside him he became multiple times more tedious than when sober. George was handed a tot of some clear liquid. It smelt like paint thinner. The place was full of women who, he realized by their insistence and handling of him, were offering him what was going on just outside the vision of his right eye. He endured half an hour of acute discomfort and rising rage, pretending to sip the hooch, having girls sidle up to him, making suggestions to which he had no idea what to say. Bugger this, he thought, past bearing it any longer, and walked out. Helle, who was talking to some girl with caked eyelashes and a beauty spot on her cheek, barely noticed. For the next two days of his visit he and Helle did not speak, except on strictly business matters, and Helle never again looked him in the eye.

But to Sylvia, he described the place in a way that implied he had been its equal, or at least its eager disciple. After all, it was not the fashion to be unequal to New York. He had roamed the streets, looked out from the Battery, moved to its music (or rather away from it), drunk in all its glamorous atmosphere. He found himself dredging his memory to describe the mansions and shops of Fifth Avenue because he thought this was what she would like to hear.

And then, because he had run out of things to say about New York, and he guessed that she would not be interested in Argentina, he told her the one thing he could relate to her as a story about lords and ladies, about seeing the Allodola Venus and Mars at Lord Buckleford's mansion, his seeing Mars on Horseback again at Lester's *estancia* in Argentina, about the missing Venus.

'What a sad story,' she said. 'Lord Buckleford, you say? Having to sell his lovely home. And imagine losing all his sons like that – so tragic.' She shook her head, then brightened. 'I can help you look for Venus if I come out with you. I'd like that!'

George smiled. As if, after all this time they might walk into some shop and . . . But then they might. Anything was possible.

'It can be our little treasure hunt,' she said, though he was not sure if she was saying it just because she thought it would please him. As they talked she had started running her fingers along the hairs of his forearm. The tickling of it, the cherry-coloured nails just in his line of vision, brought him back from these memories to the glitter of light and the smell of the river. And to her. In his hungry mind, each touch felt like a stroke of hope and possible fruition. He stopped talking, drawn too much back into the present to remember more.

'George?' Sylvia stilled her fingers, but left them resting on him. With the other hand she reached down for the oblong plastic box. 'I made a strawberry gateau.'

'How lovely.' He was full of a desirous, trance-like feeling.

She needed two hands to open the thing on her lap. Inside, resting on a sponge ring, the red shine of strawberries set like jewels into whipped nests of cream.

'Oh my word,' he found the presence of mind to exclaim. 'What a woman you are!'

Sylvia laughed, seeming gratified and he saw tiny suns reflected in her eyes. 'Mum taught me to make a good cake. All for you, George.' She gave him a long, deep look, then reached up softly and kissed his cheek. As she moved slowly away, he was caught by the sight of her ear, the fleshy pink lobe, a dark wisp of hair curling down her cheek in front of it. It seemed to show him something absolutely female, the secret shell tunnel of ear, the pearl nestling in the lobe. Her ear filled him with tender longing.

Pulse drumming along his veins, he took her in his arms, his lips seeking out hers, which were offered to him, full and warm. Everything else was forgotten. He wanted this to go on and on, here, somewhere, anywhere . . .

'George, dear . . . ?'

She drew back, tapping his arm, amusement in her eyes. The

gateau was still in its box on her lap. 'I'm going to drop this . . . Let me cut you a slice, shall I?'

He surfaced, like someone pulled back from the brink.

2.

In that night's balmy darkness, the moon like a tiny rent in the sky, George took Monty out to stretch his legs. The dog, having idled all afternoon, was eager as a pup. He dragged George down the drive and, before George could think about it, to the chalk path along the edge of the downs and Maggie and John Wylde's farm.

A faint chill was settling over the fields. The night sweats of plants reached him in the darkness: cow parsley, honeysuckle, a heady mixture which brought back to him the smell of Sylvia's scent. Sylvia . . . A besotted array of emotions passed through him.

He hesitated, then followed the dog's determined course towards the farm. Monty could obviously smell something and was surging forward. George let him off the lead. What harm would it do? He hadn't seen Maggie even in passing for weeks. He bought his eggs on his Saturday afternoon trips into Didcot once he'd shut the shop. He wasn't going to meet her out here now. And if he did . . .

A pang of affectionate regret went through him. Dear Maggie. He was already in a simmering state as a result of his extended farewells to Sylvia. They had paused on their journey home, tying the boat up in their secluded spot under the willows upstream of Wallingford. She had allowed him – for the first time and so briefly he felt she might be carrying a stopwatch – to move his hand over her breasts. And oh, what magnificence . . . but after not more than a few seconds she seized his wrist.

'We'd better not go too far, had we, George? Not here.' While he was thinking that they had not in fact gone anywhere, she was gazing into his eyes with an air of serious social responsibility. Supposing, her look said, a child were to come past? He remembered the little girl perched on the bow of her father's sailing boat and tried not to sigh.

Not here. Those words seemed full of promise. Full of longing, he stood there in the dark, concentrating on the thought of that pearled ear, the contours of those breasts. An ache solidified in his chest, that longing to clasp his arms around a warm, giving body, to be held in return.

'Tell you what,' he'd said as they parted. 'Why don't you come over to my place this weekend – Sunday, when the shop's shut? I'll come and pick you up and I can show you around.'

My place, where there was seclusion, privacy . . . Sylvia readily agreed.

He paused at the foot of the Wyldes' drive, calling softly for Monty. There was a dim glow of light from the farm. Standing in the darkness he smiled, thinking of Maggie's pink, kindly face, her rough hands, her lying slack and naked on that bed. What he felt for her was surely a kind of love, even if they had been right to retreat from one another. Turning to walk home, whistling for the dog, he thanked her inwardly and hoped that she was all right.

Ten

1.

Stepping out of the front door a couple of days later, at the beginning of the working day, he saw Kevin halfway across the drive, at a standstill and clutching his daily parcel of sandwiches as if overcome by some biblical-type event.

'All right, Kevin?' George enquired in passing, on his way to the barn.

'Oh – y-yeah. Thanks, Mr Baxter. Mornin', Mr Baxter.'

George began to revise his tentative view that Kevin had hidden depths. Any such depths seemed to be trickling away rapidly into the main drain. The lad scuttled after him into the barn, going to look for his overall with a dazed expression.

'Morning, Alan, Clarence!' George greeted them.

Alan, already at work with a chisel at the bench, looked round and said good morning. He had an edgy air all the time these days, on account, George realized, of whatever his wife might be getting up to. Clarence, contemplating a Regency tea caddy in mahogany perched on slender claw feet, made a sound in his throat which George chose to interpret as an amiable greeting.

'Taken a bit of a bashing, that, hasn't it?' George said, looking at the chipped edges of the box. The lid comprised five sections, four of them sloping up to meet a rectangular flat top, the sections divided by pale boxwood stringing, much of which looked as if a rat had chewed on it.

Clarence shook his head, tutting like an RSPCA volunteer facing a battered puppy. The caddy had clearly been treated very carelessly, but George decided to head off a torrent of woe on the subject. Moving closer to Clarence, with a jerk of his head towards the coat hooks at the other end of the barn where Kevin was robing up, he said quietly, 'What's up with the lad?'

'Huh,' Clarence said. 'Can't get any sense out of him. Caught sight of *her*, that's what.' A jerk of the head. 'That wench.'

'Wench? Oh – you mean Sharon?' Rather to his bemusement, Sharon's ominous figure had started appearing in the kitchen not twice, but thrice a week. Vera was evidently in need of Help on a large scale. Sharon had arrived this morning, already for the second time this week.

'Sharon, is it?' Clarence said with distaste. He leaned towards his tools with a sour expression as Kevin began to advance towards them. 'Huh. Well – I s'pose anything warm'll do.'

The kitchen, on his return, was presently occupied by Vera and by Sharon, dressed in her usual brown garb. The radio was on, sound crashing out of it.

'Do I use this cloth for the upstairs, Mrs Day?' Sharon was asking loudly, as George ventured in. Though she treated Vera with an almost exaggerated respect, George thought he could detect an underlying thread of contempt towards all of them. But then, he told himself, he so often got women wrong. And with a mother like Brenda, from the pub, how could Sharon really be otherwise? In any case, Vera did not seem to notice any undercurrent.

'Use the cloths I've left up there, love,' Vera said. 'You'll see the Harpic – just take the Vim up with you. You can do the bathroom now, quick, while no one really needs it – or do you, Mr Baxter?'

'Er, no – far from it.'

Sharon – unhurriedly – drew on a pair of yellow rubber gloves, picked up the Vim and with what George could only feel was a withering look up and down his person, slouched towards the stairs in black lace-up shoes. There was something Soviet about Sharon, George decided.

'Vera,' he hissed once she was safely gone. He eyed the transistor radio. Vera took the hint and turned it off. 'How old did you say that . . . person is?'

'Seventeen.' Vera was digging around in her basket and brought out a newspaper.

'Are you *sure*?'

'Quite sure. Look, Mr Baxter – you won't have seen this.' She opened the *Reading Mercury* and spread it on the kitchen table, pointing. 'Terrible – look.'

ARMED BURGLARS HOLD ELDERLY LADIES
IN ALL-NIGHT ORDEAL

'Oh good heavens.' His eyes hurried down the story. 'Lady Byngh!'

The burglary had happened in the small hours. Three men had broken into Greenburton House, one with a loaded pistol. They tied up Lady Byngh and her housekeeper and spent several hours ransacking the place for items of value, thought to be antiques and silver, which they carried off in a van. It was only when the milkman arrived at dawn that they were able to call out for assistance. The two ladies were taken to the Royal Berkshire Hospital, suffering from minor injuries and shock.

George looked up into Vera's sorrowful eyes.

'Poor old thing,' she said. 'She didn't deserve *that*. But she does live away from everyone, all the way up that creepy drive – and only that funny old dear for company . . .'

'I wonder what they took,' George said. 'I don't know what she had up there, but they could've emptied half the house in that time.'

'Yes, that's right – Chalk Hill Antiques. Can I help you?'

George, passing along the hall the next morning, heard Vera's telephone voice from the office. He went to the door in case help was needed.

'Oh – Lady Byngh.' A nervous deference entered her tone. Leaning on the doorframe, George felt his innards tighten fractionally. Until that moment he had been feeling quite relaxed. There was no Sharon lurking in the kitchen today. And it was only two days until Sylvia was coming to the house, a prospect which offered acres of Sunday afternoon time, privacy and who knew what else, an unknown towards which his mind kept veering helplessly.

'How are you?' Vera asked. She managed not to say 'love' as she would have done to most people. 'What a terrible time you've had. We read about it in the paper . . .'

She was interrupted down the line by what sounded, from where George was standing, like a Cairn terrier barking, though it appeared it was actually Lady Byngh. Vera removed the receiver from her ear briefly and gave it a look of consternation.

'Oh – no,' she interjected during a pause in the racket the other end. 'He's not here, I'm afraid.' She met George's eye and winked. 'He's gone to see another customer . . .'

More canine sounds jerked out from the telephone.

'This afternoon? Yes, I think . . .' Vera paused as if consulting a diary. 'Yes, Lady Byngh, two o'clock should be—'

'*Woof . . . Yap . . .*'

'*Sharp*. Yes, Lady Byngh.'

2.

The drive of Greenburton House branched off the road at the edge of Aston Parva village, beyond a perimeter of land owned by the racing stables. George found himself steering along a tunnel of predatory-looking conifers. After squinting in the glare through the Vanguard's windscreen, he now found his eyes widening to admit enough light in the green-tinged gloom. At the other end, he emerged to a circular sweep of grass-pocked gravel in front of the imposing house. The centre of the drive was occupied by a fountain topped by a stone dolphin, its mouth angled to spout water into the air. But there was no water and the dolphin's mouth was chipped and dry.

George parked beside Lady Byngh's red and black Daimler, which gave off an air of both disdain and dishevelment, its number plate still hanging off.

It had once been a fine house: Georgian, generously built, with three gables in the roof and the front door set in the middle. Mellow bricks could just be seen beneath the ancient wisteria that seemed almost to have ingested the house. The roof was lichen-covered and missing tiles; the door and window paint were chipped and leprous; flowerbeds were a tangle of weeds, grass and climbing roses. George stooped to look at the pink rosettes – Orléans roses, he was almost sure – which had mingled with the tributaries of wisteria flowing from its thick corkscrew trunk.

He felt the heat bearing down on him as he stood looking up at the house. He sensed the plants giving out moisture into the breezeless air. The only sound was of bees, stirring languidly round the flower heads. He could feel himself simmering, his whole body patched with moisture. But this was no place to remove his jacket. He stood with it swinging open for a moment, inviting the non-existent breeze to cool him and sought the shadow of the house, along a flagged path edged with desiccated leaves. His spirits sank. Even standing outside the black front door, he was aware of the seeping smell of stale cigarette smoke.

The bell pull was a metal handle in the wall on which he yanked, resulting in a mellow tinkling from the belly of the house. This was followed immediately by the Cairns' enraged yapping, interspersed by an occasional 'woof' from the Labrador. George realized he had little idea who might answer. Had there not been mention of a housekeeper?

There was a pause long enough for the dogs to give up any expectation of imminent events and save their energy for the final push. In the resulting quiet, George heard the approach of erratic, slapping footsteps weaving inexorably closer. The huge iron latch snapped upwards.

As the door opened he heard the clicking of dogs' toenails on stone and the barbershop trio of barking advanced towards him, borne on a gust of air flavoured with cigarettes, dog and a general grottiness. Standing before him was a woman not far off his own height, a figure of hunched, heron-like boniness, clad in a diaphanous, silver-grey dress. A lurching pearl brooch tugged on the material to the left of her flat chest. In her left hand was a cigarette holder, with a half-burned cigarette in it.

'Back!' she commanded in a cracked, screeching voice in which George thought he detected an American accent. 'Get back, you damned critters!'

A pair of silver-rimmed pince-nez clung on halfway down her pointed nose, a chain undulating each side of her shinbone face as she spoke.

The dogs obeyed, seeming chastened, though the bulbous Cairns had a brief go at yapping and making little dashes back and forth. The elderly golden Labrador stood with its head half lowered but eyes raised to George with the same fixed look he had seen from Lady Byngh's car, as if inwardly screaming for assistance.

'Bertie, Jack, quit that – now!' Silence arrived, abruptly. 'That's better.'

She peered at George over her spectacles and he found himself regarded by unnervingly pale grey eyes. Her hair, George saw, must once have been a generous, wavy headful. It still had substantial body to it. It was steel grey and swept back into some bun affair at the back. Pearl-drop earrings pendulated at her neck. She also had good cheekbones and might once, he realized, have looked rather interesting.

Before she could speak, a voice that was unmistakably Lady Byngh's assailed them from somewhere upstairs.

'*Percy?* Is that Baxter?'

Without turning her head, the woman yelled, 'Yup!'

Muffled instructions followed from upstairs which seemed to be completely ignored.

'You are Baxter, I presoom?' A hand like a bony flipper

extended towards him and his own disappeared momentarily into its cold clasp.

'George Baxter. How do you do?'

'How do *I* do? Hah!' This was followed by a long drag on the cigarette and a turn of her head to puff out smoke. 'Come on, I'll boil some water for carfee.' She turned, then back again. 'Oh – I'm Percy by the way. Full name's Marguerite Persimmon. I'll take you up to Eleanora in a moment.' She pronounced the name in five syllables: El-e-a-no-ra.

Up, he thought? Surely to goodness he wasn't going to have to meet Lady Byngh in her bedroom?

He passed through the quarry-tiled porch, benches like church pews on each side, beneath hooks bearing mackintoshes and sagging jackets. The pews were littered with old newspapers, dog-leads, old gloves and a couple of threadbare tennis balls the colour of ancient moss.

The smell of smoke increased as he entered the house. One of the Cairns who had been lingering ran up to him, yapping.

'Hello, old chap.' George bent to stroke its scruffy coat, a development the dog greeted with every sign of ecstasy, rolling on to its back.

'I wouldn't encourage the stoopid critter,' Persimmon remarked. 'Go on all of you, git! Lie down!' She moved into the main body of the house with her singular gait, legs widely spaced, one foot slapped down flat, then the other. Here the sound was muffled by old Turkish rugs, so grubby and trampled that their pattern had vanished into a uniform silt colour.

'They didn't think to steal those,' Persimmon said, pointing down at them. George felt he could hardly blame them.

'How is Lady Byngh?' he asked. 'I gather you had the most terrible time.'

'Spitting mad,' Persimmon shouted over her shoulder. 'She's still in bed after what those lousy louts did. They made a night's work of it I can tell you. Look—'

She gestured into the room to her left. Through the filmy stuff of her sleeve George saw the anatomy of her spindly arm extending.

'Oh dear me.' He was standing at the threshold of a dining room. 'I see what you mean.'

'They couldn't be bothered with the table. Too difficult to load, I suppose.' Persimmon planted her feet and gathered her arms in close to her, the left hand to her mouth with the cigarette. She stared resentfully at the mayhem.

In the middle of the room, on a stained but once high-quality crimson carpet, rested a long table. From what he could see, it was a mahogany pillar and claw design, three sets of four splayed legs each gathered into a supporting pedestal. Other than the lower part of the legs it was impossible to make out much of it. A dark red chenille cloth sagged from its top. This was burdened with such a towering array of clutter – rows of cardboard cartons, albums, books and various sedimentary layers of *stuff*.

'Oh dear, they did leave you in a state,' he said, imagining that the burglars had hurriedly thrown the contents of the room onto the table. 'What a terrible way to—'

'No, *no*,' Persimmon interrupted tetchily, with a hand gesture like the flap of a crow's wing. 'They never touched this. They just took everything from around it – all the chairs, and El-e-a-no-ra's darling bur-*eau*.'

George uncovered in himself a certain fellow feeling with the burglars. Even for a decent mahogany dining table, that lot was not worth tangling with.

Their progress upstairs, he following Persimmon's strange, deliberate gait, was punctuated by calls from the upper regions.

'Percy – hurry up! What are you playing at?'

Marguerite Persimmon gave no reaction to these interjections whatsoever. George braced himself for the state of the bedroom and what he might find in it. The smell of smoke had not lessened as they ascended. Reaching the landing, they entered a passage, its carpet threadbare but elegantly patterned in green, black and gold. There was a nicotine-yellow tinge to all the walls. Persimmon stopped at a door opening to their right.

'Here he is, dearie,' she announced, at once retreating. 'I'll make the carfee.'

To George's surprise the carpet ended at the door and he found himself treading bare, brown-painted boards, with only a small rug by the bed. It was a simple room, a single iron bedstead up against the wall to the right, sunlight, in a slanting fall through the window, lighting a strip of the dusty boards. To the other side were a dressing table and mirror and chest of drawers. Other than that, there was one wheelback chair.

'Good afternoon, Baxter.'

Her tone was as commanding as ever. George felt himself bridle inwardly. He dragged his gaze away from the chest of drawers, a bow-fronted thing in ash, and confronted the bed. His surprise at the simplicity of the room was compounded by the sight of Lady Eleanora Byngh, sitting up very straight against her pillows. Her hair, surprisingly dark for her age, which he realized was rather less than he had assumed, was brushed and pinned severely back from her face. Apart from the fact that she was wearing a pale blue nightgown with frills down the front – she was not a woman he would have associated with frills – there was something almost nun-like about her appearance. Most striking of all was the radiating spectrum of colours from her eye and down the right side of her face.

'Ah – oh dear,' he said, taken aback.

'Should have seen the other feller,' Lady Byngh said grouchily. She reached across herself to stub out her cigarette into a saucer on the bedside table. A wince of pain passed across her features but she said nothing. 'Fetch that chair, Baxter,' she ordered. 'And sit down.'

He settled on the upright chair, wondering if Lady Byngh had ever been acquainted with the word 'please', while she shuffled through a few sheets of paper. Without looking up, she commanded, 'Open the window a crack, will you, Baxter? It's getting too warm in here.'

His mind rebelled. *What did your last slave die of?* Crossing the creaking floorboards, he raged inwardly at the way her manner instantly reduced everyone about her to a minion. It was like being back in the army! What an insufferable, rude old bag she was. Any sympathy he had summoned up at hearing of the assault on her was fast draining away. He raised the sash, which to his surprise slid easily, giving a view of the unkempt garden, though at least the grass had been recently mown. Why did she occupy this simple room, he wondered. There must be much grander ones at the front. It occurred to him that this was not her room at all, but a spare one into which she had moved especially to meet with him. He realized he ought to ask how she was feeling and turned to do so, but she got in first.

'Right. Sit. I want you to help me.' Her peat-coloured eyes tracked his return to the chair. 'Percy will be up with coffee soon but it takes her an age. She is well into her seventies.'

'*Is* she?' George said as he sat. 'Good heavens. Is she an American?'

'Canadian – once, anyway.'

He found the presence of mind at last to ask after Lady Byngh. Was she recovering well from her ordeal? He managed his kindest, most gentlemanly manner, despite everything.

'Yes, yes,' she said dismissively, clutching her papers. 'A couple of cracked ribs. The face. I'll be all right. Now, Baxter –' She pushed herself a little more upright. George looked away, disquieted by the thought that some movement might release the precarious-looking fastening at the neck of her nightgown. As she moved, a whiff of perfume stole through the lingering smoke. 'I have, as you know, been robbed. Common little guttersnipes the pair of them, though they did know what they were looking for, I'll give them that. I've a list of all I *think* they've made off with. I may add to it of course. You're to help recover my things.'

George managed to swallow a rising remark that he was neither a member of the police force, nor of her personal staff.

'Put the list out to your colleagues – fellow dealers or whoever they are.' She gave an imperious wave of the hand. 'No doubt some of it will turn up quite soon. They didn't seem the sharpest knives in the drawer. But the worst of it is, they stole the Hepplewhite, the one your man polished up for me.'

'Yes – Miss Persimmon told me,' he said. 'I'm so sorry to hear that.' Secretly he wondered if this might be a blessing.

'Of course, I'm quite distraught,' she announced, not sounding so in the least. George wondered if anyone would ever be able to recognize that Lady Byngh was distraught beneath her, at best gruff, but more commonly rude and aggressive manner.

'However,' she went on, 'fortunately, Roderick need not be without a wedding gift. I have a plan B. Ah – here comes Percy.'

Persimmon's exertions on the staircase were audible long before she appeared.

'Let me . . .' George half rose from the chair.

'No!' Lady Byngh barked, so that he descended again swiftly. 'Don't interfere. She gets very put out.'

An erratic clumping of feet, accompanied by rattlings and clinkings, preceded Persimmon's entrance: a shove of the shoulder against the door and the manoeuvring of an unfeasibly vast tray. George watched with apprehension as she wove across the room to the chest of drawers, which offered the only bare surface, and deposited it with a crash of bone china. A teaspoon leapt to the floor.

'I brought you some boo-doir biscuits,' Persimmon announced, lifting the plate as George hurried over to retrieve the spoon. On the dressing table, he noticed, were enough things – picture frames, brushes, bottles – to persuade him that this really might be Lady Byngh's bedroom.

As the coffee-pouring took place, Lady Byngh recited the toll of her losses from her list: the Hepplewhite bureau, eight dining chairs described as Chippendale, a lady's work table with chess set on top, a wash stand, a Windsor chair, Chinese vases and numerous other items of china, tea caddies, various other treasures and gold jewellery.

'From India,' Lady Byngh elaborated. 'Not the sort you could actually wear, of course. Dreadful, heavy, native stuff. But solid gold. It belonged to Mother.'

'Huh!' Persimmon interjected, shuffling over with little white cups of coffee. '*Mother!*' she added with apparent venom before heading for the door.

'Thank you so much,' George called after her, even though he did not much care for coffee. She made another low 'huh' sound, but gave him a nod of acknowledgement.

'Fetch plan B, Percy!' Lady Byngh shouted after her.

'That's what I'm doing!' shrieked Persimmon.

While they waited for the whole stair-climbing business to begin again, Lady Byngh tapped the list in her lap, covered with her looped handwriting. He saw with surprise that her hands were rough, the nails chewed and broken.

'Most annoying,' she said. 'I'm most concerned about the boy's wedding. My nevew, you know.'

'I suppose you could buy something,' George ventured. 'I mean, if you no longer have anything of more sentimental value.'

She fixed him with a look of baffled contempt. 'My dear, one doesn't *buy* antiques – one inherits them.'

George swallowed. 'If that were the case, one would hardly make one's living selling them – would one?'

Lady Byngh gave him another look of distaste, one that seemed designed to eliminate his very existence. He forced down the mutinous rage rising in him. It's just her upbringing, he told himself. She can't help it. Poor old dear, clinging to her things. He took a bite from one of the sugar-coated biscuits. It tasted of dust.

Persimmon reappeared, in surprisingly good wind after her ascent, George thought, a newly lit cigarette in its holder in one hand and a silver teapot in the other.

'Plan B,' Lady Byngh said, showing signs of brightening. Her face lost some of its grouchy bullishness. She added something George did not understand, which sounded like, 'Ba-lo Percy.' One of those Indian orders, he guessed. Watching Persimmon deliver the thing to the bed, George realized that though she had her own style of cantankerousness, he could not detect any resentment in her manner at being so ordered about. She had perhaps long been a servant, he thought, watching her depart through the door again.

'Now, Baxter.' Lady Byngh thrust the teapot in his direction. 'I want you to look and see if this will do for Hughie's boy. It's got to be something good. I don't want to let the side down. Percy's given it a good polish. Those awful louts didn't find this – it was at the back of a cupboard.'

George was tempted to tell her at this point that the marvellous Hepplewhite bureau, about which so much had been heard, was not in fact the pure treasure she imagined. But he kept quiet. That particular news did not reflect well either on himself or Lady Byngh.

He handled the teapot, examining it. It was a well-proportioned piece, of medium size, with the streamlined grace of an ocean liner.

'Very nice,' he said at first sight, praying inwardly, *don't let it be plate*. Eager people were forever coming to him to sell what they assumed were solid silver heirlooms, only for him to have to enlighten them that the silver part only went skin deep. Even before he turned this one over, he was pretty sure it was the real thing. The first of the hallmarks on its slightly concave base confirmed it. He began to breathe more easily.

'Will you tell me?' Lady Byngh urged. He was surprised by the sudden softness of her voice, containing something close to humility. 'I've never know about silver marks. Well,' she startled him with a gruff chuckle, 'or about much else, come to that. I'd like to know something about it.'

George turned to look at her. Her face was intent and there was a youthful eagerness in her eyes that touched him. Silver was something he knew about, relished. 'Certainly,' he said. He pointed the lion out to her. 'See this one? The lion passant, sterling silver.'

'So it is solid silver?'

'Ninety-five per cent at least, yes. Now, see this one?' She leaned to look and gave a gasp of pain.

'Sorry – let me hold it closer. That mark is the monarch's head. You see, in the period when this was made there was a tax to be paid on silver – from 1784 onwards. The monarch's head was a duty mark. It started then because they needed money to fund the American war – the War of Independence, that is. But I'm sure it continued to come in very handy.'

'Ah –' She peered closer, sounding uncertain. 'So . . . oh dear, I don't remember much. Schooling a bit patchy. I read up on whatever I can, but . . .Who's that supposed to be?'

'Well, see these other marks?' Enjoying this small authority, he pointed to an 'O' to one side and a crowned leopard opposite it. 'The leopard means it's a London piece. That's the London silversmiths' mark. And every year they'd mark them with a different letter. So far as I remember, "O" would be round about 1810. So, that makes the monarch George the Third.'

'I see.' She was steady now and interested; somehow more normal. 'And the last one – those initials? The maker?'

He was careful now, diplomatic. The initials CB were set close above GB. He happened to have seen them before.

'Yes – they were a husband and wife partnership. Caroline and George Blakeley.'

'You surely don't mean it was made by a woman?'

Her sceptical tone got under his skin. He forced a smile, cradling the gleaming thing in his hands. 'Actually, it's possible. There were women silversmiths, skilled ones. But they may have overseen the business together, managed other craftsmen. It's hard to be sure.'

She stared at him. God, he thought, it was hard to like the woman.

'But is it *good*?' She was insistent, almost childlike.

It was good enough, he thought. After all, would the fortunate Roderick have a clue anyway? Though not rare or outstanding, and just one of thousands of items of the period crafted by smiths all over London and elsewhere, it was still an honourable piece.

'It's very fine,' he told her. 'I'd say it would make an excellent present – and it'll be much easier for you to send.'

'Thank God for that.' Lady Byngh subsided suddenly into the pillows as if a string holding her taut had been cut. 'Got to do my best for Hughie's boy.' She closed her eyes for such a long pause that George thought she had drifted into sleep. Relieved, he was about to rise and creep from the room when she opened them again, looking perfectly alert.

'I su-ppoose,' she drawled, 'you imagine that Percy and I are a couple?'

Her face crinkled, possibly in amusement at the sight of George's inability to bring forth a single sensible word in reply to this. In fact the thought had not crossed his mind. His only observation had been to wonder that Lady Byngh seemed to have reduced Persimmon, as she did everyone, to an object at her beck and call and nothing more.

'Not all women who resort to "shacking up" together are lesbians, you know.'

'Er, no. *No*,' George agreed fervently, though this was a generalization that until this moment he had not found it necessary to formulate. Heavens above – thoughts scrambled ineffectively in his brain – why did he always seem to get into things like this, without ever asking to? 'No, quite.'

'Percy has only been back with me for the last couple of years in fact. I was married once, you know. Look—' She nodded peremptorily across the room. 'There on the dressing table.'

The dressing table, with a toilet mirror on the top, was draped with a length of turquoise silk, parrots threaded through in red and gold. Among the feminine bits and pieces he saw two framed photographs.

'The one at the front is my brother – poor darling Hughie,' Lady Byngh instructed.

'Ah.' George groped for something positive to say. For some reason he came out with, 'Families are a great blessing, aren't they?'

'Huh,' Lady Byngh retorted. 'I'm glad you think so.' He felt foolish, wondering why he'd said it. It was hardly something he knew for himself.

He glanced back at her for a second from the faded picture of an earnest, round-faced young man in cricket whites, with unruly-looking waves of hair. There was a slight resemblance between them, in the set of the face, the heavy brows. He couldn't help but think that the boy looked a trifle gormless. From her tone he concluded that poor darling Hughie was no longer with them. Killed in one war or another, he wondered? Perhaps the same went for Lady Byngh's erstwhile husband.

The other frame displayed a classic wedding portrait of the period: softly focused in sepia with an abstract studio background. The groom, with thin, tapering handles of moustache and brilliantined hair stared at the camera with apparent resentment. He had on some sort of uniform, though George was not sure which one – something colonial-looking. Beside him, the veil lifted back from her face, sat a surprisingly mature-looking woman, dark hair pulled back under a pearl tiara, emphatic brows and the same eyes he could feel watching him now as he examined the picture. The young Eleanora Byngh's features gave the impression of gritted teeth, rather than abundant joy.

'Last ditch,' Lady Byngh commented. 'Thought I'd better give it a try. Play the game as one was expected to. Mother wanted to net him because he was a stray baronet. Ghastly mistake. Of course, poor old Archie went and got himself shot by the Japs in the jungle somewhere, the silly boy. But I'd bolted long before then. Six weeks after the wedding, in fact.'

'Six weeks?' George was too astonished to measure his response. 'My goodness – that can't have gone down very well.'

Lady Byngh snorted. 'My dear, you have no idea.'

3.

Exhaustion settled on him as he stepped out into the rose-scented afternoon; a heavy-headed longing to do nothing but sleep. Even with his jacket and tie flung on the back seat, sleeves rolled, the heat was soporific. The air seemed to slump in through the opened windows, even in the cool tunnel of conifers. He rejoined the glare beyond, the unbroken blue of sky, the green ripple of barley across the hillside.

By the time he got home it would be almost four. An hour until they shut up shop. Customers seldom came in late on a Friday. He could have a cup of tea instead of that vile coffee, a quiet hour in the office, perhaps even a snooze? He breathed in, then let out an airy sound of release. It felt as if he had been in Greenburton House for several days. In fact, it had been barely an hour and a half.

As he turned into the drive of Chalk Hill House, it was immediately obvious that something was up.

Vera, arms folded, was standing at the front door, Alan on the gravel in front of her, making agitated motions with his hands. At the level of Vera's knees, George could just see Monty's head looking out, ears quivering as he adjusted his gaze to whoever was speaking. The dog had a bewildered air, which George immediately began to share.

Seeing him arrive, the two of them stopped arguing and stood waiting, Alan pink and het up, Vera tight-lipped, mutinous. As George climbed out of the car, he glimpsed Clarence and Kevin sloping back into the workshop, from where they had been watching the goings-on.

Monty tore out to meet George as if in delight that an intermediary had arrived on the scene.

'Hello, old chap.' George grabbed a moment's refuge in stroking the dog's jowls, then straightened, with an imminent feeling of being about to sink once more out of his depth. Monty wandered off to sniff round the shadiest edges of the yard.

'Is something wrong?' he asked, attempting a brisk air of authority.

Alan gestured at Vera, as if towards someone beyond help. '*You* tell 'im,' he said. 'Go on.'

'It's just—' George had never heard Vera speak like this before, bitter and resentful. '*He* says I've done wrong. We had one of them knock-you-uppers round . . .'

'Knockers!' Alan erupted. 'You can't even get that right!' George was surprised and appalled at the way he spoke to her, but he tried not to show it.

'I see?' he said encouragingly. He knew a number of the knockers who worked the area, men who did not have shops but who worked door to door, buying and selling on. George had nothing against most of them. The ones he knew were lively characters who got about quite a bit. In fact there were one or two he had asked to keep an eye out for him – 'Venus on horseback, old boy? Unusual. Still – if I see her I'll tip you the wink.' And he'd had some good deals through them, often celebrated after with boozy meals in pubs around the county.

'Who was it?' he asked. 'Not old Arthur Salmon, or Reg Dickson?'

'No,' Vera retorted. 'I'd've known who *they* were. This was a gingery chap, said his name was Charlie Bird.'

'Oh yes, I know.' George recalled him. A younger bloke, used to be a greengrocer before he decided he could make more out of antiques.

'I *told* you, Vee!' Alan insisted. George was struck again by the crouching force of his anger. He seemed ready to explode.

'Yes, but he wasn't anyone *I'd* seen before,' Vera said. 'I mean, I can't just let anyone in. How'm I supposed to know who you can trust? Anyway, all I did was say you weren't here and he should come back. That's all.'

George was at a loss as to what the problem was. If Charlie Bird was after something, he'd be back. Deals were like women: they brought out male persistence.

'Well, never mind,' he said, tiptoeing through the mysterious turmoil that all this seemed to have aroused. 'No harm done.'

'Huh!' Alan folded his arms now and stared at the ground.

'Vera – could you please go in and take Monty with you?' George suggested. 'Put the kettle on – I'll be in in a moment. Alan, a word, please.'

Alone, the two men stood in silence. George felt a drifting apathy move through him. The easiest thing would be just to go inside, have a sit down and a cup of tea. But he was disturbed by what he had seen. He roused himself to speak.

'Something else bothering you, Alan?'

Alan's head jerked up, arms unfolded and his whole lanky height seemed to increase.

'She shouldn't be giving orders around 'ere.' The words poured out, as if he had been longing to say them. 'It's not her place. It's not . . . it's just not right.'

'But . . .' George attempted, but the flood had only just begun.

'Twenty years we've been married. Twenty! And now she goes round handing out orders, tells 'im to go away – and the feller, Charlie, 'e comes out to the workshop and d'you know what 'e says? 'E says, "Who's that old dragon in the house then? I ain't seen 'er before." And a few other things 'e has to say which I won't repeat.' Alan leaned towards George, his face distraught. 'That's *my wife* he were talking about, Mr Baxter. How would you like it, eh? Seeing your missus getting—' He gestured with his hands again, palms up, as if waiting for the right words to settle in them. 'Getting above herself, as if she's too good for the rest of us – oh!' He turned away and strode off, as if from an unbearable thought.

'But no harm's been done, you know, Alan,' George started after him, but Alan flapped his arm as if warning him to keep his distance and walked away, shaking his head.

In the kitchen, he found Vera at the sink, arms folded again, staring out over the garden. Monty was sitting at her feet looking up at her, his natural expression of woe suited to the times. The kettle whispered in the background.

'It's all right, Vera,' George said from the doorway. 'You really haven't done anything wrong – I don't blame you for being cautious. Old Charlie'll be back if he wants something.'

He heard a sniff. Vera turned, red-eyed, a handkerchief screwed up in one hand.

'I haven't changed all that much, have I?' she appealed.

He hesitated. She had. He could see it. She read his hesitation right.

'But why's that *wrong*? I'm not doing anything so bad! I cook his dinner every night. I do everything . . . I've always had a lot of energy, see – for a whole lot of things.' She looked across the kitchen, a dull expression in her eyes. 'More than him, I suppose.'

George struggled for words. He saw Alan's confusion, hurt, his fear, even if there was no rational reason for it. For a second he tried to picture himself if Win had branched out suddenly, made even some small change. It was hard to imagine. Would he have quaked and raged like Alan?

'He wants me to be just like his mother,' Vera said bitterly. 'Creeping about, waiting on everyone hand and foot, husband, three sons. She's a skivvy to them. Not one thought in her head that doesn't belong to them. And the thing is, it's not as if it's made her nice or anything. She's a bad-tempered old . . .' She shook her head, then stared ahead of her. 'There's that song – I heard it on the tranny again yesterday. Times they are a-changing. They are, aren't they? And I *want* them to. I don't want to be like old Ethel Day. Am I wrong just to want something else except fetching and carrying and . . . And *pastry*?'

George pulled out a chair from the table and sat down. He looked up at her.

'You're a very able woman, Vera. I don't see how it's wrong to use your head when you've got one. But old Alan – I s'pose he thinks you're going off somewhere where he can't keep up with you.'

Tears ran down Vera's face again. She wiped them with the handkerchief. 'I know. I do know, Mr Baxter.'

'Look,' George said. 'Go and get him. Both of you, knock off early. It's nearly time to shut up anyway.'

Vera didn't move. 'He wants me to go back so that everything's exactly as it was before. I'm worried what will happen if I don't.'

Should he be telling her to obey her man, he wondered? Do anything he wanted – wasn't that the required advice? But it wouldn't seem to come out of his mouth.

The kettle was working itself up to the boil. He got up to turn it off.

'I don't know what'll happen either.' He turned to her with a shrug. In a gentle voice he said, 'But take him home now, eh?'

4.

There was a storm in the small hours of Sunday morning and when George woke from what felt like no sleep at all, everything outside looked washed fresh. It was not only the slams of thunder that had kept him awake; it was his own thoughts. He had writhed this way and that, catching the sheet round his neck and generally getting in a mess.

Sylvia was due to come tomorrow – today now. Having not seen her for a few days, she seemed to him, in the dark night hours, distant and strange. He was filled with cold doubt, as if she was something alien that he had grafted on to his life which might make him grow wrongly. At the same time, the thought of her attentive eyes, her luscious shape and his own aching need for physical connection wound him into a state of such nervous expectation that he had even less hope of getting back to sleep.

Shouldering through these misgivings and fantasies was his unease about Vera. First thing on Saturday she had telephoned the shop.

'I'm just calling to say that I'd like to take the half-day off today, if that's all right.' She sounded dreadfully subdued.

'Yes of course, Vera, quite all right,' he said, while his mind stumbled through grim possibilities. Was Vera hiding at home because Alan had blacked her eye? Should he be asking if she was all right? Before he could assemble any words of concern, she concluded, 'Thanks, Mr Baxter. I'll see you on Monday.' Which was at least reassuring.

Alan came into work, kept his head down, avoided meeting George's eye and got on with it. All afternoon, after shutting up shop, George tended the garden. He hoed up the potatoes, weeded between onions and broad beans and tied up a few sprays of pink Albertine rose. He worried. Then he sat out at the back and worried more. He was not used to misery among his staff and it was not what he wanted. Strictly speaking it was private, a marital thing between the two of them, yet he could not escape the feeling that it was his fault. His encouraging Vera into more involvement had upset the balance of things, as if to the Days their marriage had suddenly become a foreign land.

He sat in a deckchair staring at the tumbling pink and white screen of roses, a silver tankard of beer in one hand, the other stroking Monty's ears. Again he considered how he would have felt if Win had wanted more independence. Would he have felt wronged? He had to own that he might have done, if he had had a sense of being neglected. But then, Vera had already been working anyway, that was nothing new. It wasn't work as such that seemed to bother Alan, but Vera's growing confidence, her authority. As if a man necessarily shrank when a woman grew. On top of that, he had been made a fool of in front of the other men. Despite his inclination to share male fellow feeling, George found he thought less of Alan for this. Let alone the business of the pies. It seemed small-minded, selfish.

Unable to make sense of it all, he stretched in his chair, then ruffled the dog's fur.

'Lock up your women, Monty,' he said. 'Or they start getting ideas.'

Monty tilted his head to look at him as he spoke, as if he might be giving the advice serious consideration.

He took Monty out as the bells were ringing for the morning service and met Eunice MacLean coming out of her house clad in a long, pale mackintosh, bound for Holy Communion.

'Quite a storm last night,' she commented, eyeing the puddles in the gutter and stooping to give Monty a pat.

'It certainly kept me awake,' he agreed. 'Cleared the air a bit too.'

'Are you keeping all right, Mr Baxter?' Her tone was formal, as ever, but held a genuine note of concern. For a moment George had an impulse to pour out to her all his concerns about Vera, to canvass her opinion. But he reined himself in. Vera would be most offended and he'd make Miss MacLean late for church. What would she know anyway, a confirmed spinster like her?

'I'm very well, thank you.' He allowed Monty to drag him onwards.

'Perhaps we might have a cup of tea together soon?' She spoke tentatively.

'Yes – marvellous. Tea, or something.' He was receding along the street. 'Not today though.' Lord, he didn't need her turning up when Sylvia was here. 'I've got a visitor coming. But soon?'

'Of course,' she said. 'Delighted. Goodbye now.'

He picked Sylvia up at two o'clock. As soon as he saw her there waiting, as ever, near the corner, his doubts of the night slipped away. Look at her, he thought, taking in the sight of her in a sugar-pink frock, her dark hair piled high. His blood surged. She was marvellous! A smile spread across his face and as he drove up to her she smiled and waved as well.

He leapt out of the car and kissed her cheek, opening the door. 'I wondered if today might be a good time to come in and meet your mother – and sister?' he asked. He didn't really want this encounter now, but felt it proper that such a meeting should happen sometime soon.

'Oh, maybe not today,' Sylvia said, settling in the front seat. Getting in beside her he enjoyed the sight of her thighs occupying the seat, knees peeping from the hem of the dress. Her nails were now a cheery crimson. 'Ma's having a sleep and Jean's worn out. She cooked the dinner today – we take it in turns.'

'How nice,' he said, pulling away from the kerb. 'What did you have?'

'Oh, you know – a bit of beef.'

He had expected something more elaborate, the exercise of cooking it having apparently had such an overwhelming effect on Sylvia's sister. But he was not sorry to be driving straight home. The afternoon was very warm, but with a breeze flickering light through the leaves. On the way back, as they chatted gently, she told him about the man who had come into the garage and lost his temper over a problem with one of his tyres and come close to punching her boss.

'Mr Green went so red in the face I thought his head was going to fly off!' she giggled and George laughed, genuinely tickled. 'People get ever so het up about their cars.'

He tried to think of things to tell her. Not about Vera and Alan, he decided. That felt a tender spot and too close. But they passed the end of Lady Byngh's drive on the way home and he told her he had had to visit there.

'Up there?' Sylvia peered at the shrouded entrance. 'Ooh, that looks rather creepy. *Lady* Byngh, though. I say.' He had known this would impress her. 'Ooh, is it really posh? I bet she's got some lovely things.'

'Not any more. She's the one who was burgled.'

'Really? Oh yes! Have they caught them yet?' Sylvia was all agog.

'No. I expect they will though. They took quite a bit of loot.'

Sylvia settled herself in the seat with a wriggle of pleasure. 'You're such an interesting man, George. Always something to tell me. I've been looking forward to today all week – to seeing your house and everything.'

'Yes,' he flashed her a gratified smile, warmed by her flattery. 'Me too – very much.'

'I can keep the dog out of your way,' he said, as they stepped inside, to her exclamations of how big it was, how lovely – oh what pretty roses! – and to the sound of Monty's bark.

'Don't you worry, George dear,' she said, sounding so game that he warmed to her further. It would be hard to feel fully enthusiastic about someone who could never get on with his dog. 'This is your house and he lives here. I'm sure we'll get used to each other. And look –' From her bag she pulled another little box of sweets.

'Look what I've got for you, poochy,' she said, waving them in front of Monty's nose. Instantly she had his rapt attention. 'Can I give him some?'

'Well, one, perhaps,' George was saying as Sylvia ripped

open the packet. She threw down a handful of allsorts and Monty golloped them all up, unable to believe his luck. He gazed up at her, still swallowing, black saliva oozing round his jowls.

'There – he'll be your friend for life now,' George said. 'But maybe one at a time would be enough.'

'Oh you're a *nice* boy, aren't you?' Sylvia said, giving the impression of someone trying very hard against opposing instincts, stroking Monty's head with the tips of her fingers while removing the rest of herself as far away as possible from his slobbery assault. 'Here – there's another one for you.'

George felt mildly annoyed. The odd sweet now and then was one thing . . . 'That's enough, Monty, settle down,' he commanded. 'I'll put him back in the kitchen now – he'll soon settle.'

When he returned, Sylvia was standing at the door of the showroom. He had explained the set-up to her.

'Oh George . . .' She turned her head, seeming awed. She had a slender neck and he repressed an urge to seize hold of her and kiss the pale nape and soft spiral of hair that rested on it. 'It's so lovely.'

She stepped inside, looking round her with an intense concentration while he watched from the doorway. Her hand caressed the complex patterns of a walnut bureau; she picked up a silver salver, well polished by Vera, or possibly Sharon. She exclaimed over a trio of English enamelled scent bottles, each exquisitely patterned.

'So pretty,' she murmured, and he could hear a hunger in her tone. He was touched, at that moment, by her appreciation of such beautiful, finely made things. Perhaps, he thought, only realizing then that this had been something that had previously seemed lacking in her, perhaps she had a fine, artistic soul after all?

Turning amid the array of splendour around her, she let out a loud laugh. 'Look at that!'

She was standing in front of a table that George had bought only that week from a house out at Kingston Bagpuize, though the pleasure had been diluted by the elegant woman who felt forced to sell it, weeping as he handed her a cheque. 'Needs must,' she said through a lace handkerchief. 'But I can hardly bear the thought of it leaving the house.'

It was a Regency table of slender Pembroke design with drop leaves, made of mahogany but, more unusually, banded at the edges with brown and black coromandel, a wood similar to ebony. It was a beautifully proportioned piece and he was just appreciating Sylvia's eye, when she added, 'It looks just like your dog!'

The remark jarred him, though seeing the four sabre legs which met in a low central pedestal, giving the table a crouched look, the flaps down at each side like long ears and the two brass drawer handles like eyes staring back at them, he could see her point.

'Oh, yes, I see!' He chose to laugh, with an inner feeling of deflation.

'How much will you sell that for then?' She was animated now, searching out the price labels tied to drawer handles and table legs. She found the one on the Regency table and looked up at him, startled. 'Three hundred and fifty pounds! For that totty little table! How much did you pay for it?'

'Er, something approaching three hundred, I believe,' he

said, trying to sound less awkward than he felt. Even though he was a businessman and used to talking prices, he was embarrassed by her fervent interest in the money side of things. How well she would get on with Lewis Barker, he thought, before pushing this ignoble thought from his mind.

'Shall we go to the back and make some coffee?' he suggested.

'So you make fifty pounds then?' She was undeterred, still holding the price ticket. 'Just on that?' She laughed. 'No wonder you drive such a nice car, George!'

'Ah, well. No guarantee until the cheque is signed.'

She wandered the room again, involved, abstracted from him. He watched with increasing discomfort, wanting to get her out of here, to distract her from her eager interest in the prices, which felt to him vulgar and uncomfortable. Sylvia had wandered to the window. Without turning to look at him she said, 'You said you had another showroom – is that it, over there?'

She explored the barn with the same absorbed attention. After, he showed her the other rooms on the ground floor of the house. In his office he had slipped the photograph of Win into the desk drawer, to avoid both Sylvia's questions about it and the mild sense of reproach he imagined coming from the portrait itself. He did not show her upstairs; the bedroom with its wide, expectant bed.

In the kitchen he booted Monty out into the garden and made coffee, still feeling jarred by Sylvia's frank materialism, which opened up a distance between them, at least for him. But as he was filling the cups, she moved close to him, seeking out his eyes, inviting intimacy.

'George? We haven't had a little kiss yet, have we?'

Heart revving up, he stopped messing about with cups and teaspoons and turned to her. Embracing her, the fleshy force of her pressed close to him, he breathed in the scent of her perfume and his mood softened. Standing on tiptoe, she reached up to kiss him, with a verve that sent a transfusion of desire through him. After a moment she drew back and looked up at him with wide eyes.

'It's lovely here. And you're so nice. I do feel so lucky to have met you, George.'

He was made tender by the sweetness of her words. Poor girl, he thought, it didn't sound as if she had had much of an upbringing. Even though 'Darling David' must have been comfortably off, he knew that it was easily possible to be dazzled, as he had once been, by the beautiful, expensive items that he sold. It was not a world everyone was used to. He was rather charmed by the idea that he might be the one to dazzle her. He smiled down at her.

'Oh, I'm the lucky one,' he said. 'Meeting such a lovely girl.' He flattered her with 'girl'. Through various means, asking about the age gap with her sister, and when Jean was born and so on, he had pinned Sylvia down to being forty-two years old. There were women who had children at that age, weren't there?

Holding her, for a moment he was filled with weariness. He was used to being married, not to all this. He did not know how to conduct a chase, the ins and outs and pacing of it all. Especially at their age. Was it too soon to expect her to be generous and yielding enough to come upstairs with him? If only he could just remove all other obstacles and lead her up there, now.

Sylvia snuggled close in his arms again. He could feel the press of her breasts against him. Kissing her, he began to surrender to the forceful sensations of arousal, the longing building in him. She stepped back.

'We'd better have our coffee now, hadn't we?' she said with a demure sweetness. She adjusted the strap on her left shoulder, under her blouse. 'Or it'll go cold.' She gazed at him in apparent adoration. 'Ooh, you are lovely.'

They sat out on the lawn, under the shade of one of the apple trees in the hot, soporific afternoon. Monty dozed on the grass between their chairs.

'I love the way your roses all match,' she giggled. 'Yellow at the front, pink at the back – so pretty! I love roses.'

'Yes,' he agreed. 'They are rather . . .' He trailed off. How to begin on the passion he felt for this beauty? For a moment he considered telling her about the rose at the window, his six-year-old consolation. But it did not feel right. And Sylvia was soon off, chattering away.

He could not help noticing, again, her preoccupation with how much things cost. She told him about the holiday to France that her mother's neighbours had been on, about the settee they had recently had delivered, about the price of clothing.

'I mean you're much better off paying the fare to go into Reading if you want to buy something nice. You can go to Heelas then – such a lovely shop. And it's so much more pricey where we are. I bought Mum a new slip last week and when I went into town I saw it for half a crown less – I mean, half a crown!'

George's mind wandered to the inviting coolness of the room upstairs, the white sheets . . . When Sylvia raised her hands for a moment in a stretch above her head, her magnificent frontage lifting, he imagined her stretched on his bed, her arms flung out . . . It was so hot. However much he tried to distract himself, in his state of half-arousal his clothes felt confining. He was filled with a claustrophobic sense of needing to move, to break through the stifling atmosphere. He was speaking, listening; especially listening. He was in control of himself, but with the itch, the need so close on him, it would only have taken a moment of contact to trigger him.

Maybe, he calculated, once we have finished our coffee, I should just ask her, outright. No messing about. They were both mature, experienced people. She might like the masterful approach. The only thing was, he just wasn't very masterful. As she chattered on to him he rehearsed the words in his head . . . *Now then – how about we . . . ?* No – how about, *Isn't it time we went upstairs?* Or perhaps the martinet approach – *Come along now!* Or perhaps, *Oh darling, come with me, I must have you, now!*

Oh God.

Sylvia put her mug down on the little table and leaned round to him. This was the moment – she was thinking the same! Any minute now they would be on the stairs, he taking her hand . . .

'I was just thinking,' she said. 'D'you know what I'd really like – if it's all right with you? I'd really like it if we went out for a drive.'

A drive. In the heat of this Sunday afternoon, she wanted to be in the car, passing between hot fields and through green tunnels of branches, the air buffeting in through the windows, in search of a 'nice little tea shop'.

So he drove and drove. He drank tea and ate toasted teacakes in a little place in Henley, watching the pleasure boats and Salter's Steamers cruising along the river's brightness and it was, Sylvia said, 'so nice'. And, he realized, it was nice. It was polite and fitting and she was happy and grateful and left him, when he dropped her off, with a smiling embrace and kisses. He was pleased that he had given pleasure and knew that she would soon want to see him again and that he should be patient and woo her as a gentleman should.

But it did nothing to relieve the ache that spread through him of simple longing to hold and be held in a spirit of whole-hearted giving.

5.

Kevin was squatting against the back wall, near the vegetable garden, eating a sandwich and apparently reading a book. This behaviour would have been unusual at any time. For nine o'clock on a Monday morning it verged on the bizarre.

'Morning, Kevin!' George said, following Monty round from the back door.

'Orghgumph,' Kevin agreed, nodding madly, his cheeks tightly stuffed. He pushed himself hastily to his feet as Monty began to show excessive interest in his crotch.

'What're you up to?' George enquired. 'Don't usually have breakfast out here, do you?'

Kevin, still trying to access a chink of free space in his mouth, shook his head at length and eventually swallowed like a python.

'No.' He was hugging a big book with a faded cloth clover. 'Just – you know – nice weather. And I'm reading my book. *Look*, Mr Baxter – I got it out of the lib'ry in Wallin'ford.'

George read the faded gold letters: Albert Jacquemart, *History of the Ceramic Art: A Descriptive and Philosophical Study of the Pottery of All Ages and All Nations*.

'Heavens, that's a big book, Kevin. No wonder you had to sit down to read it. Not in French, is it?'

'No – but it's full of words!' Kevin advised. He recited: 'Vitreous, lacquer, arabesque!' And beamed.

George could not help but warm to this endeavour. 'That's jolly good, Kevin. Good for you. Now – I'm about to open up. Time to go to work.'

He was nervous about how things might be with Vera, but she arrived in good spirits and they stood in the kitchen, catching up with Saturday's events. Sales had included a large oak chest from the barn and a George the First gilt mirror. And no, he told her – the knocker, Charlie Bird, had not come back.

Vera looked downcast. 'I'm very sorry, Mr B. I might have lost us a deal there.'

'Oh don't worry.' He liked the way she said 'us'. 'He'll be back if he wanted anything. It's not important.'

There was a pause as she leaned on the handle of her basket and gave him a direct look. 'So did you have a nice day yesterday?'

He had only passingly mentioned that he would be having a visitor in the afternoon, but Vera seemed – somehow – well aware of who that visitor had been.

George grew vague and drifty. 'Oh—' He started to move away. 'Yes, very good – thank you.' He wasn't really sure why he didn't want to talk to Vera about Sylvia. He just knew that he didn't.

'Mr B?' Vera looked down into the basket as he turned back to her. There was another pause. Much as he didn't want to, he realized he should ask after her and Alan.

'Everything all right, Vera?' It came out more breezily than he intended. He was jingling the change in his pocket like mad. 'I mean – I don't want my . . . anyone here to be unhappy. You know, good morale and all that!' He laughed, rather too uproariously.

Vera gave him a crooked smile. 'I think I've managed to settle him down. We had a bit of a talk when we could, when the boys weren't around. Came to a few agreements.'

George smiled. 'Oh, good!'

'I was wondering,' she went on. 'You know you've got a little compartment in your fridge where you can keep things frozen – ice cream and that? You never have anything in there and if I make a job lot of pastry I can keep some in mine and another lot in yours for when I need it, see. Get a bit ahead of myself.'

George agreed instantly to what seemed a remarkably simple way of keeping the peace. Vera went and pushed a rectangular package into the freezer compartment.

'There – that's a big help,' she said, filling the kettle.

Now things were more relaxed, and wanting to make her laugh, he told her about finding Kevin. 'I really think the lad might have hidden depths.'

'Huh, I don't know about that.' Vera was darting about the kitchen. 'You know why he keeps hanging about round the back, don't you? He's waiting for *her*.'

George frowned. 'It's not her day to come in.'

'It is. She's got to go to the dentist tomorrow instead.'

As she spoke, a looming brown figure passed the kitchen window and pushed open the back door.

'Ah – morning, Sharon!' George greeted her.

His teenage cleaner paused on the threshold with an expression suggesting that this salutation was the most fatuous thing she had ever heard.

'Mornin',' she said, ambling over to the sink, past Vera, who gave George a wink behind Sharon's back.

'Kevin was looking for you,' Vera said, with an air of mischief, putting her radio on the windowsill.

Sharon slowly swivelled round, holding a pair of yellow rubber gloves. 'Kevin?'

George couldn't help but admire the sheer concentration of scorn she managed to compress into one word.

'Yes,' Vera said. 'I think he's rather keen on you. D'you like him?'

Sharon stared at her. 'No.'

It was as if she had spat on the ground.

JULY

Eleven

1.

The car was squeezed into a field gateway. A fragile arc of new moon hung over the fields and sprays of hawthorn scratched against the windscreen. The few cars that passed seemed very close, faintly rocking the car.

Sylvia had suggested it, in that voice she used, thrumming with promise. They were on their way back from a meal at a very nice riverside pub. 'Shall we pull over, George – just so's we don't get back too soon?' They were only a couple of miles from her mother's house.

Once again they were wrapped round each other about as far as you can be wrapped when closely accompanied by a steering wheel, handbrake and gear-stick. Sylvia's pungent scent filled the car. Her lips tasted of lipstick and, faintly, of tartar sauce. George settled his arms round the plump fullness of her. Slowly, he moved his hand up her back and then, with burglar-like stealth, round under her arm towards her buoyant left breast which was making itself known, insistently, close to his chest. Just as the surface of his palm made contact with the delicious, rounded shape, Sylvia seized his wrist, removed his hand downwards and drew back a fraction.

'Now, now,' she said, before reaching round to play a finger-tip along the grooves of his ear, a sensation he found maddening at a variety of levels: ticklish, arousing and perversely teasing. He shifted his head out of her reach.

'Oh don't you like that? I'm *sorry*.' In the almost complete darkness she moved her face close to his, her eyes very wide. She seemed to be searching him with that sudden humility that would often come over her and remould his doubts – why am I pursuing things with this woman, why, exactly? – into a melting sense of protectiveness.

'You're so good to me, George. And it's been such a lovely evening.'

They had sat eating, looking over the water as the sun went down, lighting the ripples, a serene stillness in the air. It had been lovely. And he felt very fine, stepping out with this attractive woman, who was *toute femme* – an expression he had heard somewhere – and being able to treat her. Even though he was spending more money and eating in a style he was not used to, he kept thinking, 'Damn it – why not live a bit?' And his intentions were honourable. He wanted to do the right thing. It was just that, locked in her arms, he could only think, what harm would it do to get a bit of an advance on things?

But this was always the story, had been now through the weeks he had been taking her out. The evenings ended like this, half-embraces in the car, or in some dark corner. But whenever he allowed himself to get involved and his hand strayed to one of the more alluring parts of her body, she slammed the brake on.

'The thing is, George . . .' Her voice was light, girlish, he realized when he heard it in the dark. 'You're such a lovely man. You're the nicest, kindest man I've ever met. It's just that a woman in my situation has to take care of herself.'

She shifted round so that she was looking towards the windscreen.

'It's the way I was brought up, dear. I'm not one of those modern girls you see pictures of, you know, in Carnaby Street and places like that. I'm really quite old-fashioned.'

'Well, yes.' He sat back as well. He could just see the moon in the left-hand corner of the windscreen. 'Yes of course.' He forced himself to say, 'That's something I admire about you.'

'Do you?' She leaned round. 'Oh I'm so glad to hear you say that! I just don't think it's right, however much you want to – and I *do*, George, don't think for a moment that I don't – to have . . . relations . . . outside marriage. You might find it silly of me.' There was appeal in her voice now. 'Or rather staid?'

'Of course not.' And he didn't. She was right. His lips agreed with her, and his mind. Of course, no decent girl . . . While his body and spirits, primed with longing, howled inside him.

'I knew you thought like me. You're such a decent sort of man!' she said, delighted. 'Only I was afraid . . .' She reached up and kissed his cheek. 'Oh George, you are a darling, you really are!'

His hand reached for the ignition. 'Well – I don't know about that . . . I do try – even though . . .' He added the next words in the small, devious hope that they might make her change her mind. Morals were a fine thing, but all the same . . . 'Even though I do long for you, Sylvia, you know that. It's been a long time since . . . you know, with Win being so ill and everything.'

'I know, dear. That's lovely.' Her right hand rested warm over his left for a moment. 'That's so nice of you to say. And I do feel so *safe* with you.'

After he had dropped her off, he drew up just along the street and reached into the glove compartment for his emergency hip flask. He tipped a generous helping into his mouth and swallowed it in three goes, the friendly, pungent fumes burning out through his nostrils.

Safe? That was a compliment, he supposed. But was that all he ever was – safe? Once again he was filled with a sensation that squeezed out from his chest and along his arms, a painful longing for he hardly knew what. He let out a heavy sigh, from the depths of him.

'Oh God,' he whispered. For a moment he felt like weeping.

He took another swig from the flask and replaced the top and the silver cup. Slowly, he drove home.

2.

Vera held out the telephone receiver to George, who was seated at his desk, mouthing, 'Lady Byngh!' and rolling her eyes. She handed it to him and retreated hastily from the office.

'Hello?'

'Baxter?' She sounded better. Physically anyway. 'Have you managed to track down my things?'

'Well, no, I—'

'I thought not. Well I'm just telephoning to tell you that the police have shown a great deal more initiative than you have, my man!'

'Yes, well that is their—'

'They've made a very good start. I want you to go and . . .'

The rest of what might have been a command became abruptly muffled and was overwhelmed by a series of crashes that seemed to involve items of crockery, something large and metallic and, more worryingly, a muted thud followed by a groan.

'Oh good heavens, Percy!' An exclamation more of impatience than concern. 'Whatever are you *doing*? Look, Baxter . . .' Her voice came on full volume again. 'Percy's taken a tumble. I shall have to go. But they've found my bureau, so . . .' She must have put the receiver back mid-sentence. Perhaps she had forgotten he couldn't hear. He was left with the burring of the line.

'That's a bit of bad luck,' he said to Vera in the kitchen. 'That blasted bureau bookcase of hers has turned up again.'

'What – the mated one?' She used this term with a knowing casualness that impressed him.

'Yes.' He wandered, frowning, to the window. Outside he saw Sharon's ominous form hanging tea towels on the line. 'I wish we'd told her now. We didn't want to disappoint her, but – good Lord, what's going on?'

Something had come flying out through the window of the barn, bounced on the grass and hit Sharon in the back of her right thigh. She paused, holding up a damp white rectangle of cloth and turned, as Sharon did everything, slowly. It was like watching a tank position its sights. Her scowling features fixed their attention on the barn window.

'Someone's just chucked a ball at her,' George said. 'An old tennis ball!'

'Oh.' Vera was on her way out of the kitchen. There was laughter in her voice. 'That'll be Kevin. He can't leave her alone.' Her steps receded along the hall, but before he found the presence of mind to move, they returned.

'By the way,' she said, head round the door, 'I've found a . . . a thing in the bathroom. Hanging up. I wasn't sure if someone had left it by mistake?' There seemed to be no guile in her question. Nor had he any sensible idea what she was talking about.

'A silky thing – sort of robe.'

Now she said it, he did recall something on the back of the door, a creamy thing with large pink flowers of some sort. And of course he guessed who had somehow left it there. He felt himself colour. It would only be Sylvia. Was this a promise, a change of heart? Did she want him to persuade her into bed? But he was now conscious that it looked to Vera as though he already had.

'I . . . I don't know,' he stammered, knowing how unconvincing he sounded. 'I haven't seen anything.'

Vera looked back at him for a moment with a serious face. 'Sorry, Mr B,' she said. 'Perhaps I shouldn't have mentioned it. I just thought I'd better ask, that's all.'

'Quite all right, Vera,' he said, too breezily, turning away. He patted his jacket pockets to give the impression that he was thinking about manly, business-like affairs. 'Must go and talk to Clarence . . .'

Vera disappeared again. He stood in the kitchen. What was Sylvia playing at?

3.

'Kevin . . .' George stepped into the workshop the next morning. 'I've a few things to do over Reading way. I'd like you to come with me.'

The men halted work with various things held in their hands: Clarence an oily rag, Kevin a wedge of sandpaper and Alan, who to George's discomfort, was watching him with an unreadable expression, a chisel. He wondered exactly what had happened between Alan and Vera. Did Alan resent him? He felt a twinge of fellow feeling, a manly, old soldiers together, 'keep the little woman in line' reflex, which clashed immediately with the recollection of Vera's hardworking competence. Why, when you came down to it, should Alan dictate what she should do or not do at work? What skin was it off his nose? Should he – oh God forbid, bowel-chilling thought – have a *word* with Alan?

Kevin brightened instantly. 'Are we going to an auction, Mr Baxter?'

'No, not today. Maybe soon.' He always felt as if he was appeasing a child with Kevin. 'Just a few things to do. We'll take the van.'

'But it's not Monday.' Kevin's brow puckered.

'No, it's not Monday,' George agreed. 'But for one thing' – he looked at Clarence – 'I've been instructed to go and get that bureau of Lady Byngh's back.'

Clarence mumbled something insulting that included the word 'mongrel'. He turned away, tutting. 'I knew that thing'd come back to haunt us.'

'I'll bring my sandwiches,' Kevin enthused. George found himself feeling grateful for the boy.

It was a pleasant drive on a warm, hazy morning, the scents of ripening wheat and barley through the windows accompanied by the tang of Branston Pickle from Kevin's stolid sandwich-munching. They passed between open fields, into the wooded slopes of the Chilterns.

'Lovely, isn't it, Mr Baxter?' Kevin said with something close to poetic fervour, as they rushed down another slope in the shade of over-arching beeches.

George agreed, eyeing Kevin for a moment. Part of his motivation for getting Kevin to come with him was to distance him from his attentions towards the lugubrious Sharon. But he couldn't quite fathom Kevin, this sturdy, rather spud-like boy beside him with his brown, soulful eyes and sudden enthusiasms. He seemed like a flickering electrical circuit, sometimes startlingly bright, while at other times giving you cause to wonder whether he was switched on at all. He mused on whether he should say anything about Sharon. Another of those fatherly moments, perhaps? But the thought of Sylvia came to him. He wouldn't have welcomed the idea of being cross-questioned on that subject, so why should he inflict such a thing on Kevin? Instead, he said, 'Still reading that book of yours on ceramics, are you?'

'Oh yes,' Kevin said, shoving the remains of his supply of sandwiches into a greasy paper bag. 'It's good, that is. The library said I could keep renewing it. No one else ever takes it out, see.'

George chuckled. 'Well that's a specialist interest, all right.'

'I like china,' Kevin said. 'The feel of it. The colours.'

'Come to think of it,' George said, 'the place we're going first, there might be some china for sale, as well as the shelves she wants me to look at. It's a Mrs Mackrell, in Caversham.'

'Mrs Mackrell?' Kevin repeated with exuberant glee. He snorted, knees twitching up and down. 'Something a bit fishy about her, eh?' And he laughed until he had to wipe tears from his eyes.

The street where they parked was lined with ornate, grey-brick Victorian houses. Kevin managed to quell his amusement in time to meet Mrs Mackrell with a reasonably composed facial expression. This was just as well, as the gracious, elderly lady seemed distressed at having to part with her elegant book-shelves. They loaded them onto the Morris and in addition, came away with four Staffordshire figures, with which Kevin was only slightly impressed.

'Not as good as the things they make in China though,' he decreed. 'Good name for it, China.' He chortled a bit more, before settling down. George was already starting to feel rather weary. It would have been far more peaceful to come on his own. But he did like to instruct the boy. Somewhere in that flickering brain was a capacity to learn.

They parked again and ate their sandwiches by the towpath under Caversham Bridge, watching swans and summer boats sliding past, before they set off into Reading. The dealer at whose business 'My Bureau' seemed to have shipped up was owned by a cheerful, balding man called Ron King. Ron wore pale suits that always seemed at least a size too big and had an off-centre look about them, the jackets listing to one side. George liked Ron well enough and they often slipped over to the Turk's Head for a pint together. The shop, however, while nothing like as bad as Lewis Barker's dump of a place, occupied three floors of a tall Victorian terrace and had a cramped, dusty feel about it.

'I've had the police here, George,' Ron greeted them indignantly. 'Uniforms in the doorway in full view. I don't like that – it gives the place a bad name. Here – it's at the back.'

He led them through to an inner room. 'I bought that in good faith, I did. Auction at Watlington . . .'

The bureau bookcase stood against the back wall. Even as George moved closer, there was already something about it that did not feel right. Was it the shape of the pedestal, the texture of the wood?

'Kevin – you come and look with me.' It did not take more than a minute. His glances at the feet, the pedestal, inside the lower drawers told him immediately. Bending close, he examined the meeting place of the top and bottom of the piece. Kevin's eyes met his, serious and interested. George would take him through the details in a moment; show him. But first he straightened up, feeling a surge of exaltation.

'It's all right, Ron – it's clean. It's a similar piece, but that's not the one. They'll have to keep looking.'

'And I,' he said to Kevin, once they were back in the van, 'will have to tell Lady Byngh.'

'Proper old tartar, that one,' Kevin said. 'Scares the wits out of me.'

George laughed. 'I know what you mean. I suppose she's had an odd sort of life. I don't think she's all bad underneath.'

'Oh but I don't think you'd want to go underneath the old girl to find out, would you?' Kevin said, breaking into further helpless chortling at his own wit. Fortunately after that, the circuit flicked off and all was silence.

4.

Once everyone had gone home, George stepped out into the mellow evening to lock up the barn. Monty plopped down the step after him and ambled to the flowerbed.

George paused in a patch of sunlight and breathed in deeply. Monty's muzzle nudged at his ankle.

'Yes, all right, old boy.' He bent to pat the tan and white drum of a body. One of the by-products of being alone was that it gave him licence to talk nonsense to the dog. 'She's been feeding you too many sweets, hasn't she?' Sylvia had got into the habit of bringing a packet of liquorice allsorts almost every time she came now, however much George tried to deter her. 'You need some exercise. I'll just lock up and then we'll go for a little tootle, eh?'

As he walked back from turning the large key in the lock of the barn door, a noise arose from the road, the insect-like buzz of an engine. He would have taken no notice, except that it drew unpleasantly closer before cutting out at what sounded like the foot of his drive. In the ensuing quiet, he heard voices. Women's voices.

He looked round for Monty. Don't bark, he urged, mentally. Monty appeared to be in a state of deep meditation, his nose buried in the bed of snapdragons at the end of the house. Fortunately, his brain could not manage too many tasks at once.

George tiptoed over to the hedge bordering the road and crept along it towards the drive. The voices grew clearer. He shoved his head half into the hedge, trying to hear better. His heart pounded. Good heavens, it was Sylvia! It would be hard to mistake her honey-sweet tones. But how the heck had she got here? Another of the voices, deep and resonant, he also knew immediately: Eunice MacLean. He concentrated on trying to make out who was with them. The third voice rose for a moment, a hectoring air to it, and he knew then. A queasy pang of dismay passed through him – it was Rosemary Abbott.

He froze, paralysed once more by the sense that women always conspired against him, leaving him with no choice . . . He was soon overcome by the absurdity of hiding on the very threshold of his own house from the woman he was supposed to be courting – he *was*, wasn't he? And what if they walked up the drive to find him with the right side of his head stuck in the hedge?

Attempting weightlessness, like someone crossing newly poured concrete, he toed it over to the front step before calling to Monty, as if he had just emerged from the front door.

'Come on, old boy – looks as if we've got visitors.'

George clipped his lead on and walked down the drive with an air of surprised and expansive welcome, feeling three pairs of eyes swivel in his direction.

Eunice MacLean, wearing a long-sleeved fawn dress, looked stiff but elegant beside Rosemary Abbott in a tightly belted summer frock of a loud pink floral design. Sylvia wore navy slacks and the emerald blouse that did wonders to emphasize her contours. Her hands were grasping the handlebars of a motor scooter, which was painted blancmange pink.

'Hello George, dear!' she greeted him, in tones which left no ambiguity about the intimacy between them.

'Ah, Sylvia, hello.' He gave a little bow from the waist, a formula that he repeated, for want of any other inspiration, in the direction of each of the other women. 'Afternoon, Miss MacLean, Miss Abbott.'

Eunice MacLean returned the greeting with a nod, her gaunt face giving nothing away. Rosemary Abbott, pink and vaporous-looking in the heat, seemed about to combust with curiosity.

'I was just introducing myself, George,' Sylvia enthused. 'It's high time I met your neighbours.'

'Well, hardly neighbours,' Rosemary Abbott attempted to contradict, but Sylvia ploughed on.

'Look –' She nodded at the blancmange-coloured Vespa. 'D'you like it?'

'It's, er . . . It's very nice,' George said, one hand writhing in his pocket. 'Whose is it?'

'Oh, it's mine, dear! I thought I'd surprise you. I bought it yesterday. I thought how nice it would be if I could come over any old time and see you.' As she spoke, George's mind presented him with an image of himself being sucked further and further down into treacherous sinking sands.

'Anyway . . .' Sylvia began to wheel the thing up the drive, 'nice to meet you, Eunice, Rosemary . . .'

'Goodbye,' Eunice MacLean said with her usual grace. Rosemary Abbott opened her mouth but nothing discernible came out of it. George gave a vague wave in their direction, not meeting anyone's eye. He walked behind Sylvia to the house, with a notion that the sands were now clasping tightly round his thighs.

Once they had parked the scooter and were safely enclosed in the house, Sylvia flung her arms round him. As ever, pressed against the fulsome, perfumed force of the woman, his misgivings, common sense and general ability to orientate himself deserted him. Her eyes beamed up at him.

'It's so lovely to be here with you, Georgie darling! The more time I spend with you, the more I can't bear to be anywhere else.' She stood on tiptoe and pressed her lips to his, before drawing back, solemn-eyed now. 'Do you feel the same?'

'Oh . . .' He gave a demented smile. God alone knew what he felt. 'Yes – yes, my dear!' After all, it was a question clearly requiring a positive response.

'Look –' She rummaged in her bag. 'Allsorts for Monty.' She held the little packet up winningly and Monty started whining and wagging his tail in anticipation. 'I want him to be my friend.'

And so it came to pass that Sylvia Newsome moved in on George's life. Now that she had her scooter, there was scarcely a day when she did not appear, after work, once the shop was shut up. And there were other appearances – day by day more items took up their place in the house. He had said nothing to her about the silky garment hanging on the back of the bathroom door and he said nothing now.

'I've never seen these before,' Vera remarked, when a pair of size five wellington boots appeared beside his own at the back door. Or, 'I see you've got some new talc,' when a container of sandalwood talcum powder turned up on the dressing table.

Vera made the remark down in the kitchen. She turned from the kettle, which was making throaty attempts to boil water through a rime of limescale. She set out the mugs very deliberately, for herself and for all the men, then turned to George with a shrewd look in her eye.

'So – when am I going to meet this lady friend of yours, then?'

Twelve

1.

George sat in the pub at South Stoke, his second pint of bitter in front of him. Sylvia, beside him, was a few sips into her second Babycham. While George hoped more beer would help him lapse into mellowness, he was beginning to find the atmosphere of the pub stifling to the point of claustrophobia. It had been all right on the boat, its very motion causing a movement of air in the sullen midday. But the pub was too crowded, the very air a soup of smoke, sweat, beer.

They had set out this lovely morning to the sound of church bells and by midday they and *Barchetta* were well on their way, another of Sylvia's gigantic picnics on board. There were chicken legs, slices of beef with a pot of horseradish, rolls and butter, tomatoes and crisps, apples, bottles of beer and chocolate cake.

'You certainly know how to feed me up,' George said. He really was grateful. If there was one thing he couldn't stand it was people being unnecessarily mean and penny-pinching about food.

'Oh I like a good picnic,' Sylvia said. 'And anyway, I *like* feeding you. You're always so appreciative.'

He set the outboard at a gentle speed and they droned along between the reeds and willows, the prow turning away little plumes of water. They looked out across the humid green of meadows and vacant, chewing gaze of Friesian cows. They peered, speculating, at the backs of riverside homes. As they approached Goring Lock, instead of going through, George turned the boat. Close to South Stoke they tied up by the bank and ate. By then, the heat had built to the point of oppression. Sylvia, peering out from under a floppy white straw hat, stretched her legs in a luxurious manner across the boat and basked, fanning herself with the lid of a Tupperware box.

'It's damned hot,' George said, boiled even in a short-sleeved shirt and – revolutionary step – no vest. 'Almost makes you want to jump in.'

Sylvia giggled. 'Shall we skinny dip? Maybe not – after all that dinner.'

The very thought was a bit much for George. They soon decided on a drink. Somewhere in the shade had been the idea, but the pub was even hotter than outside.

Amid the boozy racket, Sylvia brought her lips close to his ear. 'Let's go and find a tree to sit under, shall we?'

On the way back to the river they found a copse, a pool of dark shade. George, feeling definitely unsteady after the accumulation of beer drinking, found himself being steered under the cover of the trees and seated with abrupt suddenness on a twiggy patch of leaves that at least had the advantage of being dry and minus thistles.

'Here you are, lovey,' Sylvia announced. 'You can just lie back and put your head on my cardi – there you go – there's room for both of us!'

She settled down to his left, rather closer than was sensible in this heat, George thought hazily. He lay on his back looking up at the sky in a floating, dream-like state, feeling as if he was only half present. Sylvia had turned on her side to face him and within moments a warm and not particularly dream-like hand crept across his chest. A finger inserted itself between the buttons of his shirt and began to stroke and tickle his skin.

He did remember it afterwards. Sort of . . . Somewhere after the tickling sensation on his chest. Normally such contact provoked him into a state of instant arousal from which he would have to make heroic efforts to disengage. Today, things were a little slower. The heat and the muffling effects of the drink made both mind and body work at half-speed like someone trying to run across a thick foam mattress. Work, nevertheless, they did . . .

So that he did remember a sluggish conversation – while the little warm finger between his shirt buttons kept up its work – about the 'the situation'. 'The situation' – apparently iniquitous and foolish – was that Sylvia was still stuck living with her mother, while she and he were so *completely* in love and battling to spend every spare second together, which made it all so much more silly and such a *waste*, 'don't you think, Georgie?'

He also recalled Sylvia raising her left leg and laying it over his own left leg so that they lay half entwined. A hopeful scenario began to bloom in his mind in which here in this shrouded copse, one of those useful components of the English countryside, Sylvia, carried away by the bubbly jolliness of the Babycham, might take it into her head to . . .

That didn't happen. But another conversation did happen about the fact that she was *longing* for him to make her his own. During this particular stage of the conversation, he became conscious of the fleshy pressure of a sizeable breast against his ribcage. And – the hand wandered about his person and hovered above the moist waistband of his trousers – would it not make sense for them to get married, so that they could share *everything*, and soon?

In this state, under the hot pressure of his flesh, he could only agree that to share *everything* seemed a very fine idea; that in fact he was very soon going to be unable to contain himself unless they did share *everything*. What was rather more difficult to recall, was how this conversation progressed from the notion of a vaguely good idea to a suddenly very precise discussion of dates and times during which Sylvia sat up, seeming much fresher and more sober than he felt at that moment and announced, 'The end of August.'

'August?' He could not quite think what the word meant for a moment. 'Oh, you mean next year?' This was rather a relief – he had been about to propose June next year.

'No, no – this August, George. We can do it by then, properly I mean. Get the banns read and everything. We've got six weeks at least.'

Somehow, by the time they were returned to the boat and chugging back downstream, he had agreed to a date – Sylvia possessing a remarkable facility for knowing the year's calendar off pat – and they were to be married on Saturday, 29 August.

2.

'I want to be seen with you, George,' she pleaded as they drove home. She told him she had taken the next day off work because she wanted to come out buying with him. 'I like seeing what you do and all the lovely things.' Her hand made its way across his thigh. 'Oh do let me come! I haven't had a ride in your van yet.'

'Of course you can,' he said. What else could he say?

'And on the way . . .' She gave a little laugh. 'I mean I've only just thought of it, but perhaps we could go and buy a ring together?'

The weather the next day was, if anything, even more stiflingly hot. By nine o'clock, Vera reported that Lady Byngh had telephoned, outraged that the bureau he had gone to investigate had turned out not to be hers.

'She was ever so rude,' Vera observed, pink-faced. 'If she was one of mine I'd've put her over my knee.'

George was glad to escape. He was in a state of disbelief at what he had promised yesterday. What on earth had he been thinking of? He couldn't seem to think straight, that was the trouble. Sylvia got him into such a state of need and desire that he was in a spin, to put it mildly. Sometimes he thought, if he could just knock her senseless and have his dreadful way with her – just get it over with – then he might be able to process his thoughts in a sensible manner.

He took the car, picked Sylvia up and they drove with the air billowing through the open windows. She, in a new dress, scarlet with white spots, was effervescent with excitement.

'This is all so nice of you, George – and so lovely of you to buy me a ring!'

This was not an intention he had personally expressed but by now it seemed to have been established as a fact.

'I know I've been married twice before, but it's still so important. A ring makes it all so special, doesn't it?'

The day passed successfully, so far as he could tell. He took her to the more picturesque places – not Twyford, but Goring and Henley, Cookham and Marlow. In a jeweller's in Marlow, he found himself buying her an engagement ring.

'Oh George!' She sounded almost faint with excitement as she pushed the ring, tiny diamonds clustered round a central sapphire, onto her third finger. She extended her hand to him to admire, a rapturous expression on her face. 'Oh you darling – I've never had anything so beautiful!'

She advanced on him, kissing his cheek. George smiled, gratified but surprised. Surely Tragic Lionel or Darling David must have come up with something similar in their time?

'Would you like me to wrap it for safe-keeping?' In a flourish of disclosure George could only admire from someone proffering what was in fact an empty box, the jeweller opened a little silk-lined case.

'Oh no – I'll keep it on,' Sylvia said. 'After all – it means we're truly engaged now, doesn't it, George?'

Apparently it did, George thought, as he signed what seemed to him an enormous cheque.

As they stepped out onto Marlow High Street, a voice assailed them at screech volume.

'Oooh! It's Mr Baxter!'

Sylvia grasped his arm, startled. They turned to see a spry figure in a little powder-blue suit, with the shingled hair and bright peeping eyes, behind spectacles, of Maud Roberts. She clapped her hands and clasped them together under her chin.

'Oh it *is* you! Oh it is *nice to see you*, Mr Baxter. But you're very naughty – you haven't been to visit me like you said you would, have you?'

As George mumbled an apology Maud came up very close and seized his free arm, her eyes now fixed on Sylvia, who was smiling in a bemused sort of way.

'Who's this then?' Maud demanded.

'This is Sylvia,' George began. He felt weary already. Maud stepped even closer and Sylvia, not wanting to be left out, shrank in nearer to him as well.

'EH? You'll have to speak up, dear – you know I'm a bit—'

'SYLVIA!' George bawled.

Maud looked Sylvia frankly up and down.

'Well who's she then? I've never seen her before.'

Sylvia, attempting rescue, held out her left hand, bearing the new ring. 'I'm his fiancée,' she purred.

'Eh? What did she say?' Maud cupped a hand round her ear. 'Is that the sort of ring I think it is?'

'She's . . .' George began. There was nothing for it. Conscious that people were already having to swerve off the narrow pavement along Marlow High Street to avoid the three people standing abnormally close together and yelling their heads off at each other, he decided to get it over with.

'SHE'S MY FIANCÉE! WE'RE GETTING MARRIED!' As he declared this to Maud and the public at large, it all felt heartily improbable.

'Ooh!' Maud laid her free hand over her heart, her blue eyes alight with excitement. But her face clouded.

'GETTING MARRIED? BUT WHO IS SHE? I'VE NEVER SEEN HER BEFORE!'

And so it went on. With eventual promises to Maud and anyone else within earshot in Marlow that he would visit her very soon to explain all (even then he wondered quite how he was going to do that), they managed to take their leave.

'Who on earth was that?' Sylva said, rather huffily.

'Oh, that was just Maud.' George gave a fond grin, which made Sylvia look even more put out. 'She's a good sort really.'

'I've been thinking, dear,' Sylvia said, clearly dismissing Maud as not worth considering any more. 'You must come and meet Mother and Jean.'

3.

'Goodbye, darling – see you tomorrow!' Sylvia blew him a kiss, making sure the two elderly ladies passing along the pavement did not miss this touching moment.

George was released at long, long last out of the door of number 29 of the solid railway terraces where Sylvia lived with 'Mother and Jean'.

'Toodle-ooo!' she called after him, so loudly – despite the fact that he was only about four yards away – that the two old ladies turned their heads again in a faintly affronted manner.

George waved, his other hand seeking out the van key in his pocket. The Morris, waiting for him in the road, felt to him vaguely like an ambulance. He climbed in as fast as he could, throwing his jacket off and onto the seat beside him. He would have liked to sit very still and begin to come to terms with the situation into which he had, in the past two days, apparently hurled himself. But though Sylvia had shut the front door, he was certain that at least one pair of eyes was watching from behind the net curtains of number 29. He started up and drove off, muttering.

'Oh George. Oh deary, deary, dear . . . Oh goodness me – oh Lord above . . .' This lamentation did not help in any obvious way. A stiff drink might help fractionally more, he thought. Did he have the flask in the car?

He drove with the window wound down, the clammy air passing sluggishly across his face. The heat of this summer just went on and on. His clothes were clinging to him, his back damp. Just beyond South Moreton, he could stand it no longer. He pulled the van off into a gateway, ran his hands down over his face and reached into the glove compartment. Flask in hand, he climbed out into the mellow afternoon.

In the field were several ponies. As he went to rest his arms on the wooden gate, the faint breeze cooling his shirt, the ponies, of varying colours, raised their heads and regarded him with chirpy suspicion. There was only a trickle left in the flask, damn it. He drained the last drops of warm comfort from it and they oozed down inside, the caress of an ally.

'God,' he said. 'What a crew.'

The terraced house had been stifling inside. Despite the heat, the windows in the back room in which he met the two gargoyles, were clamped shut. George felt an even higher degree of sweatiness come over him than he had been experiencing outside. His neck began to prickle under his collar. He wiped his palms stealthily on the sides of his jacket.

'Mum,' Sylvia announced to the seated females. 'I've brought George to meet you. George is my new fiancé – look at the lovely ring he's bought me!'

George could now recall barely a word of the conversation that had followed. He had not been in the house above ten minutes and there had been no offer of tea or any other sort of hospitality – thank heavens. Imagine having to stay any longer in that prison of a room. It was stuffy as hell and crammed full of grim furniture: two massive armchairs in scuffed, toffee-coloured leather; a utility table and chairs, the table covered by a drab embroidered cloth; brown linoleum on the floor. The mantelshelf, of bile-coloured tiles, held an array of knick-knacks of a spectacularly depressing kind: cheap little jugs, children with exaggeratedly large eyes, china Alsatians . . . In the middle squatted a wood-cased clock which ticked with such ponderous slowness that it felt as if time itself was heading for oblivion.

It was not the quality of ornament itself that dragged at him. He was not a snob. Obviously not many people decorated their houses the way his wealthy customers liked to. But this place was mesmerizingly cheerless, permeated by a mouldy vegetable smell mixed with the odour of stale coal dust. He found it stifling, horrifying.

On top of which was the sight of Sylvia's kith.

The mother looked impossibly old. His mind raced. If Sylvia was in her early forties, the sister – a glum, stolid-looking creature – must be considerably older. Then how old was this mother, with her clicking false teeth and grey straggling hair? She wore a sickly orange frock and grubby sheepskin slippers.

She got to her feet, clasping thin, veined hands together and seeming at a loss. Her eyes were watery and not unkind. He could see Sylvia staring, her face seeming full of fierce, explosive feeling, as if willing her mother to say something.

'So – you're going to marry Sylvia, are you?' She seemed neither surprised nor pleased nor dismayed by this possibility. She might have been asking the milkman if he would leave an extra pint.

Jean, the sister, in a tweed skirt and sleeveless white knitted top, said nothing and sat staring ahead of her.

'Sit down then, won't you?' Sylvia's mother said. He realized he had never even learned her name.

'That's it, George, dear – do sit down for a moment,' Sylvia purred at him. She remained in the doorway, leaning on the frame. There was no sense that he would be staying long.

He sat at the edge of one of the predatory-looking armchairs. The heat only seemed to get more intense. His temples were throbbing. Brimming in him was a sense of dismay that was fast turning into panic. He had promised – somehow! – to marry this woman. This was what he would be marrying into. He tried to salvage some of his own basic decency. It was Sylvia he was marrying, not her mother or sister. She was quite separate from them and he was being unkind. They were probably very decent people when you got better acquainted with them.

But beneath this reasoning, inchoate feelings seethed . . . A second's flash of memory showed him a heavy door closing, a black jacket swaying gently behind it . . . Claustrophobia which was about more than this stuffy room swelled in him, an outraged sense of having been duped, yet a familiar paralysis that left him unable to assert himself, to protest or escape . . .

Standing by the field gate, he tilted the flask up again. One warm drop flowered on his tongue. As he righted his head again he felt a breeze and darkening atmosphere: a storm gathering at last. He then saw that a paler brown creature stepping towards him across the pasture was not a pony at all. It was hands smaller, the ears longer, with a meal-coloured muzzle. A delighted tenderness spread through him.

'Hello, little moke,' he said, leaning closer over the gate.

The donkey took a few steps more towards him, its ears straight and alert. It watched him with a gentle expression. Its very being brought back the suck of mud on his boots, the pull on his legs, head bowed against the wet, the reassuring warmth of the mule beside him.

'Come on . . .' He held out his hand, clicking his tongue. The donkey stepped forward, and reached its head just close enough for him to stroke the silky give of its nose.

Slowly, so as not to alarm the animal, he climbed over the gate, glad no one could see this ungainly operation. The donkey showed no objection to his arrival and he stood beside it, stroking the creature's mushroom-coloured coat.

'You know, I once had a good friend like you,' he murmured into the twitching ears. 'She was a mule of course, bigger than you and darker than you too. Lovely, she was. Clotilde was her name. I called her Lottie. Poor old Lottie.' He thought for a second, glancing at the sky turning thick and grape-coloured over the fields. He felt the pressure in his head, his body.

'I don't think I ever talked to anyone the way I did to Lottie. Well, maybe my dog – but those were different times, during the war. I suppose none of us were quite ourselves. She was a beautiful animal, Lottie was. I always got the feeling she understood what I was saying.' He sighed. 'She met a very terrible end, I'm afraid.'

The donkey, unmoved by these disclosures, lowered its head to snuff at the thin grass near the gate, but it didn't move away. He gave it a final pat and went back to the van.

By the time he reached home, the sky seemed to be pressing down all around them, a deep mauve grey. The wind was getting up, buffeting back and forth. As he climbed out of the van, lightning crackled across the sky followed by thunder, low and still far off. Inside, as he quieted Monty with a dish of food, he heard the rain begin in an elongated swish of sound.

4.

He poured a tankard of homebrew and, Monty at his heels, went and sprawled in a chair in the back sitting room, comforted by the familiar smells of coal dust, beer and dog. He was exhausted, he realized, yet so strung up that no sense of rest would come to him. The rain made him feel imprisoned in the house, solitary and full of pent-up emotions.

How was it that Sylvia managed to lull him when they were together? A sense of horror stole through him. That sister; the mother! And now he had actually promised to marry her, had bought a ring and she was making arrangements by the hour. In a month's time he would be married – she would have moved in here.

Lifting the silver tankard, he took a mouthful and swallowed as soulfully as if it was hemlock. That body of hers . . . All summer she had kept him in a simmering state. She was in the right, of course, he corrected himself. Sexual relations only within the state of marriage – nothing wrong with that. But in his longing he had only so much as to hold her and was so tormented by desire that he seemed to lose all mental capacity.

He closed his eyes. In the cave of his body he could feel the blood drumming round. His nerves flailed about like loose wires. He was promised to this woman. Quite how had he allowed this to happen? What was it he had seen in Maud Roberts' eyes when they met her? Was it incredulity at the news that this was the woman he was going to marry? Or had he imagined that? You could never be sure with Maud.

'What the hell am I going to do?' he groaned. Monty raised his head, assessed this question as rhetorical and subsided again. The only short-term solution that presented itself was to go and fetch another helping of beer. He went to the kitchen, Monty's nails clicking on the floor behind him. Rain hurled itself at the window. He stood in the kitchen in his socks, feeling sorry for himself. All the same, he didn't want to become an old soak, boozing all evening. Better have some tea. He had just filled the kettle and switched it on when Monty erupted into barking so loudly that he jumped, an unpleasant sensation.

'Damn it, hound – what's the matter with you?'

But the dog had already dashed, roaring, to the front door. Surely no one could be out there in this? A horrible suspicion came to his mind. Not Sylvia, not again? But surely she wouldn't have climbed aboard that absurd pink Vespa of hers in this weather to come and talk his hind leg off all evening again?

As he walked along the hall there was a tap on the door. Bracing himself, he opened it. The sound of sheeting rain increased. On the step, hands gripping a black umbrella, weeping, was Maggie.

For a few moments there were no sounds except Monty's whines of greeting and Maggie gulping and sniffing. George left her umbrella to drip on the hall tiles, stood her wellingtons by the door and led her to the kitchen. He hung her rain-spotted jacket over the back of a chair. She was wearing a long, flowery skirt and pale green blouse. George handed her a towel and Maggie wiped her face and hands, but not as if she was thinking of what she was doing. As she handed it back to him, her face crumpled and she began to cry again.

'I'm sorry, George, for crashing in on you like this, only John's gone to the pub – *as usual*.' These last words were delivered with a venom he'd never associated with Maggie, 'And I need to . . . I knew you'd understand.'

'Of course,' George said, hoping to goodness he was going to. He stepped over to stand before her and gently prompted, 'What's the trouble, old girl?'

'It's Linda,' Maggie burst out with more sobs. 'Linda, my eldest, my baby girl – she and her husband are going to live in Australia!'

'Ah – oh!' George said. A skein of muddled emotions twisted in him. Relief – he'd thought it was going to be some sort of trouble with John; disappointment – he'd thought it was going to be some sort of trouble with John. And a bewilderment which even in those seconds made him wonder whether he could ever be cut out to be a father. Was Linda's departure really such dreadful news? The 'baby girl', who presently lived somewhere on the outskirts of Oxford, must be getting on for thirty, so far as George could remember.

Trying to sound a fraction more helpful, he added, 'Oh dear.'

'I knew you'd understand,' Maggie said, eyes streaming. 'I can't believe it – the other side of the world! How can they even think of it? It's cruel, that's what it is. He says he's going to work making cars. I mean, why can't he carry on making them here, instead of taking my girl all the way over there?'

She looked up at George with red-rimmed eyes, her face swollen and raw. 'I can't even imagine it,' she concluded.

'Well,' George said. He raised his hands, then unsure what to do with them, reached into his pocket for his handkerchief. 'You never know – it might be nice.' He handed her the handkerchief. 'It's clean.'

'But it's so far away,' Maggie wailed, pressing the hanky to one eye, then the other. 'And John – I know he doesn't like it. He's as upset as I am. But he won't say – not a word . . .'

The kettle boiled. George stepped over and switched it off. Turning back to Maggie, he was about to offer her tea, but he saw something in her eyes, a frank, hungry look which he could only answer with a look of his own. She stepped towards him and they reached for each other. It felt familiar and reassuring to hold her, to kiss the damp auburn top of her head.

'Maggie, Maggie,' he murmured, half tender, half despairing.

Her arms tightened round him in the straightforward, kind, needful way she had. Feeling himself held and needing himself, he cradled her head against him. Sylvia held him, of course, but any moment when he allowed himself to relax into wholehearted desire, she pushed him away again.

'Oh God, George,' Maggie said into his chest.

All his pent-up need fastened on her, reached out for her. He fumbled for her hand.

'Come on, my dear,' he said.

They climbed the stairs together, hand in hand, like children.

In the bedroom, knowing that for once this was a woman who would not toy with him, he began to let himself go, kissing her deeply, allowing the full surge of desire to course through him.

Seeing her again, the generous pinkness of her as she lay back on the bed, he almost wept. All his senses focused hungrily on this one act, of aching, needing . . . And at last someone was here for him. She was here. She came with tears and he with a cry of relief and freedom.

He held her as they cooled on top of the bedclothes, letting her cry it out. It was sweet to feel the brush of her hair against his skin and her warm solidity. He knew he did not belong with her or she with him, now any more than before, but he felt a huge rush of fondness for her.

'You know,' he said, as the fit of tears quietened, 'you did say you wanted a bigger life. For things to expand.'

'Did I?' she said in a bleak tone. 'Yes, I s'pose I did. I just—' She pushed herself up on one elbow and looked down at him. In the gauzy evening light her face looked older, sadder. There were more lines around her eyes than he remembered. 'I don't think I meant quite this big. I was thinking of a nice little trip to France, maybe . . .'

'Well,' he tried, 'life is full of surprises.' Even platitudes were in short supply. He struggled to think of something deep to follow this but nothing came to him.

'Huh. Well this is one I could have done without.' She lay down again. 'It's a shock, George, it really is. But I s'pose I'll have to come to terms with it.'

He reached over and stroked her belly, reacquainting himself with the feel of it, soft, yet also strong. He stilled his hand on her and they lay in a pool of quiet. George just made out the sound of Monty's toenails clicking along the hall floor.

In the silence, her mind must have slid back to thoughts of the world enlarging suddenly, against her will.

'Tell me . . .' She snuggled close to him, on her side, like a child demanding a story. 'What was it like where you went? Argentina, you said? What on earth were you doing there?'

He would always remember Helle's face when they visited that swanky dealers on Fifth Avenue. Paul Lester was there, a thin, austere-looking man in a long dark overcoat. He was English. They were introduced – Lester, a businessman from Buenos Aires; George, agent for the Black brothers, the London dealers. Helle, who kept trying to poke his nose in, never really got a look-in.

'I'd never met anyone like Lester before,' he told Maggie. 'He looked like a Methodist preacher, but I realized – well I didn't have to realize because he told me soon enough – he was one of the richest men in the world. *Baron* Lester. Even bought himself a peerage, I found out later. '

'Where did he get all his money from?' She sounded puzzled.

'Meat. All those cattle across the plains of Argentina. Refrigeration – packing and exporting meat. He had one of the biggest outfits at the docks in Buenos Aires . . . This was 1928 and by then he'd made a fortune – through the Great War of course. Bully beef for the troops. What he wanted, though, was furniture for his place in the country – *estancias*, they call them. It was being built at the time. He wanted European furniture, especially English and French. He looked at all the catalogues I'd brought, very quietly for ages. Then he said – never left me any choice really – 'I want you to come with me. There'll be good business in it for you.'

'But why did you have to go? Couldn't he have just ordered it?'

'That's what I wondered. He could command whatever he wanted. But he insisted I go. I never quite worked it out – it was all very peculiar. I came to the conclusion he was actually lonely and wanted someone to show off to.'

George paused; swallowed. Everything about Argentina, his first views of Buenos Aires, between the plains and that great brown river like a sea, the stench of it, of blood from the slaughterhouses, of the water, of decay and poor human lives and desperation and money – all of that, fascinating as it had been, was overlain and tainted by the Lesters.

'He took me by seaplane.'

Maggie gasped. 'His own plane?'

'Not his own – but they'd just started up a service down that way and he had the money to charter it when he wanted. He was rich beyond . . . you know, he said to me, "People think the British live well in India. But it's nothing to what we've got here in South America. Here we live like kings – we *are* kings." Anyway, we flew from New York, along the coast. It was an experience, of course. Like sliding across a map. Only time I've ever flown, in fact – there and back. He took me to his factory and then we drove out to the country place.

'It was a palace in the making. Absolutely enormous – I'd never seen anything like it. Turrets and gables and what seemed like a quarter of a mile of house – let alone all the land around it, all red earth, polo horses. I was terrified really. He wanted me to tell him how to furnish it. He didn't have a clue and I didn't have much clue either, not in a house that size!'

A queasy feeling arose in him at the memory. He had seen it not long after walking into the vast house – on a side table. He had walked towards it, hardly believing, a feeling of the hairs standing up on the back of his neck. There, the horse, the warrior, muscled, armoured: Mars on Horseback. It felt like reacquainting himself with a friend. He leaned over it, hardly breathing. At the side of the base, the imprint of a tiny black bird.

'Like him, do you?' Lester had said as George stood astonished, transported back to Lord Buckleford's grand, sad manor in Sussex where he had seen the two gods, exquisitely together. 'It's a valuable thing – but apparently nothing like what it would be with its pair. Now, if I could get my hands on her . . . I'm keeping an eye out; somewhere there's a matching Venus – worth a fortune together.'

Trust Lester to talk only about the money – no word of the fineness of the thing. He did not start on this with Maggie.

'I spent four days there. The furniture part wasn't too bad as it turned out. Everything had to be on a grand scale, obviously. Lester ordered a lot of stuff from the catalogues. He hardly seemed to care what. They were just things to acquire. He had no sense of beauty, of proportion . . . Once I was actually there he seemed to lose interest and got his wife to choose most of it. She was pleasant enough, had quite a good eye. I wired London and tried to explain the problem, which boiled down to more and bigger. But Joe and Walter Black knew what to look for. I left it to them in the end and they wired back suggestions to her – Inés Lester.'

'Other than that . . .' It was hard to explain the Lesters, the at-odds atmosphere between them despite their devoted appearance. Or the effect they had on him over those days – a sense of being scraped out and emptied, yet at the same time poisoned and humiliated. 'It was . . . repellent. I've never met anyone like Lester before or since. One of his things was tax –

not paying it, that is. The British government were after him. He owned some huge pile in Hampshire so he hadn't fully left the country. But he knew every trick in the book not to pay up.

'Everything was about money. Just about everything he said was some form of showing off. He had stables full of polo horses – dozens of them – and a whole staff of grooms. He made me ride with him. There was no choice – he spoke and everyone jumped. I had never ridden a horse before and it was bloody terrifying. Lester kept *barking* orders at me. "For goodness' sake, man. Can't you even do this, or do that?" – depending on what it was I'd done wrong each time. It was like being at school again, only worse because this man was a . . . He was a bully. And a money-making machine, as if there was nothing else. Even the furniture, the house – all of it was about showing off. Every meal we ate, that was all he talked about: the business, his shares in the railway, how he was working it to get a complete monopoly over the trade . . . He was the most boring man I have ever met. Anyway, that bloody horse could tell a mile off I didn't know what I was doing and it soon began to jitter about and threw me off.'

He heard a faint sound of amusement from Maggie. In retrospect it did seem funny. He could not describe to her the acute sense of shame and humiliation he had felt at the time. Lester made him feel it, wanted him to feel dominated and put down. George saw the contemptuous curve of his lips as he struggled to remount, his right buttock and thigh stabbing with pain.

'The thing was, he had all this – money, house and all that. The wife, Inés, was beautiful. Half Spanish. She said her father had been an English railway engineer, working over there. Met her mother in Rosario. She was nicer than him. She pandered to him. But she was bored, I think.'

'No kids?'

'Not then, no – no doubt they were on his list of future acquisitions. He wasn't young but I don't think they'd been married all that long . . . I really don't know how she put up with him. That was a gilded cage if ever I saw one.'

He wanted to stop talking now; stop before his mind ran up against that afternoon, that soft knocking on the heavy wooden door . . . By the time Lester sent him back to New York, it was as if his inner self had undergone a scouring, a quiet revolution. He would never, ever live just for money. If that meant a smaller life, so be it. Paul Lester did not live so much as stand with his head tilted back, mouth stretched open like a grotesque fish, to catch any and every thing that might fall into it. This cold, predatory man had sickened George to his very core.

Lying here now he remembered that vow, taken on the sea-plane back from Buenos Aires, staring down at the leaden ocean; the vow that he would never be anything like Paul Lester. He would live a life filled with beautiful things made by human hands, not by machines . . . He would never take things that were not his to have . . . And yet now – this brought him up with a jolt – here he was with Maggie . . .

Her voice came to him. 'You're not doing a very good job of persuading me I ought to see the world.'

He laughed, giving her thigh a gentle squeeze. 'Oh – I'm sure it wouldn't be like that. That was pretty unusual.'

'You all right, George?' Maggie said after a pause. 'You managing?'

'I'm getting married.' Even as he said it he could not really believe it. Laughter came then, taking him by surprise. He felt his whole body shaking with it. Maggie shot up beside him.

'Married? Who to? And if you're getting married, what're you doing in this bed with me?'

This was a question so pertinent that he had no reply to it.

'So who? Is she from the village?'

'She's called Sylvia Newsome,' he said. 'She lives in Wallingford.' He started laughing again. It seemed the only thing to do.

Maggie's greenish eyes stared at him in utter perplexity. 'Well . . . congratulations,' she said uncertainly. 'That's lovely. What the hell's so funny?'

He sobered himself, ashamed, and lay quietly. Maggie leaned closer, hair tickling his cheek. He could see that the flesh of her face sagged more than before.

'What's up? You don't look all that happy about it.'

He was overcome by that cold feeling of helplessness. He was promised and that was the truth of it. You didn't break a promise.

'Oh, you know. Pre-nuptial nerves.' He forced his lips into a smile. 'Out of practice I suppose.'

He and Maggie said a sweet goodbye, but he knew and she knew that everything was different now. The exuberance of their lovemaking the year before had faded. Each of them was older, more weighted down by something – above all, today, by the knowledge that this must not happen. Not again. He thought of Maggie's world, enlarging against her will. Of his own, of his engagement to Sylvia which he saw, with a terrible stab of realization, was not the expanding horizon of which he had dreamed, but would make his own world even smaller.

'Goodbye, my dear,' he said, as she slipped her boots back on at the door. The rain had stopped. The sky offered an optimistic brightness and his body felt momentarily lighter, as if on the verge of a dance.

Maggie smiled with affectionate sadness. 'Bye, George. And thanks.' She reached up and kissed his cheek before stepping outside. Turning, she said, 'I hope things . . . You know.'

He watched her walk away in her black wellies, the umbrella held rolled in her left hand. She didn't look back.

Thirteen

1.

As the next week passed, George's life took on an increasing sense of fractured unreality.

There were the small things, like walking, one morning, into the bathroom in the not unreasonable hope of relieving himself, only to encounter Sharon's brown-clad haunches rearing up before him as she leaned over to clean the bath.

'Ah, er – oh!' he exclaimed, already retreating as Sharon's heavy features turned on him in a look of scowling disapproval.

'Sorry!' he called, scarcely wondering why he felt bound to apologize in his own house, let alone bathroom.

Later that morning, a fruit pie – not something that had featured much recently – appeared in the refrigerator, only to have disappeared again a few hours later when he had actually decided to eat a slice of it. He stood for a few seconds staring at the empty shelf. Was he starting to imagine pies?

The strangest and largest eventuality of all was that he was apparently on the point of getting married to Sylvia Newsome and no one else knew – except for Maggie. Well, and Maud, sort of. That particular day he spent fully occupied – other than with glimpses of domestic oddness – with business. He listened to the requirements of customers and to Clarence on a long and obscure matter of French polishing, and also spent some moments instructing Vera on a few aspects of book-keeping, all of which she grasped before he had finished speaking. All the while, repeating in another layer of his mind was the drumming of the wedding march: *pom, pom te pom*, *POM, POM TE POM* . . . It seemed, even though it was emanating from inside his very self, to be played in a mocking sort of key.

He kept repeating to himself, I'm getting married to Sylvia Newsome.

Now, after his sexual rescue by Maggie, all this seemed even more improbable. It was like a parallel-story world that did not coincide with his real life. Or at least it didn't until that evening.

Since the storm, the weather had returned to warm sunshine but with a touch of freshness to it, a hint in the mellow angle of the light that they were reaching the waning point of summer. The rain-soaked rose heads turned up to the sun and their scent filled the garden.

The sunshine also meant that Sylvia was back, soon after six o'clock, on the buzzing pink Vespa. Vera, who was engrossed in totting up numbers had not, as she would usually have done, left for home.

'I made a quick pie here at dinnertime,' she confided to George. 'I thawed out a bit of the pastry. I hope you don't mind. I popped it home – helps me get ahead of myself a bit.'

She made this confession while on her way out through the front door, basket in hand, and in doing so was confronted by the arrival of the pink motor scooter. George had been full of misgiving that something like this would happen. The game was very definitely up.

'Hello, Georgie!' Sylvia cried, beaming at him from under her white helmet as she swept past to the spot by the garden gate where she now always left the Vespa. She was wearing a dress of pink and orange flowers, with short, puffy sleeves. The dress was rucked up by the necessity of straddling the bike, revealing plump, white knees.

Vera halted; stared. She swivelled round to look at George. George, determinedly, did not look back. He watched Sylvia with what he hoped was an expression of calm benignity.

Sylvia's feet could be heard crunching on the gravel. She approached, twitching at her skirt hem to return it to a more dignified position.

'Vera,' George said, with a now-or-never plunge within, as if diving into rapids, 'may I introduce to you Sylvia – my fiancée?'

'Hel-*lo*,' Sylvia gushed, seizing Vera's hand. George suppressed a smile. He could see that this, in its way, was Sylvia at her best: warm, forthcoming, irresistible. Her brown eyes were signalling happiness and enthusiasm, her scarlet lipstick lips turned up in an ecstatic smile.

Vera managed to insert an uncertain, 'Er, hello,' into the exchange before Sylvia was off again.

'I'm *so* excited,' she prattled. '*So* nice to meet you. I've heard such a lot about you – you're the person who cleans the shop, aren't you?'

'Well, rather more than that,' George attempted.

'We'll all have time to get to know each other better when I move in,' Sylvia said, beaming. 'Dear George . . .' She turned to him for a second before returning to Vera. 'Look at my lovely engagement ring! I don't want to be a show-off but he has such good taste – it's so pretty, isn't it?' She extended her hand. Vera stared at it, expressionlessly.

'I'm so lucky to have met George . . .' Sylvia put one arm

round the back of George's waist, the other hand resting on his upper arm. 'He's *so* marvellous. But then of course you know as much already.'

George began to wonder if Vera was all right. He had never seen her so silent or so thunderstruck. She was gazing at Sylvia with a sharp, musing expression. What was up with her? Unease stirred in him.

At last Vera spoke. 'Ah. Well.' She made her face smile. 'This is a surprise. What did you say your name was?'

'Oh *sorry*,' Sylvia said, swooping forward again to hold out her hand. 'Sylvia. Sylvia Newsome.'

'Vera Day.' She shook hands properly this time, seeming to relax now, though she still seemed dazed. George felt ashamed. He should have confided in her.

'Well,' Vera said, looking from one to the other of them. 'I'd better be off home now. Congratulations to both of you. I hope you'll be very happy.'

2.

Vera was very quiet the next morning. Ominously quiet. No Beatles songs: the radio was not switched on. Even her hair looked stiffer and more bouffant than usual, as if embalmed in hairspray. By the morning tea break George felt bound to ask if anything was wrong.

'No,' Vera said, passing out of the kitchen with raised eyebrows. 'Of course not. Why should there be?'

George sighed. Was she in a huff? Why was it so hard to tell with women? But he did know enough to surmise that when a woman would not look you in the eye, trouble was probably on its way. He increasingly had the sense that his home was becoming a terrain more mysterious to him than familiar.

The following day he was due to go out. He approached Vera in a brisk, 'we are here to do business' manner.

'I've promised to go and see Mrs Mackrell again,' he told her. 'Poor dear – she's having to sell something else.'

'Umm?' Vera said, seated at the office desk with her back to him. George wondered why he suddenly felt like the employee, trying to make appeasing noises.

It was on the tip of his tongue to ask Vera again if anything was wrong – Alan complaining, perhaps? – but he remembered the expression on Vera's face when she'd met Sylvia and decided he did not necessarily want to know the answer to this.

'While I'm over there,' he went on, attempting obliviousness, 'I think I'll go on up Oxford way . . .' He had no particular reason to visit Oxford. He realized he was looking for excuses to stay out of the way.

'Ah,' Vera seized on this and at last swung round. There was something tight-looking about her today, George felt. The hair again. 'There's a Mrs Parker in Peppard . . .'

This was hardly Oxford, but he didn't think he'd argue.

'She wants you to come over and look at a few of her things. Oh, and . . .' She bent to consult the notes in front of her. The side of her hair shone like metal. It was brushed back with pristine smoothness. 'There was a call from a Dr Hargreaves – well, from his secretary.' She frowned. 'Bit vague. Something about a house clearance but he wasn't sure exactly when he'd be able to be there. Just that he wanted you to come and . . .' She looked up in irritation. 'Oh *I* don't know. The woman sounded addled to me. If that's the sort of person running a doctor's surgery, all I can say is, heaven help them.'

'Well yes, quite,' George agreed. 'Right-o then.' He took the details, ordered Monty back into the kitchen and went outside. He was about to take the car, but on second thoughts, went and climbed into the Morris. If there were things he could bring back, he might as well do it straight away.

He steered out of the drive and away up the hill, the chalky downs spreading in front of him, with a lightening sense of freedom. Escape! A day out, a nice pub on the way back somewhere, depending where he ended up. And he could at least break free from all the confusions of the fair sex for a few hours.

Or so he thought.

Mrs Mackrell was as moistly emotional as she had been on his last visit as she parted with an elegant walnut china cabinet – 'Mother would break her heart' – so much so that it crossed his mind to write the poor old dear a cheque and tell her to keep the damn thing. But he could already visualize Vera's face when this piece of accounting came to light. Business was business.

The two dealers he visited in Oxford were both, thankfully, men. By mid-afternoon, mellow from a couple of unexpected but most welcome pints and some chappish conversation, he turned towards home along the prettiest back routes. In the high cab of the Morris he meandered through the Chilterns, humming scraps of half-remembered songs. As he flashed past a field, somewhere between Nettlebed and Stoke Row, with a heart-leap of pleasure he thought he saw a cluster of donkeys. He decided his mind was playing tricks. They must be ponies – no one had that many donkeys. Finally he reached the lush lanes of Rotherfield Peppard.

He parked beside a hedge comprising a bulging mixture of copper beech and hornbeam with swirls of clematis growing along the top of it, which bordered the house he was due to visit. As he slid, stiff-legged to the ground, he heard the 'pock' and bounce of a tennis ball from the other side of the hedge. Someone, a young girl by the sound of it, gave a cheer.

'I say, Julia!' a woman's voice tinkled above it. 'Jolly good shot! You *are* getting good. Oh yes, and you too of course, Lucinda.'

The house, end on to the road, was long, Tudor and decked with yellow climbing roses. Golden showers, George thought, and smiled. They looked splendid.

He opened the green wicket gate and knocked on a front door of the same colour. The place felt empty. Realizing he might never get an answer, he was about to set off along the side of the house when the door opened abruptly and with some vigour. A wholesome female appeared, compact and strong-looking with brown hair in a neat bob, enquiring blue eyes and cheeks moistly pink from her leapings around the court. She was clad in the minimalist garb of tennis whites, a snip of a skirt well north of her knees.

'Mr Baxter?' There was laughter in her voice. 'I'm Mrs Parker. How very punctual of you. Do come in.'

'I thought no one was in,' he said, for something to say, adding, 'I was admiring your roses.'

'Ah, yes . . .' she replied vaguely, her back to him already.

George was thrown by the sheer amount of flesh on display. He had already taken in that the shirt was short-sleeved and very low at the front. Muscular little thighs disclosed themselves below the skirt. She was not a large woman, but he seemed to be able to see most of her, he thought, averting his eyes so completely towards the floor that he almost walked into a beam.

'Oops, careful!' she chuckled, glancing back.

Despite the heat George felt glad he still had his jacket on, though there was no real logic to this thought.

'I came racing inside,' she said, pausing at the foot of the stairs, which were muffled snugly in crimson carpet. 'Rather hot I'm afraid, not to say dishevelled. We were playing tennis – my daughter and a friend.'

'Ah, yes.' George thought he had better look up, in case of seeming rude or worse, peculiar.

'Now, the thing is, Mr Baxter . . .'

Her face, previously dimpled and cheerful, collapsed into dolefulness. The large blue pools of eyes filled with tears.

Oh dear God, George thought, not another one.

'I've recently inherited some . . .' She swallowed. George saw it in her throat. 'Some things, of Mummy's, you see . . .'

George gave a slight bow. 'My condolences.'

A tearful story followed involving protracted illness in which whisky seemed to feature in some way; the troublesome practicalities of finding suitable nurses, the searing awfulness of a house clearance.

'I mean, I just couldn't bear to part with it all. Not at first. Boxes and boxes! Mummy was not herself you see, at the end. And she was rather unusual even before – so clever. But then being clever isn't always . . . If she could only have stayed off the . . . Anyway, I mustn't go on.'

She fished a hanky out of her waistband and blew her nose with unexpected heartiness before tucking it back in again.

'What I really need is someone just to *take it off me*. All of it. D'you see? Otherwise I get so hopelessly emotional. Robert – that's my husband – says it's not good for me. Look, come out and I'll show you.'

Outside he could just hear the noise of the tennis game again. Close to one end of the house stood a Victorian brick outbuilding, in which Mrs Parker showed him a not especially alarming, he thought, number of items. There were boxes of china and a few items of furniture.

'These are Mummy's things.' She picked up a small, flower-patterned plate and looked soulfully at it, before replacing it. 'I've no idea if they're worth anything – but they meant the world to her.' This brought on another bout of sniffing.

George looked round, light-hearted. A feeling of easy competence overcame him and a hint of male protectiveness. This was going to be easier than he had thought. And he could ease the burdens of this poor lady.

'Look,' he offered. 'It's not so very much, is it? If you're agreeable I'll take it all away – I've got my van with me. When we've had a chance to go through it all we can telephone you with an offer for whatever is saleable – and an inventory of course.'

'Oh – that would be just marvellous!' She clasped her hands together under her chin, the lips turning up in what he saw was a perfect Cupid's bow. She really was quite a looker when she smiled. '*Thank* you, Mr Baxter.'

'Right,' he said, reaching for the edges of his jacket to take it off. 'Well I'll just get started . . .'

A small but arrestingly strong hand clasped his forearm. He caught a sweet tang of something expensive in the perfume line and a hint of womanly sweat. Mrs Parker's peachy face was suddenly close to his.

'There's just one more thing, Mr Baxter. 'The painting. It's upstairs.'

George opened his mouth to disavow knowledge of painting in any form. However, Mrs Parker, who he guessed to be about thirty-five and did not have to guess was in the prime of her life and muscular as a dray horse, was already steering him back towards the house.

'I'm afraid it's in my bedroom,' she announced with a coy tilt of her head, when they reached the stairs. George had already assumed this. He had noticed, over the years, that a certain kind of woman had a tendency to want to show you the interior of their bedroom. It was a queer thing, but there it was. He could usually follow the hints and signs and find ways of rebuttal. But in this case, being in the garden he had not seen it coming and was also not accustomed to being dragged to a staircase by the arm.

Politeness dictated that she precede him up the stairs. A glance, before he ducked his head in self-preservation, showed him the little pleats of the skirt flicking upwards with each step. Forcing this image from his mind he prepared something diplomatic to say about the painting, which he already knew he did not want to take away with him.

'Here we are, Mr Baxter – and you must have another name?' She skipped up onto the creaking top step. 'Do call me Rosamund.'

'Er, George,' he admitted – ill advisedly, he was quite sure.

'*George*,' she purred, her round face beaming at him, all traces of grief over Mummy quite gone.

'Now – do come in. My little room. Do mind your head.'

She unlatched the wooden door and both of them ducked to enter. George had an impression of ceiling beams, latticed windows and a wide bed with silky peach-coloured coverlet. The perfumed smell grew stronger.

'There you are, you see.' Rosamund Parker, beside him, gestured at the wall above the bed. To George's abundant relief the painting was not, as he had more than half expected, some garish oil painting of a disrobed female prone on a couch.

'Lovely, isn't it?' he heard her breathe, close to his ear. He became aware that she was nudging against his arm. Some part of her was, anyway, and it was not one of her hands, which were clasped demurely in front of her. Heat rose at the back of his neck and even more perturbingly, in his groin. 'Mummy always said it was done by one of the disciples of Constable – sadly not by the great man himself.'

This had a ring of truth. It was a lovely, gentle pastoral: river meadows, the line of water in meandering perspective, a spring day with cattle grazing.

'You plan to sell it then?' he asked, inching gradually away from the fleshy pressure on his left bicep.

'Oh no! It's far too perfect to sell. I just thought you might be able to,' her voice dropped, huskily, 'give me a tiny . . .' The breast was back, insistent. 'Just an idea, a clue how much it might fetch if I did, George.'

She inched round to face him, looking up at him, one hand now on his arm. The invitation in her eyes was so blatant that it sent desire through him like a shock. Good God – what the hell was he supposed to do now?

'You're a nice man, George, I could see that as soon as you arrived.' She reached out and her warm palm stroked his cheek. The perfume filled his nostrils again. He saw the soft texture of her neck, the little cushion of flesh under her chin. Observing him flinch she laughed sweetly. 'It's all right, we're all alone. The girls will never come up here.'

Keeping her gaze fixed on his, cheek dimpling as she spoke,

she said, 'How would it be if I took my top off? I've only got on the teeniest little—'

'No!' George forced himself into action, stepping back from her before she could touch him any more, lead him into burying his face in those breasts, into the dreamland blur of physicality from which he would not wake until he had taken her and emerged horrified the other side. He ran his hand over his hair as if suspecting it might be already rumpled in some incriminating way.

'Now this must stop,' he said sternly, as if to a child. 'You're a married woman, and—'

'Married to a plank,' she said sulkily, withdrawing from him. 'No fun at all, let me tell you.'

'Well . . .' George found himself feeling sorry for her. He tried to keep up the fatherly tone. He must be at least twenty years her senior so he could carry it off. 'I'm sorry to hear it my dear, but he is your husband and this is no way to—'

'But George – just a bit of fun?' An irrepressible grin spread across her face. 'You look like a man who would be great fun in bed!'

This was flattering to hear. All the same, he wondered how many tradesmen who looked 'great fun' were acquainted with a painting possibly in the school of Constable that they just had to see.

He smiled back, unable to dislike Rosamund Parker. 'No,' he repeated. 'Really – no, my dear. But it was nice of you to offer.' He gestured towards the door. 'Let's go down, shall we?'

'Look,' he said, in the hall, 'I haven't loaded the van. I think I'll send my man round to collect all your mother's boxes and things. I think that would be best.'

'All right.' She stood with her arms folded now, faintly sulky he thought, though he could not tell exactly what was in her tone. Perhaps she was wondering what his 'man' would be like. As he said goodbye and let himself out, he wondered if Clarence would be treated to a sighting of *the painting* when he came to do the pick-up.

On the journey back between fields just turning gold with ripe wheat and hedgerows hanging with elderberries, he found himself full of cheer. He burst into song. Not a bad afternoon really. Some good pieces from Oxford. An offer from a rather inviting lady – nobly refused, he reflected. He had shown a principled dignity along with a certain sympathy. Should he stop for a pint somewhere on the way? He decided he had had enough at lunchtime. Home, James. The weekend. Peace and quiet!

Still *pom-pom*-ing he swept in triumph down the chalk-edged road into the village. The 'GREENBURY' sign seemed to welcome him with a homely smile. He swung the Morris with a flourish of speed into the drive.

Where a truly horrifying sight met his eyes. Women. A cluster of floral shirtwaister frocks in front of the house. And they were, all too obviously, waiting for him.

3.

He parked the Morris, trying to pretend he had not seen them. Head down, he gathered his things from the seat of the van, wondering whether he should keep up his pretence and try to escape round the back into the garden. It was the Cronies and Vera out there; he had glimpsed enough to know that. He closed his eyes for a few seconds. All he wanted – longed for, as for a fading dream – was his chair, a pint of homebrew with Monty at his side, and a quiet, empty house.

Bag under one arm, he opened the van door and slid to the ground, slamming it behind him. Perhaps, he suggested to himself, the women were in fact gathered coincidentally for a general natter that had nothing to do with him?

This flare of hope spluttered out as soon as he began to walk towards them. They fell silent and watched him: Vera, Rosemary Abbott, Pat Nesbitt (minus spaniels) and Eunice MacLean.

'Evening, ladies!' he hailed them, in a bid to take command of the situation.

There was a long and uncomfortable pause as they looked at each other; seeming, he thought, unprepared for whatever it was they were obviously awaiting.

Vera took the initiative and stepped forward, looking upset

and fraught. She straightened her arms at her sides in her pale blue dress. Something dangled from one hand – a newspaper, he saw.

'Mr Baxter, I –' Her voice was husky. She seemed close to tears. 'I'm so sorry. But you'd better come inside with us for a moment. We . . .' She glanced round at the others. 'Well, we need to talk to you.'

George looked at them all. Eunice MacLean, in a green and white frock, looked elegant, her bony face solemn and giving nothing away. Pat, in a peach floral affair, seemed strangely incomplete without the dogs. She tried to give him a smile, but beneath the blue-eyeshadowed lids her eyes seemed full of tragedy. Rosemary, in a bright pink skirt and white blouse, hair set like concrete, was not wearing her customary air of self-righteousness. She looked – they all looked, he realized – pained and sympathetic. The way they had looked when Win was ill.

'Better get on with it then,' he said.

He led the way inside. A mighty woofing began from the kitchen. George immediately felt the need to have Monty at his side as possibly his only ally in this so far mysterious conversation, but, as they filed along the hall to the sitting room, Rosemary Abbott immediately said, 'Do keep that dreadful dog away from us, won't you?'

'He's been fed,' Vera told George. 'He'll be all right for a bit, won't he? But would you like me to make you a cup of tea, Mr Baxter? I expect you've had a hard day.'

George was already beginning to feel the need for a good deal more than tea.

'It's all right, Vera,' he said. 'Let's just have you all say whatever it is you've come to say.' He had an inkling that this was something to do with Alan. Some sort of female ganging-up that he could not yet understand. 'Do take a seat, ladies. Monty'll calm down in a minute.'

'It might be best not,' Eunice MacLean said. Her deep voice and her manner, as usual gave a sense of grace and gravity to the situation. 'We don't intend to trouble you for long. We did feel, though, that we might lend Vera a little support for what she needs to say to you.' Eunice stretched her lips into a tactful smile.

'It's a disgrace,' Rosemary Abbott remarked with sudden fervour, but Pat Nesbitt shushed her with a hand on her arm.

'Let Vera speak, Rosemary,' she said. George was surprised at Pat's firmness. 'Don't jump the gun.'

George would have liked to sit down but amid this standing company, did not feel he could. Guesses hopped in his mind like frogs. Alan? Or was this something to do with Lady Byngh? Or some imagined slight that he had given one of them?

He looked at Vera. Her eyes met his, waiting for him to prompt her.

'Well – you'd better let me have it,' he said. 'What's happened?'

As the others stood round, Vera held out the newspaper in her hand, folded to a particular page. It was the local paper, he saw, the *Mercury*. She handed it to him, pointed to one of the small announcements. 'Here – look.'

'Mrs Edna Cook of St John's Road Wallingford would like to announce the engagement of her daughter, Sylvia Ann Newsome, to George Oswald Baxter of Chalk Hill House, Greenbury . . .'

He read no further. Not that he was not surprised. Sylvia hadn't wasted any time. And seeing it there like that was a shock. She hadn't said anything to him about announcing it in the paper. The reality of it came to him with an unpleasant twist in his guts. But he knew he was going to have to marry Sylvia now he had promised. It seemed the only thing to do. He still could not see what the trouble was. His not telling them?

'Yes, well . . .' He looked at Vera. 'Sylvia's obviously rather excited about it all. But we did tell you . . .'

'I *knew* it!' Vera said, emphasizing this certainty by hurling the newspaper away onto the seat of a chair. She seemed energized. 'That's just the thing, Mr B. As soon as I saw her the other day, I knew there was something not right. I couldn't sort out in my mind what it was at the time, but I *knew* that I knew her from somewhere . . .'

'The thing is, George,' Rosemary Abbott blurted, puce-faced, 'you can't marry the woman. She's duped you. She's an imposter and according to Vera, she's a gold-digger – and a marriage-wrecker!'

'Now wait a minute,' George said, steamed up by Rosemary's bossy accusations. 'What on earth d'you think you're doing, coming in here and—?'

Vera held up a hand to stop him, with such command he could only obey and admire.

'For heaven's sake, Rosemary, let Vera tell him,' Pat Nesbitt hissed in the background. She held her hands clasped in front of her as if at a prayer meeting. Eunice MacLean was doing much the same.

Vera spoke gently, but firmly, almost as if the others were not there.

'I went home,' she went on, 'and I kept saying to Alan, I *know* her from somewhere. That person who Mr Baxter says he's going to marry. And Alan kept telling me I'd got it all wrong of course and that I should mind my own business. But it was nagging at me. But when I saw this in the paper, I knew immediately who she was. I went to school with her, in Didcot. Her name's not Sylvia at all – well it wasn't then. It was Cook. Lillian Cook – that's who she was.'

'She's a marriage-breaker!' Rosemary asserted again.

'That's another thing, you see.' Vera looked down, speaking sorrowfully. He was touched to see that this conversation was truly painful to her. 'I didn't know Lillian really. One reason I remember her is because she was always a looker. But she was two or three forms above me.'

'*Above* you?' George said.

'Yes,' Vera said with an injured air. '*Above* me. I suppose she told you she's twenty-one? That'd be like her, by all accounts. Anyway, I lost track of her after school but I do remember, later, hearing about David Newsome. He was one of the town solicitors and she was his secretary. He was a married man with children. She lured him away from his wife. Caused havoc, she did. I mean I didn't even live in the same town but I heard about it. He was besotted with her. But the wife had a breakdown and all sorts. Lil was after his money, no doubt about it. She led him a hell of a dance once they were married. His children turned against him. Poor man died of a heart attack in the end.'

This last detail at least tallied with what Sylvia had told him, George thought. He sank into the nearest chair.

'She really doesn't sound very nice,' Pat Nesbitt suggested with a hint of a nervous laugh. 'Though I'm sure she can be very charming.'

'Insidious more like,' Rosemary Abbott declared. 'A snake.'

'We really are very sorry to bring such tidings,' Eunice MacLean said. 'But we felt it was courageous of Vera to want to tell you. And surely better to be in the picture.'

'Yes,' George agreed. He lowered his head. 'Yes, quite.'

His heart was pounding. He laid a hand over his chest. For a second he thought about David Newsome and his heart attack and took a deep breath. He did not know what he felt, not yet, other than infinitely foolish.

'Of course,' Vera said, trying to soften things. George looked up again. 'It's not up to us to say whether you should marry her. I know it's lonely for you and everything. But at least if you do, you'll know what you're taking on. And maybe she's changed . . .'

'Oh don't be absurd – he can't possibly marry her!' Rosemary Abbott interjected.

Vera turned on her a look of command that must have astonished everyone in the room and appeared to be about to speak, but she held back. Rosemary Abbott's face turned a high colour. She opened her mouth then closed it again and looked away.

'I think it's time we left,' Eunice MacLean suggested. 'Vera, we three will go, but perhaps you might stay for a little while?'

George raised his head. Things were falling into place in his mind, a shower of emotions – relief, uncomfortable insight, grief at what he would now not have; anger at the way Sylvia had gone about taking him in, shame at the way he had allowed her to . . . Yet, in the face of this truth – for he could see it was the truth – he felt suddenly strong.

'Ladies – I need to take all this in.' He gave a wry smile and got to his feet. 'What a fool – and there's certainly no fool like an old fool, is there? I am grateful to you – I truly am.'

Pat Nesbitt stepped forward in her girlish way and to his astonishment he saw that she had tears in her eyes.

'It's just that . . .' She extended her hand, then withdrew it. 'We do so *care* about you, George.'

The others murmured agreement, nodding – even Rosemary Abbott. George lowered his head, so touched that he had no idea what to say.

'Well, that's, er . . . That's . . . Thank you . . . I, er . . .' He looked up at them all again. 'It looks very much as if I shall have to call it all off, doesn't it?'

When Vera had shown the Cronies out, she came back to him, looking emotional. There was a round pink patch on each of her cheeks.

'I'm ever so sorry, Mr B. But I do think you're better off out of it. You can do a lot better than that, a lovely gent like you.' She put her head on one side. 'What will you do?'

'Do?' He imagined confronting Sylvia. No. 'I'll write to her. First of all, anyway.'

Vera met his eyes. She nodded. They stood in silence for a moment.

'Would you like me to cook you some tea before I go?'

'Oh no – I'm perfectly all right, thanks, Vera. I've got some nice sausages.'

She gave a pitying smile. 'You'll look like a sausage soon.'

'It's OK – you go on home to Alan.'

'All right. Well – see you tomorrow,' she said.

He followed her to the door.

'Don't fret too much, will you?' she said. 'She won't, I'll bet you that. She was always a bit of a cow, Lillian was, to be honest.'

'Thanks, Vera,' he said gently, as she left.

He went to the back to let Monty out for a few moments before pouring himself a tankard of homebrew and taking it into the sitting room. He sat for a long time, as the light faded, stroking the dog's ears as he sat beside him.

AUGUST

Fourteen

1.

Late-afternoon sunlight slanted across the downs, peach-gold and mellow.

George stood at the highest point of the track, his back to Greenbury's Iron Age fort, looking south over the fields. He could feel the warmth like a hand on his right cheek. Monty snuffled about in the grass in front of him, the tip of his tail like a white flag above the green.

There was a whiff of smoke in the air from stubble burning some fields away, the atmosphere tinged with blue. Even though it was a beautiful evening, it seemed to him there was a doomy, threatening feel to the sunlight. The month was drawing to a close, the days turning their face from this long, golden summer, each one's passing edging the season downwards into cold demise of the year.

He was still in his shirtsleeves though and cotton trousers, hands pushed into his pockets as he stared across the as yet unburned stubble close by, each stalk clearly defined by its own tiny shadow in the low-angled light. He saw the midnight blue of a crow, its back end swinging from side to side as it picked its way between the stalks.

He had not been up here since February, since his unholy dash from the funeral.

Yesterday, after shutting up shop, he had walked to the cemetery at the edge of the village, to visit Win's grave. It was not quite the first time, but he was not given to loitering at gravesides. He only had a dim idea of where his mother was buried. But these last weeks had brought him back to himself and lowered him into a mood of remembrance, of sadness and of awareness of growing old. This, he knew, was a reaction to his folly, his crazed wish for youth and for more – more of everything. He owed it to Win and to his past to take her flowers, at least from time to time. In his stupid excitement he had neglected her. He had clipped a few remaining blooms of Albertine, her favourite pink roses, and gathered rosemary and bay to mix with them, enjoying the sweet and pungent scents together.

In loving memory, Winifred Baxter:
28.9.1917 – 17.2.1964

'My wife.' He had whispered it, with a sense of wonder, of affection. She was my wife all that time. And most likely my only wife now, he thought.

'You know, old girl,' he told her, still under his breath, 'I've made a proper fool of myself.'

The grave offered neither reproach nor advice. Even so, he had turned away with a sense of vague comfort. He felt that Win might have laughed, somehow, despite it all. This was the way of things, he thought: gain–loss, up–down, beginning–end.

Standing now, looking at the bronze-tinted land about him, he remembered the snow and the bereft silence of that February afternoon. It had ended with his sudden vision of a life enlarged, of newness, hope, family.

A sour, bereft feeling filled him. According to Vera's reckoning, 'Sylvia Newsome' must be in her late forties. Knocking on rather, to produce a child. Not that, he saw now, she had ever mentioned any intention of doing so. Nor had he ever asked her age outright. She had dropped hints: he had assumed. More fool him.

Monty ambled back and sat looking vacantly at him, shifting on his huge front paws like a seal. Grasping eventually that no one was moving anywhere, he settled in the grass with a grunt and lay panting, pink tongue lolling to one side.

George had not hesitated after Vera's disclosures. All his doubts about Sylvia – her brash materialism, the tedium of her conversation, the ghastly pink Vespa and the way she had overfed his dog and steam-rollered him towards marriage – all came into hard-edged focus and shoved him out of self-delusion.

In the small hours of Saturday morning, in a night with no sleep during which he had both wept and raged, he had written a letter, typing it in his office to make it formal and official. By dawn he was setting out in the car, a shred of crescent moon still over the fields, to deliver the letter stealthily by hand. On the way home, as the sun came up, lapwings wandered in the fields and the sweet expectant smells of morning streamed through the window. He experienced a new, champagne feeling of wellbeing and found himself singing.

'*Bloody* Mary pom pom pom . . .' Once again he was startled and bemused by himself.

Dear Sylvia, [he resisted the temptation to add 'or whatever your name is']

I'm sorry to say that I have decided . . .

After typing this he sat for a full ten minutes, wondering if – and what – he had in fact decided. Keep it brief, he thought. Brief and to the point. Feeling stronger, he continued,

. . . to break off our engagement. I do not feel it is right. Things have moved too fast and I am not ready to remarry. I do not see this changing in the near future. I think it best that we do not see each other again.

My sincere apologies and good wishes for your future,
George Baxter

He wondered about asking her to return the several guineas' worth of engagement ring for which he had forked out, but decided against it. It seemed small-minded.

He was on edge all that day, thinking Sylvia might turn up at the house. That evening, to be on the safe side, he took himself off to the Barley Mow. This did not turn out to be especially soothing to his nerves. On his way in he met John Wylde coming out. There were exchanges of 'How do?' and 'Evening, John!' which seemed to satisfy the demands of social engagement on that front. But a fearsome sight met him behind the bar: not only Glowering Brenda, but beside her, wearing a genetically similar scowl, stood Sharon. Even more startling, Sharon was wearing a straight purple frock, which as well as fitting tightly as skin over her considerable frontage, was low cut and sleeveless, revealing her candle-white arms and cleavage in startling quantities.

'Oh, er, hello Sharon.' He nodded in the mother's direction and continued breezily, 'Didn't know you had a job here as well.'

Before Sharon could get a word out, George found himself assailed from along the bar.

'Eve'nin, Mr Baxter! Come for a noice point, have you?'

On a stool at the end of the bar from where he could ogle Sharon with doggy devotion, was Kevin. Sharon cast him a look both withering and glum as she pulled George's pint. Kevin brightened even further.

Having returned Kevin's salutations and paid for his pint, George retreated, grateful that Bill and Roy, his drinking mates, were there to regale him with dilemmas involving engine batteries and the storage of onions. Hot news was that someone had stolen Graham Turner's car. He never seemed to have much luck, it was concluded.

George sank into the comforting pond of pub talk, amid the smells of bitter and cigarettes, the bursts of sudden laughter.

He went several nights in a row, just in case. And then a letter arrived from Sylvia. George found himself feeling gratified that she had had to fork out for a stamp. It contained, in a looping hand, two sides of invective: ' . . . heartbroken . . . Such humiliation . . . never been treated . . . not the person I thought you . . . gentleman . . . in reality . . . scheming bastard . . . devastated . . . mother . . . shock . . . endangered her health . . .' That was just the first page. He stopped reading. He noticed there was no mention of the ring. He felt sad and also soiled.

He tore the letter into the tiniest pieces and scattered it on the compost heap.

Gazing out now over the fields, he moved to the lip of the path, from where the land sloped down and away, and lowered himself to sit on the grassy edge. Monty half raised himself to shuffle closer and sit beside him, looking philosophical, or vacant, it was hard to tell, but probably the latter. George sat, sensing that his own expression was probably similar. He heard a vehicle labouring up the road over the downs, a bee's vibration on the pale head of a scabious flower to his left.

The dying beauty all about him only increased the melancholy which had settled in him all this month, however much he kept busy and tried to appear cheerful in front of Vera and the others. They were full of kindness, asking if he was doing all right. He felt sad and ashamed. As a result of trying not to appear as if he felt sad and ashamed, he was being ridiculously cheerful.

Once more he considered flight; just taking off on his own. Last time he had sat on this hillside, though, his outlook had been one of panoramic glory, of him bestriding a backlit, blossoming world where all that he had never had might at last be possible. This time, he visualized himself a lonesome old gent in a squashed trilby, all hope spent, stepping out from some cabbagewater-smelling lodging house, hunched under a doomy sky as he stared over the beating, lead-coloured sea. This not altogether optimistic vision almost brought him to tears.

At least at home I've got plenty to keep me busy, he thought: the business, the garden. But as for women . . . He was filled with a despondency even greater than the one he'd felt at his seaside cabbagewater imaginings.

'Well, Monty . . .' He flapped the dog's ear that was closest to him back and forth in his hand. 'I don't think I'm much of a goer with women, do you? I was aiming a bit high. No – all that's not for me, old boy. It's just going to be you and me from now on. You and me and a few good solid Chippendale chairs. You can always rely on them. What d'you think of that?'

Monty eyed him for a second, looked away with a dispassionate air and continued panting.

SEPTEMBER

Fifteen

1.

The languorous late summer waned. There would not be many days left for trips along the river in *Barchetta*, lounging in the reeds with beer and sandwiches. The garden was full of down-facing rose heads. His crop of potatoes and onions was in sacks in the garage, beans and courgettes, blackcurrants and raspberries all gathered in and apples hanging on the trees. The Virginia creeper leaves splayed across the house and barn were tinged with red.

It was time, George decided, after this month of lugubrious mourning, to Pull Himself Together. Enough 'poor me'. There were things to catch up with.

Rosamund Parker's boxes of stuff, for a start, which had been in the storeroom at the back of the barn for several weeks now. George had despatched Clarence to Mrs Parker's house with the van to pick up 'Mummy's' legacy of items. Curious, he had awaited Clarence's return.

Clarence had climbed down from the cab of the van, as inscrutably sour-looking as ever.

'Well, Clarence – get on all right? Nice lady, Mrs Parker, isn't she?'

Clarence, not meeting his eye, walked round to the side of the van and emitted a sound that was somewhere between

'*Ummm*' and '*Phwoor*', followed by prolonged throat-clearing. That was all George managed to get out of him on the subject of his visit to Rotherfield Peppard, though he couldn't help observing that since then Clarence had been looking oddly cheerful, even had a spring in his step.

When Vera came in to work on George's first pulled-together morning – a Wednesday as it happened and a Sharon-less day – he eyed her carefully for signs of strain or misery. Had he missed difficulties between her and Alan, in his own self-absorption? She arrived with her basket, wearing a pale green dress with white spots and white heels, her hair neat and freshly 'done'. She seemed happy enough, he thought.

She appeared to have forgotten to bring the radio and there was a friendly silence in the kitchen as they made their first morning cuppa, Monty snoozing on his bed. Then both went to talk at once. Each stopped, laughed.

'Ladies first,' George said.

'No – you're the boss.' Vera grinned.

How nice she was, George thought again, how cheering with those gappy teeth and nose that wrinkled when she smiled.

'Well, all I was going to say was . . .' He paused, fiddling with a silver teaspoon. He felt fluttery with nerves, almost as if about to ask her for a date. 'I've been thinking, Vera – about the business. Bit of a fresh start after all that's happened and so on . . .' He looked down at his shoes, clearing his throat.

Vera listened from the other side of the table, across the mugs.

'What I was going to propose is that we put your position here on a more formal footing. I'd like to make you manager. Properly. A pay rise and so on, of course . . .'

Vera's reaction took him quite by surprise.

'Oh, Mr Baxter!' She was all blushes. She fanned her face with one hand and had come over tearful as well. She burrowed in her basket for a hanky.

'I'm sorry,' he said, perturbed. 'I didn't mean to . . .'

'No,' she said, muffled, from behind a white square of cotton. 'It's –' She gave her nose a forceful blow. 'I'm . . . I'd be ever so chuffed, if only . . . I mean . . .' Suddenly, she smiled. 'D'you really think I could?'

'Well yes, of course,' he said. 'You're doing it anyway, aren't you?'

Vera's face sobered. The kettle boiled and she fetched it to fill the teapot for them and for the men in the barn. She returned the kettle to the hob and stood across the table from him again, her hand on the milk bottle.

'All I was going to say when I came in was, I've seen this little bit of training I could do in book-keeping – over in Didcot. It's not much, but it might help.'

'Well that's a splendid idea,' George urged her. 'Though you don't really need it, Vera. You've got on top of things very well as it is.'

'I'd like to.' She poured milk into the mugs, seeming deflated. There was a silence before she looked up at him again. 'I think we'd better leave it there for now, Mr B. Alan being the way he is. Me being sort of, you know, promoted like that, I mean – I don't think he'd like it. It's . . .' She shrugged. 'Just the way he is.'

'I see.' George thought he saw tears in Vera's eyes, but she turned away, reaching for the tray. 'Well – as you like, Vera. The offer's there. You let me know if you change your mind, won't you?'

On her way out with the drinks, she turned again. 'Oh – by the way, that Dr Hargreaves' secretary telephoned again. And Lady Byngh . . .'

'Oh?' George said warily, dreading the thought of another visit to Nicotine Towers.

'She was quite chatty actually,' Vera reported. 'Evidently the police have found her dining chairs.'

'Really?' A memory of the heaped table at Greenburton House came to him, the musty, dust-coated clutter of it all. Fine dining did not seem to feature in the Byngh household. Or fine anything for that matter. 'Well, good.'

'She said that the old dear who lives with her has broken her wrist.'

'Can't say I'm surprised.'

'And the nephew, was it . . . ?'

'Nevew,' he mimicked. Vera giggled.

'He was pleased with the present, she said.'

'Oh – good.' He did feel pleased. It had mattered to the old girl, he could see. Not that she was *that* old, he corrected himself. About his own age in fact. He was relieved. Perhaps now she'd stop keeping on about her blasted . . .

'And she said was there any sign of her Hepplewhite yet?'

George groaned.

2.

Several days passed. Vera said nothing more about her possible new job title and George, unsure of the fragile checks and balances of the Day household, did not like to raise it.

He flung himself into practical things, avoiding the whirlpools of quiet reflection that could drag him down into longing and self-pity. Dead-heading the roses was soothing. And he cleared out his office, destroying old ledgers and receipts that had sat dustily unheeded on the shelves for years. During the process, once more he came across the newspaper cutting of the trade fair in Buenos Aires. He stared at it, a surge of shameful sensations inside him. He separated it from the other sheet of paper and tore it up, adding it to the pile of waste paper. The picture of the Allodola Venus on her rearing horse he propped on his desk.

'For old times' sake.' He leaned down and peered at her, remembering the visceral reaction he had experienced that time he saw her, at the extraordinary perfection of the craftsmanship, her beauty, almost as if he was in the presence of something holy.

'Where are you?' he whispered. 'Where did you go?'

'What's that?' Vera asked, later. He told her the story as she gazed at the grainy picture.

'She does look lovely,' she said, propping Venus back on the desk. 'So – did you tell anyone? That the other one's in Argentina?'

'Well, no – apart from Joe and Walter Black, but they've both passed on now. Who would I tell?'

'Funny really,' she said. 'You're the only one who knows, then.'

'Yes, I suppose I am,' he agreed. 'Although he's still only half as good without her. They were always meant to be a pair.'

Mrs Parker's boxes were another task facing him, but he looked over them, stacked in the store at the back of the workshop, with a sense of defeat. He couldn't face beginning on it. One day when it was fine, he thought, he'd get Kevin to sort through them.

Overall he had a feeling of his days being at a halt, stalled, while life swirled on around him and without him.

Monty moulted copiously; Clarence announced, with aberrant glee, that he was 'taking the old girl away' for the weekend. It was his and Edith's ruby anniversary.

'I'm surprised he even knows what that is,' Vera commented.

And one morning, as George walked round the side of the house, he interrupted two figures perched on the low wall, shrouded by the heads of pink Persian roses, deep in . . . Deep in Kevin talking. He had his back to George as he approached.

'. . . so it all depends, see, on the firing – how hot you do it. With this one I'm on about, it's silicon paste – that's got clay in and white quartzose sand – and if you get it really hot it goes translucent . . .'

Sharon was half turned to face Kevin, her eyes like huge coals in her pasty face, gazing at him with every appearance of raptness, mouth hanging a little open. It was she who caught sight of George. Kevin, seeing her eyes focus behind him, turned.

'Hello! Er, jolly good – carry on!' George said, hurrying round to the back door.

Amazing, he thought. Kevin seemed to be in the process of learning Jacquemart's book off by heart. He grinned to himself.

'Mr Baxter?' Vera came out of the kitchen. She sounded apprehensive until she saw his expression, which made her smile as well. 'What's tickling you?'

'Oh – Kevin's out there wittering on about pots and Sharon's lapping it all up as if it's the most enthralling thing she's ever heard.'

'P'raps it is,' Vera laughed. 'Amazing what a girl'll sit through though, isn't it?' She became serious again. 'Can I have a quick word?'

This sounded serious. They went into the office. George sat down and turned the chair to face Vera.

'I've been thinking, Mr Baxter, about what you said – me being manager and that.'

'Yes, I see,' George said, aiming to sound neutral. She was going to turn it down, he thought – Alan playing up, wife getting ideas above herself. He found himself disappointed.

Vera clasped her hands in front of her and spoke in a calm, considered way.

'I haven't said anything to Alan yet, not as such. If I said yes, just like that, I know he'd feel as if you'd put me above him in some way. It's his pride, you see. He's a man, and, well – you know . . . Anyway, I've thought of a way round it, if you were to agree.'

George waited.

'Thing is, I think if you were to give Alan a sort of title as well, it might work all right.'

George was nonplussed. What did she have in mind? *Sir* Alan?

'If you gave everyone a name for their job – say for Alan, Head Restorer, or Clarence could be Head Upholsterer and French Polisher.'

'Oh, I *see*.'

At first sight this seemed to George absurd, especially as they were the only staff in the place. Head of what? But he realized Vera was far more likely to have any idea of whether this would work or not. With a faint smile, he said, 'What about Kevin?'

'Oh . . .' Vera's face relaxed. 'We can think of something to call him. He's apprenticed under Alan so you could call him Apprentice Furniture Restorer or something like that. Something that made him under Alan – Alan would like that, I know he would!'

George found himself laughing at her enthusiasm. 'So – you think we might get away with it then?'

Vera beamed back. 'I think we might.'

Within a couple of days, everyone was settled. Even Clarence, to George's surprise, seemed honoured to have a title bestowed upon him. He stood tall.

'Head Upholsterer and French Polisher,' he repeated in his creaking voice, trying out the words by which he had informally described his work for decades. 'Edith'll like that, I reckon.'

Alan greeted the news with bashful pride, as if it was an accolade long deserved.

'Yes,' he said, pulling his shoulders back. 'That's me. That'll do nicely, thank you.'

Kevin seemed less bothered than anyone else, since he already knew he was an apprentice.

Vera's elevation to Manager passed almost without comment.

3.

A few days later, George slowed the van just past the end of a narrow side road and reversed into it.

'Where the hell is this damn place?' he muttered, swinging the vehicle back the way he had come. He had been chasing to and fro along these lanes in the Chilterns, trying to find the place for his final call that day. By now he had got to the point where he would rather have searched out a pub and a nice pint than this blasted place.

Before he'd set off in the morning for a day out, visiting other dealers in the area, Vera had come to him with another telephone message.

'Dr Hargreaves is going to be at the farm all this week apparently – it would be a good day to call on him. It's his mother's place evidently – she must've died. Toke's Farm, it's called.'

Seeing the location, across the toll bridge from Pangbourne, up Whitchurch Hill and beyond, he decided to leave it until last. Now he was cursing having had to come here at all.

His spirits had sunk gradually all day, after an optimistic beginning. There had been several misty-moisty days indicating that summer was truly in its dying throes. Today, once again, the sun was shining with a benign autumn richness. If the leaves were beginning to turn, preparing, cell by cell, to shrivel and die, it was imperceptible today. There was a vivid warmth to everything, the trees and hedges a thorough green, sky blue as blue, hopping rooks a shiny ink-black, everything sharply outlined and clear.

He had driven in a country-lane loop, first to a call at Abingdon, then up to Oxford and back to Dorchester, where he knew another front-room dealer called Ernie Greaves, who was always happy to share a pint or two in the White Hart at lunchtime. Ernie was a cheerful, pink-faced man with endearingly unsteady jowls which always reminded George of Monty. Ernie, being an optimist, usually made you feel better. But today, by the time Ernie had chuntered on about his wife, his elder daughter and her husband and sons, George left Dorchester feeling dragged low by the fresh confirmation of his own aloneness. No brothers and sisters, no wife, no children. And, despite numerous women in his life, still no one to call his own.

If he were someone else who he knew, he would feel sorry for him.

After lunch he went to Henley, then Reading. He had a satisfying collection of new stock filling up the van. Rolled in protective cloths in the footwell were a couple of Empire-period ormolu and bronze candlesticks and a blue-coated Toby jug with – a rare thing – its lid. In the back were a selection of stools, a couple of bookshelves which were guaranteed to sell, some brass hunting horns and a coal scuttle and fire irons. In Oxford he found an ornately carved Armada chest, which it had taken two of them to lift onto the van. And last of all, he had loaded up a set of mahogany Chippendale chairs and a good mahogany dining table. It was easy to transport as it separated into two parts, each supported by a pedestal leg with an extending leaf which could be fixed between the two.

From a business point of view it had been an excellent day. But as he rolled along through Warborough and Nettlebed the beauty of the day seemed to mock him. The old longing was upon him: a physical ache of need to be held and comforted while at the same time feeling his own sense of unworthiness. He felt like letting out Monty-ish howls.

'Where's my girl?' he wondered out loud. 'The girl for me? Where oh where can she be?'

As he came to pay at the toll bridge, he realized he was visibly muttering. The girl in the booth looked warily at him. If only he had brought Monty with him, he thought. At least then his disconsolate mutterings would not seem so deranged.

'For heaven's sake,' he lectured himself as the van climbed the hill, 'snap out of it, you miserable old sod.'

After another few laps of the hillside lanes on the north bank of the Thames, he at last spotted a track off to the left that he had missed when driving the other way. Coming from this direction there was a visible signpost, black letters on white, though it was snarled up with ivy and brambles: TOKE'S FARM.

The van bumped along a track clogged at the sides with nettles, brambles and overgrown hawthorn hedges which scratched against the sides of the van. George wondered about his suspension and grumbled that this Dr Hargreaves or his wife or whoever was there had better have something worth selling after all this.

Farm buildings came into view. Just as he neared the gate, he saw another sign, a long varnished wooden thing like a banner to the left of the road, with black lettering stained on it:

Come unto me, all ye that labour and are heavy laden,
and I will give you rest.

Oh marvellous, he thought. Bonkers as well as miles from anywhere.

He drove in through the open gate and braked at the side of a brick and timber barn and behind a bottle-green Volkswagen Beetle. Did this belong to Dr Hargreaves? It seemed an unlikely vehicle. For a moment, once he switched off the engine, there was absolute silence. As he opened the door and slid out, the barking began and three black and white springer spaniels came tearing towards him from somewhere across the yard.

'Hey there,' he said, not worried by them at all. They were all wagging tails and happy leaping at his legs. 'Now, now – there's no need to make such a racket, is there?'

Apparently satisfied by this, they all rushed off, back the way they had come. George straightened up in the easeful warmth and strolled across the yard. There was a shimmer of gnats in the air and farm smells of manure and musty barns. He could hear the dogs yapping in the distance.

The farmyard was deeply rutted, potholed and scattered with dusty, ancient-looking straw. The place needed a damn good sweep. The gabled farmhouse was to his right and around the yard were outbuildings, stables and storage rooms, all in mellow brick. A heavy-looking iron trough containing green water stood along the side of one of the barns. Everything looked ramshackle, nettles and weeds sprouting from the foot of walls. A buddleia was growing at an angle out of the farmhouse chimney stack and weeds poked out of gutters. He did not trouble himself to roll his sleeves down and look formal. This was a farm after all.

The dogs had gone quiet, but after a moment he thought he heard other sounds and a voice in the distance. He moved forward a few steps and waited.

She came round the corner of a building, from what must have been a paddock. His eyes stretched wider at the sight moving towards him. The sheer loveliness of her! She was right in every detail as she walked across the yard: long-legged, hair a sleek brown, a soft, mealy-coloured muzzle, those extended ears held at an alert angle and soulful eyes looking out with a gentle, enquiring expression. There she was. He was quite sure, in that moment, that she recognized him.

'Lottie?' His voice came out huskily.

'Actually, this one's called Minnie, though I agree, Lottie would suit her even better.'

George now took in the fact that, holding the rein of the mule's halter was a female, who he took to be some sort of stable hand. She was tall and most generously built, he noted, with a round, open, pink-cheeked face and wide grey eyes. The eyes held a frankly mischievous expression. Her hair – long and coiled back into some chaotic wispy arrangement – was brown, but the streaks of grey in it did not escape him. She was wearing the most enormous pair of dung-coloured slacks – army surplus, he wondered? – and a khaki short-sleeved shirt with streaks of mud and grot all over it. The body round which all this was wrapped was magnificently strong-looking and well made.

'Are you the chap who's come to rescue me from this blasted house?' she said, advancing closer with the mule in tow. The spaniels dashed here and there around her. She extended her hand towards him, then withdrew it for a moment to examine her palm before holding it out again. 'It's all right. Safe to shake. Dr Hargreaves.'

Dazed, George felt his hand clasped in a strong grip. During this bracing handshake he admitted to being George Baxter who had come about the house sale.

'I don't quite . . .' He stumbled on. 'You mean, *you're* Dr Hargreaves? My manager gave me to understand that . . .'

'I was a chap? Not to worry – happens all the time. The secretary rang from the practice in Basingstoke. You find that however much she says "she" people still hear "he" when they think of a doctor. Anyway . . .' She turned to the house. 'This was all my mother's. She died a little while back. Good sort in her way, but a complete crank, especially after she was widowed. It takes some women that way. She's been rescuing donkeys lately – there's a field full of the little buggers behind there.'

George followed the gesture of an impressively sculpted arm, as did the spaniels, seeming hopeful that she was throwing something for them. They looked mildly cheated as she lowered it again.

'She started taking on the poor little beasts of burden and gradually people got to know. They send them to her. But now – what in heaven's name am I supposed to do with eleven donkeys at my time of life? Well, at any time, come to that.' She was beginning to sound heated. 'Never mind all the rest of the clutter in there.' She patted the creature beside her. 'Minnie's the only mule.' George felt her eyeing him with amused curiosity. 'You seem rather taken with her. Who's Lottie?'

'I was placed with a mule train during the war – just for a short time. Monte Cassino.' He explained what had happened to Lottie. To his surprise, the words fell out of him with ease. But even speaking about it in brief like that, he felt a raw tightness at the back of his throat, as if every grief and longing in him must come pouring out and for which this glorious woman, who he had only just met, must be the receptacle.

Dr Hargreaves listened. Her eyes filled with a sympathy that softened her face.

'Brutal,' she said. 'Brutal times.'

'Yes,' he agreed. 'And these innocent creatures in the middle of it.' He stroked Minnie's nose, its warm softness a memory, vivid and comforting.

'Oh I'm not sure she's that innocent.' Dr Hargreaves patted the mule's neck. 'She's got a naughty sense of humour this one. Now look,' she went on, business-like. 'I can give you a quick walk round in the house but we can't possibly settle everything today. There's a lot of stuff. I don't know about you, but I'm gasping for a cup of tea. How about we have one before we get started? We might as well stay out here. The house is demoralizing. I'll just go and return Minnie to the paddock as you're here – thought I'd groom her but it can wait. Then I'll get the kettle on.'

George gave Minnie a farewell pat, then stood watching, hands in pockets. The mule held her ears at a relaxed half-mast now as she walked beside this powerfully built woman. After a moment George realized he was standing there with his mouth open.

*

Inspiration seized him as Dr Hargreaves returned from the paddock and strode back into the house, the dogs at her heels. Hurrying to the Morris, he let the back down and pulled out two of the spare rolled offcuts of carpet that he carried to cushion furniture stacked in the back. He laid them side by crimson side over the clearest patch of ground he could find in the sunlit yard, stamping them flat. He was impishly excited now. Moving at speed, he jumped up into the back, thanking high heaven he had bought the Armada chest first rather than last so that it was not in the way, and lugged out the two sections of table. He felt a great surge of energy.

My strength is as the strength of ten . . . Schoolroom poetry floated across his mind. *Because* . . . *My heart is pure?* No – he was no Sir Galahad. He felt strong because of her.

Her!

By the time his unexpected hostess emerged from the house carrying a tray, George was settled with a nonchalant air (though quietly sweating) on one of two Chippendale dining chairs which he had carried, half running, to set on the carpet beside the mahogany dining table, its two ends now bracketed together. On the table, carefully spaced, were the two bronze and ormolu candlesticks, at the base of each, a bronze sphinx.

Dr Hargreaves was already walking at speed when she left the house, surrounded by spaniels. He watched her face register the scene before her. She stopped; her feet, in their heavy leather boots, firmly side by side.

'What on *earth*?'

She put her head back and loud, unrestrained, and from George's point of view highly appealing gurgles of laughter tumbled out of her. She straightened up, took another look and started laughing again.

'What a *marvellous* surprise,' she said, bringing the tray over. She laid it on the table: a big crock teapot under a yellow knitted cosy, white mugs and a slab of dark, treacly cake. 'It's all right – there's a mat under the pot, won't do any harm,' she said. 'What a lunatic, mad hatter's tea party!'

George beamed at her. He loved having caused such delight.

She stood back and chuckled again, cheeks round and pink, her face more alive, George thought, than any he had ever seen. Oh this woman – what a woman! He was seized by an excitement he had never felt before.

'Do you always dine in style like this when you're on the road?' she asked, chuckling again as she sat down on the other chair. Her khaki-encased thighs spread across the seat.

George tried not to stare. She was a mess; filthy, dishevelled and utterly entrancing.

'No.' He chuckled. 'Not often anyway. I thought we might as well be comfortable.'

'I can't tell you how welcome this is,' she said, lifting the lid of the teapot to stir its insides. 'The house is . . .' She put the lid back on and sighed. 'It's a tip – but so austere as well. My mother lived like a Puritan. Even the mattresses seem to be purgatorially thin. She was completely outward directed, never thought of her own comfort at all. Which sounds unselfish but that's not quite how it was – not if you were in her family. Sorry – mustn't start. But she was thoroughly exasperating at times.' She frowned, pouring the tea and handed him a cup and saucer, white with a silver rim.

George held it up. 'Is this . . . ?' He peered under the saucer. 'Lenox?'

'Is it?' Dr Hargreaves said. He thought she looked impressed. 'No idea. I know it's American. Wedding present I think, originally.'

'Ah,' George said, thinking, 1920s.

'Sugar, Mr . . . ?'

He reached to take the sugar bowl from her. 'Thanks. Baxter – but do call me George.'

'Yes of course. And my name's Elizabeth. Cake? Shop I'm afraid – ginger, I think. I don't really bake. Never seem to have time.'

'I don't suppose you do,' he said, though barely able to imagine her life.

He sat back, an arm hanging down, relaxed. One of the dogs pushed its nose into his half-curled hand.

'Hello.' He patted it. 'These your mother's as well?'

Elizabeth rolled her eyes. 'Yes.'

'Good job I didn't bring my dog.'

'Which is?'

'Basset hound. A large male.'

'Ah – very entertaining.'

'Yes – he's a good old boy.'

Elizabeth Hargreaves gave him one of her direct looks for a moment, as if sizing him up. She was forthright even in the way she looked at you with those lively grey eyes. George wondered if he ought to find her terrifying, but did not, somehow. She sank back into her chair.

'These are comfortable, for upright chairs,' she said.

'Yes. Nicely designed,' he agreed.

The dogs all hovered close by, alert to the presence of cake. The way he had arranged the table meant they were facing the house. George tried to concentrate on the view before him. Glimpses of Elizabeth were so diverting that for caution's sake, he realized he would be better off looking elsewhere. She took several gulps of tea and a bite of cake, seemed to relax even further and gave a satisfied sigh.

'Well,' she said. 'This is definitely the most high-class picnic I've ever had.'

4.

Much later he drove home in the balmy night. There was a half-moon hanging. Chalk tracks leading off the road glowed white against the darker vegetation. There was a still, expectant feel to the air as if something was due to happen, as on Christmas Eve.

Vera would have fed Monty, he knew. He had had no supper himself, nothing since that sticky chunk of cake. But at this moment he was in such a state of bejanglement that he felt he would never need to eat again.

He had spent four hours in the company of Elizabeth Hargreaves, only the last part, briefly, engaged in the original purpose of the visit – looking round the house. He knew two things for certain. One was that he was well advanced in the process of being utterly, overwhelmingly, bowled over.

The other was that Elizabeth, unmarried – 'I've never turned out to be the marrying kind' – difficult (according to 'Mother', RIP) and touchily independent, had cleared away the teacups and brought out a bottle of red wine and two glasses and had been in no apparent hurry for him to leave.

'Oh – I tell you what there is in the house . . .' She set the glasses down, ran in, then out again with two candles and a box of matches. 'All right to use those?' She nodded at the candlesticks.

'Of course,' he said. 'That's what they're for.'

The wicks lit easily, flames tall in the still evening. George watched her face as they talked. Elizabeth was not young. He would not kid himself again. There was grey in her hair, deep laughter lines round her eyes, he could see. But there was such energy. There was life in abundance.

'I've got this two-week break,' she said, pouring wine. 'To sort this place out so far as I can. And then I'll be back at work. But at least I can try and make it some sort of a holiday. Here we are – cheers!'

Conversation had flowed from the start. It was extraordinary, he thought. Elizabeth had said, 'So, do tell me about yourself.' The first thing he had come out with was, 'Well – my mother died when I was four years old.' The rose looked back at him through the latticed school window just for a second, the kind, pink watchfulness of it, his infant consolation. As the sun sank and the light turned orange then edged into grey, he talked about his childhood, the school and the war and Win. Elizabeth listened. She did not make him feel he was talking too much, though now, he thought, surely he had been. Why had he said all those things? Why plunge in like that?

He had forgotten to be in awe of her because of the way she listened as if it was important. In the dusk, she told him that her father had been a vicar, 'a decent soul', as she put it. Her elder brother was killed at Anzio and the other was a vet who lived in Orkney.

'So there's no one else to see to all this.' She waved a hand towards the farmhouse. 'My mother wasn't easy.' Her tone stiffened as she spoke of her. 'She had what I think of as vicar's wife syndrome – a compulsion to keep trying to do good even when it drives everyone else round the bend. In fact I think –' She considered for a moment. 'I don't think she liked herself very much, underneath it all. It was a way of trying to compensate, to prove she was useful in some way.' Elizabeth took a sip of wine. 'All I can say is, Lord protect us from people who try too hard to be good!'

'Isn't that what you do – good?'

Elizabeth twisted her wine glass back and forth by its stem as it rested on the table. She spoke without looking at him.

'I was in London through the war. I didn't qualify until part way through. Then, when I'd trained to be a GP and they were asking for people to work in the so-called overspill towns, I thought, that's where I'll go. It's unfashionable, but my goodness – necessary. There aren't nearly enough women doctors. Some of the chaps are very good, of course. But others are patronizing and obtuse beyond belief. A patient from our practice died recently of cancer. One of my colleagues had told her she was imagining the symptoms. You know – the way you do go round imagining that you're in extreme pain.'

The anger was unmistakable, despite her measured tone. He could listen to her forever, he thought. Her voice was smooth, strong. Time picked up speed and charged past. Darkness fell, bringing night smells, the half-moon, the flit of bats between the house and barns. One of the donkeys let out a creaking bray, just once, and they laughed.

As they finally made their way inside to take a now rather tipsy look at the house and its contents, Elizabeth said, 'So – do you always go out equipped to set up an impromptu dining room wherever you go?'

George laughed. He was full of a sense of carefree euphoria. He did not care if he stayed out all night. Even walking beside this tall, rumly dressed, deliciously shaped woman in the pale silver light felt like one of the most exciting things he had ever done.

'I'd been out buying – around the area. It's something I do, every week or two.'

'How fascinating,' she said. 'And how lovely, to spend your life surrounded by beautiful things.'

'Your mother had beautiful things.'

Elizabeth considered. 'Well a few, yes she did – but she was faddy. She was making a collection of antiques at one time. As soon as she got involved with the donkeys, she dropped all that – hardly seemed to give it a thought later on.' She looked into his face. 'I should love to come and see your business.'

'Oh,' he said. 'You must.' He hoped he spoke with more restraint than he felt.

By the time he had walked round the interior of the old farmhouse, a turmoil of papery clutter and general neglect amidst which he spotted one or two pieces of furniture of genuine value, he knew he had to see this woman again, *had* to. As soon as possible. He would come back tomorrow, he promised. Then he could make a proper valuation in daylight.

'Well there's no mad rush,' she said. 'As I say, I shall be here for two weeks . . .'

That night, he could barely be bothered to sleep.

5.

'I thought you sorted all that out yesterday?' Vera said, when he announced that he would have to spend a few hours at Toke's Farm.

'I made a start.' He was opening and closing drawers in the office desk as if distractedly in search of something but in fact to avoid Vera's gimlet eye. 'It's chaos over there.'

'What're you looking for?' Vera asked, with an edge of severity.

'I . . . er . . .' He fumbled in the top drawer before closing it again.

'Kevin's keeping on about those boxes,' she said. 'Did you say you wanted him to sort them out?'

'I . . . Yes.' He was already going out of the door. 'Not today. We'll get round to it. Must be off.'

This time he took the car. The springer spaniels greeted him like an old friend. Looking round Toke's farmyard as he walked to the house, it seemed even more neglected and mouldering in hard, revealing daylight. A good many tiles were missing from the various roofs.

He paused at the door for a moment, felt the movement of his blood. Like a stag, he thought. A stallion. Manly blood. Oh for heaven's *sake*, man, just get on with it.

He rapped on the door. *Now she'll come. Now: her footsteps behind the door, her face, her arms, the whole of her . . .*

The door swung back. Her smile went through him. She was more than he remembered, and taller.

She was wearing a frock; primrose yellow dotted with blue flower sprigs. The belted waist emphasized her magnificent proportions. On her wide, strong-looking feet were brown leather sandals. She exuded health and capability.

'You're very prompt.'

'Yes . . .' He remembered to inhale. 'I . . .'

She was already turning away.

'Cup of coffee?'

They spent so long talking over coffee and biscuits – she was as intrigued by his expertise as he was by hers – that it was a good while before they got started.

'Come on,' she said at last. 'We'd better get on with something. The dresser in the dining room, you said?'

It was an enormous thing, oak, intricately carved. It was also stuffed full and piled with books, papers, framed photographs, all of which so far as he could see were of landscapes, not people, except one that was of a black Labrador.

'It'll take me the best part of a fortnight just to clear this thing out,' Elizabeth said. 'I mean *look* at it!'

'Umm . . .' George pretended to consider it seriously. 'For all you know, there might be a whole family of passing pedlars living in there.'

Elizabeth glanced at him. She laughed. He loved the unrestrained gurgle of it.

'Joke not – anything's possible in this place.'

'Look – I'll take that once you've emptied it. I can sell it for you. Let me go and look at the other things. There was that desk upstairs.'

There were not many items of any real value, he realized, seeing the furniture in daylight now. A mahogany kneehole desk, the surface of which would need a lot of succour from Clarence and a plain oak commode with the ceramic bowl still in place. He wanted to find more things, to help Elizabeth, but the other furniture was mostly late Victorian and of no use to him.

However, poking about in one of the back rooms downstairs, its filthy window making what was in fact a day of cheery sunlight seem one of thin grey cloud, he saw something draped with a blue chenille cloth. On top was a rough wooden box containing clothes pegs. Pegs and cloth removed, he bent over. This was more like it.

It was a moment before he realized Elizabeth was watching him from the doorway.

'Found something?'

He straightened up. 'Nice little piece – look. It's a *torchère* – mahogany. Chippendale, I'd say.'

Elizabeth frowned. 'A what? I remember it – I always thought it was a side table.'

George dusted it with the end of the chenille cloth. The circular top was edged with a brass inlaid gallery, like an ornate little fence around it.

'A stand for a light – candle usually. Cabriole legs – very elegant. I'd say George the Second. I was just checking it over because there was a fashion in the twenties for putting them together from the foot posts of beds. Usually an eighteenth-century bed – they'd put a top on it and some tripod feet and off you go. But this is a genuine one – only thing is, it would be worth more as a pair.' For a second, Venus trotted through his mind again.

'Oh!' Elizabeth seemed excited. 'There's another one upstairs – stuck away somewhere. How exciting!'

They beamed at each other.

'I'll show you,' she said. 'But what I came to ask was . . .' She spoke with a slow, mock seriousness. 'Whether you might feel obliged, by the sheer weight of the job, to stop and have some bread and cheese with me?'

'I think,' he replied, also very serious, 'I might.'

They also felt obliged to finish off the remaining wine from the night before and, because there was so little, to open another bottle because a half a glass each seemed neither here nor there. Lunch went on rather. They were still seated at three o'clock, chattering about her patients, his boat, the army.

'I really must get going,' George said, after a comfortable few moments of silence. Less comfortable was the thought of what Vera was going to say when he got back.

'Before you do, let me show you the rest of the mokes,' Elizabeth said. 'And you can say hello to Lottie.'

'Minnie, I thought you said.' He followed her across the yard.

Elizabeth turned, eyes mischievous. 'I don't really think she'll mind, do you?'

They stood at the gate. Only when he looked across the field did it occur to him that this was the place he had glimpsed the other day, from the road at the far side. Donkeys – he hadn't been hallucinating, he realized, now he could see it all from this angle. In fact he seemed to be seeing his whole life from a new angle.

Clouds slid across the sun; its brightness came and went. Elizabeth leaned her elbows on the bleached wood, hands pressed to her cheeks. Her gaze took in the field, the long-eared creatures in varying shades of brown, dotted across it.

In two weeks she'll be gone, he thought. His chest twinged at the thought.

'There's a woman nearby,' she said, 'less than a mile away, who was a friend of mother's. She'll keep an eye on these little chaps. And she'll have the dogs. For a while. But they'll have to go in the end.' She swept a hand in front of her. 'What do I do with them?'

'Quite a plateful she's left you with,' he remarked. 'On top of everything else.'

'Yes,' she said, still staring ahead.

He was about to apologize, feeling he had been rude about her dead mother, but she turned to him, her expression vulnerable.

'Thanks. That's . . . I've got no one else to talk to about it all really. Mother never discussed her plans with me. She wasn't the sort. Couldn't admit any kind of weakness – such as being mortal like anyone else. We were never close anyway.' She looked across at the donkeys again, but he caught a second of the hurt girl in her eyes. 'She got on better with animals.'

6.

When he returned the next morning, the second *torchère* came to light in the upstairs bathroom, a dank room smelling of mouldy linoleum. This time it was draped in a length of once-white muslin on which sat a dying spider plant. When he pointed it out to Elizabeth, she burst out laughing.

'I knew I'd seen it somewhere,' she said. 'Oh she really was the end – and it's so damp in here. It can't have done it any good!'

In her laughter, once again he thought he could hear other emotions, waiting to catch like tinder. He detected the gloss of tears in her eyes and looked away, busied himself with writing a label, so as not to embarrass her. For all her brisk toughness, these days of sorting were taking their toll on her.

He progressed around the house, examining things, jotting notes, tying on a label here and there – making, in fact, a huge meal out of a job that in most places he would have done in a quarter of the time. Elizabeth was mostly elsewhere, getting on with other things.

Now and then he heard her moving about in the house, or calling to the dogs outside. The sound of her voice made him leave the job he was doing and hurry to the window to see her walking across the yard, often heading towards the stables at the end, still in her sandals. Her voice now felt familiar – more than familiar. It was as if he had heard it within him all his life, or been waiting to hear it. It sent a pulse through him, of rightness, of tenderness, of belonging. He hurried back to work in case she turned and saw him watching.

Later he heard her come upstairs as he was toying with buying the toilet mirror in one of the bedrooms. It was not especially old, but the carved wooden frame was complete and attractive: it would sell. He heard her stop at the door and he turned. She leaned against the doorframe. A wavy lock of hair hung over the left side of her forehead.

For a moment they looked at each other in silence. It was a pause that felt, just for a second, laden in some way. Then, from the paddock, they heard the rasping outburst of a donkey. Both of them smiled.

'Are we winning, d'you think?'

'Yes – we are,' he said. 'I've been through most of the house – if that's all there is?'

'That's really all the furniture,' she said. 'Although there's a whole heap of goodness-knows-what in that barn across there – boxes mainly, I think. You can have a look if you like.'

Anything, he thought, to put off having to leave her.

'Cup of tea?'

'Lovely!' he said jovially. 'I'm afraid I can't provide a table and chairs today.'

'Never mind. We can take a couple out. Hardly up to your standards though.'

He followed her downstairs, intensely aware of everything: the movement of her hips beneath the limp cotton of her dress, the curling wisps of hair gathered at each side of the back of her neck, the lightness he felt, as if he was floating, flying.

At the bottom of the stairs she turned and said, 'Will you stay for supper?'

At once and with a mental apology to Monty, he agreed.

'I'll do the spuds,' he said.

Elizabeth gave him a look. 'I'm impressed.'

'I've had to learn to fend for myself.' He ran water into the old square sink and searched for a sharp knife. Opening a drawer, he found a battered collection of implements and chose the least blunt-looking. 'Well – with Vera's help.'

'She sounds rather a character, this Vera. Is she married?'

'Oh yes – her husband works for me as well.'

'Quite an outfit you've got there.' She opened the packet of sausages and started snipping the twisted membrane between each.

George explained about Vera and Alan. About the pies.

'Ah.' Elizabeth laid the naked sausages on the grill pan. 'So many women with bags of intelligence and not enough to do. I see it all the time. Makes them ill, some of them.'

'She's doing well. The only thing is . . .' Digging the peel from the potatoes with a hopelessly blunt knife, he related his initially unsuccessful attempts to make Vera his manager, until she lit upon the idea of job titles. Elizabeth yelped with laughter at that.

'Oh now there's a woman who's got her head screwed on all right.' She shot the sausages under the grill. 'Sounds wonderful.'

'Why don't you come and meet her? Come and see my place? You said you wanted to.'

Elizabeth turned to look at him. She was solemn, as if something important had been said.

'You're making a proper meal of those potatoes.'

'Blame the knife,' he protested, holding it up.

She looked him in the eye then. He put the knife down. Surprising himself as he did it, he walked round the table and stood in front of her.

After a second's quiet meeting of her gaze, he said, 'My God, my heart's going fit to bust.'

She looked shy, blushing, this woman of his. This wonderful, capable woman who stood before him.

'Mine too,' she said.

Seeing her permission, he reached out, his hand unsteady and gently stroked her cheek. He felt brim-full of all the words that longed to pour out from him, but for the moment he could not begin.

Sixteen

1.

'Come out buying with me, will you – next Monday?' he said as they parted that night.

He did not stay late. That first kiss, standing in her mother's kitchen in the middle of cooking, had taken him so far that there had to be a pulling-away. He felt washed along by a propulsive force. This time it was by the power of his own feelings, not by the will of someone else. It was a place he had never been to before.

Holding her for the first time, the firm loveliness of her, he wanted all of it, now – to have her, to pour out promises of loving her forever. Unlike with Sylvia, there was something deep down that he knew he could trust, as if even in this new, heady place, the ground under his feet was firm. But even so.

Both of them felt the need to draw back, as if alarmed at the rushing speed that was overtaking them. Elizabeth became brisk, brusque almost, for a few moments. But they cooked, singing Louis Armstrong hits, Elizabeth dancing across the kitchen with a plate of singed bangers, singing 'Ain't Misbehavin''. They ate sausage and mash and mustard at the kitchen table, friends at ease, chatting amiably.

Soon afterwards he left, with the invitation for Monday – the sort of measured invitation, he thought afterwards, that you might make to a person who you had not earlier kissed in a way that made your life rock with discovery.

And today was only Tuesday.

He managed to wait until eleven the next morning.

A fine rain was falling and the shop was quiet. All he wanted was Elizabeth. Peering out of the office to check whether Vera was about, he heard no sound and closed the door. Dialling her number like a spy, he glanced round in case anyone was looking. He was surprised at his own force and audacity.

By the third ring his heart was bashing away.

'Dr Hargreaves.' Her voice was clipped, professional. This was frightening.

'Dr Hargreaves?' he said, with exaggerated formality. 'It's Mr Baxter. Chalk Hill Antiques.'

There was a second's pause before he heard a delicious chuckle.

'Is it, now?' Her tone was warm and teasing. He beamed. Had it not been for the curly telephone cord he would have two-stepped round the office. 'And why would you be calling me, sir?'

'Because frankly,' George launched in, nothing ventured, 'the prospect of going through the rest of today – let alone another day – without seeing you is so dismal, that . . . Look, Elizabeth, come over, will you? D'you have time?'

'Of course I've got time,' she retorted. 'Other than the job of clearing up all my mother's bloody mess and worrying about the future of eleven asses, I'm completely at a loose end.'

George grinned, enjoying her voice so much that he forgot to speak.

'Hello? Are you there? What time shall I come, then?'

*

This is love, he thought in a sober, rather worried moment, gazing pointlessly at his print of Canaletto's Doge's Palace.

'Are you with us, Mr Baxter?'

Vera was at the door, frowning. She seemed tetchy this morning, unless he was imagining it.

'Oh – yes! Yes, yes.' He turned, trying to give the impression that he had not just spent who knew how long staring at the wall. 'Why?'

'That Dr Hargreaves seems to have been leading you a proper dance,' she said, reaching for the accounts ledgers on the desk. 'What time did you get in last night?'

'Oh,' he remained vague. 'Not late. Soon after you left.'

'Well the phone kept ringing all afternoon.' She picked up some scraps of paper in the desk and read from them. 'A Mrs Ashbury. I couldn't make her out. Something about a golden angel but she sounded gaga to me – either that or she was in the middle of a sandwich. Then Mrs Chatwin telephoned – you know, the snuff boxes – and some man from I think he said Upper Basildon, Sir somebody. Very cagey, wouldn't say why, but he's going to call back . . . Although come to think of it, he said something about a silver . . . salver? I think it was that. Said it was' – she peered at the scrap paper – 'gadrooned?' Rolling her eyes, she put the notes down with a grumpy shrug. 'Whatever that means. He sounded half-cut as well.'

'Hmmm,' George said. 'Yes. Right.'

Vera sat down at the desk with the accounts and turned to glance up with a look that seemed to cast doubt on what George was still doing there.

'Is that all, Vera? I need to have a word with Clarence – he'll need to transport Dr Hargreaves' furniture.'

'Yes, nothing else,' she said. As he left the room, she added, 'Your dog might like a walk though – with *you*, for a change.'

No, he definitely wasn't imagining it.

All afternoon he kept thinking *she's coming*, his whole body beating with excitement. The only distraction was Kevin, insistent that the day was fine enough to bring Mrs Parker's half-unpacked boxes out from the barn and start rootling around in them. George decided it was safest just to let the boy get on with it if Alan could spare him, and allowed himself to sink into a reverie.

Love, he kept repeating. Love, love. Oh yes indeed.

But other thoughts chilled through him. Two weeks. She was only here for two weeks. *I've never been the marrying kind.* What did this mean? Was she the kind to play with him? See him as a diversion for a week or so? He was not used to women like her. She seemed to like him, but she was so fiercely competent and independent. Did she really see anything in him? Already he could not help himself. All he could do was hope.

The day clouded over gradually but George was too obsessed to notice. When Elizabeth was due, at four o'clock, he hurried upstairs to the bathroom. No good being caught out with a full bladder at the wrong moment. Just as he reached the landing he heard the roar of Elizabeth's green Beetle and Vera's voice down in the hall.

'Typical, isn't it? Quiet as the grave all afternoon and just as we're getting to closing time . . .'

George, trapped in indecision about which forces of nature he should allow to take their course, hovered on the landing. There was a tap on the front door, the light sound of rain as it opened and women's voices. This, he realized, must be what it was like introducing a loved one to your mother. He closed his eyes and waited, as if for an explosion.

'Yes, do come in,' Vera said, without a trace of her former grouchiness. 'Turned wet suddenly, hasn't it?' The door closed. There was a second's pause. 'Can I help you with anything or were you just hoping for a look round?'

'I'm Dr Hargreaves,' Elizabeth said. 'I think you've spoken to one of our secretaries on the telephone.'

There was a pause, which George could only interpret as mystified.

'*You're* Dr Hargreaves?' Vera said. 'Oh. I mean – I thought . . .'

'I was a man?' Elizabeth finished for her. 'Yes, I'm sure – not to worry. You're not the first and I'm sure you won't be the last.'

There was a burst of female laughter. George breathed. He clasped his hands together. It seemed safe to creep into the bathroom.

When he emerged the two of them were still standing in the same spot.

'You must be ever so clever.' Vera's tone was solemn. 'A doctor. I've never met a lady doctor before. And to tell you the truth . . .' She lowered her voice. 'Our Dr Gregory is a nice man really, but there have been times when I could have done without having to go into certain things with him. Especially when Alan – that's my husband – was having problems with his . . .'

George decided it might be time to appear.

'Ah, Dr Hargreaves,' he said from almost the top of the stairs. He was just about to launch into a business-like speech about the collection of things from the farm, when thunderous knocking began on the door.

'Mr Baxter!' They heard Kevin's muffled voice. Vera hurried to open up.

As George reached the ground floor, the door swung open to reveal his Apprentice Furniture Restorer on the step, his face shiny with rain and radiating explosive urgency.

'Look, Mr Baxter!' he cried with no preamble.

He was holding out a small plate which showed unmistakable signs of having been used as a plant holder and was smeared with ashy-looking soil. By the grimy look of Kevin's shirtsleeve he had attempted to clean it off with his cuff.

'What is it, Kevin?' George could feel Elizabeth and Vera watching him.

'This plate – out of them boxes. This is old, Mr Baxter, I know it is. It's Chinese. And *old*.'

George took the plate from him. It was about five inches across with a raised edge divided, flower-petal-like, into curves. Its glaze was heavily crackled and beneath the dirt, the bland, unpromising colour of chicken soup.

'Well . . .' George turned the plate over. There was a Chinese character on the underside, inscrutable to him. He considered it in silence and knew he was out of his depth. 'What makes you think . . . ?'

'It's the feel of it – the crackle. I just *know*,' Kevin insisted. 'Look at it – it's *lustrous*, that is.' With desperate passion he added, 'You've got to believe me, Mr Baxter!'

For want of any other solution, George promised he would take the plate to a specialist he knew in Marlow. At last Kevin and Vera retreated and he and Elizabeth were left alone.

'He seems a bright spark,' she said, looking amused.

'He certainly has his moments,' George said, locking the front door.

'D'you think he's right?'

'I somehow doubt it – but no there's no harm in asking. Anyway – you definitely made Vera's day.' He helped Elizabeth out of her dark blue mac. Beneath, she wore a straight grey skirt and pearly grey blouse. Her hair was pinned back elegantly. 'You look lovely.'

'Oh?' She sounded truly surprised. 'Well – thank you.'

'Now, come on through – there's someone else I want you to meet.'

'Gracious,' Elizabeth said. 'That sounds ominous.'

He led her to the kitchen, lost in rapture. Here she was – in his home!

'Now this,' he said, opening the door, 'is Monty.'

Monty, caught unawares, had been fast asleep on his bed. He raised his head, ears held out at an angle and face squiffy from sleep, as if to say, 'Uhh?' Deciding he had better rise to the occasion since there was a genuine visitor present and not just Vera, he heaved himself to his feet and staggered across the floor.

'Oh my goodness,' Elizabeth laughed in delight. Of course she knew he had a basset hound, but now the full bizarre, stinky reality was before her. 'What an absolutely marvellous dog! Look at the size of those paws!'

She dropped to her knees and nuzzled against Monty's ears, stroking him and sending him into a state of sleepy delirium. This, George decided, was definitely his woman.

2.

They drank tea and once he judged that everyone else would have gone home, he showed her round: the showroom in the house and the barn. At first she said, 'So beautiful,' and 'Lovely,' looking round at the furniture, his arrangement of it, the sheen of wood grain, the colours singing out of china and enamel, the rich upholstery. Yellow roses were still in bloom at the front of the house, but the back was draped in showers of pink and apricot, white and crimson, dripping and radiant. By then Elizabeth had gone quiet, as if in some reverie, but she gasped when they stepped out of the garden door.

'Oh.' She gazed in silence, taking it all in.

He knew in that moment that something had shifted. He had found a way to her, completely. They stood by the door, her blouse spotted with rain after their dash across to the barn. She turned to him, shy and serious.

'How lovely, to know all about this, George. To work with this around you every day. And this . . .' She looked across the garden. 'It's all so astonishingly beautiful, so fine.' She turned to him again. 'You're fine. You're a marvellous man, George.'

He reached for her hand.

*

The bedroom no longer felt like his and Win's, but his alone. The sheets were a clean white space on which he could now write love: the utter, expanding, in-over-the-head sense of it that he felt with Elizabeth. In this new country, all roads opening before him seemed to lead somewhere adventurous and delightful.

Closing the door behind them, he stood before her and she returned his gaze, candid, giving. She looked down, shy suddenly, but with dimples appearing in her cheeks. He saw her then as she might have been as a little girl, pink-cheeked and stolid, with those challenging eyes.

'Don't expect too much, will you?' she said. 'Now I've got to this age, my body looks rather like a bean-bag.'

'Elizabeth.' He put his hands on her shoulders. 'You're just lovely – to me.'

'Ah, well.' She blushed. 'Thank you. But that remains to be seen.'

'Are you, er . . .' He thought of Maggie. 'You know, protected? Taking any of those pills or anything?'

Elizabeth looked at him in astonishment and started laughing so wholeheartedly that she had to sit on the bed.

'And what would you know about those pills, George? No, I'm not on "those pills" – though if I needed to be it would not be difficult. I am a doctor, remember? My dear, how old exactly do you think I am?'

'I don't know.' He really didn't. He had barely considered it. She was just Elizabeth, and that seemed all that was necessary.

She stood up and laid her palms on his chest. Desire coursed through him.

'Tell me your birthday.'

He told her.

'Well,' she grinned. 'There you are – I'm two days older than you.'

'*Are* you?'

'So – over the hill,' she said, with dignity. 'No need to worry about pills.'

Again their eyes met. George pulled her gently into his arms. There she was, the shape of her, his woman, nestling into him. This, this loving touch, this woman, was all he needed. It was desire and tenderness and comfort; it was peace.

'There's no need to worry about anything, my love,' he said.

He linked one hand with hers and they moved towards the bed.

They lay in the darkening room, rain still falling and the scent of roses stealing through the window.

After their lovemaking, so intent and generous and his discovering the wonder of her; after their solemn coming back from this, the communing of their pulses, of mixed sweat and limbs, Elizabeth lay with her face close to his and told him in a sweet, surprised tone that she loved him.

And later, as they lay together, his belly pressed against her back like a protective shell, he said, 'You know, my darling, I've never had this before. Not like this.'

'Me neither.' There was an emphasis, almost a bitterness to her tone. 'I've known men – I won't pretend there haven't been a few. But nothing where I've felt so . . .' She searched for the word. 'Right. Tender. Almost from the beginning.'

'It's a bit like an egg, isn't it?' he said, inspired. 'You get the white, sometimes – or you get the yolk. But you don't get the whole egg very often.'

He felt a giggle pass through her. She wriggled round on to her back and looked up at him with laughing eyes.

'God, this has been quick, hasn't it?' She raised her head and kissed him. 'The whole egg.' She laughed again. 'Yes. But . . .' She leant up on one elbow. 'You do realize this doesn't mean I'm going to marry you or any of that sort of thing?'

A pang. So what did it mean then? He had a momentary kick of rejection, almost of vertigo. *Didn't* this mean marriage? It did for most people. But Elizabeth was not most people.

'Who said anything about marriage?'

'All right.' She lay down again with the air of someone who has made her point.

'By the way,' he added, serious now.

'Umm?'

'Just in case you wanted to know – you don't look in the least like a bean-bag.'

3.

All the time, they were aware of this as a stolen interlude, these days until Elizabeth had to be back in her surgery in Basingstoke.

They could barely stand being apart. They did what they had to do each day – he to run his business, she to sort out Toke's Farm. He did not feel he could desert the business in the daytime, but he promised he would come at the weekend and help her clear the barn. They saw each other every evening. Elizabeth stayed the night, driving off early. Did anyone notice, they wondered? What would people say? Did they care? Not, they decided, much.

It had not remained secret for long.

'I thought she seemed a nice lady,' Vera said, the day after Elizabeth's first visit. 'Fancy her being a doctor! She looks too feminine for that sort of thing.'

George had given what he hoped was an inscrutable smile.

'You like her, don't you, Mr B?' Vera said.

'I, er . . .' He couldn't quite decide where to look.

Vera walked off, laughing.

Within twenty-four hours there was a spate of visits from the Cronies, transparently hoping for a sighting. Rosemary Abbott, for the first time in months, appeared with a cake – this time an innocuous Victoria sponge – and happened to find Elizabeth at the house. She treated her with lofty hostility.

'Oh, I don't doubt she means well really,' Elizabeth said afterwards. 'But I've met many a Rosemary Abbott on the wards. They don't believe in female doctors because they want to direct all their virgin lusts and worshipful instincts towards the male consultants. They'll hardly so much as give you the time of day.'

George thought this was a mite harsh. The cake, of which Elizabeth had eaten a hearty share, was rather nice and had a generous seam of strawberry jam through the middle. But he supposed cake was hardly the point and decided not to argue.

Pat Nesbitt, 'just passing' and happening to be bearing a punnet of blackberries – 'we're overrun!' – was deemed to be a good sort.

Another afternoon, Elizabeth disappeared for a bafflingly long time. She was gone for so long that although George still had the shop open and things to attend to, he began to feel anxious and petulant in the face of more of Elizabeth's independence. The green Beetle was still outside so what was she playing at?

She walked in at half past five.

'Where on earth have you been?' By then he was just relieved to see her.

Elizabeth put her bag down on his office desk and looked at him with a sombre expression.

'Actually, I was having tea with your neighbour, Miss MacLean. What an absolutely extraordinary woman.'

George acknowledged his respect for Eunice with a nod,

though this still did not seem to explain what she and Elizabeth could have discussed for two whole hours.

'Did you know her fiancé was executed by the Nazis?'

Of course, he had had no idea. Elizabeth's eyes were round with sadness.

She told him the story as they walked Monty along the edge of the downs. Eunice, having grown up in France, was interned after the fall of France, with her parents. Her lover, who was half French, had remained in England after studying at Oxford, and was recruited by British Intelligence and captured in France.

'He died in Buchenwald,' Elizabeth said. 'So they never even had a chance to marry. And she's a marvellous person. She spends a lot of her time working for Amnesty International – d'you know it? It's a new organization that works to free prisoners of conscience around the world.'

George didn't know. He hadn't known any of it and felt ashamed that he hadn't. He wasn't even sure that Win had known either. Eunice had evidently not seen him as someone with the sensitivity to tell such things to, whereas Elizabeth . . .

'Now she,' Elizabeth had said, 'is someone I could be friends with around here.'

'It's ridiculous,' Elizabeth said the next afternoon when he visited Toke's Farm. They were looking over the fence at the renamed mule, Lottie. 'I feel like a lovelorn teenager – like those two you've got working for you.' She had witnessed the mooning about of Sharon and Kevin's fact-laden blatherings with much amusement. 'I'm trying to clear out that damned house and all I can think about is being with you – in bed.'

George laughed, loving her frankness. 'I know the problem.' He stroked Lottie's nose, feeling as if his face was endlessly smiling these days.

Elizabeth came and put her arms round him. George held her close. He was drunk on her, his body somehow attached to hers, his bloodstream and pulse and cells at one with hers, even in her absence.

4.

Nature was tilting into red berries and gold. The garden was now full of rose heads, their petals beaten off by a few days of rain.

They spun through the countryside in the Morris.

'Shall we take the car?' George had asked.

'Oh no!' Elizabeth said. 'I'd like a ride in that van of yours. And I can help you put things in it.'

To George's amusement, she had helped Clarence when he made two trips over to pick up the items from the farm. George could have gone himself: sending Clarence contained an element of mischief-making.

'Well he's a proper old fossil, isn't he?' Elizabeth said afterwards. 'You'd think there was a charge every time he opened his mouth. There's something quite dapper about him though.'

'Really?' George said. He would have to take another look at Clarence, obviously.

'Very Bohemian,' was Clarence's only remark when he got back to Greenbury from Toke's Farm.

George had spent a good portion of the weekend helping Elizabeth clear the barn of her mother's accumulated belongings. The house was so empty now that it echoed as they walked around. Clarence had taken the best pieces, a house-clearing business had most of the rest, leaving her only a bed, the kitchen table and a couple of chairs. It was much more hospitable sleeping over in Greenbury – but there was still the barn. George had taken the risk of bringing Monty over, not liking to leave him all day. After a riotous first introduction, when the spaniels leapt about him far too energetically for Monty's comfort, they all came to a truce. The spaniels soon found the basset habit of ponderously sniffing your way about the place far too boring for their own tastes.

They had shifted – and burned – what seemed like a lifetime's collection of old papers, from theatre programmes to personal effects. There were boxes of Elizabeth's schoolbooks, postcards, loose copies of Elizabeth's father's sermons.

'Heavens,' Elizabeth said, dismayed. 'She really didn't throw *anything* away.' George thought he saw her wiping her eyes at the sight of some of these things, perhaps at the notion that her mother had actually cared enough to keep them, but he left her to her privacy and said nothing.

They worked their way through the dusty piles of things, finding a rough patch of land round at the back near the field to light a fire and feed all the papers into the hungry flames. Tonight when they got back, they would finish the job. There was only a bit more to go.

But now, with his girl beside him, George set out on his Monday buying circuit. The weekend spent with her had been so blissful that he could hardly believe it wasn't a dream. They drove along the lanes. Some fields were ploughed into furrows now, others still striped with ashen stubble. It had stopped raining and the air was fresh and bright. They chatted, sang, or just sat as the mellow miles passed, in a silence that was a delirium of contentment.

George chose that day's route with more than the prospect of deals in mind. He wanted to show this woman beside him in the yellow and blue sprigged frock again, so confident and generously made, some of the dealers, and show her to them. They had driven to Marlow first, where his china expert hummed and hawed over Kevin's plate.

'I'm not certain, George. This Chinese stuff – not really my field. He may have a point, but . . .' More head-shaking. 'I think you need to take it to London.'

'I suppose I'll have to send it to Sotheby's,' George told Elizabeth, 'or we'll never hear the end of it. And if it turns out to be valuable, Mrs Parker ought to have the money for it, by rights.'

He toyed with the idea of calling on Maud Roberts, since they were in the town. But no. Not today. Fond as he was of Maud he could foresee complications.

'Hello, Maud – I'd like you to meet my . . .' What did he call Elizabeth anyway? Not fiancée, that was for sure. Mistress? Girlfriend? Nothing seemed quite right. 'Meet my friend . . .'

'Eh?'

'My . . . er . . . LADYFRIEND.'

'*Who*? That's not the girl I saw you with before – the one you said you were going to marry!'

'No, well that was all a bit of a—'

'*EH?*'

Maud would have to be dealt with another time.

So far they had looped east; Beaconsfield and Windsor, sandwiches by the river near Maidenhead, a leisurely drink in a pub before Camberley and now . . .

'The last one,' George told her, 'is Twyford. I thought I'd take you somewhere so you can see how *not* to do it.'

As he drove, George reached out and rested a hand on Elizabeth's thigh. She laid her hand over his for a second. The very touch of her, the warm, fleshy leg under her cotton dress sent a pulse of joy through him. But there was a souring, that for all his delight in her, would not leave him. She did not want him, ultimately. If she was not the marrying kind, what hope was there for him? What future? He did not want such thoughts to spoil this or any other moment, but they sat in him like an undigested meal.

'Eyes on the road,' she instructed.

'Now – Lewis Barker, where we're going . . .' he said. 'Dear oh dear. Place reminds me of a Victorian workhouse.'

As they stepped inside the cheerless, cobweb-decked 'showroom' on the edge of Twyford, Elizabeth made a comical face at him. 'See what you mean.'

Lewis appeared, a black and tan sports jacket hanging open to reveal a shirt of broad blue and white stripes stretched over his looming belly. The usual half-burned fag tilted down from under his moustache, which in itself looked like an uneven line of tobacco stuck to his upper lip.

''Ullo, George!' Lewis hailed him from quite some distance. Drawing nearer he removed the cigarette to exhale, eyes narrowing against the smoke. 'Sniffing around after one of my best finds again, are you?'

Eyeing Elizabeth, he added, 'Who's this you've got with you then?' He gave a theatrical bow, holding the cigarette out to one side. 'Good afternoon, young lady.'

George could already sense Elizabeth bristling.

'Ah, Lewis,' he said. 'This is my, er . . .' Terminology defeated him again. 'This is Dr Elizabeth Hargreaves.'

Lewis Barker held the cigarette higher and raised his chin in a faintly mocking fashion.

'Doctor, eh? You one of those university blue-stocking types then?'

'No.' Elizabeth looked at him with a steady disdain. George watched with admiration. 'I'm a medical doctor.' She held her hand out. 'General practice.'

Lewis shoved the cigarette back between his lips and, having little choice, shook Elizabeth's hand. He gave a snort.

'No – you're having me on, aren't you? You're never a doctor, little slip of a girlie like you!'

'Well,' Elizabeth said, turning away to look around. 'We don't have to saw people's legs off *every* day you know. As a matter of fact, I trained at Barts – that's St Bartholomew's in London. One of the best teaching hospitals. So, any problems – haemorrhoids perhaps . . . ?' She turned in time to catch Lewis Barker's bewildered expression. 'Piles, dear,' she said sweetly. 'I'm the woman to go to.'

'I think we'll just look round,' George said hastily, leaving a sour-looking Lewis to his fag end. 'Masterful,' he whispered to Elizabeth. 'Absolutely masterful.'

She eyed him. 'Mistress-ful, in fact.'

Lewis had the usual collection of dark and demoralized-looking furniture: chests of drawers piled one upside down on another, dressers, wardrobes, oak chests, all packed in so you almost had to scramble through tight spaces to see things. The roof, made of corrugated asbestos, had a few windows in it, all filthy, the light seeming strained through muslin.

George picked his way round, selecting a couple of items. He noticed that some of the goods already had labels attached to them with SOLD stamped on in red.

'I see quite a few of these have gone already,' he called to Lewis.

'Ah, yes.' Lewis, recovering his irritating buoyancy, came over to join them. 'Had a dealer from America in this week, as a matter of fact. Very wealthy man – some sort of oil family, I think. Money to burn. Bought a whole load of stuff. I'm just waiting for the shipping company to collect it.'

They made their way to the back. Dust-thickened cobwebs sagged across the corners. A piece of furniture almost at the end caught George's eye. It was pushed back against the wall and tied to the key in the upper keyhole was another of the SOLD labels. As he moved closer, the piece came into focus. A bureau bookcase, mahogany, rather odd feet on it. Looking more closely at it, it was familiar. Very familiar.

'Lewis,' he called, keeping his voice casual. 'Nice piece, this – who sold it to you?'

'The bureau bookcase?' Lewis was standing quite a distance away. 'Oh – I picked it up at auction. Caught my eye – Hepplewhite, of course. It's a corker, isn't it?'

'Very nice,' George agreed. 'Mind if I take a look?'

'Be my guest,' Lewis said.

Elizabeth stood watching, with respect.

George opened the upper doors of Lady Byngh's bureau, as if admiring the workmanship. Out of the corner of his eye he could see Lewis Barker lumbering closer, along the narrow aisle.

'Been nicely restored,' he remarked. A nod to Clarence.

George bent over, taking his time. He opened the bottom drawers one by one, poked and prodded, closed the last one then straightened up, regarding the bureau with a regretful air.

'Very nice piece, Lewis – but what a shame. You do know it's mated, don't you?'

'What the hell was all that about?' Elizabeth seemed torn between irritation and infection by George's hoots of laughter as they drove away. She gave in and chortled at the sight of him wiping his eyes at the thought of Lewis Barker's face.

'Stop – you're going to crash the damn thing in a minute. *Tell* me.'

He pulled over, as soon as he could. The 'Hepplewhite' would soon be on a ship to some mansion in the USA. There was no more danger of it turning up round here.

'That,' he said, looking at Elizabeth, still full of mirth and leaning over to kiss her, 'is what you might call a truly great climax to end the day.'

Or so he thought.

5.

'That may not have been the most truthful way out,' Elizabeth said as they drove home. He had related to her the saga of Lady Byngh and the intended wedding present that had just resurfaced. 'But it was probably the kindest, in the end.'

George smiled, gratified. 'I think it was,' he said. 'Sleeping dogs I think, in that case. And Lewis will get his money for it so he won't be bothered.' Lewis just didn't like the fact that he hadn't noticed.

He didn't add his further observation that the bureau bookcase, which was on the point of being shipped out, would more normally be accessible near the door. But Lewis was keeping it squirrelled away at the back of the warehouse. He may not have known it wasn't genuine, but Lewis clearly had some idea that he was handling stolen goods. Let's hope the shipping company get there quick, George thought.

He looked at Elizabeth seated beside him and smiled at the sight. Her body, full in all the right places, eyes looking out with a gentle expression, strands of hair flying about in the air through the window, all filled him with a sense of wellbeing. It was Monday and just about closing time for the shop. Everyone would be going home. They could call in and drop off today's new purchases without any complications from the workshop staff, or a pile of tasks from Vera. Then they could drive to Toke's Farm, he would drag out the last load of junk from the barn while Elizabeth cooked a meal, they would open a bottle and eventually they would climb up to the bedroom, her hand in his . . . There would be lovemaking, and all the talk, the laughter . . . The evening stretched like a carpet of bliss before him. Everything he needed – such happiness!

They achieved the first part all right. Vera was just leaving as they arrived and exchanged a few words. They stowed away the things from out of the back of the van, lifted Monty aboard instead – in the open back as it was so warm – George dashed back inside for a nice bottle of Chianti he had ready and they hit the road again.

The evening air blowing into the cab smelt of late-summer leaves and, faintly, of smoke. He had never known it was possible to feel quite this happy. He shared this observation with Elizabeth, who smiled back, radiant herself. He saw the years unfurling ahead; this life, Elizabeth beside him. Which made him, out of a moment of unguarded fantasy touch her knee and say, 'We shan't have all this carting back and forth when you move in, shall we?'

'*Move in?*' Elizabeth sat bolt upright. He could feel the glare of her eyes even though he thought it prudent to keep facing forwards. 'What in heaven's name makes you think I'm going to move in with you? Good God – I've only known you for about ten days!'

'But . . .' he attempted.

'Look – I've told you, or at least I thought I had . . .'

She had, but it seemed wrong to him. It wouldn't settle in his mind in a way that he could accept. Wasn't that what men and women did – live together, get married?

'I'm not the sort to get married and settle down as a wifey. I'm a *doctor*, George. It's taken me a great many years and an awful lot of work to get where I am and believe me – there's a crying need for women doctors out there.' She seemed very imposing suddenly, sitting there next to him, arms folded in defence across her chest and so crisply articulate. 'Women desperately need someone to speak for them and understand their problems from the inside . . .'

'But I didn't mean . . .' He was wretched, hurt by this attack.

'I love you, George. I do . . .'

These words sank into him like a stone in mud. Did she? Oh thank God, thank God. But she was so *cross*. He was taken aback by her anger – as if she had to hold on very tight to something under attack. It wasn't that he had meant to attack. Not in the least. All he wanted was to be with her, in any way possible. He almost felt like weeping. They were driving along the back road now, towards the farm track. He wanted to brake the van, for them to get out, for them to hold each other and for things to be all right again. They could go inside, open his bottle, talk and talk . . .

'I seriously and absolutely do,' she went on. 'But don't think I'm just going to roll over and spend my time . . . I don't know, making *jam*. Not on your life.'

'I really wasn't saying that,' he said, as mildly as possible, though he felt anguished and bruised. He didn't want to row. He hated rowing. But they seemed to be doing it all the same, as if a chasm had – unbearably – cracked open between them. 'Jam? No of course not! Please, Elizabeth – don't . . .' He swung the van along the track. She had turned away and in a strained silence they crawled along the ruts until he could pull up in the yard. The spaniels came hurtling out of the barn, Monty leapt up roaring in the back.

In the midst of this mayhem Elizabeth touched his arm and said, not frostily exactly, but in a neutral tone which did not exude warmth, 'I'll put the kettle on. Why don't you get started in the barn?'

6.

He paused in the doorway of the barn, looking along its dusty, cobwebby space, which was now almost empty. The dogs had cleared off somewhere and all was quiet now. At the far end were the remaining cartons of stuff belonging to Elizabeth's mother. Pushed in beside them, in the far right-hand corner, was a tangle of rusty tools. Soon the job would be done and all of it gone.

George felt the swell of disconsolate feeling develop in him as he began on the boxes in the barn's now crepuscular light. He felt truly wretched, hurt and angry, foolish and a tad self-righteous.

Why had he kidded himself into thinking he could have a relationship with a woman like Elizabeth? Other chaps often said educated women were trouble and here he was with this one – so independent and bolshie. And she certainly didn't want the things for which he longed – a settled, affectionate married life. She didn't even want to live with him at all, apparently. So what in hell's name did the woman want with him?

He reached the closest box and landed a kick in the side of it. A soggy, unsatisfying kick. Pulling back one of the flaps he saw that it seemed to be full of seed catalogues, the top ones disfigured by grubs and damp. God in heaven, was there nothing that Mrs Hargreaves had not hoarded? Among the innumerable boxes they had found caches of letters, which Elizabeth had taken to put in drier storage for sorting out when she found the time. They were one of the few things they had not put to the flames.

Grumpily he gathered armfuls of the Suttons catalogues and chucked them into the wheelbarrow until it was full and he could push them round to the heap at the back where they would light the fire. He did this a number of times, glad of the physical activity, such was his pent-up hurt and disappointment. But all the while his unhappy mind was whirring.

Win. Oh Win, Win! During that half-hour he suffered an acute, nostalgic longing for her. He had not appreciated her. He had been a terrible man, a faithless man – a fool. Never, he thought, hurling more catalogues into the barrow with a mean sort of energy, had he given her enough credit for being the kindly, conventional and, yes, biddable woman that she had been. Win had never moaned about making jam. In fairness, he had to acknowledge that a compelling reason for this was that she had never actually made any jam and was quite happy with a jar of Robertson's from the grocer's. But all the same. Win wanted marriage, like a normal woman. She had wanted children, though that had not come about – but all she had desired was the quiet, married life, man plus woman, that most people expected.

Why had he been so discontented, he wondered now? There he had been, in a gentle, undemanding landscape with a predictable layout of fields, hedges, barns, villages . . . Now he felt as if he had strayed off the edge into the unknown, like in the old maps – the mysterious, foggy territory where 'there be dragons'. Where you never quite knew where you were or what might be crouching there in the murk . . .

He shoved the barrow out through the barn door. No Elizabeth coming to apologize, he noted sourly, all at odds with himself. Perhaps her sort, the dragon sort, never did – they always thought they were right.

As he emptied the barrow onto the bonfire pile again, the niggling thought occurred – was Elizabeth waiting for him to apologize? But what did he have to apologize for? All he was asking was for something normal and straightforward . . .

On and on his mind went, jabbing and harrumphing. But he started to find that the boxes he was emptying were full of things related to antiques – magazines and catalogues – and a part of his attention began to be engaged. He had reached the seam of Mrs Hargreaves' antiques phase. There were a few magazines about pottery that perhaps he should put aside for Kevin.

Yet at the same time he was thinking, Right, That's It. I'll do the decent thing and finish the job. I might as well eat supper with her now she's cooked it. But I'll tell her it's all over. Clearly we're not on the same wavelength. Wheeling the barrow, he started composing valedictory speeches, trying to achieve the right balance of assertion and fairness. He rehearsed various beginnings: 'The thing is, Elizabeth . . .'; 'It's obvious by now that you and I don't see eye to eye . . .'

Muttering, he went back to the barn, dumped the barrow and flung open one of the final boxes. More antique stuff. At least this was a bit more interesting.

'My word,' he said, impressed. 'She certainly got about.'

He found himself sorting through a pile of auction catalogues, almost all dated sometime during the war. She must have made a habit of going to auctions to take her mind off things, he thought. There were catalogues for sales at the big London auction houses, Christie's, Sotheby's, as well as Philips, Hamble and Moorland, and other more local outfits. She must have gone for the pleasure of it more than to buy things, he thought. After all, when you came down to it there had not been all that much in the house.

Sitting back on his heels, he flipped through some of them, intrigued to see what had been on sale during the war. So absorbed was he that he only heard Elizabeth's call, 'Geor-orge?' across the yard with a fragment of his attention. He opened a catalogue from Christie's, yellowed at the edges, the sale in September 1943.

'Geor-orge! The food's ready.'

The word caught his eye on the second page, jumped out at him like a white brick in a black wall: *Allodola*. 'Venus on horseback, bronze, C17th, Allodola, height 14" – considered to have been one of a pair . . .'

His pulse had speeded to a crazed thudding, any other thought long left behind. He kept staring at the page, willing it to divulge more information, for the alluring figure on the bronze horse to come galloping from the page and show herself to him, to prove that she was . . . Surely it was . . .

'George . . . ?' She was at the barn door as he leapt to his feet as if he had been stung, scattering the other catalogues.

'Look!' He charged at her, finger jabbing at the catalogue. 'It's her – it's got to be. I've *found* her, Lizzie – found her – at long blooming last!'

'What? Who?' She was laughing at the sight of his face.

He grabbed her shoulders and swung her round, 'hooraying and jigging with such exultation that all Elizabeth could do was join in with something much the same.

OCTOBER

Seventeen

1.

Before he had opened his eyes that morning, his senses woke gradually to the warmth emanating from beside him in the bed, to the gentle sound of breathing. He moved his hand, reaching for her and met her long, firm back. Turning over, he pressed his cheek against her – his woman.

Joy, utter joy. It was the weekend, she was not on call and she was here, able simply to be with him. Two days stretched out before them, autumn days of whirling leaves and bonfire smoke, of walks on the downs and cosy afternoons, even perhaps putting a match to the fire. And her, here – this glorious, maddening, loveable woman beside him.

Elizabeth's two-week stay at Toke's Farm had been over for some time. She could not put the house and land up for sale yet because of the presence of Lottie and the donkeys, but the house now stood all but empty and she had to return to her surgery. George had once visited her Basingstoke flat and had been taken aback by its bleak functionality. Elizabeth had apologized.

'I know you always need to make everything beautiful.' She looked round the white walls of the flat almost as if seeing the place for the first time. 'It's just – well, I suppose I'm forever busy. And it's never been somewhere I saw as being my home long term. More of a perch.' She smiled at him. 'It's one of the many things I love about you – that you bring so much beauty into my life.'

She always came over to Greenbury when she had time off.

Last night she had managed to get away in good time and fell on the shepherd's pie George had made with great enthusiasm, saying she had barely eaten all day. Even though they spoke almost every evening, there was always plenty to catch up on – his customers, her patients.

'So,' she had said as they sat digesting, sipping at good red wine. 'Your Mr Howard's very pleased to have heard from you, by the sound of things?'

'Group Captain Howard, if you don't mind,' George admonished.

Elizabeth gave a mock-obedient nod. 'I stand corrected.'

George had contacted Christie's straight away after finding the catalogue with the Venus in it, asking about the 1943 sale. Christie's promptly supplied an address in Trowbridge, Wiltshire.

'Of course,' he had said to Elizabeth as this progressed, 'she could have been sold on several times by now. But at least we're on to her.'

Elizabeth seemed to understand how the Allodola Venus had captivated him, that she was also tied up with the sadness of the place, the dead sons followed by the dead wife, such beauty in the face of a tragic family. That evening at the farm he had told her the bare bones of his visit to the Americas, about Paul Lester in Argentina, of coming face to face once again with Mars on Horseback, in Lester's possession.

'Are you absolutely sure it's the same one?' Elizabeth had asked. 'They weren't churning out replicas all over the place?'

George laughed. 'No, no. The Allodola was a most refined Florentine workshop. Each of them is unique, with the little skylark in silhouette. And it's a relatively unusual depiction from that period, having the gods on horseback – especially in the case of Venus. This was the thing, you see – Lester knew they were worth a mint if he could just get his hands on the other one.'

'So . . .' Frowning, Elizabeth rested her chin in her hand, elbow on the table. She was looking especially lovely in the gentle lamplight, her hair softly gathered back from her face. 'You're the only person, at the moment, who has a good idea where each of them might be. So now what?'

George sat back. 'Yes I am – possibly. It doesn't make any difference to anything, really, except that I've always wondered, ever since I heard they'd been split up. I suppose the current owners would like to know, but I can't even be sure that Mars is in the same place still, after all this time.'

'So what about this ghastly Lester person? Are you going to ask him?'

'Lester? Oh, he's dead,' George said. 'Died two or three years ago. It was in the paper: Baron Paul Lester – one of the ones who managed to buy a peerage off Lloyd George when he was Prime Minister, when he was trying to top up the country's coffers after the Great War. Lester left an immense fortune and three daughters. So no, he's not going to get his hands on Venus now.' He took a pleasurable sip of wine. 'All the same – it'd be interesting to know whether they've still got their Mars.'

As well as writing to Trowbridge, he had racked his brains to recall an approximate address for the Lesters' *estancia* and sent off a letter of enquiry there as well.

Within days of sending his first letter, he had a fulsome reply from Gp. Capt. Reginald Howard of Trowbridge, Wilts. Yes indeed, he and Marjorie, his wife, were in possession of the Allodola Venus and a great joy she had long been to his family. His wife, who had a marvellous eye for such things, had bought her at auction during the war while he was away. He could be assured she was in good hands. If Mr Baxter were to discover any further information as to the whereabouts of the Allodola Mars on Horseback, they would be most interested to hear and thanked him most profusely for taking the trouble to contact them.

As George's sleepy thoughts wandered over these developments that Saturday morning, Elizabeth stirred beside him and began to move.

'I'll definitely prescribe penicillin, yes,' she murmured.

George felt a second's pang at yet more evidence of Elizabeth's other life, of her work even dominating her dreams, before giving himself a ticking-off. Just think about today and stop fretting, you silly old fool, he told himself.

That evening in September when he had found the auction catalogue with the Venus in it had been a wonder to him of frankness and tenderness and making up.

'I love you,' Elizabeth had said, with stirring earnestness. 'I truly and absolutely do.' She reached across the table for his hand and said, 'Can't we just stop trying to predict exactly how all this is going to go and just start off one day at a time? We have an awful lot, you know, just as we are.'

George had swallowed hard, both the specific mouthful of mashed potato he was eating and her offering of wisdom. He nodded, with the beginnings of elation inside him. All his hurt and rage of the early evening had vanished. God, how he loved this woman – even if for now it meant only seeing her at weekends and the occasional evening in the week. What did it matter if it meant living in this new frontier country where you built a new section of the road every day? Why, he asked himself, feeling faintly heroic, would he want to retreat back to the stifling ease and certainty of the old days – those days he had so often longed to escape? He wanted adventure. He wanted a new, pioneering life in a new country – and he wanted it with her.

In the warmth of the bed he snuggled close to her and closed his eyes. In a minute he would get up and put the kettle on and make tea and they would sit in bed and chat. And, come to think of it, as he had forgotten to tell her last night – he had a little surprise this morning, for Kevin. But for now, warm and in perfect comfort, he was in heaven.

2.

Kevin had looked as if he might actually expire with excitement when George told him, after his conversation in Marlow, that he planned to parcel up the chicken-soup-coloured plate from Mrs Parker and send it to be assessed at Sotheby's.

'*London*,' Kevin breathed. George rather regretted not having done the boy the favour of making this announcement at a moment when Sharon was in earshot as well.

By the third day after he had despatched the plate, he began to hope to goodness that Sotheby's would hurry up and get their finger out on the subject. Not a day passed without Kevin's earnest enquiries as to whether he had *'heard from London?'*

The call had come eventually – yesterday, a damp October Friday afternoon. Vera called George to the telephone, from which he heard the smooth, educated tones of one of the ceramics experts at Sotheby's. It was quite late in the afternoon. Smiling to himself, George saved the news for the next day. Sharon would be there – and Elizabeth.

The morning was bright and windy, leaves circling round in the drive and blustery air blowing in their faces.

'Vera,' George said, once everyone had arrived. 'Call everyone over to the house, would you? There's something I want to say.'

'What are you up to?' Elizabeth asked, having been unable to prise any more information out of him other than that Kevin was in for a surprise.

'You'll see.'

'Come inside for a moment, will you?' he said as the men from the workshop trooped over. As they passed into the hall, George saw Sharon's trunky legs disappearing upstairs. 'You might want to stay and listen to this, Sharon,' he hailed her. The legs stopped. The brown-cardiganed figure descended until she could lean over the banisters looking, it had to be said, rather magnificent. Kevin beamed up at her and, to George's astonishment, he saw a shy, almost coy smile tug at Sharon's full lips and she looked down, blushing.

Vera and Elizabeth were waiting along the hall. Clarence and Alan stood side by side. Alan seemed more relaxed again these days, George observed to his relief. He was startled to notice that Clarence, with his overall hanging open, was wearing a rather natty brown suit and tucked into the top of his shirt was a red cravat.

'I say, Clarence,' he exclaimed. 'You're looking very dapper today.'

Clarence fidgeted in a bashful sort of way and cleared his throat to announce, 'Well, Edith and myself are off to the races this afternoon.'

'Well, jolly good,' George said. Clarence was definitely perkier these days. Whatever the reason for this, he did not need to know.

'Now,' he announced. 'I thought you might all be interested to hear that I had a telephone call from Sotheby's yesterday.'

'Oh! What did they *say*, Mr Baxter?' Kevin cried, before sucking in a huge breath and appearing, in his excitement, to forget to release it again.

'That plate you turned up . . .' George was in the process of leaving a further dramatic pause, until it occurred to him that it might be better if Kevin started breathing again. 'It's, er . . . It appears they think it's really rather good.'

Kevin seemed unable to utter a word but he did at least exhale loudly.

'The chap said he's sure it's genuine, for a start – by the mark and the quality of it. So you were right there. Said it's "Guan yao stoneware" . . .'

'Guan yao!' Kevin erupted into reverential speech. 'The imperial kilns!'

'Well yes, quite,' George agreed, having no idea. 'Thirteenth or fourteenth century, he thought. Not the rarest of pieces but still much too good to be used as a plant holder, that's for sure. Well done, Kevin – very well spotted.'

Sharon's mouth was slightly open, for no apparent purpose other than expressing awe. Elizabeth was leaning against the side of the stairs, arms folded.

'Well *done*, Kevin!' Vera said. She patted his shoulder, before adding a motherly kiss on his cheek, which made Kevin blush furiously. 'Is it worth a lot of money then, Mr B?'

'We'll see when they auction it, won't we?' he said. 'Thing is though, Kevin, whatever it fetches, the money is really due to Mrs Parker. It was her mother's.'

There was not a flicker of disappointment on Kevin's face. In fact George thought he had scarcely ever seen anyone look so happy. Kevin was not interested in the money.

'So I think we'll ask Sotheby's to go ahead and auction it, and then perhaps you should be the one to go and tell Mrs Parker and give her the cheque – don't you think?'

Kevin seemed to grow. Standing suddenly tall, he held out his hand to shake George's. For a fleeting second, a glimpse appeared of a person of new stature. 'Course. If you think so, Mr Baxter.'

'That's a good lad. Marvellous.' It was his turn to pat Kevin on the back. 'Oh,' he added. 'And while you're there, don't let Mrs Parker go showing you any paintings, will you?'

Kevin's brow crinkled. 'I don't know anything about painting, Mr Baxter,' he said humbly.

Afterwards Elizabeth, who George had filled in on the antics of Mrs Parker, tutted at him. 'You're a very naughty man,' she said. She looked at him in wonder. 'It's all go round here, isn't it?'

When the fuss had died down and the men filed out to the workshop again, Vera said, 'Well I'm going to put the kettle on. Oh – and Mr B, there's quite a bit of post. I think you'd better take a look. Some of it's *foreign*.'

George headed obediently to the office, a flicker of excitement inside him. Among the envelopes on his desk, amid the white and brown, was a blue one, addressed in a looped script – from Argentina.

He could hear the women distantly in the kitchen, laughing together. Taking a paper knife he slit along the edge of the thin, blue paper and pulled two sheets from within, both delicate as onion-skin, the writing ornate and impeccable. The signature was from someone called Paula Lester Rodriguez. He ran his eye quickly over it. Yes, the figure he had written to them about was still in the *estancia*. Yes, it was in good condition.

Another paragraph began. He frowned. The woman was dwelling on his visit, on the dates when he had come to Argentina in 1928. He read on, until he came to the closing sentences of the first page, which stopped his breath and made him stand holding the letter before him in disbelief.

3.

'So what the hell happened in Argentina?'

Elizabeth was sitting up beside him in bed. She was naked, hugging her knees and as he lay, George could see the prominent little arc of bones in her spine, the treacle-coloured mole on her right shoulder blade. He could hear the concern in her voice as well as the attempt to protect herself by putting on a professional exterior, when the part of her that loved him was bewildered, even afraid of the odd state into which he had sunk. All day he had managed to keep it to himself, until the others had gone home at dinnertime.

While he had sat, distractedly eating lunch, Elizabeth had pressed him. What was wrong? He seemed so absent.

'Will you come up to bed?' he had found himself saying. He found he needed comfort, enormously; needed to be held. They had simply undressed and climbed back into the refuge of bed, nothing more. And then he told her.

'This is all a bit of a bombshell,' he said, as she sat up beside him.

'To put it mildly.'

He wanted to reach out and touch her, draw her to him, but he seemed frozen into immobility. He felt . . . he could scarcely begin to know what he felt. The only clear thing was that he was lying here beside Elizabeth as she sat, crouched almost, and that her shape, the side of a breast, the round of her cheek that he could see from where he lay, provided a deep comfort. He could feel the light roughness of the sheet over his flesh. These were certainties.

But with them came the lines of this woman's letter – a woman in Argentina.

'I am sorry – this must come as a great shock to you. Only now am I certain for myself, since you mentioned the dates when you visited my parents. I think, Mr Baxter, that you are my father . . .'

In terms of any graspable reality, he was still tottering along the long path of the last thirty-six years, trying to catch up. The fermentation within him of bewilderment, of a pole-axing rage, of shame, of – potentially, eventually – joy, was sloshing about in a murky brew well out of the access of his conscious mind.

Elizabeth turned, rearranging herself beside him and leaned over him, her eyes full of loving concern. She stroked his forehead. 'Whatever it is, my darling, try and tell me. It's always better out than in, in the end. This woman – could she be right?'

He met her gaze for a second. 'I . . .' He had to look away, beyond her, to the corner of the window. 'She could be, yes. She just possibly could be.'

The letter, shocking as it was, touched his heart. Through the lines telling her understanding of things, the basic facts that she knew, George felt from Paula Lester Rodriguez, by the end of it, a sweet and girlish sense of need.

'My father,' she had written, 'or the man I thought was my father, passed from this life two years ago. I was even named after him. But only when he was laid to rest, my mother, Inés – you may remember?'

Oh yes, he remembered.

'It was then, at last, that she told me and my sisters the truth. My father was a clever man, but not a kind or an easy one. Even after he was gone, it cost our mother heavily to tell us, but she was sure that we should know the truth, even though it did not show either of our parents in a very good light. My mother is a brave woman – I have seen that many times. But when it came to my father, she was in his power. In fact, although she is strong, she was in some ways afraid of him and afraid that he would leave her all alone.

'We are three sisters. I am the second. The first is Estafania, and my younger sister is Isabella. And we are of three fathers, none of them the person we believed to be the true one. My father was a proud man. He had to be right, to win in everything in life. He could be cruel to get what he wanted. And he had almost everything he desired, except for one manly thing. He had no fertility. No seed. He had money and he had power, but not the power to make for himself a son. Always he made arrangements to have whatever he needed and children were one of the things he needed. And you were one of the men who he arranged to provide them.

'I am shocked and sad so that I can hardly express it. Now I am married with children of my own, my son and daughter, I feel the strength of family, the importance of truth. This must come as a great shock to you too, Mr Baxter. But if you are my father, I would now like you to know it and if it is possible, I would very much like to know you.'

Elizabeth continued to sit up beside him as he started talking. She seemed to sense that it would be easier for him if she was not looking at him. She drew her knees up tighter into her chest and rested her chin on them, still and attentive.

George looked at the miracle of her there, the dark frizz of her hair down her back, the curve of the muscle beneath the pink skin of her arm. He reached out and rested the back of his hand against her thigh.

He could only think in fragments.

'I knew there was something odd about him taking me all the way down there. To show off, I thought – and of course he did, constantly. No wonder . . .' He drifted for a moment, thoughts all at odds like a pile of sticks thrown down. 'I knew at the time there was something peculiar about the whole set-up. And . . .' The letter came back to him. 'According to her, they already had a child by then!' The extent of the deception enacted on him was appearing, piece by piece.

'Estafania,' Elizabeth said.

'There was just no sign of a child anywhere . . .'

Paula had told him elsewhere in the letter that Estafania, who would then have been just over a year old, had been taken to stay with Inés's mother throughout George's stay.

'He made out that it was all her fault. He actually said to me that she was barren – that was the word he used. I thought it was cruel of him. Indiscreet . . .'

He stared up at the wall over the bedroom door, the angle where wall and ceiling met. So many years he had lain here in this room and only now he was noticing the blue hint of mould along the join and a weightless strand of cobweb across the corner, as if he had never seen them before.

'He made me go riding with him – he had all these polo horses. It was a total disaster. I didn't want to go but he wasn't the sort of bloke you could say no to. It was the second day I was there and I didn't exactly cover myself in glory . . . Anyway, he sent me back to the house, said he had things to do, that he was going to stay on at the stables. All very important. Everything Lester did was terribly important, of course. I couldn't get away fast enough. When I got to the house, she – Mrs Lester, Inés – was, well, she was nice to me, that was all. Friendly. She must have been about ten years older than me and I was feeling pretty fed up. I'd come off the horse, you see. Bloody great bruise on my backside the next day. She told me not to worry, that horses can be difficult with you at first. And she made me some English tea. Then I went along to get washed and changed.'

He had undressed, hung his jacket on the back of the door and was standing in his vest and underpants when Inés Lester came in. A soft knock at the door and she was there in the room with him.

'I suppose I thought for a second that she had come to the wrong place. There were so many rooms . . . Or that she'd come to deliver some message – but it was quite a walk and she could have sent one of the staff for that. In fact I barely had time to think about it at all. She had changed – she was wearing this long, silky thing, dark, like wine, down to her ankles. And she said . . .' He closed his eyes for a moment, hearing her voice, exactly after all this time, that smooth, accented English. 'My dear boy . . .'

She closed the door and came over to him, laid her palms on his cheeks almost as if he were a little child. He stood there with his heart banging away, feeling her staring into his flushed face but unable to raise his eyes. Her figure, so close, was astonishing to him, the belt of the robe drawing the silk fabric tightly across her chest. She was ample, maternal. She was *there*, right in front of him. A scent came from her, a perfume which seemed to wake every nerve of him.

He had so few clothes on that within seconds of her touching him, her hand sliding down his chest, lowering to his belly, his own arousal had become mortifyingly obvious. He made a sound of protest.

'Paul will not be home for hours,' she soothed him. 'Come . . .' She drew him into her arms with an almost motherly gesture, pressing him close to her. Her caresses progressed downwards until he was hopelessly lost to her. Aged twenty, he had never made love to a woman. She overwhelmed him in seconds.

'Let me undress you, my dear.'

She was bending, looking up at him with those dark eyes, the wheaten hair loose over her shoulders and the robe now falling open. He felt more and more like a child being put forcibly to bed as she peeled off his underpants, his vest, and taking his hand, led him to the waiting sheets.

For a few moments they sat side by side, she still half covered and he defencelessly on view.

'She even held my hand; she sounded sorry, almost. She said, "My husband is very preoccupied with business. We have no children – it is my lack, my curse. It is a great grief to my husband – it makes me less attractive to him." I thought she was going to cry. She seemed vulnerable, lonely. She said, "Sometimes every woman wants a little more. A little company. Let me lie with you.'

Confessing – it felt like a confession – the bare bones of it now, to Elizabeth, the memories flooded him: Inés Lester's face below his as he lay over her, his own helpless impulses steered by her and she, her legs around him, holding him deep inside her.

'I couldn't have stopped her if I'd tried,' he told Elizabeth. This felt like the worst confession. 'I feel – have always felt – such a fool. When she'd gone, I was covered in her, in *us* – the sticky mess of it. All I wanted to do was wash. I felt dirty, to the core. Twenty years old, a beautiful woman – not my type, but lovely in her way – comes and gives you the thing you've spent all this time wondering about. Making a man of you. Of course, it had given me pleasure – but it was all wrong. Something about that place, about her . . . All I could feel was ashamed, as if I'd been . . .' He turned his head away. 'Disgraced.'

The sense of passivity, the paralysis he had felt, washed over him now. How his dark jacket had shifted on the door as she closed it behind her.

'I feel so ridiculous.' He was close to weeping, but he contained himself. Elizabeth turned to look at him. She lay down gently beside him. He felt himself laid bare in front of her, all the corners of him that had lain in dark reserve.

She did not touch him, but looked intently at him, her eyes full of understanding.

'Strictly speaking, she assaulted you. It's not only women

who can be assaulted. She took what she wanted with no thought of you. She was like a rapist.'

He looked at her, astonished. 'I've never thought of it like that.' It went through him, an electric pulse of rage. He shot up in bed. 'And the worst of it was, it was all a *scheme*. They planned it. Like a bloody baby farm!'

'They *were* horse breeders,' Elizabeth pointed out. He was grateful for her professionalism. She was not cold or unconcerned, but calm and objective. 'They were materialists. And in her case desperate as well, I should imagine. Paula did say her mother was afraid her father would leave her. But yes, they just took what they wanted.'

'They used me – like a stud horse!' He was so incensed, he got up and paced back and forth across the bedroom. 'How can anyone behave like that – it's . . . it's . . .'

'Why don't you come back and lie down?' Elizabeth leaned up on one elbow. He thought he detected a repressed amusement in her eyes and only then it occurred to him that enraged pacing when you're stark naked lacks a certain gravitas. He climbed obediently back into bed.

'You think they planned it together?' she asked.

'From what the girl says, yes,' George said. 'She certainly played her part. He brought the man home, she did the business. But they somehow pretended the children were his blood children. No wonder there was a strange feel to the place.'

'Look, my darling . . .' Elizabeth's arms took him in and he lay, held as if he would never fall again. 'They sound like a completely ghastly pair. Hideous. Him especially. And they took advantage of you.'

He watched her face, her lovely, miraculous face, needing her comfort, her insight.

'It's not this young woman Paula's fault though, is it?' she said gently. 'Nor her sisters'.'

His former impression of Paula's sweetness had been replaced by mistrust after reviving his memories of the Lesters. 'But what does she *want*? She might be just like him.'

Elizabeth looked at him with a certain severity. 'George, if you remember, it was you that wrote to her in the first place. Look, she's a – let's see – thirty-five-year-old woman. She says she has two children and not long ago she discovered that the already difficult man she thought was her father had been lying to her all her life. It seems to me she might want someone who is truthful, kind? A father she can respect – love, even? Children aren't their parents, you know. Heaven knows – if I thought I was just a reproduction of my mother . . . She sounds a nice young woman. Nicer than her parents. George, my lovely, you now apparently have a daughter and two grandchildren who are showing signs of wanting to get to know you. If the worst comes to the worst, they are in fact several thousand miles away. But it's not all bad, is it?'

Even with the seismic disturbances currently going on in his head, even though he was a long way from taking all this in, George had a glimmering sense that she was right. He looked back into her smiling grey eyes.

'No, I suppose—'

'You can expect good things, you know,' she interrupted.

He felt a warmth spreading through him. He pulled her close, so close. 'Can I?'

'You can,' she said.

NOVEMBER

Eighteen

1.

'I can't come over tonight.' Elizabeth's voice had come along the line last night, filling him with a throb of longing. 'I've got a very poorly old chap here I've got to get into hospital. I'll see you tomorrow, all right, darling?'

He really was going to have to get used to this, he lectured himself as he drove to Wallingford the next morning, trying to free himself of the resentment that intermittently stole through him in these situations.

He parked the car in the field next to the bridge and waited for Monty to emerge from the back with his usual combination of scramble and flop. Monty stumbled off across the grass for a lengthy pee against one of the bridge arches, nose raised simultaneously to sniff the air, which was crisply cold and edged with the smoke of leaf fires.

'Come on, you old fart. I've got a little treat for you today, as well.' In his pocket was a little box of liquorice allsorts. After the glut Monty had experienced with Sylvia, he had been keeping the dog off sweet things for a bit. But what was the harm in him having one or two now and then?

He clipped the lead on and led him up the steps and over Wallingford Bridge, his other arm laden with rug and picnic basket, round to where *Barchetta* was moored. He had chanced not taking her out of the water yet, though it was so late in the year, for days like this – for the odd trip on the river before the winter wet and river fogs closed in.

Folding the rug he laid it on the steps and sat waiting for Elizabeth, Monty beside him. He marvelled at the dog's capacity to wait for indefinite periods when he had no idea what he was waiting for, something intolerable to the human mind.

It was one of the most beautiful days George could ever remember: the nose-nipping cold and low-angled sun poured onto the yellow and rust of remaining leaves. The water was still as glass, giving back the inverted double of all the beauty along the river: the bridge arches and gnarled trunks of willows, the flat, cloudless sky. He sat, thinking about Elizabeth.

Since she'd telephoned last night, and on other occasions, he had had to cope with himself, with her having a demanding job and a life of her own, with the fact that he could not expect her just to give up everything for him, as if he was the only one who needed anything.

'I'm yours, darling,' she kept telling him. 'I want you and no one else. I've never met anyone who makes me feel the way you do, George – truly. We must be together as often as we possibly can. But it's not as if we're going to have a family' – though I *do* have a family, apparently, he wanted to say, still trying to get used to the idea – 'and I can't just stop doing everything I do – everything I *am* – to be a conventional wife in the way you're used to. For one thing, if I did, I'd bore you senseless – and I'd certainly bore myself.'

It was true. It was not what he was used to. It took adaptation that he had not expected. At moments he felt sore and rather sorry for himself. But it was one of the roads he was learning to walk in this new country of love.

Everyone had been learning to adapt over these months. Vera had, to his surprise, been Elizabeth's staunchest advocate from the beginning.

'Oh, I think she's marvellous,' she kept saying. He remembered clearly a conversation in the kitchen, not long ago, when Elizabeth's visits had become established enough for everyone to regard their relationship as something enduring. Vera was sorting out cleaning things in preparation for the arrival of Sharon. 'A lady doctor! So clever. Marvellous. And Alan thinks so too.'

'Does he?' This seemed, to George, rather to contradict the impression that Alan had always given of disapproving of women who exhibited any sign of brain activity.

'Oh yes,' Vera said. Her hand reached into her basket and emerged with a packet of Brillo pads, which she placed on the table like a chess piece. 'A *doctor*. My goodness. But then I suppose . . .' She gave George a coy look, going pink. 'If you both – I mean, it's obvious you're mad about each other, Mr B! If you were to – I mean when you get married I suppose she'll have more free time then.'

In those seconds George was surprised not just to hear, but to experience what Elizabeth meant. There it was again, the immediate assumption that she, everything she stood for or had achieved would be at his disposal – would in fact be disposed *of* – for the sake of a marriage.

'Oh I don't think we'll get married,' he said, making busy with running a mug under the tap. 'We're quite all right as we are. Elizabeth has her practice and so on. She'll keep her place and come over here to visit . . .'

He became conscious that Vera was standing very still, one hand in the basket, interrupted in the act of taking something out. She was staring at him as if listening to some sound in her head that was inaudible to him.

'Not . . .' She hesitated. 'Not get married? You mean . . . ?'

'I mean . . .' What did he mean? He came over to the table. 'At our time of life . . . Look, we're not going to have any children . . .' He had not even begun on Paula with Vera yet. Had hardly begun on it himself, except to write her a kind reply. One hurdle at a time. 'Surely we can work something out for ourselves?'

Vera gazed at him, seemingly awestruck. 'But – what will people *say*?'

He shrugged. 'I have no idea.' This was quite untrue. He had a pretty shrewd idea what tittle-tattle would go on. Rosemary Abbott for a start. 'I suppose we'll find out, won't we?'

'Well.' Vera tugged a skein of new dusters out of the basket. He thought she seemed huffy but was not quite sure. Perhaps not huffy, he corrected. Just trying to get used to newness, as they all were. 'You never know with people, do you?'

'No.' He relaxed, propped against a chair. 'I mean – who would have thought gloomy old Sharon would have the patience to listen to Kevin hour after hour, droning on about pots?'

Vera looked up at him then and they both laughed.

'Darling?'

He turned, heart a-leap at her voice. 'Lizzie!' His world was complete.

Elizabeth was on the steps, clad in her dung-coloured trousers, a lumpish tweed jacket and leather boots and holding a cloth bag in her hand. George struggled to his feet as Monty lurched into squeaking, tail-wagging greetings.

'Hello, you daft old thing!' she said, stooping over Monty. She straightened and kissed George. 'Hello – other daft old thing.'

She held the bag out. 'Just a few bits and pieces. Haven't had much spare time.' He saw she was pale, dark shadows under her eyes. 'I was up nearly all night in the end. Emphysema – dreadful.'

'Oh darling,' he said, contrite, laying an arm across her shoulders as they went down the steps. 'You should have stayed in bed.'

'Not at all – I wouldn't miss this for anything. I'm pretty used to it.'

'Anyway – plenty of food. Vera's made us a pie.'

Elizabeth dimpled. 'Good old Vera. Not rhubarb?'

'No, thank heaven – apple and blackberry.'

'Oh, yum. Peace offering, d'you think?'

'Oh, I don't think there was any war. Just some adjustments. It's more of a . . . let's call it a blessing. Yes?'

Elizabeth was smiling at him. 'She's a one, that Vera. Yes – a blessing.'

A fact that he kept to himself was that it was also a celebration, of a kind. Vera had passed him in the hall yesterday with what he could only describe as a wicked grin breaking across her face.

'I'll just say one thing, Mr Baxter,' she said cryptically, not even stopping. 'There's been a sighting.'

George looked at her, disquieted. What the hell was she going on about? Was he supposed to know?

Vera turned, the grin fully on show. 'A little bird told me that a certain dealer from Twyford has been spotted walking out in Reading – with a certain not-so-young lady from Wallingford!'

Good Lord – could this be true? 'What – Sylvia? With *him* – *Lewis Barker*?'

Vera winked and carried on walking. 'That's all I know, Mr B.'

'Well, well – good luck to them both.' George stood outside his office and chuckled for quite some time.

It was a serene, beautiful day. The light was rich and elegiac, the grass a farewell green, leaves ablaze to create burning bushes in yellow and burnt umber, the sky a screen of duck-egg blue. All this, the placid river gave back, reflected. Coots and grebes scooted away from the gentle advance of *Barchetta*'s prow. The larger pleasure boats had been taken off the water for the winter and all was serene. They had the stretch along towards Goring to themselves.

Mostly they sat quiet, smiled at each other and at Monty's ambivalent gruntings, linked hands now and then, taking it all in in a spirit of contemplation.

With each mile, passing the backs of houses, the elegant railway arches spanning the river, the serene loveliness, George was filled with a merry, miraculous bubbling of happiness at the promises of life.

Despite the irregularity of his relationship with Elizabeth, the sky had not fallen in. He wondered if it was partly because she was a doctor. It seemed to wrap her in a protection of sacred awe that no one was inclined to trespass upon.

Last night, a little hang-dog because Elizabeth was unable to come, he had wandered over to the Barley Mow. At first he was startled to see, among some of his other pals, Maggie and John Wylde.

'Hey there, George!' Roy called out to him, raising a brimming pint in his direction. 'I gather there's a rather special lady knocking about at Chalk Hill Antiques these days?'

George wasn't too sure about 'knocking about' as a description, but amid all the laughter and ribald back-slapping he took no offence. He was rather amazed by how pleased they all seemed to be.

'Come on, Brenda – pull him a pint. Got to keep his strength up!'

Brenda complied, with her usual thunderous expression.

'All change round here,' someone else said as they stood round the bar, raising their tankards. 'Our young Maggie here – off to Australia.'

George had been trying not to look at Maggie, but hearing this he could hardly not do so and their eyes met. Maggie's face held a look of swelling excitement, a grin barely contained.

'It's my Linda,' she explained as if this was news to him. 'Just about to go off and live there, see.'

'My word,' George said. 'That's a big step!'

'And I'm going over there to visit – for a whole month!' She looked radiant, proud of herself and younger again. More the Maggie he remembered. He made the expected noises and they all talked of other things.

Later, after all the chat and a couple of pints, he passed her on his way out. Maggie turned, seeing him. For a second she grasped his upper arm and squeezed it.

'Good for you, Maggie,' he said. 'Off on your travels.'

'I know.' She squeezed again. 'And you – you be happy, George, all right?'

As they both smiled goodbye, she gave him a wink.

They tied up for a time against a sunlit bank and drank steaming beakers of coffee from the Thermos he had prepared, the rug over their knees. Elizabeth's cheeks were pinker now. She looked revived. The sun was still warm on their faces. A goose honked, further down somewhere. The water stretched out each side of them, moving inexorably on its mission to the sea.

For a satisfying moment, George thought of Lady Byngh's bureau bookcase bobbing along in the hold of some cargo ship across the Atlantic.

'Show me, then,' Elizabeth said. A letter had arrived, he had told her. Paula's eager reply – and photographs. He had been reassured by her letter, the polite, sweet tone of it. And the pictures – oh, those pictures.

'I have had these photographs taken especially,' she said. 'To show you the little statue. But I also wanted to show you my children, my Esteban and Alessandra. They are so interested, so excited to hear of you.'

Elizabeth took the two pictures from him. One showed a family group – Paula, a lovely-looking woman with pale hair like her mother's, her serious, slender husband Carlos, who, she wrote, was an anaesthetist in Buenos Aires – and the two children, ten and eight years old. Alessandra, the younger, looked like a mini-version of her mother.

'Oh my . . .' Elizabeth's voice deepened with emotion. 'Oh George – how very lovely.'

She turned to the other picture and gasped. The statue of

Mars on Horseback, with his helmet and spear, rested on a fine-looking dining table. Standing to the left of it, in front of the table, was the boy; a round-faced, amiable and galumphing-looking boy. The moment George set eyes on him was when he had become sure without any doubt.

'He's you!' Elizabeth said. She gazed at it. Gently, she began to laugh. 'He's the absolute image of you!'

George's face broke open in delight. 'He is rather, isn't he?'

'Oh my darling.' She looked at him solemnly. 'This is astonishing. You must go and see them – or invite them here.'

He laughed. 'Well . . .we'll see. One day at a time.' He put the pictures away. Monty sat between them, looking idly from one to the other, wondering when the food was going to appear. George flicked him a piece of liquorice and Monty caught it perfectly, snapping into action.

'Fancy a slice of pie?' he said, into the calm.

'I thought you'd never ask.' Elizabeth raised her plastic cup and clacked it against his. 'This is heaven, my darling – cheers.'

'Go on, Lizzie,' he said on a whim, only half meaning it. 'Say you'll marry me?'

'No!' She pretended to pout. 'I won't – but I will love you. Promise.'

He beamed at her. Life, eh? Each day seemed more full of wonder than the last in this new landscape he had come so far to find, which was the same old country, here all the time, waiting for him.

'Cheers!' he said and leaned to kiss her pink, air-cooled cheek.

Acknowledgements

Firstly, my thanks to Oxford Narrative Group for all the encouragement, company and fun along the way: Helen Matthews, Alison Knight, Rachel Norman, Kit de Waal, Helen Newdick, Benedicta Norel, Pat Whitehouse, John Vickers, Rebecca Watkins, Serena Appella, Paul Walton, and at Oxford Brookes University to James Hawes and Tobias Hill.

Also to the brilliant community of Leather Lane Writers.

I owe a debt of gratitude to my agent Darley Anderson for his support and enthusiasm for this book, and to Clare Wallace at the agency for her helpful comments.

At Pan Macmillan, a huge thank you to my editor Victoria Hughes-Williams for her patience and editorial insights, to Amber Burlinson for excellent copy-editing and to Jeremy Trevathan for going the extra mile.

Much gratitude to the Pan Macmillan reps who work so hard to get all our books out there – especially Keren Weston and Kate Bullows.

Also to Graham Wells of Summers Davis Antiques in Wallingford for taking the time to read and check the text.

And above all to my husband Martin – for loving support, terrible jokes, Bassett hounds and so very much more.

*

Apologies to the people of Blewbury to which Greenbury's geographical location corresponds. However, all characters in this story are fictitious and any passing resemblances are entirely accidental.

If you would like to keep in touch:

Abi has a website: www.abioliver.co.uk
and is on Facebook: www.facebook.com/AbiWriterOliver
and on Twitter: Abi Oliver @AbiWriterOliver